DANGEROUS DREAMING

The dazzlingly handsome spectral stranger smiled as Rowena raised her eyes to his face and then backed away with a gasp. If he smiled at her, it meant he could see her, all of her, naked as the day she was born. She tried to conceal her breasts, but he stopped her by gently taking her wrists. There was nothing illusory about his touch, or his warm body as he took her in his arms, or the unmistakable proof of his rising desire pressing against her, or the unbelievable sensations that went through her as he kissed her. Her lips parted as his tongue slid sensuously against hers. An incredible yearning filled her, and when he picked her up to carry her to the bed, it was what she wanted more than anything else. . . .

Rowena was dreaming, of course. Soon she would wake, and all this would be gone. But what if it wasn't?

The Halloween Husband

THE HALLOWEEN HUSBAND

by

Sandra Heath

A SIGNET BOOK

For Natalie

SIGNET
Published by the Penguin Group
Penguin Books USA Inc., 375 Hudson Street,
New York, New York 10014, U.S.A.
Penguin Books Ltd, 27 Wrights Lane,
London W8 5TZ, England
Penguin Books Australia Ltd, Ringwood,
Victoria, Australia
Penguin Books Canada Ltd, 10 Alcorn Avenue,
Toronto, Ontario, Canada M4V 3B2
Penguin Books (N.Z.) Ltd, 182–190 Wairau Road,
Auckland 10, New Zealand

Penguin Books Ltd, Registered Offices:
Harmondsworth, Middlesex, England

First published by Signet,
an imprint of Dutton Signet,
a division of Penguin Books USA Inc.

First Printing, September, 1994
10 9 8 7 6 5 4 3 2 1

Chapter 1

It is a fact that there are ghosts and other unearthly beings, denizens of another world that marches alongside ours. Some are dark and intent upon evil, but others are benevolent and concerned with the welfare of those they've left behind.

The spirit of Lady Margaret Melcombe was of the latter persuasion, and at the first stroke of midnight on Halloween, she was released from her portrait in the great hall at Melcombe Manor to use the next twenty-four hours to save her descendants from penury, and the ancestral home from the dread prospect of sale. The other portraits in the hall watched her intently, for each one contained the phantom of a long-gone Melcombe, and throughout this disastrous year of 1810, all of them had become increasingly concerned about the family's dire financial straits.

Perhaps it was as well Melcombe was situated in Exmoor, that mysterious southwesterly corner of England where Halloween and the supernatural are believed in most, for this certainly facilitated Lady Margaret's liberation from the constraints of oil and canvas. It was good to be able to move again, she thought, as she hovered above the worn stone flags of the house she'd never ceased to love. She smoothed the rich folds of her silver gown and then glanced around. She'd been eighty-two on leaving her earthly life, but only forty in 1695, when her portrait had been painted, and for that mercy she was now very grateful. It would have been even more pleasing if she'd had the foresight to be recorded at twenty-five, but one shouldn't be too fussy she thought as she looked with approval at her old home.

Generations had passed since she'd been mistress of this rambling half-timbered Elizabethan house, but it still meant as much to her as ever. Melcombe Manor and its dashing master hadn't been considered good enough for an earl's daughter, as her aristocratic father had never ceased to point out, but she'd lost her heart from the first moment she'd seen Henry Melcombe, and throughout her life he'd remained her only true love. They'd made their home here and the London house in Pall Mall, and together they'd made the estate very prosperous. That prosperity had endured down the years. Until now, that is.

A flicker of anger passed through her brown eyes. The Melcombe line had always been blessed with common sense and financial wisdom, but these desirable qualities had been conspicuously absent where the late William Melcombe was concerned.

The wretched fellow had been grossly incompetent with money, although in his favor it had to be conceded he'd been warmhearted and kind. His wife and children certainly still missed him greatly two years after his death. However, there was no denying that the debts they had now were entirely due to his mismanagement. Then, after bringing proud Melcombe Manor to its knees, William had promptly contracted influenza, given up his inept soul, and slipped away into the hereafter.

But, oh, the angry spectral fingers that had wagged on his arrival! Every portrait in the house had trembled with disapproval, and it had been more than a year before he'd been permitted to rest easy in his frame in the principal bedroom, where his worried widow slept so fitfully every night. There he still skulked, hiding away from both worlds, and refusing to shoulder his responsibilities.

The Powers-That-Be, who controlled the supernatural, granted many specters a little liberty each year, but every new wraith enjoyed the undisputed right to a day to do whatever he or she could for the benefit of grieving dear ones. But William hadn't taken advantage of either privilege. He sulked cravenly in his frame when he should have tried to put matters right. Life had to go on for his widow, daughter, and three sons. Not only that, the house itself had to be protected, and that was why his ancestress felt obliged to request a little freedom now, because only on Halloween were spectral abilities enhanced.

But as she hovered there in the moonlit hall, she didn't quite know where to begin. She had so little time to accomplish something which at this moment seemed unaccomplishable. How was she going to fill those empty Melcombe coffers and prevent the house from having to be sold? All that had occurred to her so far was the usual strategy—the swift and advantageous marriage of the family heir. But the situation facing her now was a little tricky. William's son and heir was only fifteen and the twins only twelve, which meant that the twenty-two-year-old daughter was the only marriageable prospect. However, Rowena Melcombe wasn't exactly a raging beauty or possessed of the vapid empty-headedness apparently deemed desirable by today's gentlemen. In fact, until now she'd only attracted the attention of one man, an adventurer who'd hastily disappeared on finding the Melcombes weren't as wealthy as he'd hoped.

Lady Margaret's lips twisted disapprovingly. Mr. Andrew Kemp was a womanizing opportunist who'd come to Melcombe that spring. He'd possessed the looks, charm, and deviousness of his kind, and everyone except Rowena had seen through him. His activities with the serving girls at the Red Lion Inn in the village had eventually reached Mrs. Melcombe's shocked ears, and she'd forbidden him from seeing Rowena again. The closing of the manor house door hadn't bothered him, for he'd already decided to remove himself to the richer pickings of London. He left Rowena with a broken heart, but nothing would convince the girl that he'd been a scoundrel.

The ghost sighed. Rowena Melcombe wasn't promising material, but she was all there was, and marrying her off really did seem the only solution. The chit was agreeable enough, and her long golden hair was certainly an attribute, although not perhaps in these modern days of short brunet curls, but she had one very singular and undeniable fault; she was studious. Wherever she went, a book went with her. How on earth was one supposed to turn her into a desirable bride? And then there was the not insignificant matter of finding the necessary bridegroom before Halloween was over!

Lady Margaret glanced heavenwards, wishing that for once the Powers-That-Be would make a few allowances. At a time like this she desperately needed her husband, Henry's, help, and she was certain the Powers knew exactly where he was. There wouldn't be any problem if only his portrait had been brought here from London at the same time as her own, but for some reason he'd been left behind in the Pall Mall house, which had now been sold to meet the first of William Melcombe's debts. Henry had somehow been lost in the confusion of the sale and hadn't been seen since, but she knew the Powers could summon him if they felt so inclined.

Thinking about Henry's portrait brought a wistful smile to Lady Margaret's lips. He'd looked so very dashing in his periwig, brocade, and three-cornered hat, and the artist had captured the twinkle in his eyes. But Henry hadn't been a mild man, and the painting also caught his capacity for ruthlessness. He was the sort of man women found attractive, and she still missed him so much that even now she sometimes wept in the seclusion of her frame. Oh, plague take William Melcombe's debts! Snapping open her fan, she drew herself up determinedly and then glided across the hall toward the grand oak staircase. It was time to survey Rowena

Melcombe more closely, to see what, if anything, could be done
with her.

One of the other portraits spoke for everyone in the house as it
called after her. "Good luck, Lady Margaret!"

She turned to incline her head, and then drifted up to the half-
landing, where moonlight flooded in through a huge mullioned
bay window. A gilded triptych hung on the wall, a saintly medieval painting of martyrdom that had once adorned Bath Abbey.
Regrettably, there was nothing saintly about the young lady
whose face graced the painting. Mistress Elizabeth Melcombe had
been a saucy baggage who'd caught the roving fifteenth-century
eye of King Edward the Fourth, a monarch known as much for his
amours as his victories during the Wars of the Roses. Having
briefly graced the royal bed and then been painted for posterity as
a martyr, she considered herself the most exalted spirit in the
house, and seldom deigned to look at her fellow wraiths, let alone
speak to them.

Lady Margaret gave her a sour glance, but then a new sound
caught her attention. A carriage was driving along the road to the
village, and she looked out at the elegant vehicle as it bowled
through the darkness past the adjacent churchyard and then on
past the manor house gates. On such a clear moonlit night it was
possible to see the young gentleman seated alone inside. He
hardly glanced at the house, but the ghost at the window found
him very interesting, for he was exceedingly handsome.

Tapping her closed fan in her palm, the phantom watched him
drive by. He had the sort of dark romantic looks she'd always
found irresistible in her earthly existence, and he was also ex-
tremely stylish. His raven hair was worn in tousled curls that became him very well, and his taste in clothes could not have been
better, from the impeccable cut of his brown coat to the starched
perfection of his neckcloth. She could only guess how his lower
half was clad, but no doubt it was as immaculate as the rest of
him. She wondered who he was. A gilded coat-of-arms adorned
the carriage door, and the coachman wore blue-and-gold livery,
which seemed to indicate the aristocracy. Her brows drew together thoughtfully, for there was something familiar about that
coat-of-arms, and indeed about the young man's flawless profile.

She continued to watch as the vehicle drove the hundred yards
or so into the village, where it pulled up by the green, outside the
Red Lion. The coachman climbed down to open the carriage
door, and as the young gentleman began to alight, Lady Margaret's curiosity got the better of her. In a moment she'd glided

through the window into the clear October night to look at him more closely.

Chapter 2

The specter floated interestedly around him as he paused by the inn door to fling a heavy fawn greatcoat around his shoulders. Oh, yes, he was quite delectable, she thought with increasing approval, for his brown tailcoat and tight-fitting cream breeches allowed her to observe every inch of his lean, hard-muscled shape.

He had to be a scion of the old nobility, for there was at least six hundred years of blue blood in that matchless bone structure. As for his eyes, well, they conjured tantalizing thoughts of bedrooms! Long-lashed and caressing, they were such a deep sea green that any unwary female would surely drown in their glance. Lady Margaret paused, for she'd gazed into eyes like that during her time on earth. She turned to look at the coat-of-arms on the carriage door and suddenly remembered to whom it belonged— Kit, Marquess of Exford, the heartstoppingly handsome lover she'd parted from just prior to meeting her own dear Henry. She surveyed the young man again. Yes, he was very like Kit.

He entered the brightly lit inn to ask the landlord for a room, and the phantom was about to return to the house when she noticed something lying on the carriage seat, next to the Bath newspaper that indicated he'd been in the spa only two days ago. The something was a letter that had fallen from his pocket and bore the heraldic unicorns of the Exford marquesses. Oh, how many times had she seen that unicorn on the gateposts of Exford Park in Sussex, near the village of Brighthelmstone?

The coachman had already returned to his seat to drive to the inn stables, and as the vehicle maneuvered into the yard, Lady Margaret floated inside to read what was visible on the folded sheet.

Exford Park, Saturday.
Justin, my boy.
    There is no easy way of conveying my wishes on this

particular matter, so I will not beat about the bush. You are
my son and heir, but you are also twenty-nine years old,
and no nearer marriage than you were twelve months ago.
In view of my failing health, and my natural but increasing
concern for the future of the title, I have decided the time
has come for this oversight to be rectified once and for all,
and unless I hear from you soon that . . .

To Lady Margaret's frustration, it wasn't possible to read any
more of what was, under the prevailing circumstances, a
supremely interesting communication. It seemed the handsome
young gentleman was not only unmarried, but also heir to the Exford title and under instructions to acquire a wife as quickly as
possible! How provident. And how infuriating not to be able to
read more. She frowned at the vellum, and then closed her eyes
tightly as she brought all her concentration to bear.

The vellum trembled, lifted from the seat, and then turned itself
neatly over before settling again, thus revealing the rest of the letter and also the name and address of the recipient: Lord Alderney,
St. James's Square, London. Lady Margaret smiled to herself.
Confinement in a portrait frame wasn't conducive to ghostly com-
petence, but at least her skills weren't too rusty, and that it was
Halloween was certainly helpful. She continued to read as the carriage jolted to a standstill in the yard.

. . . and unless I hear from you soon that the situation is to
be rectified voluntarily, I will act by proceeding with the
Beaufort match I put to you last winter. Lady Clarissa will
make an excellent wife, and Beaufort women have an admirable record when it comes to providing their husbands
with children.

   That is all I intend to say. It is now up to you, but be
warned, my patience is running out and I will not brook
further excuses.

                                             I am, etc.
                                             Exford.

Lady Margaret drew a long breath and smiled. Providence
wasn't disposed to be merely kind, it was being positively generous! On the very night a bridegroom was required, an eminently
suitable gentleman happened to arrive in Melcombe. And what a
gentleman. Justin, Lord Alderney, was a paragon and certainly deserved better than a Beaufort. In short, he deserved a Melcombe!

Lady Margaret glided out of the carriage, much to the perturbation of the inn cat, which arched its back and spat as she wafted past. But the phantom wasn't in the least concerned with mere animals, for she had much more on her mind. Not the least being how to make Justin want to marry someone like Rowena.

Lady Margaret returned to Melcombe Manor and continued up the staircase to the principal bedchamber where Rowena's mother tossed and turned in the immense damask-hung bed. Mrs. Maria Melcombe was pale and drawn, and beneath her lace-edged night bonnet her brown hair was turning gray. She was making herself ill with worry, but had yet to confide the seriousness of the situation to anyone, including Rowena.

William Melcombe's portrait was on the wall opposite the bed, and Lady Margaret gave him a dark look. Resplendent in powdered wig and best peach-striped silk coat, he was of amiable enough appearance, if not exactly handsome, and he'd never lost his manly figure. But his lack of financial acumen was somehow evident in his soft blue eyes, which bore no trace of all of Henry's sort of flintiness. Even now he was avoiding her gaze, and she knew he wouldn't respond if she spoke to him. She did so nevertheless, knowing the sleeping woman couldn't hear ghosts.

"Well, sir?"

Silence.

"I trust you're ashamed of yourself, for I'm certainly ashamed of you. And now you compound the felony by lurking uselessly in your frame, showing no inclination whatsoever to rectify your multitudinous errors. I vow I am almost tempted to see that something dreadful befalls you."

She was rewarded by the flicker of alarm that entered his glance. "Ha!" she cried then. "So you *do* hear me!"

"Yes, I hear you, Lady Margaret."

"It speaks!" she observed scathingly. "Well, sirrah? When do you intend to lend a hand in this?"

"I can't."

"Can't? Won't, more likely."

"Whatever I touch goes wrong. I'd only make matters worse if I started meddling again."

"Worse? How can they possibly get worse?" Lady Margaret snapped. "What a contemptible malingerer you are, to be sure. I can't imagine what the Melcombes did to deserve you. Very well, cower there if you must, but don't expect a peaceful eternity, for I'll see it's denied you!"

With that dire promise she glided through into the next room, which was occupied by the twelve-year-old twins, Stephen and Paul. She hovered by their bed, her lips pursed thoughtfully. With their fair curls they looked angelic, but in fact they were the very devil, and Halloween was their favorite time of the year because it gave them license to torment. The festival had another name, Mischief Night, and in the twins' case it could not have been better described. They were in their element, dedicating themselves to "guising," as the pursuance of Halloween misconduct was known.

Guising was an ancient tradition, especially on Exmoor, and consisted of children hiding their identities with blackened faces or masks, and then dressing as ghosts, witches, demons, and fearsome beasts in order to go from house to house demanding to be recognized or rewarded. Other favorite activities consisted of exchanging farm animals, black for white, male for female, or single beasts for many, and also removing farm gates and tossing them into ditches or streams. Doors of adjacent cottages were tied together and then knocked, much to the fury and frustration of those endeavoring to open them, and the turnip lanterns placed on gateposts to protect homes from evil were stolen and fixed to poles to be brandished at bedroom windows.

All these activities were expected on Halloween, but Stephen and Paul Melcombe took everything much further. Last year they'd gone so far as to creep into Widow Longman's cottage and leave a small clay model of a hideous witch that cast a monstrous shadow over the wall when the wretched woman entered with her night candle. She'd been so frightened she'd been confined to her bed for a week afterward.

On that occasion the twins had also dressed as demons and carried lighted torches to leap out of an alley in front of the Reverend Grantham, whose disapproval of pagan Halloween was only to be expected, but whose faith had been severely rattled by such convincing acting on the boys' part. They'd pranced threateningly around him, chanting devilish names, then they'd set fire to his coattails. He'd been forced to sit in the horse trough outside the Red Lion, and had then required assistance home to the vicarage. Needless to say, his next sermon had been a thunderous condemnation of such heathen celebrations.

However, perhaps the worst of the twins' sins last year had been the business with the Exmoor staghounds. The hunt had been due to meet on Melkery Beacon on the first of November, and accordingly the hounds were kenneled not far from Melcombe. When the Halloween bonfire had been lit on the village green, the boys released the hounds. Mayhem had reigned for nearly an hour as the exasperated villagers helped the huntsmen gather the excited dogs, and Stephen and Paul had wisely made themselves scarce.

Faced with so many complaints, Mrs. Melcombe had had no option but to punish the twins severely and promise everyone they'd be confined to the house this year. But the futility of such a promise was only too plain. Boys will be boys, and if they wish to get out, then they find ways and means of so doing.

Lady Margaret knew they had something especially mischievous planned for this year, for she'd observed them whispering together in the great hall. She wished she knew what they were up to, but ghosts' hearing was no more keen than that of the living. Blue-eyed little saints these two had never been, but now they were what was commonly termed, "a handful," and their mother was no match for them. If finances had permitted, they'd have been at Eton by now, where some of their high spirits would have been suitably curbed by their peers. Lady Margaret flicked her fan open again. If all went according to her wishes, and their sister married Lord Alderney, these scamps would soon be at Eton after all. And not before time!

The shade pursed her lips thoughtfully. Chastisement was long overdue in their case, and even though she only had one day in which to complete the task of saving Melcombe Manor, she nevertheless meant to set aside sufficient time to teach them a salutary lesson. They thought Halloween pranks were rib-tickling in the extreme; well, she'd tickle their ribs for them!

Continuing on her spectral way, Lady Margaret made one more stop before reaching Rowena, and that was to look for a moment at fifteen-year-old Lionel, the Melcombe heir. Like the twins he should have been at Eton, but the best his mother could afford was a daily tutor. He was a shy, gangling boy, but he had promise. He'd make an excellent master of Melcombe when the time came—provided Melcombe was still in the family.

Lady Margaret glided toward Rowena's modest room at the very end of the passage, overlooking the rear gardens. It was no accident that the studious chit had elected to have this particular room, for it was close to the back staircase, which gave convenient—and furtive—access to the library below. The one sensible instruction Rowena's father had issued during his otherwise foolish existence had been to forbid his daughter to read so much. But she disobeyed him. If only he realized how many times she crept up and down that wretched back staircase with a forbidden volume concealed beneath her shawl! By now the scholarly little minx's head must be filled to bursting point with Shakespeare, Marlowe, Milton, and Chaucer, and if there was one thing gentlemen loathed in prospective wives, it was over-education.

Seized with disapproval, Lady Margaret swept into the room. She expected to find it in darkness, but instead there was candlelight, not because the occupant was once again engaged upon illicit reading, but because Rowena Melcombe was standing naked looking at herself in the cheval glass!

Chapter 3

Lady Margaret was so startled she flew right through the room and out the window, only stopping when she reached the walnut tree. There she paused for a moment. She must have imagined it! Turning, she glided back again, only to find that she had most certainly not imagined anything. Rowena was still there without so much as a stitch to spare her modesty. Taken aback, Lady Margaret retreated to the top of the bed canopy to watch.

Rowena was unaware of the presence in the room as she studied herself critically in the glass. Turning first one way and then the other, she tried to be objective in her assessment. Did she have a passable figure? She wasn't the willowy shape that was all the mode now, for her breasts were too full and her waist too small. If only hourglasses were the thing! She touched her nipples, which all too frequently had a habit of making themselves embarrassingly apparent through flimsy summer gowns. The new curate had scarcely been able to tear his gaze away at the August garden party, when she'd been wearing her white muslin and the humid air had suddenly turned cool. Thank goodness it was winter now, for heavier materials weren't as uncomfortably revealing.

She continued to examine her reflection. She had good skin, she supposed. It was smooth, pale, and unblemished, and as for her legs, well, they were one of her better points. Yes, she approved of her long thighs and small ankles. And her eyes were reasonable. They were clear and almost lilac, with unexpectedly dark brows and lashes. Lastly she studied her long blond hair, which didn't please her at all. It was thick and wretchedly straight, and it seemed to positively recoil from the indignity of pins!

She wasn't a beauty, and she knew it. Nor was she brainless and simpering, as seemed to be the requirement if one was to succeed in the marriage mart. No, she was just herself, and therefore unlikely to snap up someone as dashing as Andrew. She lowered her gaze for a moment, for she knew what everyone said of him. But she still didn't believe he was an adventurer. He'd really liked her, and if he'd suddenly left Melcombe, it was for some pressing private reason, not because he'd found she wasn't an heiress. She hoped he'd come back home one day to prove them all wrong.

She looked at her reflection again. Tonight she was intent upon Halloween, and whether or not there was any substance to one of the superstitions attached to the occasion. It was all in the name of serious research, of course; romantic foolishness did not enter into it! Everyone said that what she was about to do resulted in the face of one's future husband being reflected in a mirror, and she intended to test the veracity of this. But as she bent to pick up the apple and comb lying at her feet, she secretly longed to see Andrew's face. Watching the cheval glass, she took a bite of the apple and began to comb her hair.

Being a spirit, Lady Margaret possessed numerous powers, but the ability to read thoughts wasn't one of them. She didn't know that worthless Andrew Kemp still meant a great deal to Rowena; all she saw was a young girl hoping to find her future husband's reflection in a looking glass. With spectral interest, the phantom floated down from the top of the bed. Unfortunately this was the wrong part of Halloween for such charms. It was the coming night that rendered such magic its full potency, but nevertheless it proved the girl was prepared to set her bookishness aside once in order to indulge a little in matters of the heart. Maybe she wasn't entirely beyond redemption after all.

Well, whether or not this was the wrong part of Halloween, the moment shouldn't be wasted. But how to turn it to advantage, that was the question? The phantom thought swiftly. Somehow Justin's reflection had to appear in that mirror, but although the letter had obliged by turning over in the carriage, the conjuring up of an image was a very different matter. It was woefully difficult to be proficient at sorcery when one had been confined to a picture frame for so long! Commanding suitable illusions was said to be easy enough after a little practice, but not when one's skills were rusty, and not if the subject of the illusion was awake.

With a grimace Lady Margaret concentrated very hard indeed, recalling Justin's every handsome feature. To her relief he soon began to form in her mind, but then she began to feel bold and smiled a little wickedly. If Rowena was naked, might it not be intriguing to conjure Justin in the same state of undress? Oh, yes, indeed it might!

Satisfied that he was correct in every masculine detail, Lady Margaret prepared to make him appear to Rowena. She waited until the moment was absolutely perfect, and Rowena's eyes were closed in readiness to count to ten before looking. Then, with a sly smile, the apparition willed him into existence, knowing as she did so that the real Justin would now start having very sensuous dreams indeed!

Rowena finished counting and opened her eyes. Her breath caught with shock as she stared at the glass, and the apple and comb fell to the floor as she turned sharply to stare at him. Color flooded her cheeks as she couldn't help glancing down at that part of his anatomy which no proper young lady was supposed to see until her wedding night.

Lady Margaret felt even more wicked then. Just how real was it possible to make him? Closing her eyes tightly, she gave the matter her complete concentration. Heaven help the real Justin's dreams!

The image smiled as Rowena raised her eyes to his face, and she backed away with a gasp, for if he could smile at her, then he could see her. All of her! She tired to conceal her breasts, but he stopped her by gently taking her wrists. There was nothing illusory about his touch; it was firm and steady. And oh, so beguiling . . . He smelled of musk, and the scent robbed her of self-consciousness. She felt spellbound, almost as if none of this were happening, and when he drew her into his arms, she went willingly.

His body was warm, and she could feel his maleness beginning to press as it rose against her. Unbelievable sensations shivered through her as he kissed her. Her lips parted as his tongue slid sensuously against hers. An incredible yearning filled her, and she was conscious of the urgency of his body, now hard and aroused. His kiss was passionate, and his hands moved caressingly over her, touching her as she'd never been touched before. Then he picked her up to carry her to the bed, and it was what she wanted more than anything else in the world.

Lady Margaret blinked. Her ghostly powers must be stronger than she realized, for this was succeeding a little too well! They were positively incandescent with desire, and young Rowena was about to surrender her all to this spellbindingly real illusion.

Then, quite abruptly, Justin's image disappeared, and Lady Margaret knew he'd awoken at the inn. Rowena was left confused and a little frightened as she lay on the bed, and quickly Lady Margaret contrived to send her to sleep. It was an ability the spirit hadn't realized she possessed, but needs must!

Justin sat up with a start in his bed at the Red Lion. Dear God above, what a dream! He was only too conscious of the luxurious sensations still washing over him. Sleep had gone, but his body felt as if it were still with the unknown young woman to whom he'd been about to make such passionate love.

He was unbearably hot and flung the bedclothes aside to get up. He always slept naked, and the cold night air was welcome as he opened the window. The sweet scent of the high moor drifted over him as he stood there, but the effects of the dream still lingered. He could recall every tantalizing detail. Whoever the lady was, he'd loved her fervently. She hadn't been a beauty, but there'd been something about her, something bewitching . . .

He smiled a little wryly, remembering what day had just commenced. It was Halloween, and he, the most levelheaded and practical man in society, was under enchantment! Then the smile faded, for the dream had nothing to do with Halloween; rather had it been brought about by his father's terse letter. Threats of Lady Clarissa Beaufort had proved too much, and his imagination had created an alternative bride.

He leaned his hands on the windowsill. His father wasn't usually a dictatorial man; indeed the opposite was more the case, but ill health had hardened him. The prospect of dying without knowing the line would continue had driven him to these lengths. Justin knew his father meant every word of the letter. Unless a bride was produced before long, Clarissa would become more than a mere threat. Dear God, the thought of taking such a horsey creature to his bed was enough to make him impotent! But the fact remained that a wife was necessary, and at the moment there wasn't anyone suitable on the horizon. Of late his activities had been confined to his mistress, Chloe, Countess of Westcote, an experienced woman-of-the-world whose husband turned a blind eye to her unfaithfulness so that he himself was free to indulge in his taste for pert little actresses and similar "bits of muslin."

Justin ran his fingers through his hair. He'd have to find a wife somewhere, but he couldn't even begin to think of anyone in particular. All the eligible young ladies he knew were dull or tire-some, without any qualities exciting enough to make them worthy of a second glance. Something would have to be done, however, and soon. Before leaving Bath, where he'd been staying with his closest friends, George and Emily Rathbone, at the house of George's aunt, Lady Beaminster, he'd discussed the problem with them. Their advice had been to abandon this present visit to cousins in Cornwall, and instead return to London to find the nec-essary spouse. Lady Beaminster was of the same opinion, and she was considered a very wise matron with considerable knowledge of such matters. Maybe they were all right. He thought for a mo-ment and then decided that that would indeed be the wisest course. He'd been stubborn to insist upon honoring his promise to go to Cornwall. First thing in the morning he'd go back to the capital.

His mind made up, he returned to the bed. For a while he lay there watching the curtains stirring as the night breeze crept into the room, but gradually his eyes closed, and soon he was asleep again. This time his dreams were unremarkable, and unlike the one that had awoken him, would be forgotten the following morning.

Lady Margaret surveyed him from the foot of the bed. She'd glided posthaste from the manor house and was immensely pleased to realize her powers had indeed extended to disturbing his sleep. His actual thoughts were hidden from her, but she guessed they would concern his dream encounter with Rowena, and, possi-bly, the contents of his father's letter. The existence of his mistress remained unknown to her, not that it would have made any differ-ence. It was as a wealthy husband that Justin was of interest to the phantom; his future faithfulness to his wife was beside the point.

Lady Margaret felt almost smugly satisfied with her efforts so far. Things really were going inordinately well. Tomorrow, or rather later today, she'd have to bring Rowena and this devilishly attractive fellow together. They'd have to come face-to-face, and both recall their shared dream, for it was as a dream that Rowena would remember what happened. Lady Margaret didn't doubt that Rowena would find Justin as devastatingly attractive in fact as in fantasy, but his reactions weren't quite so easy to predict. The male animal was frequently guilty of thinking only in terms of se-duction, not the honorable estate of matrimony, and although the dream had aroused his desire for Rowena, it didn't necessarily make her his ideal bride!

Pondering how best to proceed next, the apparition drifted out of the window. She swooped low over the village green, where the coming night would see the entire neighborhood making merry around the Halloween bonfire. But for the moment she wasn't concerned with village celebrations. The saving of Melcombe Manor and its occupants was her task, and she meant to do it to the best of her ability. Now more than ever she felt that the solution lay with finding Rowena a husband, and after observing Justin more closely at the inn, Lady Margaret was convinced beyond all shadow of doubt that he was ideal for the purpose. She needed to think, and to rest, for leaving her frame was proving unexpectedly tiring.

The ghost glided silently back to the manor house, where she was soon comfortably reinstalled in her place. Just a few hours, that was all she needed. In the morning she'd be as fresh as a daisy again. She closed her eyes.

Chapter 4

Something jolted Rowena from her sleep the following morning. She awoke quite abruptly and lay there with her heart pounding. Alarm pulsed through her, but she didn't know why.

The mantelpiece clock pointed to half-past eight, and daylight shone faintly through the dusky pink velvet curtains. The paneled room was shadowy as she sat up wondering what had startled her into such sudden wakefulness. Even as she wondered, there was a scream, and she knew it was the second one. It came from the maid tending the fire in Lionel's empty room. He was at his lessons in the library, and a maid always came at this time to rake the ashes and lay fresh coals.

Rowena flung the bedclothes back to go see what was wrong. The two bedrooms were at the end of the house, away from everyone, and she knew she was probably the only person to have heard anything, but as she got out of bed, she realized she had nothing on. Not a single stitch! She snatched up her cream woolen wrap, for there was no time to wonder why she'd neglected to put on her nightgown the night before.

As she reached Lionel's room, there was a clatter as the coal scuttle fell to the floor. The terrified maid was standing with her hands pressed to her mouth as she stared at the fireplace. She was plump with carrot-colored hair and freckles, and there was coal dust on her gown and apron as well as her hands.

Rowena put a gentle hand on her shoulder, but the maid almost fainted at the unexpected touch. She was trembling so much her teeth were chattering, and something of her fear began to transfer to Rowena, who glanced around a little uneasily.

"Whatever is it, Sally?"

The girl pointed at the fireplace.

Rowena looked. There wasn't anything, but when she went closer, she distinctly heard the sound of stifled boyish laughter coming down the chimney from the empty attic room above. She glared angrily up into the sooty darkness and then heard what had frightened the maid. Beside themselves with glee, the twins began to make terrifying moaning sounds and wail Sally's name.

The maid whimpered and hid her face in her coal-stained hands.

Rowena called furiously up the chimney. "Stephen! Paul! You stop that immediately and come down here!"

She was rewarded by the abrupt silencing of the ghostly sounds, and then by softly hurrying steps on the bare floorboards as her brothers made good their escape. There was no point trying to catch them now, for they were past masters at escaping retribution and would soon be shinning down the drainpipe into the stable yard.

She went back to the weeping maid. "It's all right, Sally, it was only my brothers."

The girl's face was smudged with coal as she lowered her hands. "M-Master S-Stephen and Master P-Paul?"

"Yes. It's Halloween," Rowena reminded her.

Sally's eyes cleared, and she bit her lip sheepishly. "I went and forgot it were Mischief Night . . ."

Rowena smiled. "Well, to be strictly correct they shouldn't start their nonsense until dusk, but that's never stopped them before. I'll see they're reprimanded." Not that it would do any good.

The maid wiped her eyes on her sleeve. "I-I thought I were 'earin' spunkies, or boggarts, or maybe even Old Bogey himself."

"No, not will-o'-the-wisps, ghosts, or Satan, just two exceedingly naughty boys who need a good lesson in how to behave."

Sally looked in dismay at the coal on the carpet. "Oh, those darned little hosebirds!" she exclaimed and immediately bobbed an apologetic curtsy. "Beggin' your pardon, Miss Rowena, for I shouldn't speak of the young masters like that."

"Don't apologize, Sally, for darned little hosebirds is what they are. They're becoming more and more unruly as the months pass."

"They were proper fond of their father, Miss Rowena."

"That doesn't excuse them. Master Lionel misses Father as well, but he hasn't misbehaved on account of it. No, let's be honest, Sally, they're just hosebirds."

The maid smiled. "Proper ones, and no mistake."

"I'll see someone is sent to help you with all this coal."

"Thank you, Miss Rowena."

Two maids were dusting and polishing in the great hall, and after calling down the staircase to tell one of them to help Sally, Rowena returned to her own room, but as she went in, she noticed her comb and the half-eaten apple lying on the floor. Her brows drew together in puzzlement. She remembered deciding to test the Halloween superstition and also beginning to count to ten as she stood in front of the cheval glass, but as to what happened after that . . .

Suddenly her lilac eyes widened as it all came back to her. For a moment she couldn't believe she'd dreamed such wanton things! But then her glance returned to the apple and comb, and she recalled waking up without her nightgown. Something very strange had happened to her last night, and embarrassing memories returned now, especially about the gentleman who'd come to her. She could recollect him in every shocking detail! But who was he? Certainly not anyone she'd really met, and as far as she knew, he wasn't someone she'd seen at any social function. She chided herself then. It was plain he was merely the product of her imagination. She lowered her glance for a moment, remembering how she'd hoped to find Andrew Kemp's reflection in the mirror. Instead she'd seen a stranger and had loved him to distraction. It was the first and last time she'd dabble with Halloween charms!

She drew the curtains back to look at the walled garden behind the house. The October morning was beautiful, with sunlight beginning to disperse an early mist. Dew-laden cobwebs covered the lawn, and gossamer floated from the walnut tree. Late hollyhocks bloomed against the garden wall, and the flowerbeds were bright with goldenrod and Michaelmas daisies. Beyond the adjacent churchyard she could see Farmer Porlock's cider apple orchard, where the crop was so heavy it weighed the branches down. Windfalls already lay in the long grass, a sure sign that harvesting was imminent.

There was something particularly affecting about fall, she thought, especially before the first frost robbed the trees of their leaves. This year everything was still in its full autumnal glory, and a riot of crimson, russet, and gold foliage lent a breathtaking splendor to the already beautiful Exmoor scenery. Beyond the creeper-clad garden wall the wide stream was almost invisible in the misty haze, although she could just see the stone footbridge. Half a mile away, but hidden from view now, rose Melkery Beacon, the tallest hill in Exmoor. In an hour's time its gorse and heather heights would be visible above the surrounding moor and tree-filled combes. It would shine yellow and pink against the matchless blue of the sky, and wild Exmoor ponies would be grazing on its slopes.

She returned her attention to the garden. Griggs, the gardener, an old man as gnarled as tree bark, carried a basket of tulip and hyacinth bulbs to plant in a fresh bed he'd prepared the day before. His shuffling steps left a trail through the cobwebbed grass, and moisture dripped onto his old felt hat as he brushed beneath a low-hanging branch. He placed the basket on the wet grass and then knelt down on a short plank of wood to commence planting.

As she watched, the twins hurried across the lawn, carrying something large, yellow, and spherical. They didn't notice Griggs at work, but he saw them and was aroused to an instant fury.

Scrambling to his feet, he waved his fist and shouted. "You bring that there pummuck back 'ere right now!"

The boys halted in dismay, but then made a dash for the garden wall, still clutching the angry gardener's "pummuck." As they scrambled over, scattering creeper leaves in all directions, Griggs continued to wave his fist after them.

"That there's my pummuck! You darned young toads!"

But they ran across the footbridge and soon disappeared from view in the mist. Griggs snatched off his battered hat and hurled it to the grass before hastening toward the house. His face was ruddy with anger, and Rowena could see he intended to lodge an immediate complaint with her poor mother.

What on earth was a "pummuck?" Knowing her brothers, it had to be something of use on Halloween, although Rowena couldn't imagine what. She sighed, wishing her undisciplined siblings didn't have quite such fertile imaginations. Their propensity for creating new mischief was quite remarkable, and before the day was out she was certain most of Melcombe would be wishing them in perdition!

With a knock at the bedroom door her maid, Ann, came in, invisibly accompanied by a refreshed Lady Margaret. "Good morning, Miss Rowena," the maid said, giving a neat curtsy that made her starched apron crackle. Her hair was fair and curly, her face round and healthy, and her eyes wide and gray.

"Good morning, Ann," Rowena replied with a smile.

"What shall I put out for you today?"

Rowena thought for a moment. "The coral fustian, I think."

Lady Margaret frowned. The coral fustian was a horrid garment. The chit needed to make the most of herself if she was soon to come face-to-face with Justin, and for that the blue dimity was infinitely better.

The phantom fixed her descendant with an invisible glare, and after a moment Rowena hesitated. "No, on second thoughts I think I'll wear the blue dimity," she said.

"Yes, miss."

Lady Margaret drew a satisfied breath. The morning had commenced excellently, and her ghostly powers were improving by the minute. If her plan hadn't succeeded by the end of today, it wouldn't be for lack of effort on her part!

Chapter 5

Half an hour later, with her hair pinned up into the neatest knot possible, Rowena left her room. Lady Margaret glided at her side, unseen and unheard.

Sally and her assistant were still endeavoring to clean the carpet in Lionel's room, and the second maid's wrath was justified. "Oh, them twins, they're as good for nothing as twopennorth of God-help-us stuck on a stick," she grumbled as she knelt with the scrubbing brush to attend to the mark left after they'd swept up as much of the dust as they could.

Sally saw Rowena passing the door and hissed a warning to her friend. "Hush up, lessen you want us in trouble!"

Rowena smiled and walked on.

Lady Margaret fluttered silently behind her and paused by the doorway. Much heartened by her success with the choosing of Rowena's gown, the spirit was feeling a little playful. Seeing a candlestick on the mantelpiece, she subjected it to her will. It

began to rock from side to side and then fell with a sudden clatter
that made the two maids jump. Pleased with herself, the phantom
flew on after Rowena, who'd paused on the half-landing to look
at the view from the front of the house.

The morning mist was threading away fast now, and a string of
packhorses was passing the gates on its way to a village deeper in
the heart of the moor. The carrier's wagon was about to leave the
Red Lion, and on the green in front of the inn the villagers were
beginning to build the Halloween bonfire. There'd be revelry in
plenty at Melcombe tonight, and the fun would go on until the
early hours.

Rowena always enjoyed the Halloween festivities on the green.
She loved all the merriment, the turnip lanterns, the stories of
witches and ghosts, the baked apples and potatoes, the silly
games, and the dancing around the flames. She also loved the fan-
tastic costumes, especially the Devil's Mare, which was a man
dressed as a hobbyhorse with a real horse's skull. His task was to
chase all the women, clacking the horse's jaw and demanding
kisses. It could only be imagined what terrible being from the
mists of time the Mare was supposed to represent, and every year
the Reverend Grantham thundered from his pulpit about hellfire
and eternal damnation. But to the people of Melcombe, the
Devil's Mare, Halloween, and everything else were just fun.

Rowena went on down the staircase and then crossed the great
hall toward the door of the dining room, but as she did so, something drew her attention to Lady Margaret's portrait. Suddenly
she found herself remembering the missing portrait of Henry Melcombe. What a pity it had gone astray, for it was the only family
portrait to ever have been lost. She smiled a little then, recalling a
strange incident at the Pall Mall house, when she'd been about
thirteen. It had happened late one night, and to be fair her father
had imbibed a little too much at dinner, but he'd sworn Henry's
portrait had spoken to him. In fact he said it had ticked him off for
being a fool, and that it had called him "Silly Billy." Her mother
had rightly been cross with him.

Lady Margaret hovered uncertainly above her. What was the
girl thinking about? What had drawn her attention to the portrait,
and why did she smile like that?

As Rowena went on to the dining room, the church clock
struck nine. Lady Margaret hesitated. Midnight was only fifteen
hours away, and she still had everything to accomplish. The phantom knew she should go to the inn now to make sure Justin didn't
suddenly decide to leave early, but before she did that, she wished

to find out about a letter Mrs. Melcombe had received that morning. It was from the London bank and under the circumstances wasn't likely to contain glad tidings.

Lady Margaret fluttered into the dining room, where Rowena had just served herself some scrambled eggs from the covered dish standing on the trivet before the hearth. Mrs. Melcombe was pale-faced and quiet as she sat at the table, her breakfast untouched before her. The ghost retreated to a vantage point at the corner of the ceiling and prepared to eavesdrop.

Mrs. Melcombe, dressed in gray-and-black half-mourning, looked very drawn. Lady Margaret glanced at the letter from London, which lay unopened beside her plate. The poor creature was afraid to read it!

Rowena hadn't noticed the letter. She sat down to pour herself some coffee. "I fear the twins are up to no good again," she said.

Mrs. Melcombe collected herself. "Er, yes, I know. I've had Griggs in here in a fine old temper about his precious pumpkin."

"Pumpkin?"

"I understand it is a squash something akin to a vegetable marrow, but much larger, and round and yellow rather than long and green."

Rowena smiled to herself. So that's what a "pummuck" was!

Her mother went on. "It seems he acquired some seeds from a fellow who'd returned from America and had managed to grow several plants in a corner of the kitchen garden, but only one fruit had developed to its full size. According to Griggs, the twins stole it this morning."

"They did. I saw them running off with it across the bridge. I suppose it's something for Halloween."

Lady Margaret supposed so, too. She'd never heard of pumpkins before, but she intended to find out why those tiresome boys had stolen one.

Mrs. Melcombe sighed. "I really don't know what to do with the twins. They're so disobedient all the time, but when I get cross with them, they seem able to charm me into forgiving them. I was determined to see they behaved themselves this Halloween, but even though I forbade them to leave the house today . . ." She shook her head sadly. "They're too much for me, I fear."

"They've certainly been busy enough already this morning." Rowena told her about the ghostly voices in the chimney.

Mrs. Melcombe sighed again. "Poor Lionel hasn't escaped their attentions either. His geography textbook was exchanged for a disreputable dictionary of the vulgar tongue, acquired from heaven knows where, and his quill was turned upside down in its inkwell. Oh, I despair sometimes. One tries one's best under arduous circumstances, and . . ." Her voice died away on something very close to a sob, and Rowena looked at her with swift concern.

"Mother?"

"Forgive me, my dear." Mrs. Melcombe searched in her pocket and took out a handkerchief to dab her eyes.

Rowena went to put her arms around her. "What is it? Has something happened?"

"Yes. I mean, no. Oh, I don't know." Mrs. Melcombe struggled to regain her composure and then nodded more calmly. "Yes, Rowena, I'm afraid it probably has." She pointed to the unopened letter.

Rowena picked it up. "The bank has written to you?"

"I fear they mean to foreclose."

"Foreclose? But, we have no mortgage, or—"

"We do, my dear. A rather large one." Mrs. Melcombe looked sadly at her. "I haven't been entirely honest with you of late, Rowena, but now I fear it's time to be frank. As you know, your poor dear father was a little, er, remiss when it came to managing finances. What you don't know is exactly how remiss. So far, with the assistance of the bank, I've been able to keep everything going, but now I'm sure their patience is at an end."

Rowena stared in the utmost dismay. How hadn't she realized things were so bad?

Mrs. Melcombe looked wretchedly at the letter and then took it up with a sigh. "Well, I suppose it must be opened," she murmured, breaking the seal. There weren't many lines, but they were to the point, and after a moment she refolded the letter. "It's as I feared."

"Foreclosure?"

Her mother nodded wearily. "Now I have no choice but to sell Melcombe Manor as quickly as possible."

Rowena was still numb with shock. "There . . . there must be another way . . ."

"My dear, do you imagine I haven't tried everything? Selling the estate is my only option. The bank believes it will provide the funds necessary to cover the debts, but points out that what is left will purchase only a modest dwelling. Our lives will be very frugal then, I fear."

Rowena blinked back tears. "You should have told me, Mother."

Mrs. Melcombe smiled fondly. "A trouble shared being a trouble halved? No, my dear, for I didn't want you to be brought low as well."

"I feel partly to blame," Rowena said suddenly, walking agitatedly to the window and staring out at the cobwebs glistening on the lawn.

"Why on earth do you say that, my dear?" her mother asked in surprise.

"I should have been married by now, but instead I'm still a millstone."

"Rowena—"

"It's true. But who wants a bookish wife? I've been selfish, Mother, for I've indulged my liking for reading when I should have been using what few attributes I have to snap up a husband."

Mrs. Melcombe got up quickly and went to her. "My dear, you mustn't think that. We're all as the Almighty made us, and nothing can change us. Besides, who is to say you would have married sensibly?"

Andrew Kemp's name hung unspoken in the air. "I still think you were wrong about Mr. Kemp," Rowena said quietly.

"I admire your loyalty, my dear, but it's misplaced, believe me. The fellow was unscrupulous and totally without honor."

Lady Margaret nodded her agreement. Indeed he was.

Mrs. Melcombe put a comforting hand on her daughter's shoulder and then returned to her chair. "I'll reply to the bank later today, informing them the property will be placed for sale as soon as possible."

Rowena bit her lip. "There isn't any alternative?"

"No. Now then, please try to put it from your mind for the moment, my dear. We have tonight's bonfire to look forward to, and I know how much you love it."

Rowena turned toward her. "It will be our last Halloween bonfire here, won't it?" she said quietly.

Her mother didn't reply.

Lady Margaret gazed sadly down at them for a few moments more and then drifted out into the hall again. Well, at least Rowena now knew how desperate the situation had become. The phantom's sadness turned to anger. This was William Melcombe's fault! Bristling with indignation, she fluttered up to the principal bedroom to fix him with furious glare.

"Good morning, sirrah," she said icily.

He shifted uncomfortably. "Good morning," he mumbled.

"I daresay you will be interested to know I've found a bridegroom for Rowena."

His eyes widened. "You . . . you have?"

"The future Marquess of Exford, no less. He's staying at the Red Lion."

William gaped. "The future Marquess of . . . ? For *Rowena*? I can't believe it."

"Well, it's not fact yet, but it will be. No thanks to you."

He drew back defensively.

"That's right, curl up in a sulk again! Oh, you really are a tiresome creature! Well, I have some other news for you as well. Because of your bungling, the bank is foreclosing, and your poor wife has to sell this house. *Our* house! Our heritage!"

He gazed wretchedly back at her from the canvas.

Lady Margaret wished it were possible to shake him out of his guilty lethargy. "How can you exist with yourself? How can you hang there on that wall, watching your wife tossing and turning at nights? You're quite despicable, sirrah!"

William felt dreadful. It was true. He was a feeble nonentity, too craven and gutless to leave his sanctuary and try to help the family he loved so much. A tear rolled down his cheek as he curled up in the frame and hid his face from the room.

"Just remember that I may yet decide to have you disposed of," she reminded menacingly. She felt no pity for him; she was too angry for that. If he felt bad now, then it served him right! She couldn't dispose of him—she wasn't a sufficiently high-ranking spirit—but he didn't know that. He'd kept out of the way so much he hardly knew anything about the world of which he was now part.

She glided out of the house and looked toward the Red Lion. To her horror she saw Justin's carriage drawn up outside.

He was leaving!

Chapter 6

The phantom sped hastily to the inn. Yes, there was no mistake, the carriage was in readiness to set off, although Justin had yet to come out. The coachman was on his seat with the reins in his hands, but was more concerned with making eyes at a saucy tavern wench than anything else.

Lady Margaret was in a quandary. Something had to be done quickly. What was required was a small accident, just enough to damage the carriage and keep it in Melcombe. The ghost cast around for inspiration, and then her glance fell upon the cat dozing on the inn doorstep. The creature hadn't sensed her presence yet, but it would at any moment, and she remembered its reaction to her the night before. Summoning every ounce of spectral menace and ferocity, she gave a dreadful shriek only animals could hear.

The terrified cat erupted from the doorstep and fled like a demon between the legs of the carriage team, which had also heard the ghostly scream. They lurched forward to escape from the noise and caught the amorous coachman unawares. He applied the brake too late, and the carriage's nearside wheel struck a stone mounting block. Astonishment was written large upon his face. What had happened? One moment everything had been quiet, the next it was Bedlam itself!

The flirtatious serving girl was rooted to the spot, and the villagers building the bonfire stared openmouthed. Nearby cottage curtains twitched, and one or two doors opened as people looked out to see what the disturbance was. Suddenly, there was an ominous splintering sound as the damaged wheel gave way, and the carriage tilted precariously over.

Lady Margaret was exultant. Oh, excellent! Nothing could have been more neatly achieved!

At that moment Justin emerged from the inn and came to an incredulous halt on seeing what had befallen his expensive vehicle.

The dismayed coachman clambered down from the box. "My lord, I—"

"What in God's name has happened?"

"I . . . I can't honestly say, my lord."

"Can't say? You were present, were you not?" Justin replied cuttingly.

"Yes, my lord. It's just . . . Well, there was a cat on that doorstep over there, and suddenly it shot off like a cannon. It dashed past the horses, they took fright, and—"

"And your mind was elsewhere," Justin finished for him, having by now perceived the serving girl. He knew the man's taste in women, and she fitted the bill in every way.

The coachman colored and said nothing. Justin contained his anger as he examined the damage.

The innkeeper had hastened out and could scarcely contain his mercenary delight. Not only would this fine London toff have to enjoy the Red Lion's hospitality a little longer, but his carriage would require repairs by the blacksmith, who just happened to be his brother! How provident.

Justin turned to him. "At least have the tact to conceal your glee, sir," he remarked tersely.

The landlord's face changed. "I, er, I was only thinking it's as well we have a good smithy here in Melcombe."

"I expect you to personally see to it that this matter is dealt with expediently."

"Me, my lord?"

"You, sir, since it was apparently your demented feline that caused the accident in the first place."

The landlord looked uncomprehendingly at him. What was he talking about? There wasn't any sign of the cat.

Justin removed his top hat and ran his gloved fingers through his hair. God damn it! He'd intended to be well on his way back to London by dark.

"The Red Lion will offer you every hospitality while you wait, my lord," the landlord ventured tentatively.

Justin looked sourly at him. "Oh, yes, of that I have little doubt," he murmured.

"You're welcome to rest inside, my lord." The landlord's arm swept invitingly toward the doorway.

"I'd prefer to stretch my legs for a while."

"As you wish, sir."

"What I wish is that you get on with the repairs without delay!" Justin replied shortly.

"I'll attend to it immediately, my lord." The man hurried away.

Justin glanced around. Well, it was a fine autumn morning, and he might as well make the most of it by taking a stroll around the village. Tugging his top hat on again, he walked away from the inn.

Damn everything. Fate seemed determined to make his life a misery at the moment. He didn't want to marry because his ailing father regarded the matter as so important, but he loved his father and in the end that was all that mattered. His friends in Bath would applaud his decision, but Chloe wouldn't like it at all.

He considered his mistress for a moment. She'd always known he'd have to go to the altar sooner or later, but that wouldn't make it any more palatable for her now the moment had come. He wouldn't give her up, though. He'd find a bride to placate his father and remove the threat of the Beaufort match, but he'd still keep his mistress!

Lady Margaret floated after him as he walked. The phantom was delighted with the way she'd delayed his departure and now took a little time to study him in the daylight. She could view him only with approval. He really was as devastatingly handsome as she'd thought the night before, an echo of Kit down the years, and he had great style, too. There was something nonchalant and dashing about the way his great coat was tossed around his shoulders. He was traveling without a valet, but no fault could be found with the shine on his boots or the knot in his neckcloth.

The spirit sighed, for somehow this nonpareil had to be persuaded that Rowena Melcombe was his perfect bride! Hovering a while to see which way he walked, Lady Margaret then glided busily back to the manor house to see if Rowena could be persuaded to take an airing in the same direction.

But at that moment Rowena was slipping out of a side door to hurry to the wicket gate into the adjacent churchyard. A cloak covered her gown, but the hood wasn't raised, and she was anxious to be alone to think about the family's financial problems. The church offered the perfect refuge. Both the Reverend Grantham and the curate were away today, and the church would be empty.

The gate hinges squeaked and the first fallen leaves rustled beneath her feet as she hurried between the gravestones toward the porch. Moisture still dripped from the yew trees flanking the gravel path from the lychgate, and gossamer drifted gently through the air. The first apple gatherers had arrived in Farmer Porlock's orchard, and their voices were light and cheerful as they prepared to start work.

Lady Margaret followed her into the cool silence of the nave. The wraith was puzzled. What was the chit coming here for? The last thing Rowena Melcombe should be doing now was hiding away in a church! She should be out somewhere where she could come providentially face-to-face with Justin!

The musty smell of ancient stone pricked Rowena's nostrils, and her footsteps echoed on the stone floor as she hurried down the aisle between the wooden pews. She made her way to the vestry, where the village women took turns to tend the stove that kept the vestments aired. There she sat on a wooden bench and stared unhappily at the floor. It was painful to think of leaving Melcombe, and daunting to wonder what was going to happen after that. How were they going to manage? What would become of them? Tears filled her eyes and then wended their way down her cheeks.

Lady Margaret looked compassionately at her. Poor child. This morning's revelation had come as a dreadful shock. The ghost lingered for a moment more and then drifted into the churchyard to look for Justin. A smile curved her lips, for not only was he conveniently close by, he was actually passing the lychgate! All he required was a little subtle persuasion to enter the church.

But how to achieve it? Inspiration eluded her this time until a slight breeze rustled through the yew trees. Lady Margaret smiled again as she looked at his top hat. Of course! A sudden strong gust of wind would send that Bond Street headpiece bowling over the wall and along the churchyard path toward the porch! But she needed to gather herself for the effort of raising a wind.

She flew swiftly across the road to the far end of a cottage garden, then, taking a deep breath, she screwed up her face with concentration and sped mightily back again. She rushed past Justin and a huge draft followed in her wake. The trees swayed and his hat was plucked from his head. She heard him curse as it rolled along the path and he hurried after it.

Lady Margaret watched eagerly as the hat bounced beneath the porch and then into the church itself, where it came to rest against the nearest pew. The wind died away, and there was silence as Justin entered to retrieve his property. As he picked the hat up, he heard the soft sound of a woman crying. Straightening, he scanned the pews. No one seemed to be there, but he could still hear the quietly heartbroken sobs. Dusting the hat, he walked down the aisle.

Lady Margaret urged him silently on. Look in the vestry! Look in the vestry! She willed him with all her might and was jubilant as at last his gaze was drawn to the door in question. She fluttered eagerly past him as he went toward it.

He saw Rowena seated inside with her face in her hands. Some of her long blond hair had fallen loose from its pins, and his gaze was drawn to those gleaming straight tresses. There was something strangely familiar about the way they fell, and about their color and texture. For a fleeing moment it was night again, and a naked girl lay eagerly on a bed, her arms stretched up toward him. It couldn't possibly be . . . Slowly he pushed the door further open.

Suddenly, she realized he was there and rose sharply to her feet. A shock of secret recognition passed electrically through them both as they stared at each other.

Lady Margaret hovered in an agony of suspense. Everything depended upon the next few minutes. Would they make hurried excuses to go their separate ways? Or would they be as attracted in reality as they'd been in their fantasies?

Chapter 7

Rowena's heart almost stopped. The man she'd dreamed about! Her thoughts began to race incredulously, seeking a logical explanation. Perhaps she was still asleep. Yes, that had to be it, for this couldn't really be happening. But as she faced him, she knew she was awake. And the expression on his face was as startled as hers, as if he knew exactly what she was thinking!

She swallowed and pulled herself up sharply. This was nothing but a coincidence. He merely *resembled* the man she'd dreamed about, and if he was startled now, it was probably because he hadn't expected to find anyone in the vestry. He must be here on church business . . .

Struggling to collect herself, she said, "Forgive me, I, er, don't usually . . ." Her voice died away lamely, and she searched for a handkerchief.

Justin also strove to regain his equilibrium. "Perhaps I'm the one who should seek forgiveness." He found his own handkerchief and gave it to her.

Their fingers brushed, and the brief contact affected them both, for it proved beyond doubt there was nothing illusory about things now.

Justin couldn't take his eyes from her. The impossible was happening. She'd stepped out of his dreams into the cold light of day. He couldn't see her figure beneath the cloak, but he was certain of every sweet detail. Dear God, he'd taken leave of his senses! There was something about this part of Exmoor that robbed a man of his wits. He cleared his throat. "I, didn't mean to intrude, Miss, er . . . ?"

"Melcombe, and it is no intrusion."

The significance of her name struck him. "Melcombe? Would it be correct to think this village was named after your family?"

"Yes, it would, Mr. . . . ?" She looked inquiringly at him.

"Alderney."

"Mr. Alderney."

He smiled a little. "To be strictly correct, I'm Lord Alderney, son of the Marquess of Exford."

Her eyes widened. "Th-then I'm doubly honored to make your acquaintance, my lord."

"I hardly imagine you feel honored now I've blundered into your privacy."

"It was nothing."

His gaze lingered on her lips. Last night he'd kissed her, he'd held her close, body to body, warmth to warmth . . .

She thought how memorable his eyes were. The color of the sea.

Conscious of the sudden silence, they both began to speak at the same time. Then he laughed a little. "After you, Miss Melcombe."

"I-I was merely going to say I was neglecting my manners. There must be someone you wish to see. The Reverend Grantham, perhaps?"

"Er, no. Actually, I wouldn't have come into the church at all if it hadn't been for the wind blowing my hat away."

"Wind?" She looked out of the leaded window at the motionless trees.

"There was a sudden strong gust," he explained, following her glance and feeling a little foolish.

Lady Margaret smiled to herself. Oh, yes, Lord Alderney, there had indeed been a gust of wind, and it was one of which any wraith could be proud!

Rowena returned his handkerchief. "So you aren't here on church business?"

"Far from it. In fact I'd have left Melcombe already if it hadn't been for some damage to my carriage." He studied her again. It was hardly possible to find anyone less like Chloe. His mistress was lovely, vain, witty, amusing, and only too well versed in the ways of the world. This country creature wasn't a beauty, was completely unaffected, and showed no sign of a quick tongue. But she had a beguiling charm and was possessed of the seductive bloom of innocence. Last night, in the sanctuary of his sleep, she'd thrown that innocence to the four winds and become a bewitching wanton. Consummation had eluded him then, and now, on this suddenly exhilarating Halloween morning, he longed for that which he'd been denied. The thought was intoxicating, like a draft of fairy nectar.

The instant this last rather fanciful notion occurred to him, he knew it would be eminently advisable to leave. He was thinking irrationally, as if he'd gazed too long at the full moon. But it was one thing to know one should go, quite another to do so. He didn't want to leave; he wanted to know more about her. And so instead of making a timely exit, he cast around for something to say. "Melcombe is very beautiful, one of the most beautiful villages I've—"

"Please don't say anything more, Lord Alderney," she interrupted quickly, fresh tears springing to her eyes.

He was concerned that he'd somehow spoken out of turn. "Miss Melcombe, if I've offended in any way . . ."

"No, my lord, you haven't offended, it's just that Melcombe is one of the reasons you found me crying."

"Would it help to talk about it? I mean, they do say that a trouble shared is a trouble halved." It was a base ploy to remain in her company, and he knew it.

A wry smile played wanly around her lips. "That's the second time this morning I've heard that expression," she murmured.

"It's a very common saying, and a very true one."

"You may be right."

"Do you wish to talk about it?"

She shook her head. "It's too dull a tale for someone like you, Lord Alderney."

"Someone like me? Should I be insulted?" He smiled.

She colored. "Oh, no, please don't think I meant to criticize in any way."

"Being a lord doesn't preclude one from wishing to help if one can," he said.

She lowered her eyes. "I'm sure it doesn't, sir, but I fear my tale remains very dull."

"Perhaps if we walk outside in the sunshine . . . ?" The suggestion ended on a inviting note, and he offered her his arm.

She hesitated. It was not strictly correct to spend time in the company of a gentleman she'd barely met, and it was a matter for disapproval if she went so far as to walk on his arm, but nevertheless she wanted to accept.

He smiled. "I'm sure a stroll in a churchyard in full view of the village can only be regarded as decorous, Miss Melcombe."

She returned the smile and slipped her fingers over his sleeve. She still almost expected to find he was a figment of her imagination and that her hand would pass right through him. But he was very much flesh and blood.

They walked through the silent church, and Lady Margaret glided delightedly after them. What an unexpectedly well-matched couple they were. Rowena had shown considerable charm, without any of her usual studiousness, and Justin was pleasingly free of disagreeable airs and graces. It had been amusing to watch their faces as they separately recalled their midnight encounter, and it was very encouraging that neither of them had cut the present meeting short. If things continued like this, she'd return to her frame tonight to the approving applause of her spectral companions.

They emerged into the daylight, and Justin glanced toward Melkery Beacon, where the dazzling purple and gold heights seemed to touch the heavens. "Now can you tell me why you were crying, Miss Melcombe?" he asked gently.

"It's the old story of family debt, Lord Alderney. When my father died two years ago, it seems he left our finances in a dreadful state, only until this morning I didn't realize quite how dreadful. The bank is foreclosing, and my mother now has no alternative but to sell the house. It grieves me to think I remained unaware of how desperately she was struggling to keep going. You see, apart from trying to keep the estate solvent, she's also been trying to provide for all of us."

"All of you?"

Rowena nodded. "I have three younger brothers." She bit her lip to stop fresh tears as she turned to look at the manor, so mellow and timeless as it faced proudly toward the beacon. "Now we have to leave here and exist as best we can in what will be greatly reduced circumstances."

Justin followed her gaze. "I can understand why you'd be heartbroken at the thought of leaving such a home," he said quietly.

"You'll never know how much I love Melcombe, Lord Alderney. It means everything to me."

He glanced at her profile. "Everything? There is no other love in your life?" He could hardly believe he'd said something so crass. It was worthy of a boy barely out of puberty! He cleared his throat awkwardly. "I wish you'd forget I asked that, Miss Melcombe. Forgive me."

"I'm not offended, Lord Alderney; in fact I feel guilty for still being a burden to my mother," she replied candidly.

"I can't imagine you're a burden, Miss Melcombe."

"You're very chivalrous, sir, but if I'd been married, there would have been one less for my mother to worry over, and I might even have been in a position to offer financial assistance." She colored a little then, for these were things no young woman should speak of to a gentleman she'd only just met. She took her hand from his arm. "Now it's my turn to apologize, sir, for I'm sure I must be embarrassing you."

"I'm not in the least embarrassed, Miss Melcombe," he replied quickly. He found her openness quite refreshing. She was like the first breath of spring after the chill of winter.

"It's gallant of you to try to reassure me, sir, but even though you aren't embarrassed, I most certainly am." She managed an awkward smile. "I really don't know why I've said half the things I have, for we are strangers."

"To be truthful, I have the oddest feeling we may have met somewhere before," he said slowly. It was as far as he cared to venture without saying exactly how he thought they'd met!

Her cheeks flamed. "Oh, I . . . I don't think we have, sir!" She was covered with immediate confusion.

He had to look away, conscious of the almost electric atmosphere that sprang up between them, and of an almost compelling urge to take her in his arms and kiss her as he had last night. A spell seemed to have enfolded him. He wanted to feel her respond as she had then; he wanted to savor the sweet moment of her surrender . . .

The force of his thoughts made him feel hot, and as a distraction he changed the subject. A little earlier he'd noticed the villagers building the bonfire. That was as safe a topic as any. "Er, it would seem Halloween is to be celebrated with great enthusiasm tonight, Miss Melcombe."

She was equally relieved to speak of something else. "Exmoor is renowned for its Mischief Night, sir."

"Mischief Night?"

"If you're still here after dark, you'll soon know why it's called that, and I fear my twin brothers are usually behind the worst of the trouble."

Still here after dark? He suddenly realized that in a very short while now he'd be leaving this place. Leaving her.

Rowena glanced up at the church clock. "I've taken up enough of your time, and now I will release you." She extended her hand. "Thank you for listening to me, Lord Alderney."

"Perhaps you'd care to return the compliment?" he suggested suddenly.

"Return the compliment?" she repeated in puzzlement, lowering her hand again.

He hesitated and then plucked words from the air. "I, er, would value your opinion on certain family matters that are of great concern to me at the moment. Perhaps we could speak at the bonfire tonight?"

He didn't want her opinion on anything, he just wanted to see her again. He hadn't even realized the request was on his lips, or that he'd changed his mind about returning to London today.

Chapter 8

Lady Margaret pirouetted joyfully in the air above them. He was staying in Melcombe! He wanted to see Rowena again! But then a thought struck the ghost, and she ceased her ecstatic whirling. What if Rowena declined? Oh, no, that wouldn't suit at all! Lady Margaret gazed down intently at her descendant. Don't you *dare* give the wrong reply now, my girl!

Unconscious of the spectral agitation in the air over her head, Rowena had been caught a little off guard by Justin's request. "I, er . . ."

"Aren't you attending the bonfire?"

"Oh, yes, we always do, it's just . . ."

"I would really appreciate your advice."

"Advice? Oh, I don't think I am qualified to advise you on matters concerning your family, Lord Alderney. I fear I must decline."

A dismayed Lady Margaret clutched her closed fan in both hands. Oh, the impossible little miss!

But the spirit reckoned without Justin's persistence. "I think you are very well qualified, Miss Melcombe; in fact, I'm certain you are. Please grant me this favor."

"If you put it like that, sir, to refuse would be churlish." Slowly Rowena returned the smile.

Lady Margaret exhaled with relief.

Justin raised Rowena's hand to his lips. "I'm very grateful, Miss Melcombe. Until tonight then?"

She nodded. "Until tonight, Lord Alderney," she murmured before turning to hurry away between the gravestones.

Lady Margaret was about to follow when something made her stay to observe Justin. Oh, to be able to read thoughts. It would be so unutterably helpful to know exactly what was going through his mind right now. The ghost glided intently around him, studying him closely from every angle, but his sea green eyes gave nothing away.

Justin watched Rowena as she left. Her pale hair still tumbled loose from its pins, and it amused him to ponder the unlikelihood of Chloe ever appearing in such disarray. Chloe wore her hair short now, but when it had been long, the mere thought of a loose pin would be enough to make her shudder. Delightfully unaffected Miss Melcombe hadn't once seemed conscious of being less that perfectly turned out. It was tantalizing to think of really making love to her, of holding her naked body close between silk sheets. He smiled at the sensuous path his thoughts were taking once more, but then his smile faded a little. No matter what he had dreamed, she wasn't a woman of easy virtue, and if base seduction was what he subconsciously intended now, he should leave this place as soon as possible.

His gaze lingered on her until she'd passed through the wicket gate into the manor house garden. Then he walked slowly down the path between the yew trees and out through the lychgate. The smile returned to his lips, and he tugged his top hat on again. He'd wait and see. He glanced up toward the sky. He didn't know what he hoped would emerge from this particular situation; he only knew he wanted to spend a little more time with intriguing Miss Melcombe. An ironic laugh escaped him then. Miss Melcombe? He didn't even know her first name!

The laugh perplexed Lady Margaret. She flew up to the top of the church steeple and watched him until he went into the inn. Was he being entirely honorable in this? The possibility that he wasn't came as a disagreeable shock, for it wouldn't do if his intention was merely to seduce Rowena. The ghost hoped this wasn't in his mind, for in the Halloween time left, there was precious little chance of finding another prospective husband for Rowena.

Halloween. Lady Margaret's lips twitched as she recalled her determination to turn the tables on the twins. Perhaps the time had come to seek their present whereabouts and see what they were up to.

Gliding farther up into the air, the ghost cast her sharp gaze over the countryside behind the manor house. Rowena had told her mother that when the pumpkin had been stolen, the boys had made off over the footbridge. From there the only path led toward the beacon. Deciding it was as good a place as any to begin her search, Lady Margaret swooped down over the manor house gardens to the bridge and then along the barely discernible path at the edge of the stubble field on the far side of the stream. Red-berried rowan trees grew along the path, and some children were gathering branches to fix to cottage doors that night. Witches were thought to fear rowan as much as they feared turnip lanterns, and homes thus protected were said to be safe from spells and evil.

Lady Margaret hovered by them for a moment. From her observations since becoming a spirit, a determined witch wasn't deterred by sprays of leaves or hollowed vegetables, but it was so seldom anyway that a witch came anywhere near remote Melcombe that these charms were deemed to be effective. It was something akin to the old joke that placing sand by the threshold kept lions away. The natural response was that there weren't lions in England, to which it was pointed out how well the sand must work!

The apparition flew on to look for the twins. But if she'd glanced back at the road at that moment, she'd have seen a fashionable gentleman driving a smart scarlet cabriolet toward the village.

Andrew Kemp tooled the high-stepping horse expertly and then slowed the pace for a moment or so as he passed the manor house. He was darkly good-looking and wore his hair in the short rather untidy style known as the Brutus crop. His olive complexion emphasized the shining appeal of his brown eyes, and his lips were full and sensuous. His greatcoat collar was turned up, and his top hat pulled low over his forehead.

After looking thoughtfully at the manor house, he drove on toward the Red Lion. He was a heartless adventurer and practiced seducer, with a score of conquests to his discredit, but his formidable skills had failed to net the rich wife he'd promised himself. And now his mercenary ambitions were being thwarted by a constant yearning for Rowena Melcombe. He couldn't put her from his thoughts, and it was playing the very devil with his peace of mind. He couldn't understand the effect she had. She wasn't a beauty, far from it, but she had a certain *je-ne-sais-quoi*, and memories of her curvaceous figure tormented his nights. He seldom slept alone, but no matter how lovely his companion, it was

Rowena he made love to. He should have seduced her when he had the chance, for maybe she wouldn't have proved as exciting as he thought. But he hadn't seduced her, and as a result she was always on his mind. That was why he'd returned to Melcombe. He had to slake the thirst she'd aroused and thus be able to forget her.

He flicked the whip, and the cabriolet skimmed the final yards to the door of the Red Lion, arriving at the same moment as Justin. The two men saw each other and nodded civilly, then Justin went to see how his carriage repair was proceeding.

Gazing after him, Andrew alighted from the cabriolet. They'd never met, but Justin had once been pointed out to him. What was Alderney doing here? Andrew smiled a little, for although Justin wasn't an acquaintance, his dazzling mistress was. Fair Chloe was as unfaithful to her lover as she was to her husband! But her inconstancy wasn't a reflection upon her feelings toward Alderney; on the contrary, she was infatuated with him. He was the love of her life and caused her more jealousy than he'd ever know. She was consumed with the fear that sooner or later he'd take a wife who might win his heart. But even though she loved him so much, she was simply incapable of being true to him. Chloe, Countess of Westcote, was as promiscuous as any Cyprian, the pleasures of the flesh were life itself to her, and if a man caught her eye, nothing would do but that she had him.

Putting Justin's wanton mistress from his thoughts, he glanced around the village green. Places like Melcombe seldom changed; they even put the Halloween bonfire in exactly the same spot every year. It was no accident he'd chosen this day to return. He knew Rowena and her family always attended the festivities, and he intended to find an opportunity to speak to her. Calling at the manor would avail him nothing. Mrs. Melcombe had him marked as an undesirable ne'er-do-well and had told him as much, so his arrival on the doorstep wouldn't be warmly greeted. In fact, there were very few in Melcombe who'd be pleased to see him again, but if Rowena still felt as she did before, then this visit would be well worthwhile. Next time he left, it would be for good, and the lady would soon be little more than a pleasant memory. Whistling to himself, he tethered the horse to a rail and then entered the inn.

The dismayed innkeeper recognized him immediately. "Mr. Kemp?"

"I'm flattered you remember me."

"Most folk around here remember you."

Andrew smiled coolly. "Yes, and I'm sure the maids in this establishment recall me with great affection."

"Hardly. Not when they found out you'd spread your favors round them all."

"Not quite all," Andrew replied, his appreciative glance following a pert little redhead as she hurried into the taproom. She was the maid who'd distracted Justin's coachman earlier.

The innkeeper wiped his hands on his apron. "If it's the hope of money that's brought you back, you might as well know there's even less of it at the big house now than there was before."

"How insolent you are, to be sure," Andrew murmured. "As it happens, the state of the Melcombe Manor coffers are no longer of interest to me." He paused, teasing off his gloves. "By the way, how is Miss Melcombe?"

"Well enough."

"From which effusive response I take it she's still here?"

The landlord nodded.

Andrew smiled again. "Excellent. Now, I require a room."

For a moment the innkeeper considered refusing, but then acknowledged how foolish it would be to turn away custom. "A room it is, sir."

Andrew's smile became contemptuous. "I note that your avarice can always be relied upon to take precedence over your scruples. This place certainly never changes."

The landlord said nothing.

Andrew glanced out into the yard, where Justin was speaking to his coachman. "Why is Alderney here?" he asked.

"You're acquainted with his lordship?"

"Not exactly. Well?"

"I've no idea why he's here. He was on his way to Cornwall, or some such place, but changed his mind and intends to go back to London. His carriage was damaged, but is repaired now, and he can leave if he wishes. He's just told me he's staying for another night."

"Just see that you give me a room that equals his. I don't want an attic."

"All my rooms are excellent, sir," the landlord replied stiffly. "If you'll come this way . . . ?"

The man led him toward the staircase, and Andrew's glance moved to the taproom doorway as the pretty redhead hurried out again. His knowing gaze raked over her, and he pursed his lips approvingly. "Well, well, you're the tastiest morsel I've encountered in a long time," he murmured, giving her a lazy wink.

She turned, flashing him a flirtatious smile, and he hummed lightly to himself as he followed the landlord up to the next floor. One thing was certain; he wouldn't sleep alone tonight.

Chapter 9

Still unaware of Melcombe village's unwelcome new visitor, Lady Margaret was searching for the twins. Suddenly, she noticed a village boy just vanishing into a copse. He was carrying a turnip and a small bag of soot. Guising implements, the phantom decided with satisfaction as she glided silently between the trees behind him. The scent of oak filled the air, and a startled blackbird fled noisily as the boy paused to glance over his shoulder before scrambling down into a hidden glade, where a dilapidated shack stood against the vast trunk of an ancient tree.

Lady Margaret heard the twins' voices greeting the boy as he went in, and she followed immediately. She found the boys inspecting everything they'd collected for the coming night, but of Griggs's pumpkin there was no sign.

The village boy presented his contribution. The turnip was small and dismissed almost contemptuously, but the soot was very well received, for the more guisers could hide their faces, the better it was.

Lady Margaret sniffed disparagingly as she looked at their disguises. Stephen evidently intended to be Old Nick himself, with a hideous horned-goat mask and a fearsome pitchfork to jab his victims. The soot would blacken his face, for infuriated people had been known to snatch masks away.

Paul was going to be a ghost and had an old sheet for his shroud. With it he intended to carry an alarm rattle acquired from a Bridgwater watchman. Lady Margaret sighed at the shroud. Did the foolish boy really imagine those in the next world deigned to be seen in such garb? No wraith of integrity would go abroad in a winding sheet! She glanced down at her own glittering skirts. One had to look one's best, for one never knew what other apparition one might encounter. And word spread. Oh, dear me, yes.

The village boy left, and after a final inspection of their Halloween trumpery, the twins went out as well. Lady Margaret glanced around again. Where was the pumpkin? It had to be here somewhere. At last she saw something hidden beneath an old sack in a particularly dark corner. Contorting her face intensely, she per-

suaded the sack to pull to one side, and the missing pumpkin was
revealed, reposing upon a rather battered, locked wooden casket.

It had become the largest, most gruesome Halloween lantern
the phantom had ever seen, and she stared at it with grudging ad-
miration. Beside such a horror the traditional turnip lanterns
looked almost meager. It was positively demonic, with fiendish
eyes and a jagged leering mouth that might have come directly
from hell itself. She was put in mind of two particularly repulsive,
malodorous entities observed passing over Melcombe recently.
Who or what they were no one at the manor had known, but they
resembled certain gargoyles on Exeter cathedral.

Lady Margaret shuddered and then surveyed the pumpkin
again. One could only ponder how this horrid thing would look
when lit by a candle and brandished at some bedroom window. It
really was too much. The twins were most definitely overdue
what she understood the Americans called a comeuppance. Her
spectral lips pursed pensively and then curved into a sly smile as
an idea began to form. But it all depended upon how much power
she could exercise over the pumpkin, which was far heavier than
anything she'd moved until now. Grimacing again, she directed
her will at the monster lantern. Gradually, it rose from the floor.
Pleased, she made it fly around the shack, but before returning it
to its place her attention was drawn to the casket upon which it
had been placed. What was inside? It had to be something interesting, otherwise the boys would not have used a lock. She tried
to open it, but couldn't. She even attempted to put her ghostly
hand inside, but her fingers passed right through it, and so at last
she made it rise into the air and shake from side to side. An interesting rustling sound was produced by the invisible contents, but
she was still none the wiser as to what those contents were.

Crossly, the phantom lowered it into the corner again, the
pumpkin on top of it. Then with a twitch of her lips, she made the
sack slither back into place. So the twins wanted to frighten innocent people with their awful creation, did they? Well, tonight
they'd find out just how diabolical a thing they'd made!

She was about to leave when she saw a skeleton hanging on the
wall. Startled, she fluttered back several feet. Surely the twins
hadn't gone so far as to desecrate a grave! No, not even they
would do that. Recovering a little, she floated closer and saw that
the bones were held together with metal pins. This was not the occupant of a graveyard, but had come from a establishment where
medicine was taught.

The spirit hovered thoughtfully. She hardly dared think what prank the boys had in mind for such a magnificent Halloween weapon. The skeleton had even frightened *her*! She glanced back at the pumpkin. Very well, if it was to be war, it was to be war. Returning her attention to the skeleton, she made it raise its arms. Then she caused the jaw to drop and rise again. After that she instructed the whole skeleton to dance about on its hook. The bones rattled quite eerily, and Lady Margaret smiled. By the time she'd finished with them, the twins would wish they'd stayed in bed. This Halloween was going to be one they'd remember for the rest of their lives!

The phantom floated back to the house to look for Rowena, but the potential Lady Alderney was nowhere to be found. The perplexed shade glided from room to room, inquiring of all the portraits, but no one had seen Rowena. At last only William was left, but Lady Margaret doubted if he could help.

He was dozing when she entered, and he gave a great start as she spoke his name.

"William?"

"Eh? What . . . ?" He struggled to collect his scattered senses.

"I'm looking for your daughter. Have you any idea where she is?"

"On the stone bench in the garden," he replied promptly.

"Thank you." Lady Margaret turned to leave, but then halted as something odd struck her. She looked at him again. "How do you know she's there? You can't see the bench from where your frame hangs."

He shrugged. "I just know. I always know where all my children are."

"Do you indeed? How very interesting."

"Interesting? I don't understand. Surely it's something every ghost is aware of, regarding its children?"

"No, sirrah, it isn't. For some reason you appear to have been granted a very special gift."

A little miffed, Lady Margaret glided away again. How very vexing that an apparition as useless as he should have such an ability. Really, there were times when she thought the Powers-That-Be were capricious to the point of lunacy!

The rather cross spirit went out into the gardens and found Rowena seated on the stone bench between the colorful beds of goldenrod and Michaelmas daisies. Lady Margaret glided over to her, expecting to see a book lying open on her lap, but there wasn't one. Instead, Rowena's hands were clasped, and she was gazing at nothing in particular.

The ghost moved around the bench. Was she thinking about Justin? Yes, of course she was; what else would produce that dreamy-eyed expression? Lady Margaret sat invisibly next to her. It would be ideal now to conjure another illusion of Justin, but that might not be possible when he wasn't asleep. It was always worth the effort, though. The wraith gathered her powers and closed her eyes tightly to summon him. But he didn't come. Drawing another huge breath, she tried again, but no image appeared, not even a faint one.

With a sigh Lady Margaret left the bench. It was disagreeable to be foiled, but what was one small failure after all her successes? She'd done excellently so far and now she needed to rest before the exertions of the coming night.

If the spirit had only known it, however, there was no need to conjure Justin before Rowena; he was there already in her mind's eye. It wasn't the garden she saw, it was his face; and it wasn't the song of the thrush she heard, it was his voice. She didn't understand what had been happening to her since midnight last night. She only knew that it was something important.

She raised her face to the warm October sunshine, and as she closed her eyes, she was with him again. His naked reflection was beside her in the cheval glass, and she was gazing at his pale masculine beauty. How perfect he was as he reached out to her. And how exciting it was to press close to him and feel the shaftlike potency of his body. She'd never known desire could feel like this. A shiver of ecstasy passed through her as once again he carried her to the bed, and she lay there waiting for him to come down to her.

But there the fantasy ended. She lowered her eyes to the grass. How it would be to finally surrender to the consuming desire that raged through her now? What would that exquisite moment be like? How would she feel when he entered her body and made it his? She trembled a little, for she knew she wanted to experience that ultimate pleasure. She wanted to submit to Lord Alderney's lovemaking. No, not merely submit, she wanted to meet him halfway, to kiss him as fiercely as he kissed her, to possess as much as she was possessed!

The strength of her feelings was suddenly too much, and she rose hastily from the bench. She felt unbearably hot and knew her cheeks were flaming with shame that she'd permitted her imagination to go so far. How on earth was she going to be able to look him in the eyes tonight?

Tonight. She exhaled slowly. She'd be with him again soon, but the hours would drag unbearably until then. Tears suddenly pricked her eyes, for she knew she was deluding herself to hope he was attracted to her. Such a man would have his pick of London beauties, and plain, provincial Rowena Melcombe was hardly likely to be of interest. She didn't know why she'd dreamed of him before even knowing he existed, but she did know dreams were fancies that lost substance when the dreamer awoke. Now she'd met him in fact, but would be wise to bear in mind that the wonderful abandonment enjoyed by her subconscious self meant nothing in reality. If she expected anything more to come of tonight, she was fooling herself. Only pain and heartbreak lay that way.

Gathering her cloak around her, she walked slowly back toward the house.

Chapter 10

The hitherto mild autumn seemed to come to an end as the afternoon light faded into a brilliant sunset. A sudden chill filled the air, and the clarity of the sky promised frost before dawn. It was sufficient excuse for Mrs. Melcombe to ask for negus to be brought to the drawing room before she, Rowena, and Lionel set off for the bonfire on the green.

Needless to say, there was still no sign of the twins, and it was as much this latter problem as the coldness of the night that prompted the request for the fortifying beverage. While she and Rowena waited for Lionel to join them, Mrs. Melcombe dreaded to think what her wayward younger sons had planned, and she repeatedly blamed herself for allowing them to virtually run wild.

Sitting close to the fire, she sipped the negus. "It's all my fault. If I'd been firmer with them over the past year or so . . ."

"You've had a great deal to contend with, Mother," Rowena reminded her gently. She stood by the window, holding the curtain slightly aside to look out at the shadowy garden. There were stars overhead now, and Melkery Beacon seemed oddly close, as if it had stepped nearer the village to join in the festivities. On a night such as this it was only too easy to believe in ghosts and witches.

Mrs. Melcombe sighed. "A great deal to contend with? Yes, I

suppose I have, but that doesn't excuse my dereliction of duty where Stephen and Paul are concerned. If only things had been different, and there'd been sufficient funds for them to be sent to Eton as your poor dear father wished."

Rowena turned from the window, her rose gown deepening to port wine in the soft glow of the candles lighting the room. "If the twins do their worst tonight, as they probably will, you at least have the questionable comfort of knowing this will be the last time they'll be able to plague Melcombe."

"A very questionable comfort indeed," her mother replied.

"I'm sorry, I shouldn't have worded it quite like that."

"Well, it's the truth, is it not? The Lord alone knows where we'll be next Halloween." Mrs. Melcombe studied her. "I've been waiting for you to say something of your own accord, but since you show no signs of so doing, I am obliged to ask you. Who was the gentleman I observed you with today in the churchyard?"

Rowena colored and turned to look into the fire. "Lord Alderney."

Startled, her mother lowered her glass. "*Lord* Alderney?" she repeated.

"Yes. He is the son of the Marquess of Exford."

"How did you meet him?"

"He, er, came into the church when I was there."

Mrs. Melcombe stared at her. "You've made the acquaintance of a nobleman and didn't see fit to mention it to me?"

"It wasn't of consequence."

"What you really mean is that you know you were more than a little rash to permit such familiarity. The exchange of a few polite words is one thing, but to brazenly walk on his arm in the churchyard quite another!" her mother replied tartly.

Rowena looked guiltily at her.

"What did you talk about?"

"Oh, only general civilities."

Mrs. Melcombe exhaled slowly. "May one inquire why he is gracing Melcombe with his presence?"

"I really don't know."

A thought occurred to her mother. "Perhaps Lady Alderney was there as well, and I failed to observe her? Was she in the church?"

"No one else was there. I don't even know if there is a Lady Alderney." Rowena couldn't disguise her discomfort. She felt most embarrassed at any mention of Lord Alderney.

To her relief Lionel joined them, and Mrs. Melcombe smiled fondly as he bent to kiss her cheek, but then he eyed the negus.

"I say, can I have a glass?" he asked.

His mother's smile faded. "You know I don't like you to take alcohol."

Rowena intervened. "Let him have a glass, Mother, for he's quite the young man now. And anyway, it's hardly fair that you and I should warm ourselves before going out, but he should not enjoy the same comfort."

Mrs. Melcombe hesitated and then nodded indulgently. "Oh, very well. You may have a glass, Lionel."

"Thank you, Mother," he answered eagerly, tossing a grateful glance at his sister.

Shortly afterward they heard the distant blowing of horns. It was the signal that the celebrations were soon to commence. The Devil's Mare hobby-horse was about to be escorted through the village to the green, where he'd put a torch to the bonfire and the junketing would begin.

Lionel helped his mother and sister with their cloaks, and then they went into the great hall, where Sally was waiting in her outdoor clothes.

Rowena looked up at Lady Margaret's portrait. "Do you remember the time Father said Lady Margaret's husband's portrait spoke to him?" she asked her mother.

Mrs. Melcombe pursued her lips crossly. "Indeed I do! Too much good malmsey, and no mistake. What was it he claimed the portrait called him?"

"Silly Billy."

"Highly appropriate at the time." Feeling disloyal for making such a remark, she turned briskly to the maid. "Have you remembered the sugar mice and bonbons for the guisers?"

"Yes, madam." The maid brought the little basket of rewards.

Mrs. Melcombe took it, and they all walked to the rowan-decked door, out into the gathering dusk of the night.

Lady Margaret glided briskly after them. She still had much to accomplish in the next few hours and was determined not to fail. Rising high into the dark air, the apparition flew to the Red Lion.

Chapter 11

At the inn Justin was dressed and putting the final touches to his neckcloth. Lady Margaret watched approvingly as he deftly tied the crisply starched muslin. He studied the effect in the looking glass and then reached over to the mantelshelf to pick up a ruby pin. The phantom's gaze followed his hand and came to rest upon the gilt-framed miniature of a breathtakingly beautiful woman with short brunette curls, lustrous hazel eyes, and pink rosebud lips. She had a graceful neck and flawless shoulders, and such was the décolletage of her gown that only the faintest hint of filmy white silk was visible. She wore a wedding ring.

Lady Margaret fluttered closer to study the likeness. The lady's name was clearly marked—Chloe, Countess of Westcote. The wraith's brows drew together. Why would he carry Lady Westcote's portrait with him? And what did the wedding ring signify? Was the lady a wife? Or a widow?

She glanced back at Justin, but he was preoccupied with fixing the pin, and so with a swift frown she made the little portrait turn slightly so that she could see the back, where inscriptions were often placed. Sure enough, there were a few engraved words. *To the lover of my heart, body, and soul, from his adoring slave. October 1810.*

The ghost drew back. There was no mistaking the meaning of this. Lady Westcote was his mistress! It was a sobering thought, and Lady Margaret retreated to the bed in dismay. If he had such a lovely mistress, then poor Rowena could never compare. But then the specter pulled herself up sharply. It was all very well to feel sorry for Rowena, but unless something was done about her father's legacy of failure, then there would be a great deal more over which to be sorry! The existence of a mistress made no real difference to the situation; Justin still required a wife, and Rowena required a husband.

Justin put on his outdoor things and then went to the window to look out at the night. Turnip lanterns twinkled everywhere, and the horns blew again as the Devil's Mare was escorted onto the crowded green. The bonfire waited, and a man handed a lighted torch to the hobbyhorse. Cheers erupted as the bonfire started to crackle.

A fiddle began to play, and the Halloween party commenced. With the horse's jaw clacking and the bells on his ankles jingling, the Devil's Mare immediately set about his task of chasing the women to steal kisses. Children in guising costumes went from person to person with their chanting demands, and the flames rose higher and higher in the bonfire, flickering on the faces of the gathering.

Justin scanned those faces and at last saw Rowena. He knew her first name now, for he'd made it his discreet business to find out. It was a sweet name that over the centuries had become little used. He didn't know its meaning, but on a night like this, when sprays of rowan were fixed to cottage doors, it was tempting to believe she was named after the rowan tree . . .

She stood alone by a tree. Her hood was raised, but he could see her profile as she watched some young men holding forks between their teeth trying to spear apples bobbing in tubs of water. It was a very wet business and drew great mirth from the onlookers.

Rowena laughed as well, and her hood slipped back just a little so Justin could see her face more clearly. She was so very different from the women in his London circle, and he wished he knew why he'd dreamed about her before they'd met. She aroused his desire in a way no other woman had. It was a strong, almost primitive feeling, and it filled him now. Tonight he had to get to know her better, to try to gauge why she affected him so.

He was about to turn from the window when something else caught his eye on the green outside. A gentleman stood just on the edge of flickering light from the bonfire, and his attention was directed unwaveringly toward Rowena. There was something familiar about him. Justin watched for a moment and then realized it was the man who'd arrived at the Red Lion in the cabriolet. His name was Kemp, at least that was how the landlord addressed him, and he seemed to find Rowena of intense interest.

Justin tugged his top hat on and went out, and Lady Margaret floated thoughtfully behind him. She knew he'd watched Rowena by the bonfire, but she hadn't yet noticed Andrew, and she was still uncomfortably aware that any interest Lord Alderney showed in Rowena might not be as worthy as it should be. The wraith could only keep her ghostly fingers crossed, for it was far too late now to do anything about it. There were only a few hours left until midnight, at the first stroke of which she'd be whisked back to her frame, no matter what she was doing at the time.

Justin emerged from the inn to a night filled with laughter, music, smoke, and the crackle of flames. Turning up his collar against the unexpected cold, he looked where Andrew had been standing, but there was no one there now. With a shrug, he made his way quickly to Rowena. She sensed his approach and turned to smile at him.

Unseen by either of them, Andrew was still watching nearby. He'd been approaching Rowena himself, but stopped when he saw her smile at Justin. His brown gaze sharpened. Alderney knew her well enough to go up to her like that? But how could it be? They'd surely only known each other for a day and yet exuded an unsettling sense of intimacy.

His eyes narrowed as he thought swiftly back over the months since he'd left Melcombe to try his luck in London. He'd made Chloe's acquaintance almost immediately and through her knew that Alderney hadn't been out of town at all until he'd gone to Bath to stay with friends. Could he have met Rowena there? Still watching them intently, he drew back beyond the flickering arc of light thrown by the bonfire.

Lady Margaret observed them closely as well, too closely to have noticed Andrew. The phantom flitted among the branches overhead, waiting with bated breath to see how they proceeded now. The next few minutes were as vital as their first face-to-face meeting in the church.

Justin removed his hat. "Good evening, Miss Melcombe," he said, taking her hand and raising it to his lips.

"Good evening, Lord Alderney."

He didn't release her as promptly as convention demanded, for it was good to touch her. It was she who drew her fingers away.

"I . . . I trust you think our celebrations are worth staying for, sir?" she said, trying to sound casual.

"Well worth it."

She managed a smile. "It cannot possibly compare with the London diversions I recall."

"Recall? Is it some time since you were there?"

"About five years. We were obliged to sell our Pall Mall house."

"But you liked London?"

"Yes. I loved to go to the theater to see Shakespeare, and I always made a point of visiting exhibitions at the Royal Academy. As for the bookshops . . ." She fell silent, realizing she was revealing the unfashionably studious side of her nature.

"You are a very serious-minded young lady, it seems," he said with a smile.

"A far from admirable trait, I fear." She looked at him. "I'm sure you'd be hard put to name a lady of quality who likes to read Chaucer."

He laughed a little. "I'm afraid that's true." Chaucer? Chloe would die rather than be expected to decipher medieval English!

"What *is* considered the height of fashion, Lord Alderney?"

"The things you probably expect. Clothes, dancing, and so on."

"And who in your opinion is the most beautiful and modish lady in London?"

He hesitated. "The Countess of Westcote," he said after a moment, for it jarred upon him to mention Chloe to her.

"What is she like?"

"Oh, she has dark hair," he replied dismissively.

Rowena smiled. "Is that all you can say to describe her?"

"Well, she's tall and slender, and she wears her hair in short curls. Oh, and I suppose her eyes are hazel."

Rowena glanced away. "So I'm not only undesirably bookish, but also everything else that's wrong when it comes to looks."

"Miss Melcombe, it doesn't bother me in the least that you are of an academic nature, and as for your looks, well, I find them very much to my liking."

Her eyes flew to meet his. "You're very gallant, sir."

"You shouldn't hold yourself in such low esteem, Miss Melcombe, for you have a great deal to commend you."

She smiled a little. "And you have a great deal to commend you, Lord Alderney."

The moment hung, and again he found himself casting around for something to distract the way his thoughts were leading. Whenever he was with her, he wanted to hold her close, and at the moment the urge was so compelling he feared he might give in. "Er, shall we walk a little, Miss Melcombe? You can introduce me to the mysteries of a Melcombe Halloween."

She accepted his arm. "There are no mysteries, sir. What you see is what it is."

He glanced at the bobbing apples. "I feel sure it would be simpler to merely pick up an apple and eat it," he observed.

"Simpler, but not half so much fun."

"I cannot argue with that."

They laughed together then, and as their eyes met, he put his hand briefly over hers where it rested on his sleeve. It was a fleeting gesture, no more than glove to glove, but it changed the atmosphere between them. The air was charged, and suddenly the feelings they'd both been suppressing were allowed to leap to the fore.

He searched her lilac eyes, where the flames of the bonfire

danced so brightly. "May I call you by your first name, Rowena?" he asked softly.

"It seems you know it already, Lord Alderney."

"I took the liberty of finding out." Hesitantly, he replaced his hand over hers.

"Must I still call you Lord Alderney?" she breathed, held captive by his touch.

"My name is Justin," he said softly, his thumb moving over her fingertips.

An unbearable excitement began to course through her. She was drowning in his sea green gaze, plunging out of her depth, and it was a sensation of exquisite pleasure.

Lady Margaret whirled deliriously around the treetops. They were in love! Melcombe Manor was surely saved!

Chapter 12

The spell was suddenly broken by the sound of Mrs. Melcombe's voice as she hurried toward them.

"Rowena?"

They jumped guiltily apart, and Lady Margaret ceased her delighted spinning to glare. Drat the woman! What execrable timing!

Mrs. Melcombe's sharp glance took in Justin before she spoke to her daughter. "Ah, there you are, my dear. I've been looking everywhere for you."

This last was added with a pointed glance at Justin, and Rowena flushed as she hastily introduced him. "Mother, may I present Lord Alderney? My lord, this is my mother, Mrs. Melcombe."

Justin drew the older woman's hand courteously to his lips. "Madam."

"My lord." Mrs. Melcombe couldn't conceal her curiosity about his apparent interest in her daughter. She'd observed them before making her presence known, and there was no mistaking the marked attention he was paying. Gentlemen of the *ton*, especially such handsome ones, did not usually pursue unremarkable country girls like Rowena, and that made his motives rather suspect. Was he another womanizer like Mr. Kemp? She hoped not, for her daughter was rather susceptible to such fellows.

Justin smiled at her. "I trust I have not offended by taking up Miss Melcombe's time?"

"I trust not, too, sir."

Justin smiled. "Miss Melcombe has been most kind. I requested a guided tour of the night's festivities, and she has very graciously consented to do the honors. For instance, I now know that here in Exmoor one cannot possibly consider the eating of an apple to be an uncomplicated business." He was at his most winning, and it would have required a rigidly formal and humorless woman to hold out against him. Mrs. Melcombe was neither of these things.

She found herself returning his smile. "Only on Halloween, sir. At other times we are as sensible as everyone else."

Justin smiled. "Halloween would appear to be a very special occasion here, Mrs. Melcombe."

"It is, sir, but not, I assure you, because we are ungodly. Oh, indeed no. Halloween is merely an excuse to make merry."

An elderly woman with a pronounced stoop walked past nearby, her sharp eyes upon Justin. She was the village wisewoman, known to one and all as Mother Tippacott. There wasn't an ailment for which she could not produce a potion, and Mrs. Melcombe swore by her remedy for rheumatism. Unfortunately, the wisewoman was also the village's most notorious gossipmonger, and it was plain she was very curious indeed about a fine lord's interest in Rowena.

Mrs. Melcombe decided to divert her attention and excused herself from Justin and Rowena. "Forgive me, but I really must speak to Mother Tippacott," she said, giving Rowena another pointed look. Conduct yourself properly, the look said, and then she hurried after the old woman.

Justin watched her. "Mother Tippacott?"

Rowena told him about the wisewoman.

"A witch by any other name?" he said with a smile.

"No, sir, we merely lack an apothecary." She smiled as well.

The Devil's Mare cavorted close by, his bells and clacking jaw warning his latest quarry, one of the inn serving girls, of his approach. The girl squealed with delighted laughter as he caught her around the waist.

The fiddler struck up another tune, and those who wanted to dance discarded their coats and cloaks to go close to the roaring fire. Justin glanced at Rowena. "Shall we join them?"

She smiled and nodded. Leaving their outdoor clothes on a bench, they mingled with the other dancers.

It was a folk dance, with couples facing each other, their hands to their partners' waists as they circled the fire. In fashionable assembly rooms it would have been merely another country measure, but on Halloween, with the flames leaping into the night, it was a pagan ritual. Their hearts beat faster and faster and soon pounded to the rhythm of the fiddle. The intoxicating music seemed to fill their veins and then invade their souls. Round and round they went beneath the starlit sky, and the bonfire flames seemed to dance with them. Justin could feel how warm and supple she was beneath the velvet of her gown. He wanted to hold her closer, to press her body to his . . .

It seemed the music would never end, but then, just as the fiddler played the final chord, the magic of the night was at last broken by the twins and their notion of Halloween fun. A terrified black horse galloped across the crowded green, scattering the alarmed dancers in all directions, because it had the stolen skeleton tied onto its back. To the gullible it was as if the Grim Reaper himself had come to Melcombe.

Justin put a protective arm around Rowena to pull her out of danger. "Dear God above!" he breathed, snatching her to safety just as the frightened animal thundered past.

Rowena stared at the skeleton and then heard some familiar giggling coming from behind her. Turning, she saw the twins and knew them in spite of their disguises. Realizing they'd been recognized, they turned and fled, looking for all the world like demons from Perdition.

The horse was soon caught, and its "rider" removed. The angry villagers didn't need to be told whose work it was, for everything bore the mark of the twins. But even as some of the men began to search for the culprits, the twins struck again. No one saw them reappear on the other side of the green and begin to toss firecrackers onto the bonfire. With an explosion like a cannonade, sparks and embers flew over the green. At first there was a shocked silence, but then the rest of the fireworks went off as well. The alarmed villagers moved well back from danger.

The twins had long gone when the final firecrackers exploded and everything became quiet again. Everyone waited for several minutes, to be sure it was safe before approaching the fire to toss back any burning wood scattered by the disturbance.

Rowena's first thought was of her mother, who would be dreadfully upset by this latest example of her younger sons' unruliness. Gathering her skirts, she hurried to where a weeping Mrs. Melcombe was being comforted by Sally.

"Oh, Rowena, how *could* they be so wicked?" she cried as her daughter reached her.

Rowena didn't know what to say. "Come, we'll go home," she said at last, putting a gentle arm around her mother's shoulders.

Justin, who'd followed Rowena, immediately offered his services. "Allow me to escort you both, Mrs. Melcombe."

Mrs. Melcombe was conscious of Rowena's unspoken reluctance to leave and on the spur of the moment decided her daughter deserved to enjoy what was left of the evening. It would be their last Halloween in Melcombe, and if Rowena wished to spend it in the company of dashing Lord Alderney, then she should be permitted to do so. Besides, her daughter was sensible and could be trusted. And so Mrs. Melcombe smiled at Justin.

"That is most gallant of you, sir, but there is no need. Sally and some of the other servants have decided to leave now, and I will accompany them. But there is something you can do for me. I realize it is perhaps a little reprehensible of me to ask on such a short acquaintance, but tonight is a little special, and it seems such a shame to allow etiquette to spoil things."

"If I may help in any way," he replied.

"I'm sure that Rowena and Lionel don't wish to leave just yet, so I'd be most grateful if you could promise to escort them back later? That is, of course, provided you intend to stay yourself."

Rowena's heart leapt.

Justin smiled. "I am staying and will gladly assist. As for etiquette, well, if it disapproves of what is a very considerate maternal request, then it does not deserve to be observed."

"You have a way with words, Lord Alderney." Then she turned to Sally. "Go and tell Master Lionel that he is in Lord Alderney's charge."

"Yes, madam." The maid hurried away.

Mrs. Melcombe prepared to join the group of servants waiting nearby. "It's so very cold tonight, I fancy there'll be a hard frost before morning. I daresay a restorative sip of rumfustian will be in order after this ordeal," she murmured, retying her cloak and glancing at Rowena. "Put your cloak on again, my dear, or you will catch cold." Then with a final smile she left them.

Justin looked toward Lionel, having watched Sally go up to him. He was deeply engrossed in the endless diversion of the bobbing apples and showed no inclination to join his sister. Most of the revelry had recommenced, and there was even a little dancing.

Stephen and Paul hadn't succeeded in bringing Melcombe's Halloween to a premature end.

Drawing Rowena's hand over his arm, Justin led her back to the bench to put on their outdoor garments. Then they sat down together.

Rowena hardly dared look at him. The electricity they'd felt earlier was with them still, and she knew the folly of feeling the way she did. It was an attraction that threatened to eclipse common sense.

He was equally conscious of the atmosphere between them. "Your brother's preoccupation gives us a little time to talk, does it not?" he said after a moment.

"Yes, of course." Please don't let her look as self-conscious as she felt. "I, er, believe you wished to discuss some problems?"

"Ah, yes, my problems. Well, I rather fear that that was a scurrilous ploy to make certain of your company."

Her heart almost stopped. "I . . . I don't understand . . ."

"I will be perfectly frank with you. I wished to spend some time with you, Rowena." He looked deep into her eyes. "If I'm breaking too many rules by speaking and behaving as I do right now, then you have only to say, and I will not offend again."

Lady Margaret hovered overhead. Oh, the suspense! Give the right response now, Rowena Melcombe!

Rowena hesitated, knowing what she should say, and what she wished to say. Folly awaited, its beckoning finger temptation beyond endurance. She smiled. "I'm breaking the rules as well, sir."

He drew her hand to his lips. "My name is Justin," he reminded her softly.

Nearby, Andrew watched with increasing amazement and jealousy. Now there was no mistaking the way things were between them! Incredible as it seemed, one of London's most sought after lords was laying siege to modest, provincial Rowena Melcombe. Bitter frustration lanced through him, and he clenched his fists. Rowena was his, and he'd do everything in his power to see she was reminded of his existence. She'd loved him once, and she'd love him again!

Suddenly, his glance fell upon the capering figure of the Devil's Mare. A cold smile curved his lips. But as he returned his attention to the two on the bench, he was glad to see their privacy was being invaded yet again, this time in the shape of Mother Tippacott. She could be relied upon to demand their attention for some time. Andrew smiled again and then sauntered slowly away toward the hobbyhorse.

Chapter 13

Lady Margaret was furious when the would-be lovers were interrupted by the wisewoman. Just how many more times would their first kiss be postponed? The phantom knew the Mother Tippacotts of the world, for every century possessed them. They were like limpets once attached, and their sole purpose was to find gossip to spread. She'd cling to Rowena and Justin as long as she could.

Suddenly, a belated firecracker exploded in the bonfire, reminding the wraith of some other important unfinished business. The twins were due their chastisement. She glanced at the bench again. The wisewoman was now seated with Rowena, while Justin stood politely. It would be some time before the old busybody left them alone, which in turn meant there was time to deal with Stephen and Paul.

Having no idea where the boys were, Lady Margaret rose high into the air in order to see over the entire village. Some turnip lanterns were being hoisted to windows, but nothing large enough to be the dreaded pumpkin, and anyway she didn't recognize the twins' costumes among those worn by the little group of guisers. Oh, where were they? There were so many nooks and crannies in Melcombe that they might be almost anywhere.

She began to search and after a while found herself drawn to the shed at the bottom of Widow Longman's garden. The specter swooped inside, only to find it empty except for all the Halloween paraphernalia from the shack in the copse. The only missing things were the twins themselves, the pumpkin, and the rattle. The boys' caps were lying on the floor, which meant they would return, but she couldn't afford to linger indefinitely when her reason for being out of her frame was to save Melcombe before midnight. The boys still had to be punished, however. Tonight's mischief was beyond the pale, and they deserved the horrible shock she had in mind.

Lady Margaret dithered frustratedly. Just how much was one phantom expected to achieve unaided? Again she blamed the Powers, for if Henry were with her now . . . But there was no point in wishing; he wasn't with her, and she had to accomplish everything by herself. Or did she? Maybe it was time for William Melcombe to be coerced into action. He claimed to always know where his offspring were, and so he could inform her when the boys returned to the shed. That would leave her at liberty to watch over Rowena and Justin.

Lady Margaret glided determinedly back to the principal bedroom at the manor house. Paying no heed to Rowena's mother, who was about to retire to her bed with the promised glass of rumfustian and who couldn't hear or see her anyway, the apparition reached into the picture frame to shake William out of his slumber.

He opened his eyes with a start. "Eh? What? Is something wrong?"

"Coming from you, sirrah, that question beggars response!" Lady Margaret replied tartly.

He cleared his throat. "What do you want?" he asked a little sullenly.

"Don't you adopt that tone with your elders and betters, sir. Henry once called you Silly Billy, and that's precisely what you are! Now then, I've work for you to do."

His eyes widened with dismay. "Work?"

"Yes. You're to keep your wits about you and let me know immediately when the twins return to Widow Longman's shed."

He swallowed. "Let you know? How?"

"By coming to the green and telling me."

"But I can't do that!" His eyes rounded to saucers.

"Why?"

"Because I haven't left my frame before."

"And whose fault is that, pray? Sirrah, do you or do you not wish to save Melcombe?"

He drew himself up resentfully. "You know I do."

"Very well. You still haven't taken advantage of your day of freedom, and I think the time has come, don't you? I need assistance if I am to watch properly over your daughter, who is progressing very nicely with Lord Alderney. Your hobgoblin sons aren't going to get away with tonight's misdeeds. You are able to let me know when they return to the shed, and I expect you to inform me the moment they do. In the meantime, I will devote my attention to Rowena."

He shifted awkwardly and said nothing.

"Where are they now?" she asked.

"On their way to Porlock's Farm," he replied without hesitation.

"Very well, that means they'll be occupied for a little while yet. I warn you now, sirrah, if you doze off, it will be the last thing you do. Stay awake and come to me *immediately* when they return to the shed."

"What do you intend to do to them?" he asked a little anxiously. "After all, they're only boys—"

"I'll do what is necessary to trim their wings. By the way, I only want you to concentrate upon them, not upon Rowena, for *I* will be looking after her."

With that she flew away again, and William stared unhappily after her. He gazed toward the bed. His wife had finished the rumfustian and was about to extinguish the candle. He'd lost count of the times he'd wanted to lie down beside her, and how many times he'd drawn fearfully back from the terror of leaving his sanctuary.

Taking a deep breath, he gingerly put a foot out, then the other one, and sat on the edge of the frame for a moment. He felt very vulnerable and awkward, especially as he leaned forward a little too much and floated free. For a moment he flapped foolishly at the air, like an overgrown fledgling forced to quit the nest, but then he gradually glided to the floor, where his buckled high-heeled shoes made no sound at all upon the polished boards.

He smoothed his silk coat and then straightened his powdered wig. His first instinct was to walk to the bed, but instead found himself gliding. He misjudged the distance and floated right through the wall into the passage, but then he gained a little control and moved gingerly back into the bedroom, where he eased himself carefully onto the bed beside his sleeping wife. The fragrance of her lavender water wafted poignantly over him, reminding him of nights during his earthly life.

It felt so good to lie there with her he almost closed his eyes, but then he opened them again quickly. He mustn't go to sleep! Staring up at the canopy, he concentrated upon his sons. They were just removing the gate at Porlock's Farm to toss it into the stream.

Lady Margaret had returned to the green only to find the bench deserted. The ghost turned this way and that, scanning the scene. She was about to swallow her dignity by returning yet again to William for the necessary information when suddenly she saw them. They were right at the edge of the fire, and Rowena had just taken a sweet chestnut from a sack and was bending down to place it close to the glowing heat. The ghost floated down to join them.

Rowena straightened and smiled at Justin. "That's what Melcombe lovers do on Halloween; they both put a chestnut by the fire and then come back the following morning to see what has happened. If the two nuts have burned gently together, they know they'll be happy together, but if one of the nuts has started away from the heat, or burst, they know they'll part."

Justin was amused. "And is this ritual supposed to be infallible?"

"I've never had cause to test it."

"Then let us see," he said, taking another chestnut from the sack and placing it next to hers.

Rowena's lips parted. "But we aren't sweethearts."

"Is there any reason why we should not be?" He knew he was plunging in deeper and deeper, but he couldn't help himself. May God forgive him if he was being false with her now, but something he didn't understand was carrying him along.

She didn't reply, and so he repeated the question. "Is there any reason why we should not be sweethearts, Rowena?"

She felt her heart miss a beat. "I . . . I'm sure there are many reasons, sir."

"Then name one," he said again, holding her gaze.

"Well, I have very little aristocratic blood, I'm certainly not an heiress or a great beauty, and I don't move in your lofty social circles."

"Rowena, that may be your assessment of yourself, but it isn't mine."

Taking her hand, he suddenly led her away from the fire, and when they'd reached the shadows beyond the flickering light, he halted again, turning her to face him. "If you only knew how I've been longing to take you in my arms and kiss you . . ."

Her eyes widened with incredulity. "Kiss me?"

"Yes. Like this." Ignoring that they might be seen, he pulled her into his arms and pressed his lips over hers.

Chapter 14

Rowena knew she should resist. And she also knew she should break free from the sweet temptation of his mouth. There was so much she knew, but levelheadedness was swept aside as she succumbed to the sorcery of desire.

As he crushed her close, she remembered the dream. She recalled how it had been when their naked bodies had come together. Those warm feelings spread through her again now as her intoxication mounted. Her breasts tingled with arousal, but although her conscience dictated propriety, there was no propriety at all in the way she felt. Now that she was in his arms, she was slave to the wanton desires she'd discovered only the night before. Beneath her demure surface there lurked a *belle de nuit*. It was as if he'd unlocked her sensuality and freed it with his kiss.

Her lips softened and yielded, and her body molded against his as they stole every last sweetness from the long kiss, each conscious of the other's excitement. Then of one accord they pulled apart, their hearts pounding and their faces flushed.

Rowena stared at him, unable to believe she'd permitted her feelings such free rein. The dream had been allowed to cross over the boundary into fact, and it was a most exquisite and enlightening experience. She knew herself now and wasn't the demure dispassionate creature she'd been brought up to be. She was vital, eager for love, and aflame with the need to be taught by this man. Only by this man, for he'd now stolen more than her kisses, he'd stolen her very soul. As she looked into his sea green eyes, she knew she loved him above all else. Above Melcombe, above life itself . . .

Justin was equally shaken. His body still throbbed sensuously, and his arms ached to hold her. Sweet Jesu, he wanted to take her here and now on the grass, with the magic and mystery of Halloween alive in the cold air around them. If there were ghosts, witches, and wizards abroad tonight, he wanted them to witness the climax of the soaring, magnificent desire pulsing through him.

Lady Margaret stared as well, her marveling gaze moving from one to the other. There were kisses and kisses, but *that* had been a kiss in a million! Its scintillating emotions had been so strong, they'd tingled over her like invisible fireflies, making her shiver deliciously.

Rowena glanced uneasily around the green, afraid she would find the shocked villagers staring at them. But no one paid any attention. She looked at Justin again, her voice trembling because of the sensations still washing through her. "I . . . I didn't know it was possible to feel like this," she breathed.

He put his hand gently to her cheek. "I promise I'm not usually given to such public displays, nor do I easily step beyond the bounds of convention," he murmured. This innocent had ignited his passion, and the joy of kissing her transcended everything.

Her gaze returned to the green. "Do you think anyone saw?"

"No, I don't. Look at them. Do you imagine they'd be getting on with their own business if they'd noticed Miss Melcombe in the embrace of a gentleman she's only just met?"

His words brought home the enormity of the liberty she'd just permitted, and she was covered with confusion. "Please don't say it like that," she begged, moving away slightly to try to collect herself.

"Forgive me, I didn't mean . . ." His words trailed away. He was as much at a loss as she was, for nothing like this had ever happened to him before.

Rowena lowered her eyes. "I know this is Halloween and strange things are supposed to happen, but how will it be tomorrow when it's daylight and Halloween is over . . . ?" Her voice died away.

"Tomorrow will not change things, but if you wish it all to stop now, you only have to say."

"Stop? I never want it to stop!" she breathed, looking up swiftly into his eyes. She felt beyond shame, beyond respectability, beyond redemption itself.

"Then it will not stop," he whispered, drawing her close again. His mouth found her parted lips, and their tongues touched for a moment, but she trembled in his arms, and he knew she was a little frightened by the power of her feelings. Her innocence touched his conscience, and he slowly released her. "Perhaps I should take you and Lionel home now," he said gently.

"I don't really want this night to end."

"Nor I, but we have tomorrow, and as many tomorrows after that as we wish." He heard the words slipping from his lips and knew he meant them.

She nodded, her eyes suddenly filling with tears of happiness. "Do you promise I won't wake up in the morning and find that this is another dream?"

"Another dream?" He looked swiftly at her. "What do you mean?"

"I, er . . . Did I say that? I meant just a dream." She found it hard to meet his eyes as she corrected herself.

He hesitated before replying. For a moment he'd been so certain she was referring to the previous night. Had she shared his dream? Had it all been as unbelievably real to her as it had for him? He brushed the improbable notion aside. "I promise it isn't a dream," he said then.

Above them Lady Margaret smiled.

The moment was a little too much for Rowena, and she seized

upon Lionel as an excuse to change the subject. "I wonder where he is? Lionel, I mean."

Justin heard the held-back emotion in her voice, and understood. "I'll find him," he said gently and then led her back to the bench before going to look for her brother.

Lady Margaret glided away with him, and Rowena was left alone. No one noticed the Devil's Mare standing beneath the overhanging branches of a nearby tree. The man who'd been inside the hobbyhorse costume throughout the evening was now lying in a cottage garden, knocked unconscious by the man who'd replaced him—Andrew Kemp.

He'd watched the kiss and seen the warmth in the new lovers' eyes. Jealous anger sliced bitterly through him. Rowena was his! He left the shelter of the tree to approach her. She heard the soft jingle of the bells around his ankles and turned with a quick smile, thinking she was at last to fall victim to the Mare's traditional antics. He pretended to caper, and as she laughed, he reached out to take her hand and pull her to her feet. It was only then that he tipped the horse's skull back to reveal his face. Her smile froze with shock as she recognized him.

"Andrew!"

"It's been a long time, my sweet Rowena," he said softly.

She stared at him, taken so completely by surprise that she was helpless for a moment.

He mistook her reaction for mixed emotions. She'd just been in Alderney's arms, and now she was faced with her former love. Maybe the time was ripe to remind her how seductive his own kisses had been. He slipped an arm around her waist and pulled her toward him, but as his parted lips touched hers, she drew sharply away.

"No!"

Footsteps were approaching. It was Lionel. The boy had run on ahead of Justin and didn't know anything was amiss. He saw only the Halloween hobbyhorse exacting his traditional dues, but Andrew released Rowena and with a low curse tugged the horse's skull down over his face again. Then he hurried away and vanished down an alley next to the inn. The faint sound of his bells died away into the darkness.

Lionel hurried up to Rowena, and then noticed her pale face and disturbed manner. "Is something wrong?"

She stared uneasily after Andrew. "Wrong? No, no of course not."

Lady Margaret returned and immediately sensed the change in

her. The chit was lying. Something *was* wrong. Her ghostly gaze moved pensively after the now vanished hobbyhorse. What had the fellow attempted? Had he been too familiar? The phantom reproached herself for having chosen to follow Justin instead of remaining by the bench.

Rowena struggled to compose herself. She didn't quite know what to do; she knew only that instinct told her to hold her tongue about what had happened. She didn't know why Andrew had returned to Melcombe, and she didn't really care anymore. This time yesterday it would have meant a great deal to her to see him again, but now, after Justin, he no longer had any place in her heart.

She managed to smile at her brother. "Have you enjoyed yourself?"

"Yes, except for Stephen and Paul." He gave her a sly grin as Justin approached. "A lord, eh? I'd never have thought it of you."

"Mother requested Lord Alderney to look after us, and he very kindly agreed to do so," she replied, but knew she was blushing. She was conscious of Justin as he reached them, and a warmth settled over her as he smiled. But then she remembered what had happened to her a few moments ago. Andrew was not only back here in Melcombe, but had forced his attentions upon her. Should she tell Justin? Or would it be better to say nothing?

Lady Margaret saw the shadow enter her eyes and became more certain than ever that something was wrong. What had happened? The Devil's Mare had been carrying out his kissing obligations all night, and he hadn't been with Rowena for more than a moment, so what could he have done in that second to so unsettle her? The phantom became uneasy. A shiver passed through her. There was something oddly disturbing in the air, and she knew it posed a threat to all she'd achieved. She wished now that she hadn't been so firm in her instructions to William, for if he'd been thinking about Rowena as well, he might have been able to tell her what had taken place.

Justin didn't notice the change in Rowena. "Are you ready to leave now, Miss Melcombe?" he asked, being careful to observe every propriety in front of Lionel.

"Yes, Lord Alderney."

He offered her his arm, and they began to walk from the green. Lady Margaret glided pensively behind them.

The turnip lanterns still flickered on the gateposts at the manor house, and Lady Margaret settled next to one of them to watch as Justin took his leave of Rowena. Lionel had already gone into the house, and Justin was careful not to linger at the door for more than a second or so. He took her hand and raised it tenderly to his lips. "I'll call in the morning," he promised.

Her fingers closing yearningly over his and her lips were so close that he wanted desperately to kiss them, but he was conscious of Lionel in the great hall. Reluctantly he released her. "*Jusqu'à demain, ma chérie,*" he whispered.

"Until tomorrow," she confirmed, and then she hurried inside.

The rowan boughs on the door trembled as she closed it behind her. Justin stood there for a moment and then turned to walk back to the Red Lion. He looked up at the sky and gave a brief laugh. Dear God, whatever he'd been expecting tonight, it hadn't been this. From hardly knowing her, he'd progressed to feeling as if he'd known her forever—wanted her forever.

His gaze encompassed the stars and the shining moon. It was Halloween, and witchcraft was all around him. He was spellbound, charmed, and beguiled, and his enchantress was so different from his previous conquests he could hardly believe what had happened to him.

Chapter 15

Lady Margaret watched from the gatepost as Justin made his way back to the inn. She was sure a proposal would soon be in the air and wished she could feel jubilant, but she was too uneasy about the incident with the hobbyhorse. Something was very wrong.

Suddenly, with panic-stricken flapping William's apparition erupted noisily through the door. "Lady Margaret! Lady Margaret!" he cried frantically, tumbling past her so swiftly that he shot clear across the road and into a tree.

She sighed irritatedly and waited for him to collect himself. Really, the fellow was a ghostly calamity! A true Silly Billy!

For a moment he scrambled about in the tree, trying desperately to grab branches to prevent himself from falling. But as he realized that his hands passed straight through them and he couldn't fall anyway, he struggled to compose himself. His wig was askew and his fine coat crumpled, but he endeavored to be dignified as he made his way back toward her.

She raised a spectral eyebrow. "Well, sir?"

"I . . . I didn't mean to doze off, truly I didn't, but it was so comfortable lying on the bed—"

Lady Margaret wasn't interested in the whys and wherefores of his dozing off, simply that that was what he'd done! "You imbecile! I was most specific in my instructions!" Too specific, she added silently, thinking of Rowena.

He was full of remorse. "I know, Lady Margaret, and I humbly crave your forgiveness, but at least I awoke in time."

"I take it they're on the way to Widow Longman's?"

"They're by the cottage next door to hers."

Lady Margaret floated up from the gatepost. "Well, since you're here, you may as well accompany me, to see how ghostly matters should really be done!"

"Accompany you?" he repeated in dismay, for it had been all he could manage to leave the house, and he'd done that as clumsily as inhumanly possible!

But Lady Margaret caught his collar and dragged him with her. "I have a feeling you may be needed after I've returned to my frame. Something is not quite as it should be concerning Rowena, and I might not have time to get to the heart of it before midnight."

His dismay increased as she hauled him bodily through the icy night air. He might be needed? But he couldn't possibly do anything on his own!

She shook him a little crossly. "Fly for yourself, sir! You're perfectly capable!"

He immediately began to flap his arms.

Lady Margaret watched incredulously. "You don't need to do all that! You aren't feathered! Just think what you wish to do, and you'll do it."

He followed her advice, and soon they were gliding side by side over the village. He glanced around and kept very close to her, for on Halloween it was only too likely that all manner of fiendish things were out and about.

Lady Margaret paused only to collect the skeleton, which she had earlier noticed propped up on a doorstep. It had another task to perform tonight! She commanded it to obey her, and it rose into the air, its bones rattling slightly as it followed William and her over the village. They all three came to the ground by the shed, and Lady Margaret directed the skeleton into the bushes nearby. It settled gently among the crisp autumn leaves, and then she took William with her toward the cottage that belonged to the village gravedigger and his pretty but faithless wife.

The twins had at last lighted their pumpkin lantern. It was fixed to a long pole, and they were holding it up to a bedroom window at the back of the cottage. The two Melcombe ghosts watched as the horrible illuminated face swayed before the panes.

Lady Margaret was consumed with curiosity as to the exact effect it would have upon the unfortunates inside, and so she left William and glided into the bedroom to watch. The bed was occupied by two illicit lovers, the gravedigger's wife and the handsome peddler who visited Melcombe every month. The gravedigger was on the village green with his rowdy friends, overindulging in Halloween cider.

The peddler was a lusty fellow, and the bed springs squeaked as he and his adulterous partner made passionate love. At first they were too engrossed to notice anything at the window, but then the twins tapped the lantern against the glass. The lovers froze, and the peddler turned slowly to stare at the ghastly face leering in at them.

After a moment's silence one of the twins used the watchman's rattle. The noise split the night, and the gravedigger's wife gave a terrified scream before hiding under the blankets. But her lover was made of sterner stuff. It was just a Halloween lantern! Maybe it was much bigger than usual, but it was still a lantern! Damned guisers! Tossing the bedclothes back, he went to fling open the casement.

The twins immediately pulled the lantern away and ran off into the darkness, vanishing among the thick bushes separating the garden from Widow Longman's.

The peddler shouted furiously after them. "You young varmints! Just you wait till I gets you alone! I'll treat you like the hosebirds you are!"

His lover peeped nervously from beneath the blankets. "Don't shout so, Joseph; d'you want everyone to know you're here with me?"

He glanced back and then closed the window again. "What's up with that darned hound of yours, eh? Don't it know about barking to warn when intruders are about?"

Her eyes were large and apologetic. "It ent the dog's fault, Joseph; I gave 'im a bone to keep 'im quiet while you were 'ere."

"Well, it certain sure worked," he replied, getting back into bed. His amorous gaze moved over her. "Now then, where were we . . . ?"

Lady Margaret glided back out to William. "Did you see where the twins went?"

"Yes, they're in the shed now," he said unhappily.

She eyed him. "I trust you accept that your boys need punishing?"

He nodded.

They flew to look in the shed. The twins were taking off their guising apparel and discussing the success of their night. There was soot on their faces and hands, and they looked like two little chimney sweeps. The pumpkin lantern was still lighted and glowed softly by their feet. Its pale glow fell upon the small wooden casket Lady Margaret had seen in the shack. It was open and inside she could see several unused firecrackers. Well, at least she now knew what it had contained. She took William's arm and drew him outside again to collect the skeleton from the bushes. He shuddered, for he'd always loathed skeletons, and he was still uneasy away from his frame.

But before Lady Margaret could explain what she meant to do with the skeleton, William looked up at the sky again and to his horror saw two ghoulish gray creatures flying idly along on scaly wings. They were about three feet tall and quite the most repulsive things he'd ever seen. As they passed, they exuded a stench like rotten meat.

Terrified, William seized Lady Margaret's arm and pointed up. She drew back in concern. The entities from last year! And now they looked even more like gargoyles. Oh, if only Henry were here now, *he'd* know what to do!

As one, the Melcombe ghosts flitted swiftly out of sight into the bushes, from where they were further dismayed to see the two hideous beings cease their flight and turn to look back. The foul smell increased as they slowly returned to circle overhead, glancing intently around. William was beside himself with dread, and Lady Margaret was alarmed. What were they searching for? Suddenly, she knew. It was the skeleton. They'd got scent of the bones! Gargoyles loved bones!

She and William drew fearfully together, watching the vile things continue to circle. After a moment one of the creatures pointed down, not into Widow Longman's garden, but the gravedigger's next door. Then they both plunged down, and there was a terrified yelping and whining from the dog that had been gnawing contentedly on the mutton bone given to keep it quiet. The skirmish was soon over, and the dog ran howling toward the cottage, its tail between its legs. The ghastly entities then rose triumphantly with the bone.

Lady Margaret and William could hear them smacking their lips as they resumed their journey, flying directly over the village green. No one saw them, for they were invisible to human eyes, and soon they were lost in the skies over Melkery Beacon. As the noxious odor faded away, the Melcombe ghosts crept thankfully from the bush, looking all around for fear of seeing something else hovering overhead. But the Halloween sky was clear.

With a deep breath Lady Margaret drew herself up. "We have work to do, William," she said crisply.

"Can't we just go home?" he ventured hopefully.

"Certainly not."

"But what if those . . . those demons return?"

Lady Margaret didn't reply, for the shed door opened suddenly and the twins came out. They'd discarded their disguises, but their faces were still black with soot. They were about to hurry away when they realized they'd left the pumpkin lantern alight. Paul went back inside to extinguish the candle, and Lady Margaret swept into immediate action. As the boy reached down to the pumpkin, she made it shake from side to side. His eyes widened, and he leapt back with a gasp.

With silent delight Lady Margaret commanded the lantern to rise to a level with the boy's eyes. It did so, and he stared with horror at the hellish glowing face.

Stephen was impatient. "What's keeping you?" he hissed from the doorway.

In reply Paul took to his heels past his twin and up the garden toward the side gate. The lantern bobbed after him, and when Stephen saw it, he gave a cry and followed his brother.

Lady Margaret turned to William. "Take over with the lantern. Keep it on their tails!"

"But I don't know how!"

"Heavens, man, I've done the hardest part and got it in the air. All you've got to do is make it chase them! Get on with it while I see to the skeleton!"

William fluttered away, his face twitching as he strove to take control of the lantern. To his relief it at last responded to his will, hovering for a moment until he made it continue its fearsome pursuit of the terror-stricken twins.

Lady Margaret applied herself to the skeleton. "Up with you, Bony!" she ordered, and it immediately lifted out of the bush. She nodded after the boys. "Off you go. We have to reach the house before them," she said, following as it flew away. They passed the other chase, and at the manor house door she made the skeleton hang in the air above the doorstep, to bar the boys from passing.

The sound of scampering feet told her Stephen and Paul were

almost at the gates. She drew back a little and watched as they hurtled toward the door, then she made the skeleton's bones rattle. The twins came to an abrupt standstill, staring with open-mouthed dread before turning to flee again, but the pumpkin lantern glided toward them through the gateposts.

Petrified, the boys headed for the gardens. The pumpkin and skeleton floated after them, and the ghosts followed. Lady Margaret found it exceedingly satisfying to observe the twins being chased by their own Halloween mischief, and she had no intention of letting them off lightly. Wherever the twins went, they found their way blocked by either the skeleton or the pumpkin, and she saw to it that they could only flee from place to place around the far end of the shadowy gardens, where their cries went unheard by those inside.

Lady Margaret was enjoying herself hugely, but William began to feel sorry for his sons. "Please let them go now," he said at last. "Look at them; I doubt if they'll ever leave the house again on Halloween!"

She was loath to give in, but had to concede that the necessary lesson had been taught, and so she called the pumpkin and skeleton from the chase, directing both to fly away into the night. They'd fall to earth somewhere at midnight; it didn't really matter where, for their work was over.

As soon as their tormentors had vanished, Stephen and Paul scrambled up the ivy-clad walls of the house and into the safety of their bedroom. Content they wouldn't forget tonight in a hurry, Lady Margaret turned to William. "A job well done, don't you agree?"

"Er, yes. Can I go back to my frame now?" he added hopefully.

"Indeed not, sir, for I have further work for you to do."

"But—"

"No buts!" she interrupted tartly. "Come, I must take you to the Red Lion."

"Why?"

"Because I'm not happy about things. Oh, don't misunderstand; I'm sure I've successfully brought Rowena and Lord Alderney together, but I have the most disconcerting instinct that it is all in danger."

Plague take her instinct, William thought sourly as he obediently rose into the air to accompany her.

Lady Margaret ignored his reluctance. "Now then, I want to show you Lord Alderney and tell you what you need to know."

She related everything as they flew, and when they reached the inn, she fluttered toward Justin's window. "Lord Alderney is in the main bedroom at the front, above the entrance." But then she came to a stunned halt in midair when another window opened suddenly nearby, and Andrew leaned his hands upon the sill to look out. "Oh no!" she breathed.

William almost collided with her. "What is it?"

"Don't you see him?" She pointed.

William stared blankly at Andrew. "Who is he?" he asked after a moment.

"Andrew Kemp."

William's face changed. "The base scoundrel who presumed to dally with Rowena?"

"The very same. You'd have recognized him immediately if you'd ever bothered to leave your frame while he was about his despicable business."

William looked hatefully at the window, for he'd heard Rowena crying into her pillow on account of this worthless blackguard.

Lady Margaret's thoughts went back to the moment she'd realized something was wrong with Rowena. "Now I understand. She must have seen him!"

"Rowena, you mean?"

"Yes. I thought it was something to do with the Devil's Mare, but it can't have been. She saw Kemp, and it shook her."

The church bell sounded through the night. It was midnight.

Lady Margaret whirled about in despair. "I have to go!"

William was appalled. "Oh, please, no!"

But she was already being drawn toward the manor house. "I have no choice. It's up to you now, William," she cried.

William scrambled desperately after her. "You can't leave me!"

"You have twenty-four hours from the moment you left your frame," she called back to him. Her speed was increasing with each note of the bell. On the twelfth she'd be locked in her portrait again.

William stared as she disappeared. Panic rose in his breast, and he looked one way and then the other, unable to put two sensible thoughts together. What was he supposed to do? He didn't know the first thing about such matters!

But then his glance returned to Andrew, who was still leaning out of the window. William's heart hardened, for he'd always despised the fellow for the cheap adventurer he was. So he'd come back in time to spoil things for Rowena, had he? Well, he wouldn't find it a comfortable matter. Indeed, no!

With an instinct born of righteous indignation, William made the window close upon Andrew's fingers. The slam almost shat-

tered the glass, and Andrew gave a cry of pain. William smiled
with grim satisfaction, but his pleasure was short-lived, for at that
moment he heard the familiar slow beating of scaly wings. He
glanced up to see the two ghoulish beings returning.

With a gasp he fled beneath the inn's overhanging thatched
eaves and then peeped out to watch. They were gargoyles, he was
sure of it, and not from Melcombe church, for it had none. No,
they had a cathedral look about them—Exeter probably.

They filled him with revulsion and fear, and he drew back beneath the eaves as the ominous winged sound continued. The
flapping was accompanied by the lip-smacking noises made when
the dog's bone had been stolen. The noisome odor drifted over
him again, and he closed his eyes tightly, expecting a clawed
hand to drag him from his hiding place at any moment, but instead the sounds began to move away, and the stench diminished.

At last he peeped out, and to his relief saw the entities flying on
out of Melcombe. They were dragging something with them. It
was the skeleton.

Chapter 16

William spent a miserable night huddled beneath the eaves, and
when dawn arrived accompanied by mist and frost, he still had no
idea what to do next. He was totally out of his depth, and only too
aware that as far as being a ghost was concerned, he was a novice.

The trees on the green were visible only as shadows, and the
cottages opposite were completely hidden from view. The smell
of the bonfire hung in the air, and smoke drifted from cottage
fires as the village prepared for the new day. Thanks to the guisers, few garden gates remained in place, and gates at the surrounding farms had suffered the same fate. Hardly any animals
were where they were supposed to be, and the business of getting
them back to their rightful owners was always a tiresome chore.
The aftermath of Halloween always took several days to tidy up
anywhere in England, but in Melcombe, which celebrated more
than most, it took a very long time indeed.

William stared at the mist. He was supposed to keep an eye on Andrew Kemp and stop him from intefering between Rowena and Lord Alderney, but there was less than a day's grace left in which to do it. Like Lady Margaret, he, too, would soon return to his frame, and then everything was left in the lap of the gods.

Leaving the eaves, William floated along to Andrew's window. The casement was closed and the curtains drawn, but even a raw phantom knew such things were no obstacle, although they did require a little conscious effort. Summoning his beginner's skills, he managed to glide into the bedroom with reasonable grace, in marked contrast to the way he'd burst so inelegantly out of the manor house the night before.

Drawing himself up, he approached the bed. Andrew lay asleep, and nestling naked in his arms was the saucy red-haired serving girl. The ghost was pleased to see how bruised his fingers were. That would teach him to come back here! William studied his face to see what had so impressed Rowena. The fellow was good-looking, he supposed grudgingly. A little Frenchified, but tolerable.

How did Lord Alderney compare? The phantom passed through the adjoining wall into the main bedroom. Justin was also asleep, his dark hair disheveled against the pillow. William moved around him, inspecting him from one side and then the other, and couldn't help but concede he was very handsome, indeed. Was it really likely that Rowena would turn from this nonesuch in favor of a mountebank like Kemp? One could never tell with women of course, for they were undoubtedly the most fickle and perverse creatures that ever drew breath—with the single exception of his beloved Maria, of course.

William floated over to the fireplace, intending to make himself comfortable in the chair in order to think, but just as he was about to sit, he noticed the miniature on the mantelpiece. Lady Margaret had told him about her suspicions concerning Lady Westcote, and agitation flurried through the ghost when he saw how truly beautiful she was. Lady Margaret had spoken of loveliness, but he still wasn't prepared. He stared at the portrait and then thought of Rowena. Oh, dear, how could Lady Margaret possibly think his daughter capable of stealing Alderney from such a woman?

Upset anew, William sat down. He was now more daunted than before and felt like giving up. Then he was cross with himself. Everything depended on him now; therefore he'd *have* to think of what to do next. He inhaled deeply to steady his concentration. It was warm by the fire and exceedingly cozy after his nighttime discomfort beneath the eaves. He was also finding this unaccustomed exercise very tiring indeed. Even passing through windows and walls required concentration, and he wasn't used to it. He settled more snugly in the chair, and after a moment Justin's mistress ceased to matter. A few minutes later his head began to nod. Soon he was fast asleep.

Rowena had hardly slept at all. She glowed with excitement after the ecstasy of her evening with Justin, and when she got up, she chose a lace-trimmed lavender merino gown she knew suited her particularly well.

Her heart was light as she went down to breakfast, but as she passed the twins' room and heard their low voices inside, her smile was replaced by anger. So the little monsters had returned, had they? Well, she had one or two things to say to them! Without ceremony she entered the room.

The boys sat up in their beds, still sooty-faced and fully dressed from the night before, and the suddenness of her entry startled them so much they shot beneath the bedclothes again.

"Yes, well may you hide after all you did last night!" she said.

Stephen peeped cautiously out. "Rowena? Is that you?"

"Who else did you think it was?" she demanded.

Slowly, they both sat up again, and for the first time she noticed their clothes and dirty faces, as well as the soot on the bedclothes. She was about to tell them off in no uncertain manner when she noticed that beneath the soot they were both very pale and frightened. Indeed, they looked quite dreadful. "What happened to you?" she asked. "I hope some of your victims got their own back?"

They exchanged nervous glances. "No, it wasn't like that," Paul said at last.

"Then what was it like?"

Stephen swallowed. "You must promise not to laugh."

"Laugh? That's the last thing I feel like doing where you two are concerned," she answered tersely.

"Well, do you remember the skeleton?"

"I doubt if anyone at the bonfire will ever forget it."

"And you know we took Griggs's pumpkin?"

She was puzzled. "Yes."

"We made the pumpkin into a huge Halloween lantern." Stephen's tongue passed anxiously over his lips, and his eyes crept a little fearfully toward the window. "Rowena, last night they chased us back to the house and all around the garden."

She looked blankly at him. "Who chased you?"

"The skeleton and the pumpkin."

She was irritated. "Oh, for heaven's sake, this isn't Halloween now, nor is it April the first!"

"Please, Rowena, it really did happen!" Paul cried.

She searched their faces. "Were you drinking apple brandy last night?" she demanded.

They shook their heads vigorously. "No!" they said together.

"Then all I can say is that some of your victims *did* pay you back," she declared. "Skeletons and pumpkins don't fly of their own accord, and I daresay there are others in Melcombe who are as capable of mischief as you. I say good luck to them, for you deserve everything you get."

"Rowena, it wasn't guisers, I swear it wasn't! You *must* believe me!" Stephen answered urgently. "The pumpkin rose from the floor and floated, and the skeleton did the same. They chased us."

Rowena raised an eyebrow. "Do you honestly expect me to believe that?"

"It's the truth," Paul insisted.

"Well, I suggest you spare Mother such a tall story, for she won't appreciate it any more than I do."

"We won't go guising ever again," Stephen promised ardently.

"I seem to recall hearing something like that last year."

"I know, but this time we really mean it. We're never going to leave the house again on Halloween. We've been talking and know we've been bad. We'll apologize to everyone, truly we will."

Rowena stared incredulously at them. "You'll *apologize*?"

They nodded.

She took a long breath. "Well, whatever happened last night seems to have done you the world of good."

"We promise to behave from now on," Paul said again.

"You must say that to Mother," she replied. "You *do* know how difficult things have been for her recently, don't you? It's never easy for a widow left with children to provide for, but it's even worse when—" She broke off, for it wasn't her place to tell them the house had to be sold.

"Even worse when what?" Paul asked.

"Oh, nothing. It doesn't matter. I must go down now." Gathering her skirts, she left them. Her fingers were crossed as she hurried to the staircase. Please let Justin call as promised. Don't let it all come to nothing.

But as she reached the half-landing and looked toward the Red Lion, she was filled with uncertainty. What if he'd changed his mind now that it was morning? What if he'd decided to leave Melcombe and forget all about her?

She crossed the great hall, not glancing up at Lady Margaret's portrait, but the portrait watched her. Lady Margaret felt thwarted. It was maddening to be confined again after her hours of freedom. It was even more maddening to have to leave a dolt like William in charge. She prayed he was using his time to good effect. Let him at least have meddled with their dreams to keep their desire at boiling point. She'd told him about the fantasy she'd conjured and could only hope he knew the importance and efficacy of such illusions. But then she sighed again, for it was surely a forlorn hope that foolish William would have done anything at all. Oh, if she was ever granted the opportunity to speak her mind to the Powers-That-Be, she'd tell them *exactly* what she thought! William should never have been allowed to hide in his frame for so long, but should have been *made* to sharpen his ghostly skills.

Blissfully unaware of his ancestress's dire thoughts, William was still snoring by the fire in Justin's room, although his ghostly noise was only audible to animals and other phantoms. His slumber ended abruptly as the bedroom curtains were suddenly flung back and the first morning sunlight flooded in. Justin was in his dressing gown, looking at the winter morning, and the wraith scrambled guiltily from the chair to join him.

The mist was dispersing now, and the sun pierced the vapor to sparkle on a crisp white frost. A wagon was drawn up outside the inn, and the landlord came out to exchange a few words with the carrier. Justin saw him and opened the window to call down to say he'd like his breakfast served in his room. The landlord nodded and disappeared into the inn again.

Closing the window, Justin turned to look at Chloe's miniature. She wouldn't like what he'd decided. It was a simple plan and had come to him in those moments of strange clarity that come between sleep and wakefulness. He'd opened his eyes and known what he should do. Emily would be delighted if she knew, but George and his aunt Lady Beaminster would no doubt be more cynical. It didn't matter what any of them thought, for as far as he was concerned, the plan was as good as carried out.

William was suspicious. Why had he looked at the miniature like that? The shade glowered at the little likeness, and then at its owner, before gliding through into the adjoining room to see Andrew again.

Andrew was dressed. The serving girl had gone, and he was writing a note to give to a village boy who was waiting by the door. He was finding it difficult to write because his fingers were so bruised, a fact that pleased the phantom. But then William's curiosity took over, and he floated closer to see what the note said.

> Rowena, I must see you again in order to repair the mistakes of the past. I should never have left and now wish to redeem myself. Please meet me by the footbridge at noon. Andrew.

William was appalled. Meet this reprobate? He trusted his daughter wouldn't be so addle-brained!

Putting his quill down, Andrew sanded and sealed the note and then handed it to the boy. "You're to deliver it to Miss Melcombe, and no one else. Is that clear?"

"Yes, sir."

"Here's a coin for your trouble. There'll be another one when you return with her answer."

"Yes, sir!" The boy's eyes shone as he took the coin and then hurried out.

William glared at Andrew, then glanced at the table where he'd been writing. The candle he'd used for the sealing wax was still alight, and next to it was the fresh neckcloth Andrew intended to wear that day. It was too much temptation for the phantom, and with a certain savage delight he managed to make the candle topple over. Hot wax scattered over the neckcloth, and the flame continued to burn for a moment or so, leaving a neat hole in the starched muslin.

Andrew cursed and extinguished the flame, but the neckcloth was ruined. Satisfied, William fluttered through the window to follow the boy, who was reluctantly admitted to the manor house when he showed the note. William flew in busily behind him, nodding a brief greeting to Lady Margaret before accompanying the boy into the dining room.

Lady Margaret gazed uneasily after him. What was going on? Why was William so interested in a village boy? She glanced around at the other portraits in the hall and saw they shared her perturbation.

Chapter 17

Rowena was seated alone in the dining room and placed her napkin on the table as she faced Andrew's youthful messenger. "Yes?" she inquired.

"The swell at the inn sent me with this, Miss Melcombe," the boy replied, handing her the note.

Justin? Color touched her cheeks as she took it, but then her heart sank as she recognized Andrew's writing. She was about to break the seal and read what it said when she thought better of it. She didn't want to resume any contact with Andrew, not now. Slowly she ripped it into four pieces and then gave them back to the boy. "Please tell the gentleman that this is my answer," she said.

William was proud of her. That's my girl!

The boy gaped at the ripped note. "But I . . . I can't give 'im these!" he protested.

"It's all the response I intend to give."

He swallowed and nodded. "Yes, miss," he muttered and then turned to leave.

Rowena gazed after him. Andrew's conduct at the bonfire had been inexcusable, and now she wished to avoid him at all costs. She hoped he would accept the torn note for the deliberate snub it was.

William was delighted with her, then fluttered out to Lady Margaret, who was as pleased as he about Rowena's response to Andrew's communication, indeed there was audible relief all around the great hall. But Lady Margaret's approval was tempered with caution.

"Mark now, for we must remain on our guard. That fellow will not give up easily. It's clear he means to pursue Rowena, and so you must be vigilant, William."

"Oh, I will, Lady Margaret," he promised, then hesitated. "Er, about Lady Westcote. I know you said she was beautiful, but you didn't say quite *how* beautiful. I don't think poor Rowena can possibly compete with such a—"

"The woman is of no consequence whatsoever," Lady Margaret interrupted.

"No consequence? But—"

"My dear sir, if she were suitable, I'm sure the Marquess of Exford would have instructed his son to make an honest woman of her. Instead, the marquess has threatened to arrange a Beaufort match for his son unless a bride is soon forthcoming."

William still wasn't happy. "She must be the loveliest woman in London," he muttered.

"Yes, and at the moment London is probably where she is. Rowena and Lord Alderney are here in Melcombe, and I've seen to it they're fired up with desire for each other." Lady Margaret eyed him. "I trust you've been putting the past few hours to good advantage?"

"I, er . . ."

Her spectral eyes sharpened. "You've been asleep!" she cried furiously.

"No! Truly, I haven't!"

"Liar!"

Hisses of disapproval came from all around the hall, and William looked nervously at the reproachful countenances.

If Lady Margaret could have reached out of her frame to throttle him at that moment, she would have done so. "William Melcombe, you are a disgrace to the spirit world. How *could* you have been so remiss as to sleep at a time like this?"

He backed away. "I . . . I'll be more alert from now on."

"You'd better be, sirrah. And don't make the mistake of thinking you're immune because I am shackled in this wretched frame! If necessary, I'll appeal to the Powers!"

Angry recriminations followed as he fled to the safety of his frame. He was a failure. The hours were ticking away, and not only was he expected to promote matters between Rowena and Lord Alderney, but prevent Andrew Kemp from spoiling things. It was too much for a wraith who'd cowered away from everything for two long years!

An hour later William was still lying low in his frame and didn't know when Justin called. Lady Margaret was on guard, however, and as Justin was shown into the great hall she managed to get word to the principal bedroom. She did so with the assistance of Mistress Melcombe in the triptych.

"Prithee, Master Melcombe, my lady requires you in the great hall!" the medieval phantom called up the staircase.

William jumped as if scalded and hurtled down to the hall to see what was happening.

Justin was waiting by the fireplace. His greatcoat covered his shoulders, and his top hat and gloves lay on a nearby table. The maid who'd admitted him was hastening to the dining room, and William followed her.

Mrs. Melcombe had now joined her daughter and at the announcement put her cup down with a startled clatter before looking accusingly across the table. "Rowena, were you expecting this call?"

Rowena colored a little. "He merely mentioned last night that he might call," she explained.

"I think you might at least have mentioned it to me. I'm not dressed to receive visitors, least of all aristocratic gentlemen I hardly know!"

"I . . . I could go out to the hall to speak to him," Rowena offered hopefully.

"Propriety precludes such a thing."

"Oh, Mother! How can propriety be compromised now when you allowed me to be alone with him at the bonfire last night?"

"I shouldn't have left you as I did last night. I was in the wrong."

"Please, Mother." Rowena looked urgently at her.

Mrs. Melcombe sighed. "Oh, dear, I daresay I'm being weak again, but with everything else on my mind at the moment, I really cannot face any bad feeling with you. However, we must be wary of Lord Alderney's motives. It has to be said that you are hardly the sort of young lady with whom he must usually mix. It may be that he intends to take liberties."

Rowena lowered her eyes and hoped her cheeks weren't as red as they felt.

Her mother went on. "You may walk with him in the garden, where I may keep my eye on you from the house."

"Thank you, Mother!" Rowena's face brightened into a glad smile.

"Just keep my warning in mind."

"I will." Rowena hurried out to the hall.

William lingered in the breakfast room, gazing fondly down at his wife. How pretty she was still, but how tired her eyes were. Remorse touched him, for it was his fault that she was in such a scrape now. Unable to face his guilt, he glided after Rowena.

Justin had turned as he heard her light steps behind him. His gaze encompassed her, taking in the fresh simplicity of her appearance. He was damned if he knew why she drew him so much; he only knew that when he was with her, she aroused such a burning desire it was as if at any moment he'd be consumed by flames. Halloween magic still coiled almost tangibly around him, and she excited him as much now as she had the night before.

He went to raise her hand tenderly to his lips. "Good morning, Rowena," he said softly.

His touch tingled through her. "Good morning, Justin," she replied.

William, Lady Margaret, and the other portraits watched intently.

Justin smiled. "I know I've called early, but I couldn't stay away any longer. I needed to be with you, Rowena."

Her heart sang with joy. Nothing had changed. The ecstasy of the night continued into the day. She gazed up into his eyes. "And I with you," she whispered. "I'll go to put my cloak on, and then we may walk in the garden."

Several minutes later, with William floating attentively behind, they emerged into the garden behind the house. The mist had gone completely now, and the sun shone from an immaculate blue sky. Their breath stood out in silver clouds, and the frost crunched beneath their feet as they left the path to cross the grass. Cobwebs hung like frozen lace among the flower beds, and leaves were falling heavily because of the sudden sharp drop in temperature. A robin sang in the creeper on the wall, and farther away curlews called on the slopes of Melkery Beacon.

They walked in silence for a moment, both conscious of Mrs. Melcombe's attentive gaze from an upstairs window. Justin spoke first, and he did so a little awkwardly, for he wished to say something exceptional.

"Forgive me if I put this a little bluntly, but there isn't an easy way of saying it. Yesterday in the churchyard you said you felt guilty for still being unmarried."

His words caught her off guard, and she drew back. "I . . . I shouldn't have said anything like that."

"I'm glad you did."

"Nevertheless—"

He put a finger to her lips and repeated his words. "I'm glad you did, Rowena, for your admission might solve my predicament."

"Your predicament? I don't understand."

He nodded. "In the interests of continuing the Marquesses of Exford, my father has virtually instructed me to marry and informs me that unless I soon find a wife of my own, he will find one for me. I hasten to add that he isn't a tyrant, merely an ailing man who fears for the future of the title. The wife he has in mind for me is a lady I cannot abide, but on the other hand until now I haven't found anyone I wish to marry."

"Until now?"

He hesitated, then took from his pocket the two chestnuts they'd left by the bonfire. "Do you remember these?"

"Yes, of course."

"You told me that if they burned steadily, happiness would ensue. It seems to me that these have burned very steadily indeed."

"It's only a foolish superstition."

"Then let us be foolish. Oh, Rowena, can't you see where this is leading? I have to find a wife, and you would solve your family's financial difficulties if you were to make an advantageous marriage."

Her eyes widened. "What are you saying?" she breathed.

"I'm asking you to be my bride, Rowena."

Overhead, William gave a triumphant huzzah.

Chapter 18

Rowena was so shaken she couldn't respond.

"Have you nothing to say?" he asked gently.

"You can't possibly wish me to be your wife," she said at last, her mind a whirlpool of emotions.

"Why not?"

"For all the reasons I gave last night when you asked why we should not be sweethearts."

"Those reasons meant nothing then, nor do they now."

"Justin, I'm a provincial nobody who hasn't been to London for some time, and when I *was* there I didn't have a season." She met his eyes. "Then there is the matter of my family's situation. It's hardly proper that the future Marchioness of Exford should be virtually penniless."

"Rowena, what does all that matter if we hold each other in high regard, as I know we do? Or am I misreading you?" He paused. "How exactly do you feel about me, Rowena?" He put his hand to her cheek, ignoring her mother's startled gaze from the window.

"I . . . I don't know how I feel. It's all happened so quickly that I feel as if I have no control over it . . ."

"It's happened as swiftly for me, but I know how I feel. You mean a great deal to me, Rowena Melcombe."

Her lilac eyes were large and uncertain. "I'd like to believe that."

"Then do so," he said softly. "Oh, Rowena, how can I persuade you this is the right thing to do? Must I remind you how we feel when we kiss?" He took her by the arms to pull her toward him.

She froze, her anxious glance flying to the house. "My mother's watching!"

"Let her watch," he replied, giving her no chance to resist as he drew her into an embrace.

Her reluctance subsided, and she lifted her mouth to meet his. It was a long and hungry kiss, and their hearts beat urgently together. Oblivious to everything around them, they were lost in their intimacy. She linked her arms around his neck and submitted to the yearning emotions tumbling through her veins. Even through their clothes she was conscious of his masculinity stirring against her; it was a sensation that robbed her of all thought of impropriety. She pressed herself to him, luxuriating in the delicious excitement his body gave her, and she returned the kiss as passionately as it was given. There was nothing innocent in her conduct, for she'd abandoned all the rules in order to follow her desire. And that desire soared exquisitely through her now, reaching out to meet him and sweeping her along in a voluptuous wave.

William fluttered incredulously around them. How could his little Rowena behave like this? Had she no shame? What of the servants, the villagers, the ancestors whose portraits looked out over the garden? Oh, this was too bad!

From the house Mrs. Melcombe also stared in amazement. Her daughter had taken leave of her senses, and Lord Alderney had most certainly forgotten he was a gentleman! Maybe he'd never been a gentleman! Maybe he was another Andrew Kemp. But even as this thought occurred, she dismissed it. No womanizer, no matter how base and calculating, would have the effrontery to make such a reckless move in front of his quarry's mother! So, could that mean Lord Alderney was in earnest when he embraced Rowena so ardently?

Mrs. Melcombe hardly dared hope that this might be the case, for the prospect of Rowena making a love match with a lord was too dazzling for words. She continued to watch, half knowing she should put a stop to the meeting, half fearing that to do so might be the wrong thing.

On the frosty lawn Justin cupped Rowena's face in his hands.

"Now will you say you'll marry me?" he asked softly, his voice trembling a little because he was so aroused.

Her lilac eyes were dark with passion. "Yes," she whispered. "Yes, I'll marry you."

In the air above them William forgot his paternal dismay about the disgraceful display of sexual abandon, and instead began to skip around giving little whoops of delight. Melcombe was saved, Lady Westcote and Kemp consigned to the past, and his own misdemeanors could at last be allowed to rest!

Justin still had Rowena's face cupped in his hands and again put his lips to hers. Their tongues moved seductively together, and his desire immediately began to mount, pulsing so erotically through him that he had to pull away. He'd never known such an urgent and compelling craving before, never been so physically enslaved by his own virility. Not even with Chloe . . .

Chloe. His mistress's name echoed coolingly through him, and he turned away slightly, running his fingers slowly through his hair as he sought to steady the riot of feelings still tingling through his whole body.

Rowena felt as if she were walking on air and struggled to regain her composure. And, as with him, someone else's name brought a sudden sobriety. She found herself thinking of Andrew, and a pang of unease touched her because she hadn't mentioned him to Justin, who surely had a right to know about the incident at the bonfire and the note this morning.

But as she hesitated, Justin turned to her again. "I cannot deny there have been others before you, Rowena, maybe far too many others, but they have no place in my heart now. What has gone before is immaterial; only the future matters from now on." He chose words that salved his conscience. He had a mistress and knew he should tell Rowena, but he couldn't. What happened where Chloe was concerned lay some way ahead. He didn't have to face it now.

What he said eased Rowena's guilt as well. "Only the future," she repeated, closing her eyes as their mouths met again. Yes, only the future mattered—the future and this man, to whom she was so willing to surrender her chastity.

He drew back slightly and gave a sudden smile.

"Something amuses you?" she asked.

"I was thinking of my friend George Rathbone and his wife Emily and wondering what they would say if they were here now."

"What do you think they would say?"

"Emily would be happy, for she is softhearted and romantic, but George would probably be more, er, cautious, as would his aunt, with whom they are staying at the moment. I fear Lady Beaminster has long since ceased to view the world through a rosy haze."

"As indeed should we if we're sensible," Rowena replied sagely.

"Do you want to be sensible?"

Her eyes shone impishly, and she shook her head. "No, I want to continue being foolish."

He laughed. "We're fellow spirits, Rowena Melcombe, although I never would have thought it. I am part of London's *haut ton*, and you haven't set foot in the capital for several years, but we go together as sweetly as if fate had meant it to be." He stroked her hair. "Much of my time has to be spent in London; will you mind that? I have a house in St. James's Square, but if you do not like it, then we will find somewhere else."

"I will not mind where we live, just that we are together."

"When do you wish us to be married? It can be very soon if I acquire a special license."

"Then let it be soon," she answered softly.

He smiled. "I adore you, Rowena Melcombe," he murmured, bending his head to kiss her again, but Mrs. Melcombe's shocked voice addressed them from a few yards away, and they started guiltily away from each other.

"What is the meaning of this?" she demanded. She'd come outside because she'd been dismayed to observe two village women on the other side of the boundary wall. One was Widow Longman, the other the redoubtable Mother Tippacott, and they'd crossed the footbridge from the field to halt in amazement on seeing the lovers. Their heads were together as they whispered, and Mrs. Melcombe knew there'd be unwelcome tittle-tattle all over Melcombe before the hour was out.

Gathering her skirts, she hurried across the frosty lawn toward them, clad only in her gray-and-white striped morning gown and shawl. But she was too concerned to notice the cold. "Well? I'm awaiting an explanation."

"Mother, I—" Rowena didn't know how to begin.

Justin spoke for her. "Mrs. Melcombe, I've presumed to ask for your daughter's hand in marriage, and she has done me the inestimable honor of accepting."

Mrs. Melcombe blinked. "I . . . I beg your pardon?" she said weakly. "Marriage, did you say?"

"With your permission."

She stared at them both. "If this is some sort of jest—"

"It is no jest, I assure you," Justin said quickly.

"But you hardly know each other, sir . . ." Then Mrs. Melcombe's breath caught on a dismayed gasp. "Or have you perhaps come to know each other a little too well too quickly? Is that what I am to conclude?"

"Mother!" Rowena's face flamed with color.

Mrs. Melcombe looked at her. "Tell me I do not need to concern myself on that score, and I will believe you."

"You do not need to concern yourself, Mother."

Mrs. Melcombe nodded. "I accept your word." She looked at Justin again. "Forgive me if I seem distrustful, sir, but I find it hard to credit that a lord such as you would wish to take as his bride a young woman who brings him nothing but herself."

"Apart from the genuine and mutual affection Rowena and I have for each other, two factors have led to our wish to marry. To begin with I have been instructed by my father to find a bride without delay or he will find one for me. Then there is Rowena's heartfelt wish to do something to alleviate the, er, dire financial straits in which you find yourself."

Mrs. Melcombe gave her daughter a reproachful look. "It's hardly fitting you should have discussed our private affairs like that."

Rowena lowered her eyes.

Justin went to the older woman and raised her hand to his lips. "Mrs. Melcombe, Rowena spoke to me only because she was deeply distressed, believing herself to be at fault for remaining unmarried."

"She should not blame herself; I've told her that."

"I find you an inspiration in every respect, Mrs. Melcombe, especially for the admirable way you have so steadfastly and properly striven to protect your family against such monstrous odds. With your leave I would be more than willing to shoulder that burden for you. If you could but accept me as your son-in-law, my fortune would be used to save Melcombe and provide for you and your sons."

She was almost overcome. "I . . . I confess that your offer is very attractive, sir, but I cannot help feeling your parents will not welcome such a lowly match for their son and heir."

"You misjudge them, Mrs. Melcombe. Perhaps you do not know that my mother doesn't come from aristocratic stock. She was the daughter of a modest Sussex landowner and happened to catch my father's eye when he was walking in Brighton. He made it his business to gain an introduction, and within a week their betrothal had been announced. They've been happy together ever since. It's true my father wishes me to marry and threatens an arranged match, but it isn't because he is a harsh man. On the contrary, it's because he's in failing health and wishes to be assured of the title's succession before he dies. Provided I have affection for my bride, and she for me, it won't matter to him whether she is titled or not, only that she is suitable, and no one can deny that Rowena is suitable, Mrs. Melcombe."

"You are very persuasive, Lord Alderney."

"I have to be if I am to gain your consent," he replied with winning sincerity.

"Have you considered all the implications? For several years now the furthest Rowena has been from Melcombe is Bridgwater or Taunton. She's a country rose, not the hothouse orchid London society will expect you to marry."

"That's of no consequence as far as I'm concerned, and besides, my closest friend and his wife will be more than glad to help me smooth her path." It was true. He knew as surely as night followed day that Emily would adore Rowena.

Mrs. Melcombe searched his face, then looked anxiously at Rowena. It was so very tempting to do as they wished, but she was afraid of making the wrong decision. "I . . . I need a little time," she said to them.

"Of course," Justin replied.

But Rowena beseeched her. "Please don't keep us in suspense, Mother, for I can't bear it."

"I only want to do the right thing, my dear."

"This is the right thing."

Mrs. Melcombe looked long and hard at her daughter's earnest face. Rowena had never been a creature of impulse, but had always given everything a great deal of consideration before acting. Now, quite suddenly, she was reckless. Was it merely a caprice of the heart? Or was it a deep and enduring emotion?

"Mother?" Rowena's lilac eyes pleaded.

In that moment Mrs. Melcombe's decision was made. She smiled. "Very well, my dear, you have my consent."

William was almost overcome, and there were tears in his eyes as he instinctively reached out to touch his beloved wife. But his ghostly hand passed right through her, and she knew nothing of his closeness in that most important and poignant of moments.

Chapter 19

"Oh, Mother!" Rowena ran to hug her.

Justin smiled. "Thank you, Mrs. Melcombe."

But after holding Rowena close for a moment, Mrs. Melcombe drew back. "There are conditions, however."

Rowena's happiness caught. "Conditions?"

"Lord Alderney, I imagine you intend to procure a special license so the wedding can take place without delay?"

"That is my hope, yes."

"Any appearance of undue haste may be misconstrued, sir, and I will not have my daughter's character questioned." Mrs. Melcombe lowered her glance, for the two village wives were still watching from beyond the garden wall.

Justin nodded. "That is more than understandable. How long do you feel we should wait?" he asked.

She smiled a little. "Oh, not very long, sir. It occurs to me that one month from today, December the first, is Rowena's twenty-third birthday, which makes it an acceptable date. A month may not be long, but is sufficient to remove any unwelcome conjecture."

"Do you wish banns to be called?" he asked.

"Not at all, sir, for although I realize such announcements are coming back into vogue, I do not regard them as essential. I merely wish there to be an appropriate period between the announcement of the betrothal and the actual wedding, and few will question the choice of the bride's birthday. But by all means proceed with acquiring a special license, for it would please me greatly if Rowena were to be married here at the manor house. William and I were married in the great hall, and I know he would approve." Mrs. Melcombe's eyes filled with fond tears as she remembered that wonderful day.

William nodded eagerly overhead. Oh, yes, *how* he approved! Nothing could be more fitting. His only regret was that he couldn't give the bride away himself.

Mrs. Melcombe looked from Justin to Rowena. "Are my conditions acceptable?"

Rowena smiled. "Of course."

"Lord Alderney?"

"I will agree to anything you wish, Mrs. Melcombe. With your leave I will procure the license as soon as possible so the clergyman and parish clerk can have as much time as possible to make arrangements."

"I'm sure they will appreciate that, sir." Mrs. Melcombe then gave a little smile. "I'm also sure the Reverend Grantham will be overcome at the honor of performing such a marriage, for he can hardly have expected to preside over the nuptials of the future Marquess and Marchioness of Exford." She paused suddenly, a little daunted at the prospect of Justin's grand family. "Lord Alderney, it occurs to me that maybe I've been a little presumptuous."

"Presumptuous?"

"Perhaps your parents will wish to arrange the ceremony?"

He smiled reassuringly. "Mrs. Melcombe, I wish the wedding to take place here, and I do not intend to inform my family until afterward."

She was shocked. "Not inform them? But—"

"My family has sufficient numbers to form a battalion, and to invite everyone would require many months of planning, but to omit some would cause offense, so my solution is to proceed without any of them. Besides, my father's health is such that he would find a grand ceremony a great strain, and he would also be too frail to consider coming here. All in all, I think it much better to present them with a *fait accompli*. Rowena and I can visit Exford Park immediately after the wedding." He smiled at Rowena. "They will welcome you, I promise."

She returned the smile, but a little apprehensively. Would such great aristocrats really welcome a daughter-in-law from a background as genteel but humble as hers?

Mrs. Melcombe shared her daughter's concern. "What if they really don't approve of the match? We must be practical about this."

"It's very unlikely, Mrs. Melcombe, but if the worst should come to the worst, I am not reliant upon my father. I have an inheritance from an uncle, and a town house in St. James's Square, which is where I trust Rowena and I will make our home. But I promise I'm on excellent terms with my parents and wouldn't enter upon a match if I felt it would deeply hurt or offend them. I'm confident they'll gladly receive Rowena into the family, and that in the fullness of time I'll succeed to my father's title and estates. My desire for haste now is to ease my father's mind by presenting him with the daughter-in-law he yearns for, and also to assist in your predicament here at Melcombe. In short I believe a swift match to be in everyone's best interest."

Mrs. Melcombe's last lingering doubts evaporated. "Lord Alderney, I am truly happy you and my daughter have so swiftly formed this attachment; indeed, it's almost as if fate has had a hand in it."

Justin glanced at Rowena. Fate? Maybe. Whatever it was, he welcomed its intervention, and he longed for the weeks to pass until the moment she became his wife.

Word of the betrothal swept through the village like wildfire and soon reached Andrew. He was eating alone in the dining room and was in a foul mood. Rowena's sharp response to his note had so enraged him that all he could think of was revenge. On top of that his sore fingers obliged him to take his time over eating, and the food was now too cold to be palatable.

The man he'd knocked out the previous evening in order to become the Devil's Mare was seated on the settle by the fire, rubbing his sore head and grumbling. His inexplicable fate had so far monopolized conversation at the inn, but the theft of the hobbyhorse costume was soon forgotten as the astonishing news arrived from the manor house.

Andrew was just about to rise from his table when the serving girl he'd spent the night with rushed in to tell the landlord what she'd heard. She spoke in a low voice, but the landlord's astonishment was such that he laughed aloud. "A wedding? Oh, come now, Daisy, I can't believe that. Why, his lordship came here only two nights ago, and I'd swear blind he hadn't even heard of Miss Rowena then, let alone asked for her hand!"

Andrew folded his napkin and rose to his feet. Alderney was to *marry* Rowena? It wasn't possible! He addressed the innkeeper. "What was that you said? Lord Alderney and Miss Melcombe are to be wed?"

The landlord nodded. "That's correct, at least, it is according to this foolish wench."

The maid was indignant. " 'Tis the truth! I got it from Mrs. Porlock, and she got it from Mother Tippacott and Widow Longman, who happened to be crossing the footbridge earlier and saw Miss Rowena with his lordship. Mr. Grigg, the gardener, says it's so as well, for he came out into the garden to do his work, and he overheard them talking with Mrs. Melcombe. Lord Alderney's still at the big house now, and a message has been sent to the vicarage, asking Parson Grantham to come as soon as he can. There's talk of a special license and house wedding on Miss Rowena's birthday, and only telling his lordship's family about it when they visit afterward. Then they're going to live in London." She grinned a little. "No groom's family and no banns, eh? Mayhap they've jumped the broomstick before they should."

"That's enough!" the landlord snapped. "The groom mightn't have any family, and as to the special license, everyone knows the quality always marry that way, banns and so on aren't for the likes of them."

"Yes, but only a month . . ." Daisy pouted, not liking being denied the chance to spread a little salacious gossip.

"Many choose to marry on the bride's birthday," he replied.

"And many *have* to marry," she insisted.

"Not Miss Rowena," he declared firmly. "Away with you now, get some work done instead of standing in idle gossip!"

Tossing her head, she stalked away.

Andrew's eyes were bright and hard. Well, well, so there was to be a fine wedding in Melcombe. He'd come all this way to savor Rowena, only to see a rival like Alderney snatch her from under his very nose! Alderney, who could have his pick of London's ladies and had one of the greatest beauties of the decade as his mistress, came here to this godforsaken corner of Exmoor to take someone like Rowena Melcombe as his bride? It didn't make sense.

Andrew left to return to his room. He paused on the stairs to wonder what Chloe would have to say about this. Losing her lover to another woman would be bad enough, but to lose him to Rowena would be deemed an unendurable insult! No title, no beauty, no wealth, and yet this West Country mouse was to become the future Marchioness of Exford. Oh, London would ring with it for months!

Chloe would be both furious and jealous, just as he was. He still intended to have Rowena, and after the snub she'd dealt him, he'd punish her severely. Not only would he take her by force, but he'd then do all he could to destroy her match with Alderney.

Tonight, when all was quiet, the prospective bride would receive a very unwelcome visit, indeed.

Andrew went on toward his own room, but was opportunist enough to try Justin's door as he passed. It opened, and in a moment he was inside. He didn't know what he thought he might find; he only knew he'd take whatever might prove useful to hurt Rowena. He'd gone through the drawers and wardrobe when he noticed the miniature on the mantelshelf. Ah! The very thing. He'd be very surprised, indeed, if Alderney had confessed to his new bride about the mistress in London. Such information might prove very upsetting for someone like Rowena. Pocketing the miniature, Andrew searched a little more, found nothing, then slipped out again.

He was just about to enter his own room when a maid hurried

past with some fresh linen. He caught her arm. "How quickly can a letter be taken to the nearest London mail coach?"

"The letter carrier goes on the Dunster stagecoach in half an hour and links up with the Bridgwater mail, sir," she replied.

"Have some writing implements sent up to me."

"Yes, sir." Bobbing a curtsy, she hurried on.

Smiling to himself, Andrew went into his room. Chloe had to be informed about what was going on, and he was the very one to tell her!

Chapter 20

Spectral joy filled the manor house. Lady Margaret was rapturously applauded by her fellow spirits, and William was granted his share of the approval. But as the other portraits chattered happily throughout the house, an uncomfortable thought began to beset Lady Margaret. They were forgetting Andrew Kemp!

She shifted uneasily in her frame. The ripped-up note wouldn't deter the scoundrel. He was totally immoral and unscrupulous, and he hadn't come to Melcombe for the good of his health. Even phantoms were ill-advised to rest upon their laurels, especially where creatures such as he were concerned. It would therefore be prudent to find out what he was up to. She called William, who was circling the hall enjoying his newfound popularity.

He came unwillingly, for her tone was sufficient warning that she had more for him to do.

She held his gaze. "William, it occurs to me we're forgetting Mr. Kemp. That won't do at all, and so I wish you to return to the Red Lion to ascertain what he's up to."

William's face fell. "Oh, but—"

"Go now, sir."

With a heavy sigh he turned and glided away, slipping out through the oriel window and then flying hastily toward the inn. Andrew's window was open, and the wraith floated easily inside.

Andrew sat at a small table. He'd been provided with the necessary writing equipment and was penning his warning message to Justin's mistress.

Red Lion, Melcombe, Somerset.
November 1st, 1810
My dearest Chloe,

It may interest you to know that chance has brought both Alderney and me to this same hostelry in Exmoor, and that he no longer intends to travel on to Cornwall. On the contrary, he has found things very much to his liking here, or rather, he has found a certain young lady very much to his liking. It seems he has acquired a bride-to-be, the very same Rowena Melcombe I came here to belatedly enjoy. Your lover has wasted no time. He arrived here the night before Halloween, and word has just spread through the village that they are to be married.

Should you suspect him of resorting to mere expediency because of his father's wishes, let me warn that I've witnessed them together, and there is no doubting their passion. As you know from me, the lady is hardly a beauty, nor even an heiress, but she certainly possesses an astonishing allure.

I understand the nuptials are to take place here in Melcombe on December the first, which gives you one month to bring the fellow to his senses. I fear the Red Lion could hardly be described as suitable for a lady of your rank, but it is all the area has to offer if you decide your presence here is imperative.

Should a journey to the wilds of Exmoor prove impossible (or unpalatable!) then I believe the happy pair will be coming to London after a brief sojourn at Exford Park. In London it will no doubt be possible to set about driving an enduring wedge between them, for the new Lady Alderney will hardly be a match for you. I will gladly assist in any plan to separate Alderney from his bride.

However, for the moment I am still in her thrall—indeed she holds a peculiar fascination for me—and I will stay on until I have tasted the delights that drew me here. Her compliance is immaterial.

I am,
Your eternal devotee,
Andrew.

William stared in horror as Andrew sanded and then sealed the letter. The blackguard intended to force himself upon Rowena? The shade turned agitatedly as he heard the Dunster stagecoach drawing up outside, and then the ringing of the letter carrier's bell. Andrew's disgraceful intentions toward Rowena were bad enough, but the presence in Melcombe of Justin's mistress was equally undesirable if the match was to be protected. There was no time to consult with Lady Margaret; something had to be done *now*! But what?

Poor William dithered and agonized as Andrew carefully wrote Chloe's Mayfair address on the letter and then left the room with it. The phantom fluttered nervously out of the window and down to the waiting stagecoach. The carrier was accepting letters from several villagers, and he touched his hat respectfully as Andrew went up to him.

Pressing a coin into the man's hand, Andrew spoke in a low voice. "See that this doesn't go astray."

"Sir." The man pocketed the coin and the letter.

As the stagecoach pulled noisily away, to the horn accompaniment of "Cherry Ripe" and the barking of village dogs, Andrew paused before going back into the inn. His face was very still as he gazed along the village road toward the manor house, where he knew Alderney was with Rowena. Tonight, when his lordship was in his bed at the Red Lion, a certain compliant serving girl would be bribed to swear upon oath that Andrew Kemp had been with her through the night. Dear Rowena was going to regret tearing up his note and returning it unanswered.

William floated busily around him, wishing he knew what thoughts were going on behind those cold hazel eyes. Whatever they were, they were damned unpleasant.

Andrew felt no prick of conscience about what he planned to do. He'd come to this remote village to enjoy Rowena Melcombe's charms, and nothing would prevent him from doing just that. With a faintly contemptuous smile, he went back into the inn, and William heard him calling for a measure of apple brandy.

The ghost was still in a fluster. He desperately wanted Lady Margaret's advice, but in his heart he already knew the first and most vital thing that must be done. The letter must not reach Lady Westcote. He set off after the stagecoach, skimming along at a commendable pace a few feet above the road. Soon the vehicle appeared ahead of him, the notes of "Cherry Ripe" still reverberating across the moor. As the coachman slowed to negotiate a hump-backed bridge over a fast-flowing river, William floated gently down onto the roof to settle invisibly between two outside passengers. The traveler on his left gave no sign of sensing anything amiss, but the other was immediately conscious of a lowering of the temperature.

Shivering, he pulled his scarf more tightly around his neck and huddled in his greatcoat. "It's suddenly got much colder," he grumbled.

"Colder?" The first passenger shrugged. "It doesn't feel any different to me."

"No different? My dear sir, it's lower by at least ten degrees!"

The other man gave him an uneasy look. Was the fellow sickening for something? Deciding that this was likely, he moved as far away as he could.

The stagecoach drove on along the winding moorland road, which at last led steeply down to the wide main street of Dunster, a large market village situated where the foot of the moor reached the narrow coastal plain. The Bridgwater mail coach was waiting to leave, and the letter carrier was the first to alight as the coach from Melcombe drew up. William swooped into action. Remembering in which pocket the man had put the letter, the wraith hovered within inches of him, concentrating hard upon the folded paper. Grimacing even more fearsomely than Lady Margaret, he at last persuaded the letter to wriggle up toward the pocket flap. As he saw the thin line of white appear, William drew upon all his strength, and to his delight the letter slipped out and then down to the cobbles. Then the wraith hurled himself along the street, raising a huge wind that snatched the letter high into the air. It flew over the chimney tops and out of sight. The sudden gust of wind took everyone by surprise. Hats had to be held on tightly, and cloaks flapped around ankles. An inn sign creaked noisily, and horses shifted nervously, knowing that it was no ordinary wind.

Triumphant, William glided back toward the moor and Melcombe. For the moment he'd completely forgotten Andrew's intention to violate Rowena.

Lady Margaret was very pleased with him, although her pleasure was tinged with a certain regret that they now knew beyond all shadow of doubt Lady Westcote was Justin's mistress and that her existence was being kept from Rowena. It remained to be seen what place Lady Westcote would occupy in his life from now on, but for Rowena's sake all the Melcombe ghosts hoped the mistress would soon be discarded.

Any delight Lady Margaret may have felt was swiftly doused when William at last mentioned the full content of Andrew's let-

ter. She was appalled, and gasps of horror swept around the hall.
"The scoundrel actually wrote that?" she cried.

"Yes." The full import suddenly swept back over William, and
he went pale.

"He has to be prevented," Lady Margaret declared to the hotly
expressed agreement of the other portraits. "Rowena's very safety
is at stake, to say nothing of the safety of the match we've striven
to bring about. William, you have until late this evening before
you have to return to your frame for good, and in that time I trust
we will have thought of a way of, er, persuading Mr. Kemp that
Melcombe really isn't a very pleasant place for him."

"You wish me to frighten him?"

"With a vengeance, sir. With a vengeance. While you rest, I will
confer with everyone in the house, and when we've decided upon
the best course, we will awaken you and tell you what must be done.
Take heart, sir, for you've done well. I'm still a little annoyed you
wasted last night, but you've done a great deal to atone for it today."

William took himself back to his frame and settled down to try
to rest. But the thought of what was intended for Rowena made
him too restless to sleep.

Chapter 21

It was late when Justin at last prepared to return to the Red Lion.
He'd spent a very agreeable day with Rowena's family and been
made to feel very welcome, even by the twins, who'd turned out
to be a good deal quieter than he'd expected. Even Mrs. Melcombe, once she'd recovered from the shock of their abject apol-
ogy, conceded they seemed almost chastened. Rowena chose not
to mention flying skeletons and pumpkins, and the twins themselves had evidently thought better of it as well, for they said
nothing to explain their reformation.

Rowena accompanied Justin to the door in the hope they'd be
able to steal a few moments together after a long day of making
wedding plans. The Reverend Grantham had readily agreed to
perform the ceremony at the house, and even the wedding list it-

self had been agreed upon. After spending their first night at an inn in Bridgwater, they planned to go on to Exford Park to see his family, and then to London.

The ceremony was to be a very private affair, with just Rowena's immediate family and, they hoped, Justin's friends, George and Emily Rathbone. He wanted George to be his groomsman and was also anxious for Rowena to make Emily's acquaintance because he trusted his friend's wife would take the new Lady Alderney under her capable and kindly wing. There might also be one other guest, George's aunt, Lady Beaminster, who by happy coincidence, appeared to be a long-lost friend of Mrs. Melcombe's.

But if the ceremony itself was to be small and private, the celebrations in Melcombe village were set to be the very opposite. Word of Rowena's grand match already seemed to have reached every corner of Exmoor, and congratulatory messages had been arriving all day. Nothing would do for the delighted villagers but that there was another bonfire on the green, with as much merry-making as possible.

As Justin and Rowena reached the front door, he couldn't help marveling again that she'd come to mean so much to him in such a short time. He glanced fondly at her modest gown and swept-up hair, which were exactly as they'd been that morning when he'd first called. He couldn't help reflecting that by now Chloe would have changed at least twice and for evening would be splendid in rich silk and jewels. Rowena was a little wren compared with such a bird of paradise, but the wren had crept past all his defenses.

He reproached himself for comparing her with his mistress, and as he opened the door, he drew her swiftly outside into the autumnal darkness and into his arms. She came gladly, raising her parted lips to his and pressing longingly against him.

His hands moved sensuously over her back and waist, exploring the soft curves that seemed created only for him. For a moment he caressed her breast, his hand moving with tender skill over its fullness and then lingering on the nipple that pressed so eagerly through the soft merino of her gown.

The intimacy of his touch sang electrically through her. She leaned back in his arms, her breath catching as frissons of pleasures rippled across her body. Her heartbeats had quickened, and her skin was so warm the November night might have been July. She wanted to go further, to be seduced completely into the physical temptation now open to her. It was so compelling a feeling, it was disturbing, and she drew back before it overwhelmed her. She had to turn away.

He understood and embraced her from behind, resting his

cheek against her hair as he whispered. "A month may seem so long, but it will pass, and then we will be free to do that which tempts us now."

"It frightens me to feel so much."

"I know."

"And I'm painfully conscious of knowing so little."

"I will be a more than willing teacher," he said softly, kissing her hair. Unbidden, Chloe swept back into his thoughts, and the guilt was so sharp he had to release Rowena.

She turned anxiously to search his face. "What is it?"

"I . . . I was just thinking that your mother might disapprove if we dally out here any longer."

"Yes, she probably will," Rowena replied ruefully.

"Then I'll go now. I'll leave for Taunton for the special license first thing in the morning, but hope to be back tomorrow night."

"I hope so, too," she whispered.

He raised her palm to his lips, kissing it tenderly. His tongue caressed her skin for a moment, and then he released her. "Sleep well, my darling," he murmured, then left her, walking swiftly out between the gates.

Andrew watched from his window at the Red Lion. The moment he recognized Justin's tall figure leaving the manor, he turned to look at the red-haired serving girl who still lay on the bed after they'd made love. Her skirts were pulled up around her thighs, and her bodice had been unlaced to free her plump breasts. She'd served to pass the time, but she hadn't satisfied the aching need he had for Rowena.

He took a coin from his pocket and went to the bed, pressing the coin between her breasts before grasping one of her nipples and pinching it tightly. "Just remember you spent virtually the whole of this evening and tonight here in this room with me. I'm going out now, but however long I take, you're just to say it was a few minutes. I'll have supper sent up, and when it's brought, you're to take it at the door and pretend I'm back here with you. Do you understand?"

Her breath caught because he was hurting her. "I . . . I'll do whatever you want," she promised.

"See that you do, and there'll be two more coins in it," he replied, loosening his hold.

"Two?" she breathed.

"Maybe more if you're an especially good girl," he murmured, bending to kiss her on the lips, then caressing the nipple he'd hurt a moment before.

She closed her eyes. He was the most skillful lover she'd ever had, and there had been many, but above all he was her first fashionable gentleman. He didn't just take his pleasure of her; he knew all the subtleties of lovemaking, and it was a new as well as a gratifying experience for her. She'd have done whatever he wanted even if he hadn't bribed her. All he had to promise was be another tumble between the sheets.

Putting on his outdoor things, he left the room, and she curled up deliciously on the bed. Let him return soon, for she wanted much more of what she'd just had. Much, much more! She didn't care what he was up to, for what business was it of hers?

Andrew had timed his departure very carefully, for he wanted to encounter Justin on the stairs. It happened exactly as he planned, and he looked down with loathing at the man who'd just come from Rowena's arms. His jealousy was such that he could no longer hold back, but had to provoke Justin in some way. He didn't intend to go so far as to risk a duel, but if that should happen, he was confident of his own prowess with a pistol, whereas Justin's skill as a shot was an unknown quantity.

As Justin passed him, Andrew deliberately jostled his arm and then went on down without apologizing.

That the encounter had been intentional wasn't lost upon Justin, who halted and turned. "Do you have a defect of the eyesight, Mr. Kemp?" he asked coldly.

Andrew turned as well. "No, Lord Alderney, I do not."

"Since you are also capable of replying, it cannot be said that your powers of hearing or speech deny you the ability to apologize for your clumsiness."

"Indeed it cannot be said, sir."

Justin surveyed him. "Then I can only presume that the difficulty lies with your lack of manners, in which case I will make allowances. But be warned that I expect you to take more care from now on, for I will not be so tolerant in future. Do you take my meaning?"

Andrew's eyes flickered. It seemed his lordship had a little more spirit than he credited. "I take your meaning perfectly, my lord." He sketched a bow.

Justin looked at him with distaste and then continued up the staircase. There was something about the fellow he disliked intensely. Kemp might be a gentleman on the outside, but beneath the veneer he was the very opposite.

Andrew watched him pass out of sight. Maybe he'd underestimated Alderney, for there hadn't been anything hesitant about his reaction. He flexed his fingers in his gloves and then continued down the stairs. He went to the crowded taproom to look for the landlord, who came to him immediately.

"Mr. Kemp?"

"I'm going out for a brief stroll. I'll only be five minutes or so and wish you to send supper to my room. A bottle of red wine, some bread and cheese, and a little cold beef."

"Sir."

Andrew smiled a little. "Make it sufficient for two. My, er, companion will need all her strength."

The landlord nodded. "As you wish, sir."

Still smiling, Andrew left the inn, making certain as he did so the landlord saw which way he turned for his walk. It was the opposite direction from the manor house. After walking a few yards in the darkness, he ran swiftly across the green and then along the road toward the manor gates.

He knew which room was Rowena's, for she'd once confided in him that she'd deliberately chosen the room above the library, near the back staircase. How provident that staircase was now! He made his way around to the rear of the house. The curtains were undrawn at one brightly lit window, and he saw Lionel and the twins gathered around the billiard table, arguing about who should sit out the first match. Passing on, he soon entered the kitchen garden and then peered through another window. The servants sat in their parlor, chattering excitedly about the wedding as they enjoyed a cup of tea. He knew they weren't likely to notice him as he slipped into the house.

The rear door opened into a whitewashed passage between the kitchen and buttery, and the lingering smell of dinner drifted over him as he stepped inside. He listened, but there was no change in the chatter from the servants. Swiftly, he passed their room to the short flight of steps leading up into the main house.

All seemed quiet as he listened again before entering the small candlelit hall where the library was adjacent to the back staircase. He was just about to cross to the stairs when he heard a slight sound in the library. A smile played coolly upon his lips. Only one person was likely to be in there now. He bent to the keyhole. Sure enough, Rowena was inside, selecting a book. A lighted candle stood on the table behind her.

Andrew straightened. How like her to retire early and to take a book with her. A few hours' bedtime reading was nothing to her;

sometimes she read on until well past midnight. Tonight she was about to have more than the written word to think about!

He went quietly up the staircase and into her bedroom directly above, in darkness except for the flickering fire in the hearth. The bedclothes were turned back in readiness, and the fresh, almost sharp fragrance of chrysanthemums filled the warm air from a vase on a small table next to the fireplace. Glancing around for the best place to conceal himself, he noticed that one of the tall windows was adjacent to the bedhead and thus not immediately visible to her when she was sitting up reading.

In a few steps he'd concealed himself behind the heavy velvet curtains. Taking off his outdoor clothes, he leaned back against the folded shutters to wait.

Chapter 22

Rowena returned to the bedroom and discarded her wrap before climbing into the bed and opening the book she'd chosen. But there were still so many thoughts and feelings singing through her that reading was impossible. Even now she felt as if she would suddenly awaken and find she'd dreamed it all.

She leaned her head back against the pillows, gazing wonderingly up at the canopy. So much had happened since she'd gone so wretchedly to the church yesterday. No, it hadn't begun at the church; it had started at midnight the night before. At first she'd been so sure it was a dream, and then merely an astonishing coincidence that Justin was so like her imagined lover, but sometimes it felt far too real for her to be sure about anything. She smiled, for the ritual with mirror, apple, and comb, was supposed to reveal one's future husband, and that was exactly what had happened! Maybe there really was magic and witchcraft on Halloween . . .

Andrew held the curtain slightly aside and looked at her. Her hair spilled like gold over the pillows, and her lips seemed to pout invitingly. She'd neglected to tie her nightgown ribbons properly, so he could see the full swelling of her upturned breasts. His gaze lingered hotly on those alluring contours, and lust rose urgently through him. In his thoughts he'd dwelt endlessly upon taking his pleasure of her; now he was within seconds of fulfillment. It would be more satisfying if she'd cooperate, but forcing her would still be reward enough for all the torment she'd caused him. It would certainly be recompense for the insulting way she'd ripped his note and sent it back. And if she thought she could look forward to happiness with Alderney, she was mistaken, for he, Andrew Kemp, wouldn't rest until he'd riven the match asunder.

Without making a sound, he stepped stealthily from behind the curtain. She was still so lost in her reverie she didn't sense the danger. She knew nothing until suddenly his hand was forced over her mouth and he'd flung himself upon her, his weight pressing harshly through the bedclothes.

Terror seized her, and for a moment she was too confused to struggle, but then her wits returned, and she strove with all her might to fight him off. He dragged the bedclothes away to prise her thighs apart, then took his hand from her mouth to kiss her. His tongue forced its way between her unwilling lips, and the more she struggled, the more his excitement mounted. He used her roughly, and his entire being throbbed with anticipation. Soon he would thrust deep into her, and he'd be master of the body he'd craved for so long. He forgot the pain in his fingers; nothing mattered to him now except the sweet imminence of ravishing her.

With a huge effort she dragged her lips away from his, but her scream was stifled as his mouth smothered hers again, devouring her with his ugly passion. A tide of dread and revulsion washed through her. He was going to rape her to gratify his lust, and she was helpless to prevent him. Her cheeks were wet with tears, and she closed her eyes to shut him out.

He ripped the thin stuff of her nightgown and caressed her breasts, taking her nipple so savagely between his fingers that she arched in agony beneath him. He enjoyed her pain, and the writhing of her body excited him beyond endurance. In a frenzy of desire he struggled with his breeches buttons to free the shaft pulsing so intensely at his loins. He had to take her now, when his need was at fever pitch—

But her suffocated scream hadn't gone unheard. William's eyes flew open, and he sat up swiftly in his frame. Rowena! Her terror was all around him, and he knew she was in the utmost danger. Without a second thought he flew urgently to her, passing through the door as Andrew was still fumbling one-handedly with his breeches.

The phantom was filled with instant fury and launched himself at the bed to place spectral hands upon his daughter's assailant. Such was the power of William's paternal rage that his touch was palpable. Andrew gave a gasp as he felt the icy grip wrenching him away from Rowena. His head jerked around to see who was there, but there was no one. His eyes widened with alarm as something invisible hurled him from the bed. He knocked the vase of chrysanthemums to the floor and then fell with a force that broke the table and jolted the breath from his body. The pulsing desire that had ruled him a moment before suddenly diminished into limp uselessness.

Rowena was still too terrified to be really aware of anything. She knew only that for the moment at least her attacker had gone, and she curled up and clung to the pillows to weep helplessly. She was oblivious to what now went on around her.

The temperature in the room suddenly plunged below freezing, and the fire flared as an arctic draft swirled up the chimney toward the night sky. Andrew glanced fearfully around the room. The candle flame streamed and then went out, leaving only the leaping light of the roaring fire. He could hear heavy panting. It wasn't Rowena. There was someone else in the room, someone invisible! Panic surged through him, and he scrambled away until he was pressed against the wall. His eyes were huge as he scanned every shadow, thinking that at any moment he *must* see who else was there.

William was shaken to realize he could actually touch someone in the living world. He sensed that it was a power born of the incredible anger still searing through him. This despicable villain had to suffer for what he'd tried to do! Swooping toward Andrew again, the wraith heaved him mightily across the room toward the fire, where he sprawled in the hearth within inches of the fierce flames.

The ghost summoned the poker, making it jab at the fire. Sparks and ash scattered over Andrew, who clawed himself away with yelps of pain. His mouth was dry, and his heart was thundering so much he feared it would burst. The eerie panting was still audible, and an icy finger suddenly touched his cheek. With an anguished cry he scrambled to his feet and fled from the room. William followed, still reaching out now and then to shake him by the shoulder.

Andrew stumbled down the back staircase, almost falling several times. He cried out with dread as he crossed the inner hall and the invisible hand clutched at him again. Flinging open the door to the kitchens, he dashed down into the passageway beyond. His boots rang on the stone floor, and the servants turned in astonishment as he ran past their door so swiftly they didn't have time to recognize him.

The cold night air snatched his breath as he stumbled out into the gardens, but if he hoped to have left his invisible tormentor in the house, he soon knew he hadn't. Ghostly hands jerked him almost from his feet, and he gave a terrified cry as he continued to flee. William kept after him, his ghostly rage still blazing like an inferno. The wraith wanted vengeance, wanted Andrew's very demise, but knew the Powers wouldn't countenance such extremes. But they would allow Andrew's precipitate departure from Melcombe, and that was William's purpose now. He wanted Rowena's attacker out of the village and wouldn't cease his tormenting until that happened.

Mrs. Melcombe had just been climbing the main staircase when she heard the table in Rowena's room being knocked over. Pausing with her hand shielding her lighted candle, she looked toward the sound. Then she heard a man cry out, and a moment later Andrew ran into the passage and down the back staircase as if the Gabriel hounds were upon him.

Rowena had mentioned his return to the village, and Mrs. Melcombe was immediately fearful for her daughter. Gathering her skirts and still trying to protect the candle flame, she hurried to the end bedroom, where she found Rowena weeping hysterically into her pillows. There was no mistaking what had happened; the crumpled bedclothes and ripped nightgown told all. The room was still ice-cold in spite of the drawing fire, and Mrs. Melcombe shivered as she put the candlestick down. As she did so, the flames in the hearth suddenly ceased their roaring and settled back to their customary flicker. Almost immediately the room became perceptibly warmer. She glanced around uneasily, for there was a very strange and almost charged atmosphere, as sometimes happened before a thunderstorm. She felt the hairs at the nape of her neck stand a little on end and instinctively glanced toward the darkest and most shadowy corners.

Rowena suddenly realized someone was there and sat up with a sharp gasp.

"It's all right, my dear, it's only me," Mrs. Melcombe cried, hurrying to her.

"Oh, Mother—"

"He's gone, sweetheart." Her mother brushed a heavy lock of

hair back from her Rowena's tear-stained cheek, then sat down on the edge of the bed.

With a sob of relief Rowena flung her arms around her.

Mrs. Melcombe held her tightly. "It's all right, my dear, you're safe now." For a while she allowed Rowena to weep, but then knew there was something very important that had to be asked. Taking her daughter's face in her hands, she looked earnestly into her eyes. "My dear, I must know if he . . . I mean, did he manage to . . . ?"

Rowena shook her head. "No."

"Are you quite certain?"

"Yes." Rowena pulled her torn nightgown over her breasts. "He w-was going to, but then . . . Well, he just stopped. One moment he was on me, the next he wasn't. I know it sounds silly, but it was as if someone pulled him away."

Mrs. Melcombe looked at the broken table, the spilled vase of chrysanthemums, and the poker lying among the scattered ashes in the hearth. "He must have been taken quite by surprise when you put up such a fight," she murmured.

Rowena followed her glance. "I . . . I don't know how that happened. I was on the bed all the time." She was bewildered. There must have been a great deal of noise, but she hadn't heard anything.

Her mother stared at her. "On the bed? But—"

"I don't know how this happened," Rowena said again.

Mrs. Melcombe recalled a strange ambience in the room, and a shudder ran through her. Just what had gone on in here a few minutes ago?

Rowena looked at the curtains where Andrew had been hiding. "He was waiting there when I came into the room."

Mrs. Melcombe got up and went to draw them back. Andrew's outdoor clothes lay where he'd left them. With a shudder of distaste she picked them up. "I'll see they're destroyed," she said angrily, "for I see no reason why they should be returned to their owner, do you?" She placed them on the dressing table and then returned to the bed, but as she sat down once more, she saw something golden lying among the sheets. It was the miniature of Justin's mistress, which had fallen from Andrew's pocket during the assault.

She examined it and read out the engraving on the back. "*To the lover of my heart, body, and soul, from his adoring slave. October, 1810.* Well, it would seem Mr. Kemp has a mistress. The Countess of Westcote, no less," she declared, showing the little portrait to Rowena.

"She's very beautiful."

"For all her finery, she still looks a woman of easy virtue,"

Mrs. Melcombe replied crushingly, turning to throw the miniature into the fire.

A discreet tap came at the door. "Miss Rowena?" It was her maid.

Mrs. Melcombe got up swiftly and went to open the door, but no so that the maid could see the bed. "Yes, what is it?"

"Oh, Mrs. Melcombe, we were all in the kitchens a short while ago when a man ran out of the house. We couldn't see who he was, and we lost him in the darkness outside. He must have been a thief."

"I, er, haven't heard anything up here. Miss Rowena and I have been together for some time. Please have the house searched to see if anything has been taken."

"Yes, madam." The maid curtsied and hurried away.

Mrs. Melcombe closed the door and looked at her daughter. "It would seem all is not lost."

"Lost?"

"No one knows Mr. Kemp was here, and I doubt if he'll brag about what he did, which means that this entire incident, serious and unsavory as it is, can remain secret."

Rowena stared at her. "But—"

"If you say anything, anything at all, you'll be compromised and your match with Lord Alderney may be over before it's begun."

"I was attacked in my own bed!"

"I know, my dear, but you were Mr. Kemp's innocent victim, and he did not take what he came for. You will still be chaste when you marry Lord Alderney, and he does not need to know anything."

"I have to tell him, Mother. It's wrong not to."

"And is it right you should risk sacrificing happiness for something you could not prevent? You didn't invite Mr. Kemp to this room, nor did you consent to anything he attempted to do."

Fresh tears filled Rowena's eyes. "Mother, I already feel guilty because I haven't told Justin anything about Andrew. If I remain silent about this as well—"

"Just contemplate the consequences of telling. Lord Alderney will learn that Mr. Kemp once meant a great deal to you, and that you've also been keeping more recent things from him. That is bound to make him wonder about tonight. He'll fear you may have invited Mr. Kemp, and his trust will be shaken, no matter how much he may love you. That could jeopardize your match, my dear, and if he calls it off, then not only will you be unnecessarily denied your chance of a very fortunate marriage, but Melcombe will be lost to us after all."

Rowena searched her face. "But it's wrong to keep silent."

"It's even more wrong to deliberately court disaster when there is no need."

"But what if Mr. Kemp tells—?"

"Tells? Monsters who attack helpless women are never man enough to face their equals, and he'd risk being brought to account if he said what happened here tonight."

"He could claim he was welcomed to my bed, and you've already pointed out that Justin is bound to wonder if it's true," Rowena said quietly.

Mrs. Melcombe was silent for a moment. "That is a chance we must take. Rowena, you must see that it is more sensible by far to hold our tongues about this. After all, Lord Alderney will still be the first man with you, and that is what matters."

Rowena lowered her gaze.

Her mother put a gentle hand over hers. "You haven't said so, but I know you love him. For you this is much more than a sensible solution to a situation. I'm right, am I not?"

"Yes," Rowena whispered, tears springing to her eyes.

"Then take my advice, my dear; put this most dreadful experience from your mind and think only of the future. You and Lord Alderney will be very happy together."

Rowena hesitated. "If . . . if that's what you advise . . ."

"It most definitely is."

Rowena gave an unhappy nod.

Mrs. Melcombe breathed out with relief. "Now then, I'll leave you and go through the motions of believing we've had a thief, and then I'll send Ann up with your usual glass of hot milk."

"No, I don't want to see her tonight," Rowena said quickly.

"Everything must appear quite normal. As soon as I leave you now, I want you to change into another nightgown, straighten your bed, and be sitting reading as you usually are when the maid comes."

Bending, Mrs. Melcombe kissed her daughter's cheek, then took Andrew's clothes to go out. She paused in the doorway, glancing around the room again. But everything was normal now. It was warm, with firelight dancing over the walls and furniture, and the unsettling aura might never have been. Maybe she'd imagined it.

As the door closed, Rowena's eyes filled with fresh tears. Lying back on the pillows again, she hid her face in her hands and gave in to the misery she felt.

Chapter 23

Rowena's physical ordeal was over, but Andrew's continued. Still hounded by William, he fled back to the Red Lion, where his ashen, disheveled appearance alarmed the girl waiting in his room. The icy draft accompanying him snuffed the candle, and she backed away as the temperature in the room plummeted. The fire began to roar, and her terror rose to match Andrew's as she saw William's indistinct shape hurtle into the room behind him.

William knew she could see him, and realized his fury had not only granted him hitherto unknown strength, but also made him partially visible to those who were susceptible. Could she hear him as well? There was no trace of his former clumsy incompetence as he faced her.

"Tell Kemp to leave Melcombe immediately!" he ordered. His voice sounded normal to him, but to her was hollow and sepulchral.

Her lips trembled, but she was too rigid with fear to say anything.

William wafted menacingly toward her. "I want him to leave! Now!"

She jumped as if stung, and her huge eyes moved slowly toward Andrew, who was cowering behind the bed. "He s-says you m-must leave Melcombe, Mr. K-Kemp," she whispered.

"Louder!" William roared at her.

"He says you've got to leave right away, Mr. Kemp!" she cried, looking fit to faint.

Justin heard her in the next room and looked up curiously from the letter he was endeavoring to write to his father. He shivered a little, suddenly aware that the temperature had dropped. Getting up to put his coat on, he returned to his seat and took up his quill again.

But beyond the wall the next world was intruding upon the present, and Andrew was still on his knees behind the bed, trying to hide from his terror. But at the girl's raised voice he ventured to peep over the coverlet.

"Who . . . who says I've got to go?" he asked fearfully.

Desperate to make him do as the ghost wished, she pointed toward William. "It's Mr. Melcombe, and he says you're to go," she said, trying to swallow, although her mouth was like parchment.

He followed her pointing finger, but saw nothing. His teeth were chattering with fear and cold, even though the fire continued to roar in the hearth and the draft forced the flames to reach up the chimney. "Th-there's no one there," he whispered, his voice barely audible.

"You'd best do as he wants, for you can't disobey a boggart," she said.

"Boggart?" Andrew didn't understand the word.

"A ghost!" she cried. "You've got to do it, sir! I'll have your horse harnessed!" Gathering her skirts, she edged past William and then fled from the room, beginning to scream as she dashed toward the stairs.

Andrew was dismayed. "Don't leave me!" he squeaked.

But William made the door slam behind her.

All the noise made Justin fling his quill down irritably. What in God's name was Kemp doing? He opened the door in time to see the frightened maid vanish down the stairs.

"There's a boggart! I've seen a boggart!" she cried at the top of her voice.

Justin raised a puzzled eyebrow. If he knew what a boggart was, he'd know whether or not to be as terrified as she evidently was. He glanced at Andrew's closed door, but no sound came from the room behind it. Lingering for a few moments more, he shrugged and then returned to the letter he was finding inordinately difficult to write.

William was still intent upon Andrew's just punishment. Advancing toward him, he seized his hair and shook his head violently from side to side.

With a cry of anguish Andrew dragged himself free and scrambled to his feet to rush to the wardrobe and fling on the warmest coat he could find. Snatching up another hat, he dashed from the room, and the door banged on its hinges behind him.

By now Justin was thoroughly exasperated. Was there a fight going on? Tossing the quill down yet again, he strode out into the passage, where a blast of bitterly cold air snatched his breath away. Andrew ran frantically past, glancing fearfully over his shoulder now and then as if something hideous was pursuing him.

The chill gradually diminished as Andrew disappeared downstairs, and Justin went curiously to the adjacent room to look inside. He expected to see someone else there, but the room was empty. Firelight flickered gently over the furniture, and the only sign of the occupant's hasty departure was the open wardrobe. Raising mystified eyebrows, Justin glanced around for a few moments more, then he shrugged again. To Hades with Kemp!

Returning to his own room, he once more resumed his writing, but it wasn't easy. His original intention had been to present his family with a *fait accompli*, but now he'd had second thoughts. Maybe it would be better to inform them of his plans after all, but the more he tried to put those plans down on paper, the more outrageous they seemed. He'd already written to George and Emily in Bath and hadn't had any trouble wording his announcement, but when it came to his father . . .

He looked up from the letter as more shouting resounded through the inn. The frightened maid had told everyone she'd seen the late Mr. Melcombe's boggart. So soon after Halloween, it was too much for most of the men in the taproom, and they huddled together as far away from the door as they could, especially when Andrew ran down the stairs again, and they all felt the ice-cold draft that followed him as William continued his pursuit.

The horses in the stables were disturbed by the ghostly presence and whinnied and kicked in their stalls. A dog began to bark distractedly, and the frightened grooms trying to harness Andrew's cabriolet found it difficult to maneuver the horse between the shafts. They'd barely completed their task when Andrew scrambled on to the little vehicle and snatched up the reins. They released the bridle, and the terrified horse started hastily out of the yard, its hooves striking sparks from the cobbles.

Andrew sped away from the Red Lion with William in full spectral cry after him. Every dog in the neighborhood began to bark or howl, and the trees on the green swayed in the blast of ghostly wind William raised as he passed by. Autumn leaves streamed chaotically through the night, and the weathercock on the church spun wildly.

The inn sign creaked and groaned, and with a muttered curse Justin gave up trying to write. He evidently wasn't meant to send this letter. Tonight this hitherto quiet country inn seemed to have become a veritable Bedlam, and it was as well he didn't have a superstitious bone in his body, or he might be tempted to think the place was haunted! He went to the window and looked out. The inn sign was still swaying, but more gently now, and a fading eddy of leaves wafted across the road before coming to rest on the edge of the green.

Everything became quiet again, and stars twinkled softly in a clear sky. He drew a long breath, turning his gaze toward the manor house. Was Rowena asleep now? He thought of her lying warm and soft between the sheets and longed to be with her. Well, soon he would be.

In the morning he'd leave for Taunton for the special license, and in a month's time . . . In the morning? Why wait until then? Kemp and his goings-on had put paid to his filial letter, and now he was far too restless to sleep. Highwaymen didn't bother with Exmoor roads because there were too few pickings, so he could be safely in Taunton by the morning if he left now. The sooner he went, the sooner he'd be with Rowena again.

With sudden decision he turned to go down to tell the landlord of the change of plan, but as he did so he noticed Chloe's miniature was missing from the mantelshelf. He glanced down in case it had fallen to the floor, but there was no sign of it. He sighed. All inns possessed light-fingered servants, and such trinkets fetched good prices. He'd been foolish to leave it out.

Putting the matter from his mind, he went to find the landlord, who was in the crowded taproom. There was a great deal of excited chatter as everyone discussed the past few minutes' strange events, but they all fell silent as he entered.

The landlord hastened forward. "May I be of some assistance, my lord?"

"Yes, I intend to leave for Taunton. Have my carriage prepared immediately."

"You're leaving *now*, sir?"

"That is usually what is meant by immediately," Justin replied a little caustically.

The landlord flushed. "I know, sir, it's just that . . ."

"Well?"

"There are things out and about tonight, my lord," the man said in a low voice.

"Things?"

"Ghosts and such like."

Justin stared at him and then gave a skeptical laugh. "Well, I don't presume to know whether you're right or not, but I do know I still mean to leave now for Taunton."

"As you wish, my lord."

"See my carriage is made ready. I'm not vacating my room, for I intend to return soon."

"To marry Miss Rowena? Yes, my lord, we all know."

"I'm sure you do."

"May I extend my congratulations, sir?"

"Thank you. Oh, by the way, would you see this leaves with the next post?" Justin handed him the letter to George and Emily.

"Certainly, sir."

Inclining his head briefly, Justin left the taproom.

The landlord turned to the rest of the taproom and shrugged. "Well, I did try and warn him there were boggarts abroad," he muttered, putting the letter with several others waiting for the morning carrier.

His brother, the blacksmith, shrugged and knocked his clay pipe out on the fireplace. "If it were Mr. Melcombe's boggart, then his lordship won't be at risk, of that you can be sure. His lordship's money will save Melcombe, and that's what matters."

The landlord nodded. "Aye, I suppose you're right. Mind, I don't like to think what that there Mr. Kemp has done to warrant such a punishment."

The blacksmith raised a knowing eyebrow. "It weren't for the fresh Exmoor air that 'e returned, it were sommat to do with Miss Rowena."

The landlord glanced nervously toward the staircase and then glared at him. "Hold your tongue!"

"I was only thinking—"

"Then don't. We want the Melcombes to stay on at the big house, and we want Master Lionel to take over when he's of age. You open your trap and say sommat as might stop this wedding, and God alone knows who might buy Melcombe. Better the devil we know."

The blacksmith fell silent, and the landlord hurried out to the stable yard to see about Justin's carriage.

William was keeping up his fiendish pursuit of Andrew, determined to make him suffer as much as possible. But the phantom overreached himself by terrorizing the horse. As the cabriolet came to the hump-backed bridge where the stagecoach had slowed earlier in the day, the animal suddenly swerved to one side, and the vehicle capsized, rolling over and over into the rapids below. The shafts and harness had broken, and wheels continued to turn. The horse dashed on, its hooves thundering into the night, but Andrew lay very still, half in and half out of the icy water.

The accident subdued William. He tried to shake Andrew, but with the sobering of his fury his new powers had vanished, and his ghostly hands passed right through the motionless figure.

William drew sharply back. He'd killed him! Flapping with alarm, the wraith hastened away, but realized as he did so that he was rushing more and more swiftly through the night. An invisible force was tugging him along, and suddenly he knew his time was up. He was being drawn back to his frame! Clawing uselessly at the air to try to slow his speed, he hurtled helplessly toward the manor.

He was out of control, tumbling like a mad acrobat as he reached the house and landed with a thud in his frame. Breathless and disoriented, he lay there for a moment or so, then got up to straighten his clothes. He still had things to do! He needed to see Rowena! And Lady Margaret had to be told he'd so overstepped the mark as to cause Kemp to meet his end!

He tried to put his hand out of the frame, but it was impossible. He was trapped behind the canvas. Frustrated, he tried again, and then he kicked the frame furiously. Damn it all, why had his time run out before he was ready? He desperately wanted to be with Rowena for a moment or so. He knew she was crying in her bed, and although he couldn't touch or speak to her, he needed to go to her. That wish was going to be denied him, as was his desire to speak to Lady Margaret.

But then he remembered that in the latter case at least he could still communicate with his fellow spirits. Taking a deep breath, he called out to the half-landing.

"Mistress Melcombe?"

There was silence.

"Mistress Melcombe!"

He heard a faint grumbling. "Oh, what is it? I'm trying to sleep!"

Reluctantly, he told her what had happened.

She was shocked. "You killed him?"

"It was an accident. I didn't meant to do it," he replied wretchedly.

"We're not supposed to go that far! Things like that are left to the Powers-That-Be, or to darker spirits!"

"I know. Oh, just tell Lady Margaret, that's all I ask." William turned his back on the bedroom and huddled in the corner of his frame. He hadn't intended to kill Kemp, just frighten him into never coming back. Well, he wouldn't come back now, that was certain!

Miss Melcombe relayed his message, and the portraits in the great hall gasped. Lady Margaret was appalled. The Powers wouldn't approve of this. No, not at all. Still, it was done now, and she'd have to face their wrath. Oh, if *only* Henry were here! He'd always been such a tower of strength, and at this moment she felt the very opposite.

Chapter 24

Justin's carriage bowled swiftly through the darkness on its way to Taunton. It was a perfect night for traveling, with a good moon and no wind. He was glad he'd decided to set off now instead of waiting until the morning. When he'd obtained the special license, he intended to purchase a wedding ring and have it inscribed with words he'd seen somewhere, but couldn't remember where. *If in love thou constant be, My heart shall never part from thee.* He looked out at the moonlit moor. He wanted Rowena to be constant, but what of his own constancy?

The hump-backed bridge was a short distance ahead, but suddenly the coachman began to apply the brakes. Justin heard his shout.

"My lord? There's something at the roadside ahead!"

Justin's thoughts scattered. Highwaymen? He lowered the window, preparing to reach for the loaded pistol he always kept beneath the seat. He could hear the roar of the rapids as he scanned the road ahead, and then saw what looked like a man lying on the verge.

The wary coachman brought the team to a standstill some distance short of the bridge. Robbers resorted to all kinds of tricks to fool the careless, and pretending to be in need of help was just one. "What shall I do, my lord?" he asked.

Justin suddenly noticed the overturned cabriolet in the stream. Kemp! Flinging open the door, he hurried toward the still figure. Andrew lay facedown and groaned as Justin turned him over. He'd regained consciousness sufficiently to stagger from the stream toward the road, but the effort had proved too much. Apart from some blood on his temple and what appeared to be a twisted ankle, he seemed uninjured, but he was soaked through, and Justin knew he wouldn't survive the cold of the November night unless helped. After the incident on the stairs at the Red Lion, the responsibility of being Kemp's good Samaritan wasn't particularly appealing, but passing by on the other side wasn't in his nature.

Straightening, he called to the coachman. "He must have attempted the bridge too fast. We'll have to take him back to Melcombe."

"There's no doctor in Melcombe, my lord, I heard them say at the inn. When one's needed, they send to Dunster." The coachman nodded ahead, where the moor began to fall away toward the coast.

"Dunster it is then. Help me lift him."

"My lord." Making the reins fast, the coachman climbed down, and soon they'd managed to carry Andrew to the carriage. A minute or so later they drove on.

They aroused the doctor in Dunster and left a still unconscious Andrew in his care before continuing their journey to Taunton.

Once he was in the warmth and comfort of a bed, Andrew wasn't long in regaining consciousness. The moment he opened his eyes he sat up with an anguished cry as he remembered the terrifying events that had occurred. For a second or so he could again feel the demonic grasp of those ghostly hands and hear the tempestuous roar of the wind as it gusted ferociously around him. Perspiration leapt to his forehead, and his already pale face lost even more of its color.

The doctor became alarmed and hastily administered laudanum, which soon took the edge from Andrew's terror. Lying back in the bed, he thought about what had happened to drive him out of Rowena's bedroom, and then out of Melcombe itself. Her father's ghost? It wasn't possible. Superstitious country knuckleheads might be taken in by such things, but not Andrew Kemp! All the same, he didn't relish the thought of returning to Melcombe. It was a hostile place and might be even more hostile after what he'd tried to do to Rowena. Not that he seriously imagined she'd risk saying anything; she had too much to lose to do that. He smiled a little. He'd succeed with her yet. Whatever it was that had saved her in that room, it wasn't going to do the same in London!

He rose the next morning and informed the doctor he was well enough to travel.

"I don't think you appreciate how desperate your condition was last night when Lord Alderney brought you here," the doctor replied.

Andrew stared at him. "Alderney?"

"Yes, sir. His lordship found you at the roadside. If he hadn't come that way, I have little doubt that you'd no longer be alive."

Andrew continued to stare at him. *Alderney* had rescued him? Oh, the sweet irony of it! Throwing his head back, he began to laugh.

The doctor looked uncertainly at him. "Sir, I really do think a rest would be advisable," he said.

"You can keep your advice," Andrew replied, drawing on his gloves. "That it was Alderney who came to my aid has done more to hasten my recovery than you can possibly imagine. Where can I obtain a post-chaise?"

The doctor gave up. "You won't find one in Dunster, sir. The nearest posting-house is in Bridgwater, but you can hire a gig here."

"Then a gig it will have to be. How much do I owe you?"

"There is no charge, sir. Lord Alderney attended to it."

The unpleasant amusement still played upon Andrew's lips. "Did he, be damned? How very noble of the noble lord." He went to the front door, and the chill morning air swept in as he paused on the threshold. "Where may I find this gig?" he asked.

"Ask anyone at the yarn market, sir."

One day later, when Justin had returned to Melcombe to be reunited with Rowena, his letter was delivered at Lady Beaminster's residence in The Circus, Bath. Her ladyship was away from home, having been sent for urgently by her sick sister in Cheltenham, and George and Emily therefore had the house to themselves. The letter reposed upon the breakfast table as they came downstairs after a particularly late night. Emily was merely a little tired, for she never overindulged, but George was feeling positively fragile.

His wife selected her breakfast and then sat down, shaking open her starched napkin and surveying him a little crossly. She was a pretty brunette in her late twenties, with gray eyes and a figure not too unlike Rowena's. Her hair was in an elegant French knot, and she wore a damson gown with a muslin ruff at the throat. After pouring the coffee, she put the silver pot down with unnecessary force.

George winced as he chose some kedgeree. "Em, I know I was a littler, er, remiss, last night, but can't you relent a little this morning? I'm not feeling at all the thing, you know."

"If you're not feeling the thing, you have only yourself to blame. Was it really necessary to make that wager with Freddie Congreve? You don't like maraschino at the best of times, so why on earth you swore to drink more of it than he could I really don't know!"

"Nor do I this morning," he muttered, sitting down and reaching across to take her cup of coffee.

Her gray eyes flashed vexedly as she was obliged to pour herself another. "George Rathbone, there are times when I wish I'd set my scheming cap at Justin instead of you!"

He smiled engagingly. "You don't mean that."

"No? I doubt very much if *he* would ever be as beastly drunk as you were last night!" she retorted.

"He's had his moments."

"On account of La Westcote, no doubt," Emily observed tersely.

George shrugged and prodded the kedgeree with his fork. "Chloe isn't the easiest of women," he admitted.

"Oh? And how would you know?" she demanded.

"Justin told me. Oh, come on, Em, you *know* I've never strayed from you!"

She eyed him. "See you never do," she murmured.

"I wouldn't dare, for I vow you have the most savage temper in all England."

"I do indeed, and I'd have a certain part of your male person removed and nailed to the wall if you were ever unfaithful."

"I believe you would, too," he muttered.

"There is no question about it." Emily sat back in her chair. "Besides, having the misfortune to know Chloe as well as I do, I don't think you'd appeal to her."

"Thank you very much!" George was offended.

She smiled. "It wasn't a criticism of you, my darling, more an insight on her. I've known the creature since childhood and can state quite categorically that you just aren't her type."

"What was she like all those years ago?" he asked curiously.

Now it was her turn to be offended. "It wasn't *that* long ago!"

"You haven't answered my question. What was she like?"

"A bud of the *belle de nuit* she later blossomed into. She was a flirt at ten and by fourteen had developed a taste for naval officers. I believe it was the uniform that drew her. I vow that if Westcote had realized what she was really like, he'd never have married her."

"He was besotted then."

"He certainly isn't now."

"No. They've been going their separate ways for some time." Emily sipped her coffee. "I wonder if Justin really loves her?"

George shrugged. "He's never confided in me." He glanced suddenly at the little silver plate of mail waiting on the table. "Well, well, talk of the devil," he said, reaching over to take Justin's letter.

Emily recognized the writing as he broke the seal and began to read. She lowered her cup as he gave a slightly incredulous laugh and then read again.

"What is it?" she asked.

"Well, I'll be blowed—he's taken our advice and is getting married!"

Emily stared at him.

He went on. "To a Miss Rowena Melcombe of Melcombe in the county of Somerset."

"I've never heard of her."

"Nor have I, although it seems the bride-to-be's mother is an old friend of Aunt Beaminster's. Read for yourself."

She took the letter and scanned the brief lines before shaking her head with disbelief. "If I were to hear this as tittle-tattle, I wouldn't give it credence, and yet here it is in black and white! It must be a love match!"

"Trust you to view it in that light," George observed dryly.

"George Rathbone, I believe you would manage to pour cold water on a pail of ice! I'm sure it's a love match, and nothing you say will convince me otherwise."

"You don't think he's acting a little, er, precipitately?"

"It's in the family," she reminded him. "Don't you remember what he said about his parents? They were betrothed within a week of meeting."

"True."

"You will oblige him and be his groomsman, I trust?"

"Of course. And are you willing to be mother hen to his bride?"

Emily smiled. "Nothing would delight me more. I like Justin very much indeed, and I'm sure I'll like his Miss Melcombe. And if she's the daughter of an old friend, I'm convinced your Aunt Beaminster, will approve as well."

"I've never heard Aunt Beaminster mention any Mrs. Melcombe."

"You wouldn't, not if they lost touch years ago. Oh, what a pity she's gone to Cheltenham." Emily's eyes began to shine wickedly. "When this gets out, it'll be the talk of society. The future Marchioness of Exford is a nobody from the back of nowhere! Well, Justin's father wanted him to marry, and it seems his wish is to be granted more swiftly than expected."

"Em, you don't think the extraordinary haste indicates the bride to be in an, er, interesting condition?" He raised an expressive eyebrow.

"George!"

"Well, you have to admit it's a possibility. Justin isn't a saint."

"Nor is he a magician. He only left us a few days ago and hadn't even met this Miss Melcombe then. I cannot deny that he may have seduced her, but there certainly hasn't been time for her to discover she is in an interesting condition, as you so delicately put it."

"Then maybe they were caught in flagrante delicto, and a pistol is being held to his head."

"George, why must you always be so cynical? Justin's letter doesn't suggest he's being coerced into anything; in fact, I'd say it's the very opposite. I still think it's a love match."

"I'll reserve judgment."

"Maybe I should remind you the groomsman is supposed to perform his duties with a glad heart, not with eyebrows raised."

"I'll be the perfect groomsman."

"I trust so."

George pushed the kedgeree thoughtfully around the plate. "One wonders what La Westcote will have to say when she hears," he observed quietly.

"She'll be furious," Emily replied with masterly understatement.

"One might as well poke a wasps' nest with a stick," George said and then looked at his wife. "You're going to have your work cut out. Mother hens are supposed to look after their chicks and protect them from the fox. Chloe Westcote will be a vixen to end all vixens when she hears about this marriage, and the new Lady Alderney will be very much her prey."

"I'm a match for dear Chloe," Emily answered tartly.

"You'll need to be."

Emily was philosophical. "Well, maybe Chloe already has enough on her hands without taking on more."

"What do you mean?"

"Jack Jermyn."

George laughed dismissively. "Oh, that! Jermyn's been pursuing her for months now, and I hardly think Justin's marriage is going to enhance his chances."

"Jack Jermyn is a very devious, disagreeable, and unscrupulous toad, and when his sights are set upon something, he's very single-minded indeed."

"Possibly, but maybe we're hazarding the wrong guess. How do we know the advent of a Lady Alderney is going to make any difference to Justin's dealings with Chloe?"

Emily stared at him. "You think he might continue the liaison?"

"He wouldn't be the first new bridegroom to enjoy the best of both worlds, and no matter what her faults, Chloe Westcote is a very beautiful, fascinating, and clever woman who knows full well how to hold a man's interest. Justin has found her irresistible until now and may continue to do so. In fact, the more I think about it, the more convinced I become that that's his intention. He's going to marry Rowena and still bed Chloe."

Chapter 25

Emily was appalled. "Is that what you really think?"

"Em, I know you regard Justin as the most of an angel there ever was, but that's because he can charm the birds out of the trees when he wishes. As I've already said—he isn't a saint. Be honest and admit he has faults."

Emily didn't reply.

George drew a long breath. "Mind you, I hope I'm wrong about his intentions regarding Chloe."

"So do I."

"Whatever happens, La Westcote won't go away meekly, you can count upon that."

Emily shrugged. "Enough of her, let's make plans for going to Melcombe." She smiled at him. "A wedding! Oh, this has cheered me up!"

"I wish I could say the same, but I feel decidedly queasy."

"Serves you right," Emily replied heartlessly, her thoughts still on Justin's news. "We must write back immediately."

George pushed his breakfast place away, beginning to find the smell of the kedgeree quite nauseous.

Emily didn't notice. "We must also inform your aunt. I'm sure she'll want to attend the wedding with us when she knows the bride is—"

She didn't finish the sentence, for George suddenly rose urgently from his seat and tossed his napkin on to the table. "My aunt can fly to the moon if she wishes, but my stomach bids me fly elsewhere!" he muttered, turning to rush from the room.

Emily sighed and picked up Justin's letter again. Society would be agog to see the new Lady Alderney, and everything about her would be minutely examined and criticized. Poor Rowena Melcombe was going to find the coming months very difficult indeed, but if she was of the right mettle, she'd emerge triumphant, and then the beau monde would adore her.

At the end of his long journey from Exmoor, Andrew's hired chaise joined a crush of elegant carriages in Berkeley Square. It was some time before it at last halted outside Westcote House, where music, laughter, and the brightly illuminated windows told him a ball was in progress.

Aware he was hardly dressed for such an occasion, and feeling too impatient to go to his lodgings to change, he alighted and made his way through the grounds to the kitchen door, where he was recognized by a footman who'd admitted him secretly that way in the past.

The kitchens were busy, and as the other servants scurried to and fro with sumptuous supper dishes for the ball, the footman glanced curiously at his rather travel-weary appearance. "Sir?"

"Would you inform Lady Westcote that I wish to speak privately with her?"

"But there's a ball, sir."

"I'm aware of that. Just inform her I'm here. She probably knows what it's about." His letter must have arrived by now.

"Sir." The footman hurried away, and it was several minutes before he returned to say Chloe would meet him in the summerhouse on the grounds.

Without a word Andrew stepped back out into the cold night. His breath stood out in clouds as he followed the path to the little pavilion at the end of the lawns. In warm months the Westcote House balls spilled out into the grounds, with lanterns in all the trees and little bowers for the guests to sit, but in the cold of winter there was no one out here, and a meeting in the summerhouse was very private indeed.

He hadn't been there long when he heard the rustle of taffeta as Chloe approached. She'd tossed a warm cloak around her shoulders, but hadn't raised the hood, so the diamonds in her dark hair sparkled in the moonlight. Beneath the cloak her gown was midnight blue, and she brought the scent of roses with her. She was by far the most beautiful woman in London, probably in the whole of England, and she certainly put Rowena in the shade. As for her talents between the sheets, they were as matchless as her beauty.

She paused in the entrance to face him. "If this isn't important, Andrew, I swear I'll never speak to you again. I've had a most disagreeable evening so far, and I'm not in any mood to—"

"I can see the mood you're in," he replied. "What is it? Has Westcote decided you must be the dutiful wife tonight?"

She drew a long breath and pulled her cloak more closely around her. "Westcote has other things on his mind at the moment. Would you believe he's in love?"

Andrew laughed incredulously, for Chloe's husband was a profligate who'd never been truly in love in his life, except perhaps when he'd first married her. The affection had been short-lived.

"It's no jest. He's smitten with Lady Jane Pankhurst."

Andrew's incredulity increased. Lady Jane was a plain, shy, rather dumpy spinster whose name had never been linked with any man's, let alone a married womanizer like the Earl of West-cote.

Chloe sighed. "It's so tedious and embarrassing, for he makes sheep's eyes at her all the time. To be sure, she is the dullest creature in London, and it is all I can do not to laugh out loud when I watch them. They're welcome to each other, for if he's interested in her, he won't bother me."

"If Westcote isn't the reason for your mood, what is?"

"I've had Jack Jermyn strutting after me all evening; he hasn't let me out of his sight, and if he did but know it, I find his dandified manners and appearance quite abhorrent!" She shuddered and then looked at Andrew. "Why do you need to speak to me so urgently?"

He was a little taken aback. "Don't you know?"

"Know what?"

"I wrote to you. Well, no matter, for I can tell you in person now. It concerns your beloved Alderney."

"Justin?" She came closer, her skirts whispering through the autumn leaves on the floor. "What of him?"

"He's found himself a bride."

She gasped and recoiled slightly. "I don't believe you."

"It's the truth. He met her on Halloween and proposed to her the next day."

Her hand crept to her throat. "How do you know?" she whispered.

"Because the bride happens to be Rowena Melcombe."

She was startled. "Melcombe? The rustic you went back to seduce?"

He gave a low laugh. "Yes, but I failed most signally, although not for want of trying."

"And you're saying Justin succeeded where you failed?"

"Yes."

"But you told me she was drab and unsophisticated!"

"So she is."

Chloe drew a long breath, then raised her chin challengingly. "I still don't believe you."

"Why would I lie? I returned to Melcombe to have her if I could, but it seems your precious Justin got there first."

"He told me he was leaving Bath to go on to Cornwall!"

"I understand that was indeed his original intention, but he went by way of Exmoor, resulting in the acquisition of a Lady Alderney on December the first."

"Are you suggesting it's a love match?" she demanded.

"After watching them together, I think it may be."

"Justin loves me, I know he does," she breathed shakily.

"I don't pretend to know whether or not he loves you, but the kisses he gives her couldn't, by any stretch of the imagination, be called chaste pecks on the cheek."

"Don't!" She turned sharply away, pressing her trembling hands to her cheeks. She didn't want to hear this, not this . . . Justin was hers!

Andrew watched her. "After the wedding they're going to Exford Park, and after that to his house in St. James's Square. I think you'll be forced to believe me then."

"Justin wouldn't do this without telling me!" she cried.

"Why? *You* do a great deal without telling him," he reminded her.

She tried to compose herself. "I still say Justin wouldn't do this," she repeated more evenly.

"He's doing it, my dear, and although I suppose I'm in his debt for my life, I still despise him as much as you no doubt despise his bride."

She searched his eyes. "In his debt for your life?"

"He rescued me from the wayside." Andrew briefly described what had happened, although without mentioning the fear that had driven him from Melcombe. "By the time I've finished," he went on, "I have a feeling Alderney will wish he'd left me where I was, for I still mean to have Rowena *and* I mean to break the match."

"You still want her?" she asked in surprise.

"More than ever," he breathed, remembering how Rowena's body had arched beneath him, and how firm her breasts had been in his hands. "I almost took her. She was struggling, but I was within moments of having what I wanted, when . . ." His voice trailed away as other memories returned, unpleasant memories that turned the blood in his veins cold.

"When what?" Chloe asked curiously, seeing the odd shadow in his eyes.

"It doesn't matter. Suffice it that I was at the very gates of Heaven when fate denied me my will."

"What do you mean to do now? I take it from your tone that you have some revenge in mind?"

"My first instinct was to urge you to go there and remind him how plain his new love is, but now I've thought again. Think about it, Chloe. Alderney has to marry sooner or later, and it's better for you he takes a nobody like Rowena Melcombe. He may find her fascinating in the remoteness of Exmoor, but it will be different here in London. She has no sophistication and could easily become an embarrassment to him, especially if she is helped toward it."

Chloe's eyes began to shine a little. "Go on," she breathed.

"Her fidelity might also be called into question if it were to appear that she was having certain, er, dealings, with me. All I have to do is behave as if she and I are more to each other than mere acquaintances and see to it that others observe my conduct. And all you have to do is provide Alderney with the sympathetic shoulder he requires when his bride's apparent inconstancy starts coming to light."

"You make it sound too easy."

"The best plans are always simple. Trust me."

She laughed. "Trust you? My dear Andrew, I would as soon trust a viper."

"But in this instance we are natural allies," he pointed out. "It's in both our interests to work together. You want to retain Alderney, and I wish to enjoy Rowena and destroy her match. It will be easier to accomplish here in London." He smiled then. "There is another reason why it might prove easy to convince Alderney his bride is seeing me."

"I'm all agog," she murmured.

"I made it my business to find out all I could about the Melcombes. Their financial situation has deteriorated considerably since I was last there, and now their bank is whispered to be foreclosing. Rowena has never made a secret of the fact that she loves her home and the village, so Alderney could soon be led to wonder if saving her family was her sole reason for marrying him. Maybe he could be persuaded that she has always loved me, but that my lack of fortune made me unsuitable as a husband . . ."

A cool smile played upon Chloe's lips. "I begin to warm to your plan, sir."

"Is it a pact, then?"

She nodded. "Yes."

"All we have to do is wait for them to arrive in St. James's Square and then commence our stratagem."

Chloe exhaled with feline anticipation. "Your little Rowena is going to wish she'd never set eyes upon Justin. He was mine before she came, and he'll be mine long after she's gone." She glanced toward the house. "I must return, or my absence may be remarked. No doubt Jack Jermyn is scouring every room for me."

"I'm still staying at Green's Lodging House in Conduit Street. You will always be able to reach me there."

"Very well." Gathering her skirts, she hurried away along the path, and after a moment Andrew followed, making his way back around the house to his waiting chaise.

As they both left the garden, a stealthy figure emerged from the evergreen shrubs behind the summerhouse. Slender, prinked, and very much the dandy, Jack Jermyn flicked his lace-edged handkerchief to brush some leaves from his immaculate sleeve. How very fortunate it was he'd espied dear Chloe slipping so secretively into the garden, and how even more fortunate he'd chosen to eavesdrop upon her meeting with Kemp. What a devious and scurrilous plan they had in mind; indeed one felt quite sorry for Alderney and his remarkable bride.

Jack smiled a little and began to retrace his steps toward the house. He was leaving for the country the day after tomorrow and wouldn't be returning until the new year, which meant he'd keep his knowledge to himself for the time being. But he'd use it when it suited him. Oh, yes, he'd certainly use it—sooner or later.

Chapter 26

The wedding day dawned cold but clear, and the village awoke with the firm intention of celebrating to the full. Another bonfire stood on the green, and there was to be dancing and merrymaking.

The Melcombe ghosts were overjoyed with the way things had turned out, for not only was the manor saved, but the family was restored to its former position. Justin had already honored part of his word to Mrs. Melcombe by attending to many of the immediately outstanding debts, and also by arranging for the three boys to go to Eton in the new year. The mortgage would be settled as soon as he and Rowena arrived in London, and thus Mrs. Melcombe would finally be relieved of the heavy burden she'd been carrying for so long.

Rowena's mother was a changed woman. No longer pale and careworn, she'd acquired roses in her cheeks and a sparkle in her eyes. She was also delighted to have found her old friend, Lady Beaminster, again. Unfortunately, George's aunt couldn't leave her sick sister in Cheltenham in order to attend the wedding, but as soon as she was back in Bath, Mrs. Melcombe was to visit her there.

The wedding ceremony itself was to take place early in the day so the newlyweds could leave in good time for the Taunton inn where they intended to spend their first night together before driving on to Exford Park. The prospect of meeting Justin's family filled Rowena with trepidation; she'd have felt a good deal worse if he hadn't been so certain they'd approve of her.

As the hour drew nearer, Justin and George were ready in such good time they were obliged to kick their heels in the gardens. They were both elegant in dark blue velvet coats and white silk breeches, and, following the age-old custom, white satin ribbon favors were pinned to their sleeves.

George glanced toward snow-topped Melkery Beacon, which seemed to drift mysteriously against the blue of the sky. "There's something about this place," he murmured, half to himself.

Justin smiled. "You've noticed."

"One can't help but notice," George replied, halting to look at him. "Em's convinced there's witchery here."

"Is she indeed? Are you equally as convinced?"

George grinned. "You know I haven't any time for such nonsense."

"But . . . ?" Justin prompted quietly.

"But when I'm here I find myself thinking about sorcery and the supernatural."

"I can't believe it of down-to-earth George Rathbone," Justin murmured.

George studied him. "By the same token, what is one to make of your marriage?" he asked quietly. "I mean no offense, my friend, but it has to be said you could have made a much more beneficial match than this. Sweet and delightful as Rowena is, I can't help but wonder how she will go on in society. London is full of *chiennes*, and most of them will be hoping to see her flounder."

"Especially Chloe?"

"Now you've brought her name into it, yes, especially Chloe." Justin looked away.

"What do you intend to do about her, Justin?" George asked.

"Do?"

"Oh, come on, don't pretend you don't know what I'm talking

about. She's your mistress, damn it, at least she was, and I'm asking if she's going to continue in that position."

"Is it any of your business?"

"No, I suppose not."

"Quite."

"From which response I deduce you'll still meet her at the
house in York Street," George said flatly.

Justin didn't reply, for in truth he hadn't yet brought himself to
face the sensitive problem of Chloe. He'd been deliberately
putting her from his thoughts, but knew that sooner or later he had
to confront the situation. For the moment, however, he didn't
wish to discuss it, not even with his best friend.

The silence made George uncomfortable. "I, er, think we'd better leave the subject, don't you? It won't do for us to quarrel
today of all days."

Justin smiled then. "We haven't quarreled."

"No?"

"No."

George was relieved. "I didn't really mean to pry."

"Oh, yes you did, and I'll warrant Emily put you up to it. She's
formed a great attachment for Rowena and has always loathed the
very sight of Chloe."

George colored a little. "I don't deny it."

"Then you may tell her I'll never make Rowena unhappy."

As they walked on, George was still thinking about Chloe. "By
the way, Justin, did you know there were whispers about Westcote?"

"Whispers?"

"That he's actually fallen in love?"

Justin halted. "Really?"

"The lady concerned is none other than that paragon of prim-
ness, Lady Jane Pankhurst."

Justin stared at him. "There must be some mistake."

"That's what I said, but Em made it her business to get to the
root of it and assures me it's definitely Lady Jane. I gather the
feeling is mutual, which may mean . . ." He allowed the unfinished sentence to fade away into a very pointed silence.

"Divorce? Is that what you're hinting?"

"Stranger things have happened, and if this particular thing *did*
happen, then Westcote will be looking for names to cite."

Justin met his eyes for a moment, then calmly took out his fob
watch. "It's almost time. Shall we go in?"

George nodded, but then caught his arm. "Allow me to say one thing more, and then I'll hold my tongue. Rowena Melcombe isn't part of the beau monde, not yet anyway, and hasn't been brought up to accept that her husband might choose to keep a mistress. Your bride may be unused to London ways, but that doesn't make her a fool, nor does it mean she lacks pride, and I believe she'll salvage that pride by leaving if you cling to Chloe."

Justin met his earnest gaze. "You've made yourself very clear indeed, George," he said quietly.

"Then pay heed."

"It's time to go in," Justin said again and began to walk back toward the house.

George sighed and followed.

In her room Rowena was almost ready. She wore a lavish white silk gown, and her rose bouquet was sprinkled with loveknots. Her hair was swept up on her head, and she wore a satin fillet adorned with orange blossom and rosebuds.

It was warm in the room, but she shivered as she looked at herself in the cheval glass. "Will I do?" she asked after a moment, turning to look at her mother and Emily.

Emily nodded. "You're beautiful, Rowena."

"Beautiful? Me? Now I know you exaggerate, for you are the one who's beautiful," Rowena replied, looking at Emily's amethyst tunic dress and flowing ivory undergown.

But Emily shook her head. "You're so glowing with happiness, no woman could hold a candle to you today," she said.

Rowena's mother nodded as well. "Emily's right, my dear. You're as lovely as any bride has ever been." She glanced at the mantelpiece clock. "Dear me, is it that time already? I'll have to see that the boys are looking as they should." Gathering her jade taffeta skirts, she hurried from the room.

Rowena turned to face Emily. "Do you think Justin will regret marrying me?" she asked suddenly.

"Regret it? Why should he?"

"Because I'm not a great catch, and for various other reasons which must by now be apparent to you."

Emily picked up the bridal posy and gave it to her. "Justin wants you as his bride, Rowena, and that's all that matters."

"Will you answer something truthfully, Emily?"

"If I can."

"Who was the last woman in his life?"

Emily's heart sank. "There hasn't been anyone of consequence recently," she replied, hoping she looked as sincere as she sounded.

"Do you mean that?"

"Why should I not?"

Rowena drew a long breath. "Oh, it's just that sometimes I feel . . ."

"Yes?"

"That he's thinking about someone."

Plague take Chloe Westcote, Emily thought, but she still managed to smile. "You must be imagining it."

Rowena smiled as well. "I feel better for hearing you say that."

Emily felt dreadful. The last thing she wished to do was be untruthful, but how could she possibly tell a bride on her wedding day that her husband had a mistress who was one of the most beautiful and fascinating women in London?

A tap sounded at the door. It was Lionel, who was to give his sister away. "It's time," he said.

Emily kissed Rowena's cheek. "I'll go down then," she said softly, then hurried out.

Lionel looked at his sister. "You look wonderful," he said.

"Thank you."

He offered her his arm, and they walked from the room.

Down in the hall the small gathering had assembled around a table which was to serve as an altar. The air was filled with the scent of rosemary, for the herb had been scattered on the floor and made into garlands. Rosemary for remembrance. The Reverend Grantham stood waiting with his prayerbook by the table, where two silver-gilt candlesticks had been lit, and the parish clerk was at another table with his register open in readiness. Justin and George waited in front of the clergyman, and Mrs. Melcombe and the twins stood nearby. The servants were at the other end of the hall.

But there were invisible guests present, spectral guests who waited as eagerly as everyone else for the first glimpse of the bride. Every Melcombe ghost gazed down eagerly from its frame, but none with more emotion than William and Lady Margaret.

As Emily hurried to join the gathering, she quickly drew George to one side. "Did you manage to ask about Chloe?" she whispered.

"Yes."

"What did he say?"

"He was equivocal," George confessed.

She was dismayed. "Then he means to keep Chloe?"

"That's my guess, but I've said all I can." George glanced toward the staircase. "The bride's coming; I'll have to stand with him now." He hurried back to his place, and Emily went to join Mrs. Melcombe and the twins.

Everyone turned as Lionel escorted Rowena down the staircase. William's ghostly heart swelled with paternal pride as he watched his daughter, and Lady Margaret yielded to a tear or two of immense satisfaction.

The ceremony began, and both George and Emily felt decidedly awkward at one particular point, when the clergyman addressed Justin. ". . . and, forsaking all other, keep thee only unto her, so long as ye both shall live?"

Justin replied without hesitation. "I will."

The Rathbones exchanged glances as the service moved on, and Lady Margaret saw. She guessed they were thinking about the bridegroom's mistress, and she shared their disquiet. Until now it hadn't seemed to matter that Justin had a mistress, but now it mattered very much. Poor Rowena was so completely in love and so heartbreakingly trusting that she was going to suffer greatly when she found out. But she was on her own now, without a guardian spirit to watch over her.

The ceremony seemed to end quite suddenly. The ring was placed on the bride's finger, and then the entry was made and witnessed in the register. Some of the maids dabbed their eyes, Mrs. Melcombe wept unashamedly, and the Reverend Grantham clasped his prayer book to his ample chest and beamed at them all.

Justin drew his new wife tenderly toward him and brushed her lips with his. "It is done now, Lady Alderney," he whispered.

Rice was tossed over them as they emerged later from the house to the two waiting carriages. The second was for Rowena's maid and the luggage, most of which comprised Emily's exceedingly fashionable clothes. George's wife had been aghast that the new Lady Alderney should arrive at Exford Park clad in anything less than the very latest modes, and since she and Rowena were much the same in height and build, she'd insisted upon lending her wardrobe.

The villagers cheered as the carriages pulled away, and the twins reverted briefly to type by tossing shoes after the vehicles. It was a custom that would have been acceptable enough if the shoes had been old and past use, but they weren't! The bonfire crackled and smoked on the green, and the fiddler played the happy couple on their way.

Rowena gazed back as the village faded away beyond a curve in the road. She was leaving her old life behind, and an exciting new one stretched ahead. Rowena Melcombe was no more, but had become Lady Alderney. She turned to smile at Justin, and her lips parted as he kissed her. A delicious thrill of anticipation quivered through her. Tonight she would leave more than Melcombe behind; she would leave her chastity behind as well.

Chapter 27

The Royal George at Taunton was a fine old hostelry in the center of the town. Darkness had long since fallen, and the courtyard lanterns had been lit as the carriages arrived.

It was a busy inn, used by both stagecoaches and mails, and the ticket office bell rang loudly as Justin alighted and turned to hand Rowena down. The smell of roast beef drifted on the cold air, as well as singing from the taproom.

Justin's eyes were dark as he drew his new wife's fingertips to his lips, biting them softly before releasing her. Excitement stirred through her. It wouldn't be long now. Soon they would make love for the first time . . . A warm blush crept into her cheeks, and she tried to distract herself by smoothing the primrose pelisse and gown she'd selected from Emily's wardrobe.

The landlord had hurried out on seeing the carriages. He bowed and wiped his hands on his starched apron. "Welcome to the Royal George."

Justin inclined his head. "We require a room for the night."

"Sir."

"Your best room, I trust?"

"Certainly. If you'll come this way?" Snapping his fingers for some men to assist with the luggage, the landlord led them into the inn. There he paused.

"I'll give instructions that the room is to be made ready immediately, sir. Perhaps in the meantime you'd care to dine?"

Justin looked inquiringly at Rowena, and she nodded.

The landlord's expert eye led him to conclude they were on

honeymoon, although they probably wouldn't care for the latter word. Honeymoon was far too vulgar for the quality, who merely "went away" or took a bridal tour. He cleared his throat. "I can fully recommend the roast beef, sir."

"The beef it is, then. Would it be too much to hope you can serve a bottle of champagne?"

The man drew himself up still more. "Of course I have champagne, sir."

"Excellent. Oh, and by the way, see that her ladyship's maid and my coachman are properly attended to. I will not have them consigned to the stables or an outhouse. They are to have proper accommodation."

Her ladyship? The man drew himself up a little more as he realized he was speaking to nobility. "Certainly, my lord." He beckoned to some maids to come and relieve his important new guests of their outdoor garments. "The principal chamber," he instructed them. "And see *everything* is as it should be."

"Sir." They hurried up the staircase.

The innkeeper smiled at Justin and Rowena. "If you will come into the dining room . . . ?" Gesturing toward an open doorway, he conducted them inside.

The roast beef proved as excellent as he'd claimed, but Rowena couldn't eat much; indeed the excitement of the day had given her a very poor appetite indeed. Perhaps that was why the champagne affected her so that when they at last adjourned to their room, she was quite light-headed. It was a deliciously warm feeling that drove away all inhibition. Tonight she would become a woman, and she wouldn't merely lie there submissively. On Halloween she'd been made aware of her sensuality, and it was an awareness that had opened her eyes to her real self. When Justin made love to her, he'd find her eager to learn. She wanted to give as much pleasure as she received, and she wanted to hold his interest after the first heady delights. She would be wife and courtesan, lady and Cyprian.

The candlelit room was spacious and warmed by a fire flanked with armchairs. There were tasseled green velvet curtains at the windows, and an old four-poster bed hung with the same material. Her nightgown was laid out neatly on the coverlet, and the familiar scent of rosemary hung in the air because her maid had tied a spray of the herb to the bedhead.

She turned to him, her lilac eyes reflecting the candlelight. "I love you, my lord," she whispered.

He drew her close and kissed her ardently on the mouth. She thought he tasted of the sea she saw in his eyes. The champagne still ran in her veins, and she pulled coquettishly away. "Is this how you seduce your ladyloves?" she asked with a smile.

The question amused him. "By marrying them? I think that would be a little extreme, don't you?"

"How do you set about seduction, my lord?"

He met her eyes. "That is an improper question, Lady Alderney."

"I'm feeling improper."

"And to confess to feeling improper is even more improper," he said with a quick laugh.

"Blame the champagne," she replied, glancing at him from beneath lowered lashes.

The glance was that of both innocent and temptress and reminded him of the paradox that was his new bride. She was a virgin, but he'd already sampled the passion in her lips and felt her sensuous response to his caresses. She wasn't a trembling maiden who dreaded losing her precious chastity; she was a warm and spirited woman who wanted to meet him halfway. The innocent in her appealed to his sensitivity, the temptress to his virility, and the two combined served to ignite the passion he'd been holding in check since first knowing her.

"Seduce me, Justin," she breathed.

He smiled and led her to one of the armchairs, where he knelt in front of her. Her breath caught as he took off her shoes and then her gartered stockings. "A pretty ankle is much admired," he said softly, "and you, my darling, have very pretty ankles indeed." He took one of her feet and drew it to his lips, kissing each toe in turn.

A trembling sigh escaped her as his fingers caressed her calf and then moved gently toward her thigh. Her heart was thundering, and her breasts had tightened, the nipples standing proud against her gown.

His eyes dark with desire, he knelt up to kiss her lips, which parted eagerly to admit his tongue. He cupped her breasts and felt the excitement of her nipples. She was ready for love. Her skin was warm and flushed, and there was rich desire in the sensuous clinging of her lips.

He rose to his feet, drawing her up too and then embracing her again. He was hot with arousal now, his loins pulsing with a compelling need to be one with her, and he closed his eyes with pleasure as she touched him there, her hand at first tentative, but then enclosing him through the silk of his breeches.

He loosed her hair so that it tumbled warmly over his hand as he bent to put his mouth to the pulse fluttering at her throat. She trembled against him as he unfastened her gown so it slipped to the floor. It was followed by her chemise, and at last she was naked in his arms. As naked as she'd been on Halloween . . . and as willing.

He lifted her onto the bed and then took off his own clothes. She stretched her arms up entreatingly toward him as she had in the dream. It was the moment when he'd awakened. But he wasn't asleep now; this was real and her body awaited.

Her lips sought his as he lay down with her, and her breaths increased with excitement as he stroked her breasts. Her nipples pressed wantonly into his palms, and she moaned with desire as once again she took him in her hand. "I'm yours, Justin. I love, honor, and obey you," she whispered.

With no silk between them now, nothing kept them apart. Her fingers curled around him, and he knew he could wait no longer. Her body was lithe and needful, resisting only a little before allowing him entry. It was a moment of expiation for him as he slid inside her. He was the first to possess her, the first to know the secrets of her soul. He savored the moment, not moving within her, but just exulting that they were joined.

Then she whispered his name, a sound so soft and loving he could no longer just hold her. He withdrew a little, then pushed gently in again. She cried out with pleasure, meeting his strokes with a natural rhythm that raised them both to ecstasy. Then their lips seared together again so his thrusts became more imperative until suddenly their passion met in a blaze of magnificent white-hot emotion.

For a long moment they lay spent in each other's arms, and tears welled in her eyes as at last she put her lips to the salt skin of his shoulder. Their bodies were damp and fulfilled, and she felt so wonderful she wanted to cry. If this was love, then let her whole existence be devoted to enjoying it with him. Just with him. No other man would ever make her feel like this.

He kissed her tears away, then rested his cheek against her hair. "Did I hurt you?" he asked anxiously.

"No. I . . . I didn't know there was such pleasure to be had . . ."

He smiled down into her eyes. Of all the times he'd made love, this was the most exquisitely satisfying. He'd taken the virgin and been served by the most knowing of demimondaines. "Oh, there's infinitely more pleasure ahead, my lady," he breathed.

"I'm eager to sample it all, my lord."

His eyes darkened with renewing desire. "I'm not sure who has been seduced tonight, Lady Alderney," he said softly.

"I'm of a mind to be jealous of those women who've enjoyed your love before me," she whispered.

"You have no need to be jealous, for I am yours now," he replied, lowering his mouth once more to her parted lips.

Her body moved to meet him, and he felt the brush of her breasts against his skin. He knew it would be dawn before they slept.

For the moment Chloe didn't exist, except in the recesses of his mind.

Chapter 28

A railed ornamental lake shone in the center of St. James's Square, and the pleasure boats kept there were frozen in thick January ice. In the early morning the capital was quiet as yet, but would soon awaken. Smoke curled from chimneys, and the first street cries echoed around the houses as Rowena got out of bed and wrapped herself in a coverlet before going to look out of the window. Justin was still asleep, but she was so nervous about embarking on her new life in society that she'd been awake for some time. Her hair was disheveled, and she shivered beneath the coverlet because she'd dispensed with her nightgown on retiring. The last time she'd worn such a garment had been on the eve of her wedding.

It was her first morning in London, since they'd only arrived from Exford Park the evening before after spending the entire Christmas season with Justin's family. It had been a happy stay, for they'd made her as welcome as he'd promised.

A milkmaid began to call on the broad pavement below. "Milk, fresh and creamy! Milk, fresh and creamy!" Pigeons were alarmed into flight, rising as one into the icy air to flutter past the equestrian statue of King William III in the middle of the lake. The street cry brought the past back to Rowena, reminding her of when her family had owned the house in nearby Pall Mall. She'd never dreamed then that one day she would be mistress of a fine residence in exclusive St. James's Square.

A church bell began to sound the hour, and Justin stirred in the canopied crimson velvet bed behind her. She turned. His dark hair was tousled against the silk pillow, and one of his arms stretched across to where she'd lain a few moments before. His eyes were still closed, the lashes resting against his cheeks, and his lips were just a little curved, as if he dreamed of something pleasing. How clear and flawless his skin was, and how oddly vulnerable he seemed with his arm reaching out like that. She could see the dark hair in his armpit and the faint gray shadow on his chin. How she loved to be with him like this, to see him so intimately, and to know that he would make love to her before they rose.

She went softly back to the bed and discarded the coverlet before slipping in beside him. He was warm and sleepy as she wriggled nearer, and his arms went instinctively around her, pulling her close. She snuggled against him, sliding her hand lovingly over his chest and breathing deeply of his exciting maleness.

His eyes opened and he smiled at her. "Good morning, Lady Alderney," he murmured.

She loved him so much she almost felt pain. "I love you, Justin," she whispered, kissing his mouth, his cheek, his forehead . . . Then she leaned up slightly, pushing her hair back from her face to look down at him with sudden anxiety. "You aren't sorry you married me, are you?"

He caressed one of her breasts. "How can you possibly fear that when I prove my ardor night and day?" he replied softly, pulling her lips down to his.

For a long moment they kissed, but even as her desire flared into swift life, she pulled back again, sitting up and turning her head away slightly.

He reached out to thread a strand of her hair between his fingers. "What is it?" he asked softly.

"I . . . I'm afraid now I'm here in London. I'm especially nervous about Almack's." She bit her lip as she thought of the capital's most exclusive assembly rooms. Almack's was the temple of high fashion, and to be excluded from it was catastrophe, but Justin had vouchers from Lady Jersey, one of the cabal of lady patronesses who ruled the rooms with almost military discipline.

"You have nothing to fear from Almack's or anywhere else," he replied gently, "Just be yourself, and the *monde* will be at your feet. Think of how it was when we arrived at Exford Park. My parents adored you and said you were the finest Christmas gift I could have given."

"They were very kind, but . . ." She bit her lip and looked away. It was true that his parents had liked her, and she them, but doubts lingered at the back of her mind, doubts she'd never voiced until now.

"But what?" he pressed. "Tell me, Rowena."

She looked at him. "But although I looked very stylish in Emily's clothes, I wonder what they would have thought had they seen my real wardrobe? Straitened financial circumstances do not permit clothes in the height of every new fashion."

"Soon you'll have the most modish clothes in town, for I've promised you a wardrobe by the finest couturières," he reminded her.

"I know, but—"

"My parents aren't under any illusions, my love," he interrupted with a smile.

"But they'd have preferred a titled daughter-in-law," she replied, unable to help giving in to the gnawing doubts.

"My mother wasn't titled," he pointed out. "My darling, they're happy I've presented them with a wife, and they'll be even happier when eventually the line's future is assured. Please don't worry about anything else, for your fears are groundless." He reached out to touch her cheek.

She caught his fingers and kissed them, drawing them gently against her teeth.

He smiled. "One thing is certain, Lady Alderney, I am more than enjoying working toward that fruitful end."

She laughed then. "And so I am, sir. There, is that not a shameful admission for a properly brought up young lady to make?" She gave him a warm glance. "I like being between the sheets with you, Lord Alderney, indeed I think I like it too much."

"One cannot like such things too much, madam."

"No?"

"No."

She searched his face. "But my eagerness is surely not entirely decorous?"

"I find it very flattering and very exciting," he replied, taking her firmly by the hand and pulling her down next to him. Then he leaned over her. "Never fear that it isn't ladylike to show your love, Rowena, for to me it is the sweetest and most adorable thing about you. You look at me, and I see in your eyes that you want me. You touch me, and I feel your desire. You turn in your sleep, and you reach out to me. And when you enter a room, I'm more conscious of your closeness than I have ever been of any other woman. My body stirs at the mere thought of you, and if we aren't together, I want you near me again. There isn't a night when I don't want to make endless love to you, nor a morning when I don't awaken needing you again. You are essential to me, as essential as the air I breathe."

"That's how I feel about you," she whispered.

He smiled. "Then we are one, my love, and you do not need to concern yourself with what anyone else may or may not think." As he spoke, he had to glance briefly away, for Chloe came unbidden into his thoughts. He couldn't postpone the inevitable, but knew he'd have to go to her today.

Rowena saw his fleeting distraction. "What is it?"

"Nothing." He smiled at her again. "Am I to understand that you and Emily are going to an art sale or exhibition this morning?"

"I believe so. I was so tired last night when we arrived I didn't really concentrate on what she was saying, but I think it was something about a sale of paintings at the Hanover Square rooms."

He nodded. "Emily adores purchasing paintings."

"I like her."

"Among London's jewels, she is one of the more precious gems."

"I think she loves you a little." Rowena studied him.

"She and I have always been very fond of each other, but that is all. She loves George."

"What will you do today?"

He pulled away from her and ran his fingers through his hair. Guilt still ran through him because he had to see Chloe, but he had other things to attend to as well. "I, er, have to call upon my lawyer. Marriage has made a considerable difference to my estate, and he needs to be properly informed." He smiled quickly at her. "As promised to your mother, I'll see to it that Melcombe is secure once and for all. Whatever happens, after today the manor and estate will fully belong to your family."

"That means a great deal to me," she admitted, lowering her gaze.

"I know."

Tears sprang to her eyes then. "I . . . I still can't believe all this has happened," she breathed. "In less than six weeks, I've not only met you and become your wife, but I know Melcombe is safe as well."

He leaned over her again. "You once told me that Melcombe meant everything to you."

"It doesn't now, for you mean much more," she replied quietly.

He pulled her on top of him, his arms locked about her waist. "I hope I do, my lady," he murmured, "for I am completely in your spell."

"Completely?" Her eyes were warm as she felt his maleness hardening against her.

"Heart, body, and soul."

"Make love to me, Lord Alderney," she whispered, lowering her mouth yearningly toward his.

He pressed her hips to his, and they both savored the imminence of lovemaking. But just as she moved to permit him entry, there was a discreet tap at the door. "Begging your pardon, my lord?" came his valet's voice.

Justin gave a low curse. "What is it?" he called, knowing the man wouldn't come in.

"Mr. Rathbone has arrived, my lord."

"Very well. Tell him I'll be with him in a few minutes." Justin gave the door a wry look, then smiled at Rowena. "Plague take George Rathbone," he murmured cordially.

"There's always tonight."

"Yes, I suppose so, but tonight is a long time away." He pushed deep into her, needing at least to feel her warmth enclosing him.

She shuddered with delight, drawing upon his tongue and sliding her hands beneath him to hold his taut buttocks. She wanted fulfillment, but not in haste. It was ecstasy just to know his hard virility was inside her, and to know that the love that filled him now would be hers when next they lay together in the bed. Perhaps before then. And not in bed . . .

She continued to hold him close for a long moment, but then broke from the kiss. He withdrew slowly, allowing her the pleasure of every inch, and at last she rolled reluctantly aside, and he got up to put on his dressing gown.

A number of town carriages stood outside the Hanover Square rooms as Emily and Rowena arrived, and it was clear the art sale was attracting a great deal of attention.

Their barouche drew up a little farther along, and the coachman climbed down to open the door for them to alight. It was still bitterly cold outside, and Rowena was glad of her cream fur hat and muff and tight-waisted royal blue pelisse. It was good to feel so à la mode, but it would be even better when the clothes were her own.

She shivered as she stepped down to the pavement, and her breath was visible in a silvery cloud. She glanced around the elegant square, which surrounded a simple central garden of grass and paths. London was well and truly awake now, and the hum of the great city seemed to fill the air. It was a strange noise, a mixture of voices, bells, hooves and wheels upon cobbles, the cooing of pigeons, and the raucous cries of seagulls.

Emily alighted as well, looking particularly pretty in peach velvet and brown beaver hat. She smiled encouragingly at Rowena. "Don't be anxious, for you look splendid and will carry this off excellently."

"I trust you're right."

"Of course I am. Rowena, you may have spent most of your life in Melcombe, but you're still gently bred, and you're most certainly a lady. Not being bang up to the mark with every fleeting London fancy doesn't make you a hopeless rustic. George and I are confident you'll do brilliantly."

"You're very kind, Emily, but I *know* they'll all be wondering when I am expected to be brought to bed. Mother may have insisted upon a month's delay before the wedding, but that isn't very long, and fingers will be counting, won't they?"

"Yes, but eyes will also be glancing at your enviably tiny waist. Rowena, why on earth do you think I suggested you wear that blue pelisse today? It's so close-fitting it would reveal anything untoward, and anyone studying you would have to concede that pregnancy did not figure at all in the speed of your nuptials."

Rowena smiled then. "I don't know what I'd do without you, Emily."

Emily put a gentle hand on her sleeve. "Justin's a good friend, and I'd do this for him even if I didn't like you." She smiled. "But I *do* like you, very much indeed, and I'm glad you're going to be in town from now on, for I've long been in need of a confidante. Acquaintances are all very well, but a really close friend is to be treasured. I trust you, and I will soon be as thick as possible."

"I trust so, too."

Emily looked at her. "You're bound to be the envy of London's fair sex for snaring Justin, you know," she said suddenly. "He's long been the object of much feminine yearning."

"Yes, I can well imagine." Rowena smiled.

"It's clear you and he are doing very well together, shamefully so, in fact." Emily grinned.

Rowena colored a little.

Emily laughed. "Oh, how easy it is to make you blush! That won't do at all, for it's not at all the thing. One must show sangfroid at all times."

They laughed together, and then Emily remembered something. "I've been meaning to ask—do you ride?"

"Of course. What a question to ask of a country girl."

"I suppose it *was* a query about the obvious. Well, since you ride, and I have a spare riding habit, what do you say to a ride in St. James's Park tomorrow? It's quite the thing to be seen in the Mall at about midday."

"I'd like that."

"Then consider it a firm arrangement."

A gentleman they hadn't noticed had been flagrantly eavesdropping next to them, and now he suddenly spoke. "Why, Rowena, what a very happy coincidence!"

She whirled about with a gasp of revulsion and fear, for it was Andrew Kemp.

Chapter 29

A faint smile played upon Kemp's full lips as he surveyed her. "Rowena?" he murmured again, removing his hat and sketching an elegant bow.

For a moment she was frozen with shock. She couldn't believe he had the audacity to speak to her after what he'd tried to do. Disgust and alarm lurched through her, and she felt physically sick as she met his eyes. She'd tried to put him completely from her mind, as if he'd never existed, but here he was, conducting himself as if nothing untoward had ever passed between them.

Emily glanced curiously at her and then looked at him. She didn't know him, nor did she like his manner. There was something decidedly disagreeable about his smile and about the lascivious way he allowed his gaze to move over her friend. Nor did she care for the familiar way he spoke. And who was he to address Lady Alderney by her first name? Not someone Rowena wished to acknowledge, that much was clear.

He smiled again. "How fortunate I should be passing, for it gives the opportunity to offer my congratulations upon your marriage."

She didn't reply.

Her silence didn't ruffle him at all; on the contrary he found it amusing. He was here this morning because he was paying one of the footmen at St. James's Square to keep him informed of her every movement. He knew she and Alderney had arrived the night before, and he was satisfied by now that she'd held her tongue about what had happened to her in Melcombe. If she'd said anything, he'd have received a call from her husband's seconds.

He'd never seriously feared being exposed, for he was certain she'd put her match first. Her silence strengthened his hand. His glance lingered on her breasts. He'd brushed aside all memory of his frightened departure from Melcombe, and here, in the heart of worldly London, it was possible to convince himself he'd imagined it all. His abject terror was a thing of the past, and now he enjoyed toying with her.

"How are you, Rowena? I vow you're looking exceeding well." He reached out, inviting her to remove her hand from her muff for him to kiss, but she didn't move.

"Rowena?" He feigned a look of injured puzzlement, giving every appearance of being the concerned and devoted admirer.

Emily turned to her. "Do you wish me to call someone?"

"Er, no, that won't be necessary," Rowena replied, struggling to collect her wits.

Andrew wasn't prepared to let her go just yet. "Aren't you going to introduce me?" he inquired, glancing at Emily.

But Emily was a match for him. "I have no desire to be introduced to you, sir," she said coldly, "and if you do not desist this moment, I shall not hesitate to call for assistance."

His smile became set, and he replaced his top hat. "There is no need for any unpleasantness, madam, for I was merely greeting an old and dear friend, although it seems that friend is loath to return the compliment. I fear the new Lady Alderney wishes to forget the past." Bowing, he strolled on.

Rowena trembled and kept her eyes downcast as she at last began to master her confusion.

Emily touched her arm anxiously. "Who is he, Rowena?"

"His name is Andrew Kemp, and I once knew him at Melcombe. He paid brief court to me, until he realized that I wasn't the heiress he hoped. Then he left."

"He seems quite despicable."

"He is."

"Rowena, far be it from me to interfere in any way, but he has the air of a troublemaker. You would be best advised to tell Justin about this."

"No!" Rowena's eyes flew to her face.

"But—"

"Emily, I'd rather forget all about it, and I'm sure now Mr. Kemp realizes I mean to cut him, he'll leave me alone."

"He didn't strike me as the sort of man to behave so obligingly," Emily replied shrewdly.

"Please, Emily, can't we leave it as it is?"

Emily was reluctant. "Rowena, Justin should be told. You're his wife and, in my opinion anyway, require his protection."

Rowena's anxiety rose. The last thing she wanted was for Justin to hear about Andrew Kemp. "Please, do this for me, Emily. You see, I haven't told Justin anything about Mr. Kemp."

Emily was dismayed. "You haven't mentioned him at all?"

Rowena summoned a smile. "No. There was nothing to tell." Her gaze was determinedly steady because she knew she had to sound convincing. "Emily, can you honestly say you've never received attentions you'd have preferred not to? Or that you've thought it better not to tell George about some of them for fear he might misunderstand?"

Emily hesitated and then returned the smile a little ruefully. "It doesn't always do to admit everything," she conceded.

Relief rushed through Rowena. "Then you'll humor me in this?"

"If you're quite sure this Kemp person will not bother you again?"

"I'm sure he won't," Rowena replied, but inside her muff her fingers were crossed.

Emily linked her arm. "Then no more will be said of it. Come on, let's go inside before we freeze."

Rowena accompanied her gladly, but as they entered the crowded rooms she was still trembling within. It had been a horrid shock coming face-to-face again with her attacker, and frightening memories moved through her like a tide. She could feel his hands upon her and taste his mouth. It was all that was abhorrent and terrifying, not at all like the soaring pleasure she knew with Justin . . .

The rooms were a great press because the occasion had been very well advertised, and there was no shortage of eager purchasers. The cream of London society strolled from floor to floor, raising quizzing glasses to canvasses and discussing merits. Rowena was aware that some of those quizzing glasses were directed toward her as well, but she affected not to notice.

As they went up to the third floor, they had the second unpleasant encounter of the morning, this time with none other than Chloe,

Countess of Westcote, who Rowena immediately recognized from the miniature Andrew had dropped in her bedroom. She had no idea that Chloe was in fact Justin's mistress, not Andrew's.

Chloe was just descending and halted in front of them. She looked magnificent in ermine-trimmed mauve corduroy with a matching hat, and her dark eyes shone pensively as she glanced briefly at Rowena before addressing Emily.

"Why, Emily, how charming you look today."

"Chloe." Emily was horrified. Why, of all the *chiennes* in London, were they obliged to be confronted by this one? She glanced uneasily at Rowena, almost fearing she'd guess the truth.

But Rowena's thoughts weren't of Justin at all. Following so swiftly upon seeing Andrew himself, she was completely rattled by encountering the woman she thought was his mistress.

Chloe looked pointedly at her, and Emily reluctantly made the expected introduction. "May I present Lady Alderney. Rowena, this is Lady Westcote."

Chloe inclined her head coolly. "Lady Alderney."

"Lady Westcote." Rowena returned the greeting, but awkwardly.

Chloe smiled, taking comfort from her rival's obvious unease. The creature was gauche in the extreme and couldn't possibly hold Justin for long. Why, she was as plain as Andrew said, which made her effect upon the opposite sex all the more extraordinary. What did men like Justin and Andrew see in her? No doubt it was her breasts, which, although too full to be modish, were covetingly firm and upturned. And her waist was commendably small, thus vanquishing the whispers that she might be with child. Added to that she plainly had agreeably long legs . . . Perhaps the creature wasn't entirely without desirable attributes.

This disagreeable realization made Chloe's mouth twitch, and she couldn't resist the temptation to belittle her rival. "Why, Lady Alderney, is it not wonderful that you and dear Emily have such similar likings where clothes are concerned? I could almost swear that your pelisse and hat were hers."

Rowena gave a faint smile, but didn't respond.

Her silence goaded Chloe still more. "Allow me to congratulate you upon your amazing match. I vow London will soon be talking of nothing else. When I heard of your sudden marriage, I said that you had to be someone exceedingly, er, exceptional, and I can see that you are."

The double-edged words cut into Rowena, but she didn't flinch; indeed she found an unexpected edge of her own. "Would that I could return the compliment in kind, Lady Westcote, but I can see you aren't in the least exceptional. Besides, what I know of you is such I'm sure you wouldn't wish it to be talked of over town."

Emily glanced at her in surprise. The country kitten had claws after all!

Chloe's eyes hardened. "I'm sure you'll soon learn a great deal more about me, Lady Alderney," she murmured witheringly.

"Yes, I'm sure I will." Rowena even allowed herself the luxury of allowing her glance to move as disdainfully over Chloe as that lady's had earlier flickered over her.

"You may also be sure you won't like what you hear," Chloe said softly. The faintest of smiles played coldly upon her perfect lips as with a curt nod of her lovely head she swept on down the staircase.

Emily looked at Rowena with new eyes. "Well, I must confess to being completely taken aback."

"Taken aback?"

"I wasn't expecting your riposte, and nor was she."

"Nor was I, I suppose," Rowena admitted. "I'm afraid I just found her disagreeable."

"That's putting it mildly. Dear Chloe is the most accomplished bitch in London." Once again she took Rowena's arm. "Oh, *do* let's get on with this wretched viewing. We've been here for ages and have seen hardly anything yet."

Neither of them noticed another figure on the staircase. Since returning to London from the country, Jack Jermyn frequently indulged in the pastime of following Chloe. His interested gaze rested upon Rowena. So this was the enigmatic Lady Alderney. He smiled, looking appreciatively at her shape. She might not be a beauty, but ah, what sweet charms she had. Alderney was to be envied his conjugal rights.

Flicking a lace-edged handkerchief over his immaculate sleeve, he went on down the staircase. His eyes were thoughtful as he recalled the conversation he'd heard before Christmas at Westcote House. He'd decided then to use it to his advantage, and he still meant to. Fair means couldn't persuade Chloe into his bed, therefore he'd resort to foul means. He wasn't quite sure yet how to use the information about the plot against Lady Alderney, but he'd think of something.

Rowena and Emily had reached the next floor and entered the first room. Rowena's steps immediately faltered as her attention was drawn to a portrait on the wall opposite. It was of a periwigged late seventeenth-century gentleman in a brocade coat and three-cornered hat, and there was something very familiar about it, from the frame to the style of the portrait itself. Could it possibly be . . . ?

Gathering her skirts, she hurried toward it, and Emily followed her in puzzlement.

"What is it, Rowena?" she asked, looking up curiously at the painting as Rowena studied the little nameplate at the bottom of the frame.

"I've found Henry Melcombe!" Rowena cried excitedly.

Emily looked blankly at her. "An ancestor, I presume?"

"Yes. Oh, yes! This painting is one of a pair. His wife, Lady Margaret, is still at Melcombe, but we thought Henry had been lost forever." Rowena gazed delightedly up at the portrait. "You're going to go home to Melcombe at last, sir," she whispered.

"And not before time," he replied sharply.

Rowena's breath caught, and she stared at the canvas.

Chapter 30

Hearing the portrait speak made Rowena's heart almost stop with shock. Instinctively, she touched the painted figure, half expecting to feel flesh and blood, but there was only canvas.

She glanced uneasily at Emily. "D-did you hear that?" she asked.

"Hear what?"

"I thought . . . Oh, it doesn't matter."

"Rowena, you've gone quite pale. Is something wrong?"

"You'll think me quite mad if I tell you, but I could have sworn the painting answered me when I said it was going home to Melcombe. I . . . I'm *sure* I heard a voice say 'And not before time'."

Emily's eyes widened a little, but then she laughed dismissively. "Oh, stuff and nonsense. If you heard a voice, I daresay it was one of the gentlemen here." She gestured around the room.

Rowena felt a little foolish. "You're right, of course."

Emily looked at the portrait. "I presume you're going to purchase it."

"You don't think Justin will mind, do you?"

"Mind? Why should he? He'll be only too happy to indulge his new bride." He should be positively *anxious* to indulge her. Emily glanced briefly away, thinking of his liaison with Chloe. It was to be hoped his conscience was playing havoc with him.

"What do I do to buy it?" Rowena asked.

"You place one of our tickets on the frame and then go downstairs to tell them. Here, let me do it for you." Opening her reticule, Emily took out a pencil and the little sheaf of tickets they'd been given on entering. Quickly, she wrote Rowena's name upon one of them, then tucked it into the corner of the frame.

"There, Lady Alderney, Henry Melcombe is yours."

Rowena smiled. "Let's go down immediately. Oh, I'm so pleased to have found him. Mother will be delighted."

Henry's ghost gazed thoughtfully after them. Unlike his fellows at Melcombe Manor, he was a hard and accomplished phantom who was used to the harshness of the city, and he had the quick, clear gaze of one who'd seen and done a great many things. Not for him the occasional paltry excursion from his frame; over the years he'd proved so useful to the Powers-That-Be they'd elevated him to a very superior and influential rank. He could move about at will and could summon up terrible forces to wreak awful vengeance upon those who'd transgressed. He aspired to become one of the Powers, and whenever he went abroad, even the entities of hell treated him with respect. He feared only the Prince of Darkness himself.

Ambitious and ruthless, he'd devoted himself to his calling, but only because he was denied the one thing he yearned for above all else—his return to Melcombe. He could move around as he chose, but wasn't permitted to go more than fifty miles from his frame, and Melcombe was much farther than that. But now, quite suddenly, it seemed he was to go home.

He watched Rowena until she and Emily left the room. Who was she, this fair rescuer who spoke so lovingly of Melcombe and Margaret? She'd heard him answer her, and that made him very curious indeed. In all the years he'd been a ghost, only William Melcombe had ever shown any awareness of him. Silly Billy was a blood descendant, and that made Henry wonder if his new purchaser was as well.

Stretching, he floated idly from the frame to study the ticket Emily had left. Lady Alderney. He knew the title, of course, for a former Marquess of Exford had once given him cause for concern about Margaret's fidelity. Kit? Yes, that was the womanizing rogue's name. Too pretty by far, and with eyes to charm Heaven

itself! This Lady Alderney must be married to one of his succes-
sors, but who exactly was she? Suddenly his spectral eyes cleared
as he remembered. Of course, she was Silly Billy's daughter,
Rowena! At the Pall Mall house she'd been a green, rather awkward girl, but her curves had promised to make her a desirable
woman. And so she was, and elegant in her London clothes. Well,
who'd have thought she'd snap up a future marquess? It couldn't
be an arranged match, for no grand aristocrat would consider such
an inconsequential bride, unless, of course, things had now pros-
pered so much at Melcombe that she'd become an heiress!

Henry scowled then. Prosperity at Melcombe? Not when Silly
Billy had been at work. It was because of that dolt's lack of per-
spicacity the house in Pall Mall had had to go and he, Henry Melcombe, now suffered the humiliation of being displayed for sale!

Still scowling, the shade floated back into his comfortable
frame. He'd had a long night dealing with the increasingly trou-
blesome gargoyles from Westminster Abbey, and he was very
disgruntled. The gargoyles had been getting above themselves of
late, and not just at the abbey, for the Powers-That-Be had received reports of their activities from all over England. Gargoyles
were loathsome creatures with quite disgusting habits, and had
never taken kindly to being kept under control. It had rankled
with them that they were attached to churches, for they wished to
be free to do as they pleased, which pleasures encompassed many
unacceptable practices. From time to time they rebelled, and now
was just such a time.

At the moment they were bent upon mischief of every descrip-
tion, and were nimble and sly enough to make catching them very
difficult. But they had one weakness that invariably led to their
recapture if they were foolish enough to indulge, and that was
their liking for butcher's shops, slaughter houses, churchyards,
and charnels. Last night he'd happened upon a group of them
raiding a poulterer in Cheapside and been obliged to chase them
up the Thames almost as far as Windsor before he'd caught one
of them and the rest fled back to their lair at Westminster. The
one he'd caught was now so firmly embedded in Thames mud it
would never escape, and he hoped its fate would serve as a warning to its fellows.

Henry's humor was restored a little at thought of the hapless
gargoyle still deep under the river. His frown faded, and he settled
back to contemplate the much more agreeable prospect of his imminent return to Melcombe, where he'd at last see Margaret
again. His anticipatory smile faltered. It had been so long he'd

probably forget what to do! But then he closed his eyes. No, that was one thing he'd never forget.

Returning from Hanover Square, Chloe's carriage entered the gates of Westcote House, but as she was about to alight, her maid hurried out to hand her a note.

"Begging your pardon, milady, but I'm to give you this as soon as possible."

Recognizing Justin's writing, Chloe swiftly broke the wax seal and read the few lines. *I must see you immediately. The usual place.*

A slow smile came to her lips, and she leaned out of the carriage to instruct the coachman. "York Street, and be quick."

"My lady." He touched his hat. He'd driven her to York Street on many occasions in the past and knew it was where she kept her assignations with Lord Alderney.

York Street lay to the south of St. James's Park, and the rented house was tucked back behind a high wall. It was very discreet and secluded, and she and Justin had spent many passionate hours there. She meant to spend many more such hours with him and would dissemble and connive as much as necessary in order to do so. A drab little nothing like his new wife wasn't going to rob her of the one man she craved! Chloe's eyes flashed as the carriage turned carefully in through the narrow entrance and drew up behind Justin's curricle.

Alighting, she hurried into the house and found him waiting in the entrance hall. He turned swiftly, and she ran to him.

"Justin! Oh, my darling!" she cried, coming into his arms and cleaving against him as she kissed his mouth. Her body moved seductively, and she pressed her knowing hands to his hips, holding him to her. It was exhilarating to feel him in her arms again, and she craved the consummation she'd been denied since he'd left town for Bath the previous October. He was an addiction, and she could never have enough of him. No other lover had ever excited her as he did, and no other lover had ever raised her to the ultimate height of true ecstasy. He flamed the blood in her veins, and she was desperate for reassurance that nothing had changed between them.

Her kiss was consciously seductive, for she wanted him now. She needed him and would surrender right here on the floor if he wished.

But suddenly he broke away, loosening her arms and placing them gently at her side. "No, Chloe," he said quietly.

Dismay swept through her. "I don't believe you really mean that."

"I do mean it." He ran his fingers through his hair.

"Because you're married?"

"You've heard?"

"I've met your bride."

He paused. "How?"

"At the Hanover Square rooms."

"Ah." He turned away.

Chloe watched him. "She isn't what I expected."

"No, I don't imagine she is."

"In fact, I thought her rather plain."

"I don't wish to discuss her."

"There's no need for her to make any difference to us," she said softly, moving behind him and slipping her arms around his waist. "Things can be just as they were before, this house, our bed here . . ." She slid one hand slowly down the front of his breeches, but he seized her wrist and turned sharply toward her again.

"I asked you to meet me so that we could end things civilly," he said.

"Civilly? How can it be civil when you discard me in favor of that insipid provincial milkmaid!" she cried.

"Please, Chloe, don't make this any more disagreeable than it already is. I wish to abide by my marriage vows, and so I'm finishing our liaison."

Her heart pounded with furious disbelief. Until this moment she'd been sure deep within she could hold him, but now her certainty was crumbling. She remembered what she and Andrew had agreed. She had to play her cards cleverly and be there to offer sympathy when Rowena appeared to be the unfaithful wife. Choking back her dismay and rage, she managed a submissive nod. "If . . . if that is what you wish," she said quietly.

He was relieved. There wasn't to be a great scene!

She raised her lovely eyes appealingly to his. "Tell me you loved me for a while," she pleaded.

"You know that I did."

"And I pleased you?"

He put his hand to her cheek. "No man in his right mind could fail to be pleased by you, Chloe."

"I'm not interested in any man, just you," she whispered.

He took his hand away quickly.

"I love you with all my heart, Justin, and I'll be here for you when you tire of her."

"I won't tire of her. Just accept that it's over between us, Chloe."

"It will never be over," she murmured, and before he knew it she'd slipped her arms around him again. Her lips closed desirously over his as she used all her remarkable repertoire of sexual talents to remind him of the erotically satisfying nights they'd spent together. She gave him no chance to disengage the embrace, for she ended it herself by turning to walk to the door.

There she paused to look at him again. "If you want me, you only have to send word and I'll come."

His sea green eyes were steady. "Yes, you probably will, but I'd be a fool if I thought you'd ever been faithful to me. I know I've been sharing your favors."

She raised her chin. "If I've turned to others for comfort, it's only because you've never given me your heart. I'd have left Westcote for you, Justin. I still would, if you asked." She gazed at him for a long moment, then opened the door, stepping out into the winter morning chill.

She didn't look back again as she entered her carriage, but the moment the vehicle drove out into the street, she lowered the blinds to hide her tears. They weren't simply tears of heartbreak over him; they were also filled with malevolence toward his wife. Andrew was right; between them they could drive an invincible wedge between the newlyweds. She didn't care what fate befell the bride at Andrew's hands; she only cared about the bridegroom.

Justin remained in the house, listening to the dwindling sound of her carriage. That final kiss had told him his interest in her wasn't completely dead, but then it would have taken a very cold man to resist the expert advances of such a beautiful woman. He glanced around at the house where they'd kept so many passionate assignations, then snatched up his hat and gloves from the hall table to leave.

Climbing on to the curricle seat, he seized the reins and flung the startled horses forward. They set off so smartly the wheels nearly struck the gatepost before he brought the team up to a spanking trot along the street.

Had he done the right thing? He prayed so, for he didn't want to lose Rowena. George had warned that his properly brought up bride wouldn't accept the existence of a mistress, but Chloe had meant so much to him . . . *Had* meant so much to him? Could he really be sure that she was in the past now?

His mouth set firmly as he flicked the whip again, urging the team along at an even greater pace. The curricle flew dangerously over the cobbles, and several passersby turned to stare.

Chapter 31

Justin hardly knew the direction he was taking, until he found himself tooling the sweating horses into Hanover Square, where he saw George's barouche still drawn up outside the rooms. Rowena and Emily were just emerging, followed by two men carrying Henry Melcombe's portrait.

Reining the horses in, Justin leapt out of the curricle and hurried toward his wife. Her eyes softened, and her lips curved into a glad smile. "Justin?"

Ignoring Emily's startled gaze, he caught his bride close, tilting her mouth to meet his. He paid no heed to the many onlookers as he crushed her to him. She was honey-sweet, driving away memories of other lips he'd kissed only minutes before. His arm tight about her little waist, his fingers moved adoringly at the nape of her slender neck as his tongue slid richly against hers.

At last he brought the kiss to a close and looked into her eyes. "You mean so much to me," he whispered.

"And you do to me," she answered, her arms still around him.

Emily smiled. "What a shockingly public display, to be sure," she murmured.

Rowena drew back self-consciously, color flooding her cheeks, but Justin took her hand, raising the fingertips to his lips. "Let everyone watch; let them see how highly Lord Alderney regards his wife," he said softly.

Emily looked at him, and he met her gaze. No word was said, but she knew he'd ended things with Chloe. She glanced suddenly along the pavement in time to see Andrew draw swiftly back out of sight. Her heart sank anew, and she wished Rowena would tell Justin about him. Every instinct informed her that reticence now was very unwise indeed, but she'd given her word to Rowena and would abide by it.

The men carrying Henry's portrait almost dropped it, and Rowena was anxious. "Oh, please take care!" she cried.

Justin looked at the painting. "What is it?" he asked.

"One of my ancestors." She smiled at him. "We feared he'd been lost forever, but I've actually found Henry Melcombe."

"Henry Melcombe?"

"The matching portrait of his wife, Lady Margaret, is still in the great hall, but his portrait was in our London house, and . . ." She broke off and smiled. "I'm sure you're not really interested in the saga of the only lost portrait in the family."

He put his hand to her cheek. "I'm interested in everything about you," he replied. "Come, I'll drive you back in the curricle."

"But, Emily—"

Emily interrupted quickly. "You go with Justin, Rowena. I'll take the portrait to St. James's Square and then go home. If we don't see each other again today, don't forget we have an appointment tomorrow."

Justin looked from one to the other. "Appointment?"

"We're riding in St. James's Park," Rowena told him. "You don't mind, do you?"

"Of course not. You're at liberty to do as you wish."

"Including purchase old family portraits?"

"Most definitely including that," he murmured, smiling into her eyes. "Especially as I've now seen my lawyer and settled Melcombe's future. Word will be sent to your mother this very day informing her that her debts are no more."

"Oh, Justin!" Rowena face lit up with a glad smile, but then the smile faded just a little. "Mother is in Bath with Lady Beaminster and won't know until she returns next month."

"Do you think I haven't thought of that? The letter will go to Bath."

She hugged him. "You think of everything, do you not?" she whispered.

"I do where your happiness is concerned." He kissed her forehead and then opened the barouche door for Emily, who held his hand for a moment as she took her seat inside.

"Justin, I must know for certain."

"Emily?"

"Is it finished with Chloe?" she asked quietly so Rowena wouldn't hear.

"Yes."

She squeezed his fingers and then let go. He closed the door and nodded to the coachman.

As the barouche drove away, Henry sat back in his frame. He'd listened very carefully to the brief exchange between Emily and Justin, as he'd listened closely to everything Justin had said since arriving in the square. The wraith's eyes were flinty with anger. Lord Alderney's handsome face wasn't entirely unknown to him. About three months earlier he'd chased some gargoyles to a house in York Street. They'd eluded him for once, but while searching the house he'd witnessed a tryst between this very Lord Alderney and his exceedingly beautiful mistress, whose name had been Chloe.

Henry Melcombe was far too much a man of the world not to know when another man of the world wasn't being entirely truthful, and it was plain to him that Justin hadn't responded entirely honestly to the questions about Chloe. The wraith's eyes were hooded and dangerous as Emily's barouche conveyed him out of the square, for if there was one thing he could not abide at any price it was adultery, especially if that adultery was committed by the spouse of a Melcombe. Henry promised himself that if unfaithfulness was confirmed, then Rowena's handsome husband wouldn't be long for this world.

Back outside the rooms, Justin had turned to draw his wife's hand over his sleeve. His fingers enclosed hers as they walked toward his curricle, and he kissed her palm as he assisted her onto the seat.

She laughed as the light vehicle leapt away over the cobbles, and her laughter carried to Andrew as he watched them leave. The new Lady Alderney had had quite a shock on seeing him again, and tomorrow at noon she'd have another such shock when he'd just happen to be in St. James's Park when she and Emily Rathbone took their ride.

For the moment, however, he had an appointment to keep. Tapping his top hat more firmly on his head, he strolled away in the general direction of Berkeley Square, where he and Chloe had arranged to "accidentally" meet at London's most fashionable confectioners, Gunter's.

In summer it was very much the thing for gentlemen to bring Gunter's famous ices to their ladies, who remained in carriages in the shade of Berkeley Square's trees, but in winter the *monde* resorted to the warmth and comfort of the shop itself. When Andrew looked in through the windows, most of the white-clothed tables inside were occupied, but Chloe had yet to arrive.

He lingered outside, pretending to examine the bride cakes on display beneath glass domes in the windows. His cane swung in his hand as he watched the reflection of the square. He could see the gates of Westcote House, and just as the bells begun to strike midday, he saw Chloe emerge.

As she reached the pavement near him, he turned and doffed his hat. "Good day, Lady Westcote," he said, sweeping an elegant bow. His courteous but formal manner was that of an acquaintance. The few passersby could not have realized there was anything more to the greeting than the civility demanded of those who'd been formally introduced.

Chloe inclined her head graciously. "Why, Mr. Kemp, it's been some time since last we spoke. I trust you're well?"

"I am indeed, as I can see you are," he replied gallantly, although he could see by her slightly puffy eyes that she'd been crying.

Andrew glanced toward Gunter's and then looked inquiringly at her. "I was about to sample an ice. Would you care to join me?" He knew the invitation was perfectly in order, for the shop was crowded.

"That would be most agreeable," she answered, accepting the arm he offered.

The air inside was sugar-scented as he escorted Chloe to a free table in the middle of the shop. He then procured two pineapple ices and sat down opposite her.

He smiled as she picked up her silver spoon. "I presume Alderney is calling it off?" he said, although to anyone watching he appeared to be remarking upon something as innocuous as the weather.

She made herself meet his eyes. "Why do you say that?"

"You've been crying. I imagine you'd be alight with happiness if all was well."

She didn't reply, but he saw how her fingers tightened over the spoon.

He spoke again. "I saw him with his bride outside the Hanover Square rooms a short while ago. He was disposed to give a very passionate and public display of connubial affection."

"Are you enjoying my wretchedness?" Chloe inquired coolly, but with an apparently amicable smile. Justin had gone straight to his wife from York Street? The knowledge cut into her. She studied him. "What on earth do you and he see in her?"

"She has a certain something."

"So I noticed. The something in question was straining her bodice to the full when I, too, saw her at the rooms," Chloe replied acidly.

"Well, I have something to suggest that might lighten your gloom."

She looked at him. "Go on."

"By her reaction today I could tell she'd held her tongue about my activities in Melcombe. George Rathbone's wife was there at the time, and she was obviously most curious when I addressed Alderney's wife by her first name and behaved as if I was a disappointed lover from the past."

Chloe's lips parted. "You went as far as that?"

"Yes."

"And?"

"Well, I'd walked on and couldn't hear, but I'm certain Rowena managed to persuade Rathbone's wife that it would be better not to mention me to anyone."

"Which leaves us where, exactly?"

"Which leaves us with a weapon, especially as I know she and Mrs. Rathbone are riding in St. James's Park tomorrow at midday. I intend to be there as well and to approach her in the same way. I think it would be prudent if you and some of your most influential lady friends were to be in the park as well to witness the meeting."

Her eyes cleared. "And I, out of concern for Justin, should then tell him what I've seen?"

"Yes."

She considered for a moment. "He won't listen," she said then.

"He will if you follow my advice. How did you behave when you saw him again? Did you show the fury of a woman scorned? Or were you the soul of wounded love, promising to be there when he needed you?"

"The latter—eventually."

"Then his happiness will be uppermost in your thoughts."

She met his eyes. "Won't this put you at risk from his anger?"

"I think not, for all I'll be guilty of is speaking to the woman who deserted me for him. He might choose to warn me off, but by then the seeds of doubt will have been sown. Your lady friends are bound to spread whispers, and Emily Rathbone is certain to tell her husband about it. As Alderney's closest friend, Rathbone will feel honor bound to inform him his new bride may not be as faithful and adoring as he thought."

"You're very cool and certain, sir."

He smiled. "I am, for I mean to make quite a scene of it tomorrow. Anyone who sees will be most intrigued, I promise you."

Chloe's spirits had lightened with each minute, and now her eyes were shining again. "I can hardly wait, sir."

"It will be an acting *tour de force*," he said softly.

But fate was to play a hand before the ride in St. James's Park. That evening the intriguers and their quarries were to come face-to-face at the Royal Opera House.

Chapter 32

Rowena and Justin sat at dinner when a message came from George and Emily to say they'd been unexpectedly offered use of Lord and Lady Holland's private box at the opera house for that night's performance of *Twelfth Night*. Mrs. Siddons herself was to play the leading role, and the production was considered to be one of the finest ever of this particular play.

Justin looked inquiringly at Rowena. "Would you like to go?"

She smiled. "See the bard *and* Mrs. Siddons? I'd love to."

He returned the smile and then nodded to the waiting footman. "Inform Mr. and Mrs. Rathbone that we will be delighted to join them."

"My lord." The footman bowed and withdrew.

Justin poured her another glass of wine, watching the way the candlelight danced in her eyes. Learning she'd met Chloe that morning had unsettled him, and now he felt compelled to ask her about it. "I believe you met Lady Westcote today?"

She paused, the wineglass only halfway to her lips. "Yes, unfortunately."

"Unfortunately?"

"I found her most disagreeable."

"She'd renowned for her beauty, not her warmth to her fellow females," he murmured.

"That was clear, even to me." She studied him. "Do you really regard her as the most beautiful woman in London?"

"It's generally acknowledged," he answered.

"Then the eye of the beholder must be dimmed," she observed scathingly.

He raised an eyebrow. "You don't agree?"

"Oh, she has a veneer of beauty, but beneath it she's very ugly indeed. She made it obvious that she disliked me on principle, and she was even base enough to let me know she recognized the clothes I was wearing."

What a *chienne* Chloe could be, he thought.

Rowena sighed. "I don't know why she singled me out. Perhaps it's because I've stepped above my station." She considered for a moment. "Or perhaps she's jealous," she said then.

"Jealous?" His eyes flew to meet hers.

"Because I've won you."

He stared at her for a moment, wondering if she knew, but her gaze was ingenuous. He laughed a little then. "I doubt if Lady Westcote has ever given me more than a passing thought," he said.

"If that's so, then she's lacking in taste as well as civility," Rowena replied with a smile.

"Such compliments will make me vain," he declared, wishing he hadn't succumbed to the urge to mention Chloe. It had been shabby of him, and he knew it.

"What should I wear tonight?" she asked suddenly.

He was relieved to talk of something else. "Er, from what I've seen of the clothes Emily has lent to you, I'd suggest the pink plowman's gauze."

"I . . . I thought I'd wear that to Almack's."

He shook his head smilingly. "Trust my judgment. The plowman's gauze for the theater, the silver lace for Almack's."

"The silver lace?"

He nodded. "It's perfect for London's most select assembly rooms."

"Then I shall do as you say."

"Now, however, I fear we cannot linger over the dessert, or we'll miss the opening curtain," he said, tossing his napkin down and getting up to draw her chair back for her.

She rose and turned instinctively to kiss him. His arm moved around her little waist, and he pulled her close. Their lips joined with swift desire, and he caressed her through the thin stuff of her gown, his arms tightening as he was seized with fresh remorse over Chloe.

Regret lanced through him that he hadn't told Rowena the truth before, for he'd just compounded the omission by more deceit. Now if he ever told her Chloe had been very much more to him than a social acquaintance, he knew it would destroy her trust, and maybe even her love. He couldn't bear the thought of forfeiting any part of her.

The door stood open to the entrance hall, where Henry's portrait hung on the wall. His gaze was sour as he watched them kiss.

This Alderney fellow was cool, he had to grant him that. To actually bring his mistress, whether former or current, into the conversation was evidence of a devious and callous nature. The shade liked Justin less and less, but was loath to set about punishing him until it had been finally ascertained whether or not the fair Chloe was still gracing his bed.

His lordship required close observation before his fate was decided, and so the ghost decided to accompany them to the theater.

Any appearance by Mrs. Siddons was guaranteed to attract a large audience, and tonight's performance was no exception. The January night was cold, but Rowena was warm in a fur-lined gray velvet cloak. The delicate plowman's gauze gown wasn't suitable for the depths of winter, but no lady of fashion could be seen at the Royal Opera House in anything sensible.

Invisible on the seat opposite, Henry surveyed her approvingly. She was a credit to the Melcombes, and far too good for Alderney! The wraith's hollow glance moved to Justin, who wore the formal evening black and white silk breeches that were *de rigueur* for the theater.

The carriage drew up at the entrance, and one of the theater footmen came to open the door and lower the rungs. Justin alighted, his breath silvery in the glow of lamps around the building. Then he turned, extending his hand to Rowena. Their fingers closed warmly together as she stepped down, and he smiled a little, his thumb smoothing her palm for a moment before he released her. As the footman slammed the carriage door and the vehicle pulled away to make room for the next one, Justin offered his arm to his wife.

Henry followed as they walked into the crowded vestibule. Another footman relieved Rowena of her outdoor things, and then Justin escorted her to the grand staircase. She knew they were attracting a great deal of attention, for by now everyone had heard of Lord Alderney's unlikely match.

Progress up the staircase was necessarily slow, not only because there was such a crush, but also because Justin had to introduce her to so many people. She was subjected to ordeal by curiosity, some of it discreet, most of it blatant. It was far worse than the Hanover Square rooms, where Justin's absence meant her identity hadn't been so readily obvious.

She was relieved when the top of the staircase came into view, but that relief was swiftly expunged when she saw Chloe approaching with her husband. Lord Westcote was somewhat portly and slightly overdressed in a black brocade coat with jeweled buttons.

He was about forty years old, with receding hair, pale blue eyes, and pouting lips, and he gave the impression of merely enduring his lovely wife's company. From the stony look in Chloe's eyes, it was clear the feeling was mutual. The Westcote marriage had been hollow almost from the outset, and now relations were very strained indeed because of his admitted affection for Lady Jane Pankhurst.

Chloe was truly splendid in peony silk and opals, with tall white plumes streaming from her dark hair. Her eyes were warm as they rested on Justin, but when her glance moved on to Rowena it became cold and malevolent.

Fluttering invisibly overhead, Henry immediately recognized Justin's mistress. He glided closer, and he saw the passion with which she looked at Rowena's husband. It clearly wasn't over as far as the lady was concerned, the spirit thought. It was then, to his utmost shock, that he realized Lord Westcote was looking straight at him!

There wasn't so much as a glimmer of surprise in his pale blue eyes, and Henry knew Chloe's husband was one of those rare humans who saw and accepted entities from the other world existing alongside his own.

Henry was taken completely by surprise, but then put a ghostly finger to his lips and shook his head. Lord Westcote gave a barely discernible nod before looking away again. So used was he to seeing phantoms that the encounter didn't bother him in the slightest.

Justin bowed. "Westcote. My lady," he murmured.

Lord Westcote nodded. "Alderney, may I extend my congratulations to you and your new bride?"

Both greetings were cool, for neither man had ever particularly liked the other. Long before his liaison with Chloe commenced, Justin had exposed Lord Westcote for cheating at cards and hadn't been forgiven for it.

Rowena was introduced and ignored Chloe as she smiled at Lord Westcote. "I'm honored to make your acquaintance, sir."

"Lady Alderney," he replied, bowing courteously over her hand.

Chloe's fan snapped open impatiently. "We should adjourn to our box if we are to see the curtain raised," she said to her husband.

He nodded, and she took his arm again as they walked on.

Rowena was about to remark to Justin that Chloe didn't improve on second acquaintance when from the corner of her eye she saw something that made her heart sink with dismay. Andrew Kemp was ascending the staircase toward them.

He halted in surprise, for he hadn't reckoned on seeing her again so swiftly, especially with her husband. But he was equal to the moment, turning it neatly to his advantage.

He swept a graceful bow. "Lady Alderney."

Justin turned swiftly, recognizing the voice before he saw the face. "Mr. Kemp," he murmured coolly, for his feelings were mixed. He may have rescued the man from the roadside, but hadn't forgotten the unpleasant encounter on the stairs at the Red Lion.

Rowena confined her response to the merest nod of her head. Her whole body recoiled from him, and she couldn't meet his eyes. Her fingers tightened over Justin's sleeve.

Henry fluttered concernedly around her. What was this? She was upset by this Kemp fellow. Who was he, and why did he arouse such a reaction?

Andrew bowed again to Justin. "I'm glad we've met, my lord, for it gives me the opportunity to express my gratitude."

"There is nothing to thank me for, sir. It's no more or less than anyone would do."

"Nevertheless, if you hadn't rescued me, I know I'd probably not have survived the night. I am in your debt, sir."

Rowena looked at Justin in surprise, for it was the first she'd heard of any rescue.

Andrew smiled at her. "May I compliment you upon your appearance tonight, Miss Melcombe? Er, forgive me, I mean Lady Alderney."

Remembering how Andrew had watched Rowena at the Halloween bonfire, Justin picked him up on the apparent slip. "You and my wife are acquainted?"

Rowena's heart quickened uneasily.

Andrew nodded. "I'm acquainted with all her family, my lord," he explained. "When you and I met at Melcombe, it wasn't my first time there. Lady Alderney and I knew each other about a year before then. I like to think we were, er, friends." He allowed his glance to linger upon her, and then he smiled briskly at Justin. "I won't detain you further, my lord. I trust you both enjoy the play." With another graceful bow he walked on.

Henry looked perplexedly at Rowena's suddenly pale face. She'd been quite unsettled by the encounter, and it was obvious, even to a ghost, that there was much beneath the surface where Andrew Kemp was concerned. Could it be that the bride was as guilty of secrets as her groom? Henry didn't like to think so, especially of a Melcombe, but there had to be an explanation for her disarray.

Justin said nothing as he escorted Rowena to Lord Holland's

box. The horseshoe-shaped auditorium was brilliant with color
and echoed with chatter as the audience prepared for the performance. Chandeliers shone over everything and upon Emily's ru-
bies as she turned to smile at them. She wore gray silk, and a
plumed fan rested on her lap. George, like all the other gentlemen, was dressed in formal black.

After a few moments of polite greeting, Justin drew Rowena's
chair out for her, then sat down next to her.

She was still unsettled by the encounter with Andrew, but she
strove to appear natural and unconcerned as she glanced at Justin.
"What did Mr. Kemp mean about you rescuing him?"

Hearing the name, Emily turned her head toward them.

"It was nothing," Justin replied dismissively. "He merely had
an accident on the road to Dunster. I found him unconscious at
the wayside when I was going to Taunton for the special license."
He put his hand over hers. "Rowena, Kemp isn't the sort of fellow I wish you to number among your friends."

"I don't regard him as a friend," she replied, conscious of
Emily's continuing gaze.

At her elbow Henry gave his descendant a dire look. She was
lying about something. But what? Her attitude didn't quite suggest Kemp meant a great deal to her, nor did it suggest the contrary. There was a mystery, and her friend Emily was party to it.
At least, to some of it.

Justin looked at his wife. "But, Kemp said he was a friend."

"He said he liked to think we were friends," she corrected, "but
the truth is he was briefly acquainted with my family, that is all."
How she managed to meet his eyes she didn't know, but somehow she found the will.

He smiled. "Good."

Troubled, Emily looked at her, silently imploring her to tell
him the truth, but Rowena wouldn't meet her eyes.

Henry retreated thoughtfully to the back of the box. What was
going on here? Whatever it was, he'd find out, and if any punishment was to be meted out, then he was prepared to do it—whether
it was husband or wife, or both.

Chapter 33

Overnight snow dusted the capital, which sparkled in the midday sun as Rowena and Emily rode slowly along the Mall in St. James's Park. It was the sort of weather that brought riders out, and the air echoed with the sound of hooves upon frozen ground.

Emily hadn't yet raised the matter of Andrew, but Rowena knew she intended to, and so postponed the moment by chattering about anything and everything. It was nervous prattle, for the incidents of the previous day had made her very anxious, especially the second one, when Justin had been present.

The truth was she didn't know what to do about Andrew. Common sense told her to take Emily's advice and tell Justin; but that same common sense pointed to the obvious consequences of such a belated confession. Might he not wonder if she did indeed have something to hide? He wouldn't be human if he didn't. And so she chattered, but it was bravado. No one glancing at the new Lady Alderney could have known she was churned up with nerves.

At last Emily couldn't hold her tongue any longer and reined in. "Rowena, we have something important to discuss," she declared.

Reluctantly Rowena halted as well. "I . . . I'd rather not."

"Yes, I know, but you really can't leave the situation as it is. It's clear this Kemp person intends to cause trouble."

"We can't be sure of that," Rowena said lamely. "Last night was purely accidental, I could tell by his face, and Justin really had rescued him."

"Rowena, it doesn't matter how accidental it was, or how indebted he feels toward Justin, the fact remains he still used the meeting to make things uncomfortable for you. Well, he did, didn't he?"

Rowena lowered her eyes. "Yes, I suppose so."

"There's no suppose about it."

"I can't tell Justin, Emily. I've left it too long now, and I'm afraid he'll be suspicious if I suddenly—What is it?" Rowena broke off as she saw Emily look past her and gasp. Turning, she saw a small group of elegant ladies riding approaching, among them Chloe. "Oh, do let's ride on," she said, quickly gathering her reins.

But Emily shook her head. "They know we've seen them, and at least two of them aren't ladies to cross. The one in crimson is

Lady Cowper, and the one in fawn is Lady Jersey. You must know they're both patronesses at Almack's and could make life exceedingly unpleasant for you and me, as well as for Justin and George, who've acquired vouchers for next Wednesday's ball. Those vouchers could be withdrawn on a whim, which would mean social calamity."

Rowena knew she was right. The importance of the lady patronesses couldn't be underestimated, and so she resigned herself to meeting them, as well as having to put up with another disagreeable encounter with Chloe. Suddenly, she found herself telling Emily about the connection she believed there to be between Chloe and Andrew.

"Emily, I have reason to believe Lady Westcote is Andrew Kemp's mistress," she said.

Emily was incredulous, but had no time to say anything because the ladies reached them and reined in. Introductions were made, and then Rowena had to force herself to acknowledge Chloe, whose smiling response was laden with an almost tangible hatred. Rowena tried not to let it bother her, but couldn't help feeling Chloe was enjoying a secret laugh at her, as if she knew something the new Lady Alderney did not.

Ladies Cowper and Jersey were among the most brilliant stars in the high society firmament. If Lady Cowper trod a new measure at Almack's, that dance immediately became the rage, and if Lady Jersey chose to wear a color hitherto considered *passé*, lo and behold, suddenly everyone was wearing it.

Such was their power that Rowena felt hesitant in their presence, and she therefore took very little part in the conversation that ensued, but she became more and more conscious of Chloe's gloating gaze. The woman was definitely enjoying something at her expense, and the knowledge would have been perturbing even if Chloe hadn't been so intimately connected with Andrew Kemp.

An urgent and freshly dismayed Emily suddenly caught Rowena's eye and nodded something further along the Mall. Rowena looked, and her heart almost stopped as she saw none other than Andrew riding toward them. She knew instinctively that he intended speaking to her again, and panic pumped sharply through her. She glanced anxiously at the lady patronesses, for she didn't dare risk his speaking to her when they were present! On an impulse she was soon to regret to the depths of her soul, she withdrew from the group to ride to meet him. Her intention was to deny him any opportunity to say anything that would raise eyebrows, but even as she made the move, she knew it was a grave error of judgment. He was already closer than she'd realized, and anything they said was bound to be just audible to the ladies.

Emily couldn't believe Rowena had been so unutterably foolish. Why, oh, why choose to go to meet him? To detach herself from them so obviously in order to speak to a gentleman was hardly the way to go on. Why do that if her relationship with him was above-board? The obvious conclusion was that some impropriety was taking place, and it was a conclusion compounded by her manner, which aroused immediate and unwelcome speculation.

Emily glanced at the other ladies and saw they were all a little surprised, but that Lady Jersey was particularly disapproving. She was looking at Andrew, whom she clearly knew and disliked. Emily's unhappy gaze returned to Rowena.

Chloe could have hugged herself with delight, for Rowena hadn't simply fallen into the trap, she'd ridden voluntarily! But Chloe's pleasure was tempered with shrewd observation as she too noted Lady Jersey's displeased countenance. Andrew was evidently beyond the pale as far as the lady patroness was concerned, and that meant that he should be beyond the pale for everyone. Chloe recalled how she'd sat in Gunter's with him only the day before, and her mind raced as she tried to remember who'd been present at the time. To her relief she couldn't bring anyone significant to mind. She'd have to take extra care in her dealings with him, for it wouldn't do for him to be the cause of her downfall as well as Rowena's!

Andrew hid a satisfied smile as he removed his top hat and inclined his head. "We meet again, Rowena," he said, being sure to say it loudly enough for the familiarity to reach the onlookers.

"Please don't address me by my first name," she replied in a low tone, loathing him with her eyes.

"I've missed you," he went on.

"I despise you," she breathed. "Why don't you leave me alone?"

"You mean too much to me," he replied, his clever glance sweeping briefly toward the nearby group, who had now fallen silent with openmouthed astonishment. Then he lowered his voice. "Why didn't you tell Alderney about me, Rowena? Are you afraid of losing him?"

She couldn't respond.

He smiled. "Oh, dear, I would appear to have put my finger on the very pulse," he murmured. Then aloud he said, "You know that I'm always here if you need me, don't you?"

She stared at him. "Why are you doing this?" she whispered.

"Because I want you, Rowena," he said softly. "I nearly had you once, and I mean to make a better job of it next time." He smiled and raised his voice again. "Never fear to lose me, Rowena."

Icy fear swept over her and she gave a sharp intake of breath, but from somewhere she found the courage to hold his gaze. "I don't know from under what stone you crawled, but I do know you and Lady Westcote are well matched," she breathed.

He met her eyes swiftly. Surely she couldn't be aware that he and Chloe were allies in this? "Lady Westcote? I, er, don't understand."

"No, I'm sure you don't, sirrah, which is why you carry her miniature with you. At least, you did before it was mislaid. She is your mistress, is she not?"

For a moment he was nonplussed, but then he gave a quiet laugh. So that was where the miniature had gone; he'd dropped it at Melcombe Manor! He answered her in the softest of tones. "You think Chloe Westcote is *my* mistress? Oh, poor fool, she isn't mine, she's your husband's. The miniature belongs to him, Rowena. I merely, er, appropriated it from his room at the Red Lion."

"You're lying!"

"You think so? Then I suggest you ask him." He smiled again. "My dear Rowena, you don't honestly imagine Alderney is in love with you, do you? It's Chloe he loves, but she wasn't free when he needed a wife. You may wear his ring, but Chloe has his heart."

Chapter 34

Rowena was stricken to the heart. It was as if the winter air had passed right through her. "I . . . I don't believe you," she whispered.

His reply was for her benefit alone, for he didn't wish Chloe's name to be heard by other ears. "That is your prerogative, Rowena, but Chloe Westcote *is* your husband's mistress. She was before he met you, and she still is. They meet at a house in York Street; I forget the number, but it stands discreetly behind a high red brick wall. He's used you most cruelly, my dear. Oh, he's given you wealth and a title, but he hasn't given you his heart. All he requires is a son and heir, and once you've obliged him in that way, I doubt he'll trouble you much."

She stared at him through a veil of tears. Please don't let it be true. Please . . .

"Face it, my dear, and remember, when you require a lover I am more than willing to oblige."

"I would sooner die."

He smiled. "I'll have you, one way or another," he said softly, gathering his reins. "I'll speak to you again soon, Rowena," he said aloud, then kicked his heels and urged his horse away along the Mall.

She was beyond worrying about what Emily and the other ladies may or may not have interpreted from the scene; her only thought was what she'd been told. Justin and Chloe? Please, don't let it be true! But phrases returned to her now. Who was it that Justin said was the most beautiful woman in London? Whose conversation had he inquired about only the evening before at dinner? And why was Chloe herself so antagonistic?

Tears wet her cheeks as she struggled to remain composed, but her shoulders shook and her throat was choked. She kept her head averted, but knew her distress was plain to see.

Emily was appalled, for the scene they'd just witnessed would be all over town before nightfall. Justin was *bound* to hear now! She knew she had to go to Rowena, and so glanced uncomfortably at her companions. "Er, if you'll excuse me, ladies . . ." she murmured, inclining her head and then turned her horse away. She could only pray that Rowena's unfortunate conduct didn't reflect upon the Rathbone household as well!

Behind her the others exchanged glances, and then Lady Jersey raised an eyebrow at Lady Cowper. "The fellow's name is Kemp, and he had the temerity to approach me for vouchers. I made it my business to inquire about him, and it seems he is nothing more than a low adventurer. His intimate acquaintance with Lady Alderney would seem to call her character into question. Do you not agree?"

Lady Cowper was forced to nod. "I fear so."

"What of the vouchers given to her husband?"

Lady Cowper sighed. "They must be withdrawn. It's unfair to Lord Alderney, but his wife would appear to be an undesirable." She looked at Chloe, about whose liaison with Justin she knew. "How fortunate this is for you, Lady Westcote," she murmured sweetly.

Chloe's response was as honeyed. "I only have Lord Alderney's best interests at heart, Lady Cowper," she replied.

"Yes, of course you do. To be sure, I'd have his interests at heart, too, for he is quite the most devastating man in town and certainly doesn't deserve such a wife as this. One wonders what possessed him, for she isn't even a beauty. And now she's been publicly indiscreet. One may do as one pleases in society, provided one does it with discretion."

Lady Jersey nodded. "Discretion is of the utmost importance," she agreed, "but it seems the new Lady Alderney is bereft of it."

The group rode on, not looking at Rowena and Emily as they passed.

Emily watched them and then looked helplessly at Rowena. "Please try to collect yourself," she urged.

"F-forgive me . . ." Rowena struggled to control her tears.

"Why on earth did you ride over to him like that? Have you any idea how incriminating it seemed?"

Rowena's eyes were haunted as she nodded. "I panicked. I knew he'd say something in front of everyone, and all I could think of was preventing him."

"We heard a good deal anyway."

"He meant you to," Rowena replied bitterly, taking another deep breath to quell the fresh sobs shuddering through her.

"Why is he doing it? Rowena, you must tell me, for the situation has now become very serious for you."

"You think I don't realize that?"

"I don't know what you realize, Rowena, for you've been very mysterious about everything. What is Andrew Kemp to you?"

"Nothing. I've told you, I was once foolish enough to believe he cared for me, but he left Melcombe as soon as he knew how parlous my family finances were. He came back when Justin was there and wanted to see me again, but I spurned his advances." Rowena looked away, remembering the final advance in her bedroom.

"He was actually approaching you when you were seeing Justin?"

"Yes."

"Oh, Rowena! If only you'd told Justin then."

Rowena lowered her eyes. It was on the tip of her tongue to confess everything, but almost immediately she thought better of it. The situation was already bad beyond belief; how much worse would it become if talk of attempted rape should begin to spread? Fresh tears stung her eyes, and her lips trembled.

Emily squeezed her arm. "It's still not too late, Rowena. You must tell Justin before someone else does. Your vouchers to Almack's are going to be withdrawn, for not only have you broken the rules today, but I fear Mr. Kemp is disapproved of by Lady Jersey. Justin at least deserves to hear about this from you, before someone else delights in telling him."

Rowena met her eyes. "Yes, and we both know who that someone will be, don't we?" she said quietly.

"I don't understand."

"Come now, Emily, you know I was wrong to think Lady Westcote was Andrew Kemp's mistress. She's Justin's, isn't she?"

Emily's dismay plunged to new depths. "Rowena, I—"

But Rowena interrupted her. "I can see from your face that it's true. You say that he deserves to hear the truth from me, but haven't I deserved the same consideration from him? I married for love, but it's plain he didn't do the same." Bitterness tinged every word.

"You mustn't think that." But Emily knew her comfort sounded hollow.

Rowena looked at her. "Why not, when it's the truth?"

"I saw him with you in Hanvoer Square yesterday, and no one could say that kiss wasn't loving. Apart from that, he told me it was over between Chloe and him."

A bitter laugh escaped Rowena. "And I stood there within inches of you, blissfully ignorant of what a fool I was!"

"It wasn't like that, Rowena. Truly it wasn't."

"I wish I could believe you, Emily," Rowena said quietly.

"I'm your friend, Rowena."

Rowena shook her head. "No. Like everyone else, it's Justin's part you've been taking." Collecting the reins, she kicked her heel and rode away.

Emily stared after her, not quite knowing what to do. Things had gone horribly wrong, and the situation was more delicate than anything she'd ever encountered. She had to speak to George. Glancing after Rowena again, she turned her mount toward home.

Chloe had left her companions and ridden swiftly to Andrew's rooms at Green's Lodging House in Conduit Street. She was careful not to go there openly, but approached by way of the mews lane leading off nearby Swallow Street, entering the lodging house from the rear and hurrying up the back staircase to the second floor.

He was waiting, as she knew he would be, and her eyes shone with malicious delight as she faced him. "I vow Sheridan himself could not have penned a sweeter scene!"

"I have to admit I was surprised when she actually detached herself from the rest of you and came over to me."

"She has no idea at all of how to go on," Chloe murmured, going to the window and holding the lace curtain aside to look down into Conduit Street.

"I've told her about you and Alderney," he said and explained about the miniature.

Chloe wasn't displeased, for she wanted Rowena to know. "So that explains the display of the vapors she gave after you'd gone." Her face appeared thoughtful. "Well, now I must tell Justin. As a friend, of course."

"Of course."

"And when she returns to the sticks in disgrace, she'll be at your mercy." She went to the door, but then turned. "Are you known to Lady Jersey?"

"Yes." His gaze cooled as he remembered the stony reception he received from that particular lady.

"It would seem you aren't a gentleman to be seen with," Chloe observed.

"Do you mean to cut me from now on?" he asked softly.

She saw the danger, for he could compromise her as easily as he'd compromised Rowena. She was too artful for that. "No, I merely mean to be even more discreet. Any future meetings will be away from the public gaze, and certainly not in places like Gunter's."

"How private?" His gaze moved sensuously over her.

She remembered how talented a lover he was and suddenly felt like sampling him again. "Come to me tonight. Westcote is out."

"Stay now," he suggested, looking toward the bedroom.

She shook her head. "I don't grace lodging house beds, sir. Westcote House, tonight."

Then she hurried down to the mews lane again and rode the short distance to Berkeley Square, but on the way Jack Jermyn's carriage turned out of a corner ahead of her, and she was obliged to rein in.

Ever eager to speak to her, Jack lowered the window glass and smiled. "Good afternoon, Chloe."

"Sir." Her response wasn't in the least encouraging.

"You're in a hurry, it seems," he murmured curiously.

"Yes, I am."

"Then I won't detain you long." He alighted and took her horse's bridle to prevent her riding away.

She was angry. "Jack, if you mean to proposition me yet again, you're wasting your time."

"Are you sure of that?"

"Quite sure," she answered coldly.

"There's no way I can persuade you to be kind?"

She lost patience. "Jack, I wouldn't submit to you if you were the last man on earth, and if I never see you again, I'll be quite content."

"From which tirade I presume I'm being unfavorably compared with Alderney?" he murmured.

"You'll never even come close to him," she said coldly.

"You still love him, do you?" He gave a thin smile.

"What concern is that of yours?"

"You'd be surprised, my dear. Very well, spurn me if you will, but you'll be sorry." He released the bridle, and she rode swiftly on.

He gazed after her. She'd indeed be sorry, for he now knew exactly how to use the information he'd so providentially overheard that night in her Berkeley Square garden.

Chloe had already put him from her thoughts as she returned to Westcote House, where she went immediately to the library to write a brief note to Justin.

> There is something vital you should know before it becomes society's sole topic of conversation. It concerns your wife's fidelity. I write as a friend and urge you to meet me without delay. I'll be at the usual place.

Sealing the note with hot wax, she rang for a footman. "Take this to Lord Alderney. You'll find him at White's at this time. Be quick now, it's urgent."

"My lady."

"And have the town carriage brought around immediately," she added.

"My lady." The footman bowed and withdrew.

It was three o'clock as Chloe left the library to go up to her rooms to change. Soon she was clad in a clinging white muslin gown concealed beneath a cloak. The afternoon light was just beginning to fade as her carriage set off for York Street. Excitement and anticipation quivered through her. Maybe she'd have no need for Andrew Kemp tonight; maybe Justin would be hers again by then . . .

Chapter 35

Justin was leaving White's when Chloe's footman hurried along the pavement toward him. "Begging your pardon, Lord Alderney, but I have an urgent note for you," he said breathlessly.

Justin took it reluctantly, for he recognized the footman's livery. He broke the seal and read. A nerve fluttered at his temple and he crumpled the paper in his hand.

Thinking he was going to ignore it, the footman spoke up hastily. "Her ladyship stressed it was very urgent, my lord," he reminded him.

"Very well."

"Sir." Relieved, the footman bowed and then walked wearily away, for he'd run all the way from Berkeley Square, and it was uphill most of the way back.

Justin went to his waiting curricle. He wanted to ignore the note, but knew he couldn't. Chloe was probably intent upon mischief, but maybe she wasn't, and if things were being whispered about Rowena, then he wished to know about it. Flicking the reins, he urged the horses away toward York Street.

Chloe waited him, and her rose perfume filled the house as he entered. She sat in the drawing room, where the first candles had been lit as the evening closed in more and more. She'd arranged herself in an elegant pose upon a sofa, the better to show off her figure through the diaphanous folds of white muslin.

He halted in the center of the green-and-gold room, which was furnished *à la Rome*. "Well, I'm here. What is it you wish to say to me?" he inquired, being careful to keep his tone distant.

She got up and went to him. "It isn't easy for me to have to tell you this."

"Chloe, I have every faith in Rowena, so if you think to make mischief—"

"I don't need to make mischief, Justin; your wife has made it for herself, and not only in front of me. Ladies Cowper and Jersey, Emily Rathbone, and several others were unwilling witnesses to a very curious and public scene in St. James's Park just after midday."

Justin became very still. "I'm warning you, Chloe . . ." he breathed, his eyes like the North Sea in winter.

"I understand you're acquainted with Mr. Andrew Kemp?"

"Kemp? What has he to do with it?"

"It seems your precious Rowena is in love with him," Chloe said quietly.

Justin stared at her, a thousand and one thoughts passing instantly through his head.

Chloe feigned sympathy. "I realize it's a shock, Justin, but she actually went up to him while we were present. We heard a great deal of what they were saying, and there's no mistake. Actually—" She paused dramatically. "Actually, Andrew Kemp isn't entirely unknown to me, although after today I shall be sure to avoid him, for it seems Lady Jersey frowns upon him. Anyway, yesterday, before I knew that, I happened to encounter him in Gunter's, and he insisted upon sitting with me to tell me his, er, woes. It seems he and Rowena met a year or so ago and fell in love, but he wasn't wealthy enough to save Melcombe Manor from debt. He said she ended their relationship because of this and told him she'd have to find a wealthy husband to save her home and family."

Justin lowered his glance. Rowena's voice drifted back to him from that distant churchyard on Exmoor. *You'll never know how much I love Melcombe, Lord Alderney. It means everything to me.*

"Justin?" Chloe put a hand out to him.

He moved away. "I don't believe any of this," he said.

"I'm only telling you what you're bound to hear soon anyway. No matter what his character may be, I understood in Gunter's that Kemp is the injured party in this. He's still in love with her and is trying unsuccessfully to come to terms with losing her to you."

"You expect me to believe that Rowena's sole reason for marrying me was to save Melcombe?"

"Yes." Chloe met his eyes.

"That isn't the Rowena I know. She hasn't a conniving bone in her body, whereas you, my dear Chloe—"

"Oh, I admit to being a scheming bitch, but in this instance I'm being honest with you, Justin. She isn't content with having broken Kemp's heart, but has to keep his love at boiling point by never quite spurning him once and for all. Did you know she seduced him into making love to her on the very day you proposed to her? He spent that night in her bed and believed she would return to him after all. She wasn't an innocent little virgin on your wedding night, of that you may be sure." Chloe exulted in the malicious lies spilling so poisonously from her lovely lips, for each one turned the knife in Rowena's back.

Justin's thoughts returned to Melcombe and the strange meeting with Kemp on the stairs at the Red Lion. He hadn't understood it at the time, but if what Chloe was saying was true . . . He turned savagely away from her. No, it wasn't true! "I've had enough of your spite, Chloe. You despise Rowena because of me, and that's all there is to it."

"I don't deny loving you or loathing her, but I do deny inventing any of this. I suggest you ask Emily Rathbone, for she was as shocked as I was in the park today. As for Ladies Jersey and Cowper, well, you may be certain your vouchers to Almack's will be revoked. There's going to be a scandal, Justin, and it's your wife's fault, no one else's. Don't think to blame Andrew Kemp entirely, for he suffers through not being able to fall out of love. He told me you'd rescued him after his accident, but what you may not know is that he has a conscience over it because of his affair with Rowena. It was on account of being so cruelly rejected by her that he drove so wildly out of Melcombe and had the accident. She'd taken him to her bed, given him that which he craved above all else, and then told him it was still over. Can you wonder that he drove so recklessly? Or that he lost control of his cabriolet at that bridge?" She put a tentative hand to his cheek, and he didn't move this time, but she knew it was because he was hardly aware of the touch. "Just ask yourself how I know so much?" she went on, her voice tightening a little with the swift desire she felt at the slight physical contact. "I know, because Kemp has confided in me, and he did so out of heartbreak after encountering her again yesterday outside the Hanover Square rooms. Justin, has she told you anything about him? Anything at all?"

"No." A nerve flickered at Justin's temple. He didn't want to believe any of it, but too many echoes were resounding through him. He became suddenly aware of Chloe's loving fingertips, and he moved sharply away. "Damn you, Chloe!" he breathed.

"I'm here for you, Justin. No matter how she may have deceived and failed you, I'm still here."

"I love my wife."

"But does your wife love you?" Chloe countered. "Ask her, Justin. Face her with what I've told you, and see then how guilty she is. She's used you, my darling, just as she used Andrew before you."

"Chloe, I swear that if you're lying to me—"

"I'm not lying. Go to her now if you must, but I'll wait here. You'll come to me today, Justin."

He turned and strode from the room, and Chloe's eyes glittered as he flung the curricle away from the house. A smile played upon her lips, and she raised her hand to her mouth. It was the hand with which she'd just touched him. She kissed her fingertips, as if she were kissing Justin himself.

Justin remembered little of the drive back to St. James's Square. The lamplighters were beginning their work, and the sky was leaden—a fitting background to the white-hot emotions that gripped him. Jealousy was followed by pain, disbelief by devastation. All he could think of was Rowena and Kemp together in her bed at Melcombe Manor. Chloe was capable of lying to get her own way, but this time he feared there might be an element of truth in what she said. There was too much smoke for there not to be a little flame somewhere.

The afternoon light had gone completely as the curricle lurched to a halt at his house, and he dashed inside.

"My lord?" A startled footman hurried toward him.

"Has Lady Alderney returned yet?"

"Yes, my lord, she's—" The man didn't finish, for Justin hurried to the staircase.

The footman stared after him. What was going on? First her ladyship arrived back in tears, and now his lordship turned up in a proper fury.

Henry also stared after him. The ghost had woken late after another tedious gargoyle night and had stirred himself to follow Rowena to the bedroom when she'd rushed past his frame, sobbing. He'd seen how distraught she was as she flung herself on the bed and hid her face in the pillow. The phantom had hovered concernedly around her. He would have considered speaking to her, except he was sure such a shock would make matters even worse when she suffered in such a pitiable state.

Now he floated down from his frame to follow Justin. A denouement of sorts was evidently about to take place, and he meant to be there. He flew swiftly up the stairs and reached the bedroom door just as Justin flung it open without warning and strode inside.

The bedroom was unlit and the curtains undrawn so the fire was reflected in the dark windows. Candlelight from the passage fell in a bright shaft over the bed, where Rowena still lay facedown. The top hat she'd worn for riding lay discarded on the coverlet, and her hair was disheveled as she slowly sat up, bracing herself for what was going to be the most distressing confrontation of her life. Her face was hot and her eyes red from crying, but her sobs died away as she looked at him. Her foolish conduct in the park had evidently reached him, but she felt equally let down by his silence over his affair with Chloe. From somewhere she summoned a steely self-control and stood to face him.

He closed the door, and the room was immediately plunged into a darkness broken only by the glow of the fire. "I believe you have something to tell me about a meeting with Andrew Kemp," he said levelly, his tone belying the chaos he felt within.

"It wasn't a meeting, not in the way you seem to think," she replied. How could he point so pious a finger at her when he wasn't without sin himself?

"What then, if not a meeting?"

"I . . . I realize I should have told you about him before now." Her voice trailed away ratherly bitterly. She was innocent of everything except having remained silent, but he'd remained silent about something of which he was very guilty indeed.

But Justin misread her silence, seeing it as an indication of guilt. It was true! He was shaken to the core. He'd been so sure of her, so content that against all the odds theirs was a perfect match. "Yes, madam, you should indeed have mentioned him before now," he breathed.

"He doesn't mean anything to me, truly he doesn't," she said quickly.

"Doesn't he? That's not what I've been hearing. Were you or were you not speaking to him in the park?"

"Yes."

"And was he or was he not heard to speak in a rather overfond manner?"

She couldn't reply. Chloe had indeed been swift to tell him everything!

He waited for a moment, but she remained silent, and so he continued. "And yesterday, outside the Hanover Square rooms?" He didn't need to hear her reply, for guilt flickered around her like a flame, and he burned in the heat.

"Yes, outside the rooms as well," she confirmed, turning to look at him through a haze of unshed tears. The questions he'd asked and the responses she'd been obliged to give conspired to condemn her. But she was innocent!

He kept a grip on his emotions, but only just. "It hasn't only been here in London, has it? It went on at Melcombe before then."

"You know I knew him then." She didn't meet his eyes, for she could feel Andrew's groping hands upon her helpless body and taste his mouth as he forced it cruelly over hers. A wave of nausea swept through her, and she began to shiver.

Justin was resigned to her guilt. "You not only knew him in the modern sense, but in the biblical sense. Is that not so?"

"No!" she cried, her eyes flying reproachfully to his face.

"Do you deny the time he spent in your bed on the day I proposed to you?" he challenged coldly.

She was stunned. "Who told you that?" she whispered, but even as she asked she knew the answer. Chloe may not be Andrew's mistress, but only a fool could not have realized by now that she was well acquainted with him. If Chloe had told Justin, which seemed certain, then she could only have heard it from Andrew himself. And it wasn't likely the truth would be transmitted to Justin; no, it would be a twisted version, with Rowena Melcombe cast in the role of wanton seductress.

"I learned it from Lady Westcote," he said.

"Ah, yes, from Lady Westcote," she replied scathingly. "And where did she tell you? At the discreet address in York Street? Was it before or after you made love to her?"

He was caught off guard, for it hadn't occurred to him she'd know about Chloe.

She gave a scornful laugh. "It seems you thought yourself undetected, sir. Undetected, and therefore at liberty to heap blame solely upon me. But let me advise you that although your accusations about my fidelity are without foundation, the same quite clearly cannot be said of you. Lady Westcote was your mistress before I met you, and she still is now. You go to York Street for your meetings, and I don't doubt you've just come from there. So much for your attitudinizing as the outraged, betrayed husband! What a hypocrite you are, to be sure!"

He was thrown on the defensive and so struck out. "Yes, Lady Westcote is my mistress, and yes, I've just come from York Street, but that has no bearing on this!"

Her heart shattered into a thousand fragments, but she held her head high. "No? Is the moral high ground the sole preserve of the male of the species? Are you saying it's perfectly in order for you to break your vows with a mistress?"

He couldn't help the contemptuously accusing words that fell from his angry lips. "The point of it is discretion, madam, and you've shown none at all. If it were not bad enough that you're seeing Kemp, you have to conduct your meetings in front of witnesses! I will not be laughed at for a fool, and wish now I'd listened when you warned me you'd let me down in society!"

She flinched, and when she replied, her voice was low and trembling. "It seems that you're only concerned with your reputation, sir. That I haven't been unfaithful is evidently of no consequence. I hadn't realized what a shallow man you are, shallow and selfish. Blame me if it makes you feel any better, but you do so without justification. I haven't been conducting a liaison with Andrew Kemp, and if he was in my bed at Melcombe . . ." She paused, trying to summon the strength to tell him exactly what had happened that terrible evening. But the words wouldn't come; she couldn't give voice to the horror of the assault.

Something snapped in Justin then, and he moved closer to her. "So you admit he was in your bed. Many a thing I could forgive, but not that! Sweet Jesus, and to think I mistook your enthusiasm for love! I should have known you weren't the little innocent you pretended to be. You were far too knowing, weren't you, Rowena? And you were knowing because you'd been rutting with Kemp and God alone knows who else before him!"

She struck his face, leaving weals on his cheek. She'd have struck him again had he not caught her wrist.

"Enough, madam," he breathed before disdainfully releasing her.

He slammed the door as he left.

Chapter 36

Fresh tears stung Rowena's eyes as she stared after him. "Oh, Justin," she whispered, then hid her face in her hands. She didn't make a sound as she wept. The wonderful dream had slipped through her fingers and shattered around her. Nothing was left.

Henry hovered close by. He was filled with disquiet and acutely sensitive to the powerful emotions in the room. They swirled so conflictingly through him, they obscured the facts. Both parties seemed equally hurt and accusing, neither admitting or denying absolutely everything. But he could tell a huge misunderstanding was taking place. He wished he knew what it was, but he didn't, and for the first time in his ghostly existence he felt unequal to the situation.

He was out of his depth and wished he had Margaret to consult with. *She'd* know what to do now; she'd always been very astute about such things. He was master when it came to gruesome hauntings, gargoyle hunting, or simply wreaking spectral havoc, but he was useless where matters of love were concerned. With a heavy heart he drifted from the room and along the passage to the landing. It would be helpful to observe Justin now that he was on his own, but where was he? As the ghost hesitated at the top of the staircase, a gentleman's cane rapped at the front door.

It was George. "Will you tell Lord Alderney I've called?" he said to the footman who admitted him.

"Yes, sir." The footman took his things and then hurried away to the library.

Henry glided curiously down, for George was plainly ill at ease about something, and from the way he glanced toward the library door, he didn't relish seeing Justin.

After a moment the footman returned. "If you will come this way, sir."

George crossed the hall, and Henry went with him.

Justin stood by the fireplace, an almost empty glass of cognac in his hand. "Yes, George?" he inquired with unaccustomed brevity.

George went to the decanter and poured himself a generous measure before facing him. "I don't need to ask if you've heard about the, er, incident in the park."

"That, and everything else."

"Everything else?"

Justin nodded. "It seems my wife and Kemp have been, and probably still are, lovers. She married me simply and solely to save her precious Melcombe."

George drank the cognac in one. "I'm sorry, Justin. I really don't know what to say, except I'd never have believed it of Rowena."

"Nor I," Justin replied with a dry laugh.

"What do you intend to do about Kemp?"

"Do?"

"You're surely not going to let this pass unchallenged, are you?"

Justin swirled his glass. "Yes, I am," he murmured.

George was taken aback. "But, he's put horns on you, man!"

"The lady would appear to have put horns on both of us, and I have no intention of challenging anyone for her mythical honor. I'll say this, though—I wish to God I'd left him to rot at the roadside instead of taking him to a doctor," Justin answered, going to pick up the decanter, but then he put both it and his glass down. "Damn it, now isn't the time to drown my sorrows," he muttered, leaning both hands on the table and bowing his head.

"Justin—"

"Look, George, I appreciate your coming here like this, but I'm not exactly pleasant company at the moment."

"That's why I've come. When Em told me what had happened—"

"I know you and Emily are probably the only ones in town who won't be relaying this with relish," Justin interrupted, giving him a quick smile.

"You wrong a number of people, Justin, for there are many who'll be sad about it."

"And just as many who'll be queueing to say they could have told me Rowena was a misalliance."

George was commiserative. "For what it's worth, I thought you'd found true happiness."

"Happiness?" Justin gave a derisive laugh and filled his glass again. "Perhaps I'll descend into my cups after all," he muttered.

"Then at least allow me to accompany you," George said, holding out his own glass.

"I'm quite capable of unaided inebriation."

"Never get drunk alone, dear boy. Didn't Nanny ever tell you that?" George smiled.

"Nanny warned me never to tangle with clever adventuresses, and what did I do? I married one!" Justin replied, returning the refilled glass.

"I still can't see Rowena as an adventuress."

"Well, she is." Justin drew a long breath. "Melcombe means everything to her," he said softly.

"Eh?"

"She said it the first time we met. Well, the first earthly time. Oh, Halloween, where is thy sting?" Justin murmured.

George was perplexed. "What in God's name are you talking about?"

"Oh, nothing." Justin stood by the fire, pushing a log more firmly into place with his boot.

"What are you going to do now?" George asked after a moment.

"Do?"

"About Rowena."

"I don't know."

"I suppose she's not really a suitable future marchioness," George admitted reluctantly.

"And maybe I'm not a suitable future marquess," Justin replied scathingly.

"You have no choice, you were born to it."

"Yes, but was I also born to be an unfaithful husband?"

"Unfaithful?" George stared at him. "You've been seeing Chloe?"

"No, but I mean to now."

"Justin—"

"George, my damned male pride has been wounded. I was so busy wrestling with my conscience over Chloe, I couldn't see what was happening under my own nose. Rowena and Kemp made love on the very day I proposed, did you know that?"

George's lips parted. "No, I didn't."

"Well, you know now, and before you start on again about calling him out, or whatever it is you have in mind, I understand he is as used as me." Justin paused and then looked at him. "Do you remember saying you could almost believe in witchcraft and the supernatural at Melcombe?"

"Yes."

"Well, right now, so do I."

"That's the cognac talking," George said uncomfortably.

"Probably." But Justin looked away, remembering Halloween, his strange erotic dream, and then the sweet joy of actually holding Rowena in the flesh and kissing her mouth . . . Witchcraft? If it was, then he'd welcomed such sweet sorcery.

George studied him. "Justin, do you really mean to take up with Chloe again?"

"Right now? Yes."

"It would be a mistake."

Justin smiled. "I know, but then what have I got to lose now? I may as well enjoy my mistress's bed."

"That's cynical, even for you, but it's not what I meant. Keeping Chloe as your mistress would be a mistake because I've heard Westcote means to divorce her and marry Lady Jane."

"I find that hard to believe."

"My source is impeccable, Justin. Westcote's prepared to move heaven and earth in order to have his way, and that means proving Chloe's adultery, his own frequent vow breaking being beside the point, if you see what I mean. So, if you wish to be named in a scandalous case, then go ahead, but don't say you weren't warned."

Henry perched on the pelmet above them, listening with intense interest. So Westcote wanted to be rid of his wife, did he? What a useful snippet of information.

Justin didn't want to know about Lord Westcote's intentions. "You've said your piece, George, and now I'd prefer to be on my own."

"As you wish."

Realizing how ungrateful he sounded, Justin quickly reached over to place his hand on his friend's shoulder. "But I do appreciate your call."

George smiled, but evidently hadn't quite finished, "Justin, I—"

Justin interrupted a little wearily. "I've taken your point about Westcote."

"It's Rowena I'm concerned with now. Justin, I don't profess to know the whys and wherefores of all this, but I do know what my instinct tells me. Don't cast her lightly aside, for I still find it difficult to believe she's guilty. I know how it appears, and I know she was foolish to speak to Kemp in the park, but I reserve judgment. You may say you're going to return to Chloe, but it's my guess you still love your wife. If that's so, you'll be a very unhappy man if you reject her because of bruised pride."

"Love can die as swiftly as it finds life," Justin murmured.

"Just pay heed to what I say. Stay away from York Street and Chloe." George put his glass down and left.

Justin went to the window. It was very dark now, and an occasional snowflake drifted idly past on the frozen air. He stared out without seeing anything. His vision was misted, and he was conscious of the unaccustomed sting of tears. But he didn't shed them.

Henry watched from the pelmet. At any other time the wraith would have scorned tears as unmanly, but not now. Justin's unhappiness was palpable, and it reached out to Henry's ghostly heart. The shade pondered what he'd now learned. Justin admitted to George that Chloe had ceased to be his mistress, but out of male vanity pretended the opposite to Rowena. And Rowena admitted that this Kemp person had been in her bed, but she couldn't—or wouldn't—say exactly what had happened. Justin saw this as evidence of guilt, but Henry wasn't so sure. Just what had taken place in Melcombe?

The specter's brows drew together in puzzlement. Something very serious had happened on the night Justin proposed, and it involved Kemp. Henry knew he had to find out what it was. The answer lay at Melcombe, but although he was able to leave his frame at will, he couldn't travel more than fifty miles. And even if Rowena sent him back to Melcombe as at present intended, and he found the truth, he wouldn't be able to return to London to deal out any punishment Kemp was due. Henry's spectral hands clenched with frustration, and again he wished he could talk to Margaret. She'd find inspiration from somewhere, whereas he couldn't think of anything constructive.

Justin downed another large glass of cognac, then turned as a tap came at the door. Hope leapt into his eyes. Was it Rowena? "Yes?" he replied.

But it was only a footman. "Begging your pardon for intruding, my lord, but the curricle is still at the door. It's snowing a little, and the groom is concerned for the horses. Will you be requiring it again today?"

Disappointment ran soberingly through Justin. "No, I won't require it."

"My lord." The footman began to withdraw, but Justin spoke again.

"Wait a moment. Yes, I do need the curricle."

"My lord."

"I'm leaving now, and should she inquire, you may inform her ladyship I won't be back tonight. I'll be at York Street if I'm required urgently, but that is something you may *not* inform her ladyship."

The footman's face gave nothing away as he bowed. "Very well, my lord."

Henry fluttered alertly down from the pelmet. York Street? He was going to his mistress?

Justin strode past the footman, snatching up his hat and gloves in the hall, then going out into the snowy night. Henry glided out, too, and sat next to him as he urged the team out of the square.

Chapter 37

Rowena heard the curricle leave and from the window watched it drive from the square toward Pall Mall. Where was he going? To Chloe? Was this to be Lady Alderney's punishment for having

caused a scandal? It didn't matter to him that his wife was the innocent victim; he preferred to salve his conscience by pointing to
her lack of discretion.

Tears shone in her eyes as she turned from the window, but
then she felt a surge of strength. Her only crime was naivety, and
she wouldn't endure unjust punishment for that! She'd been bru-
tally attacked and threatened by Andrew Kemp, and now Justin
accused her of welcoming those despicable attentions. It wasn't to
be tolerated, especially not from an adulterous husband who admitted to having a mistress!

She struggled to regain her composure. She'd ascertain whether
Justin had gone to Chloe and then decide what to do, for the
empty life stretching before her was too dreadful to contemplate.
Justin was everything to her, but she had her pride and dignity. If
he meant to withdraw his kindness and show her no affection at
all, then she would leave rather than endure such unhappy humiliation.

She rang the bell and then held some candles to the fire so the
room was well lit when her maid came in. The girl's manner told
her the terrible argument between Lord and Lady Alderney was
all the talk below stairs.

"Ann, I wish you to tell me something," Rowena said, facing
her.

"My lady?"

"Where has Lord Alderney gone?"

The maid lowered her eyes uncomfortably. "I . . . I don't know,
my lady."

"You never were any good at fibbing," Rowena murmured.
"He's gone to York Street, hasn't he?"

The maid looked reluctantly at her. "Yes, my lady, but he said
you weren't to be told. And . . ." Ann glanced away again.

"Yes?"

"And he left word he wouldn't return here tonight, my lady."

"Which makes it all very clear, does it not?"

Ann remained unhappily silent.

"Very well," Rowena declared with brisk decision. "You and I
are going to return to Melcombe. We'll leave tonight."

The maid's eyes widened. "Tonight?"

"Yes."

"But it's dangerous to travel after dark!"

"We can reach the Golden Cross at Hounslow. That's the first
stage out of London, isn't it?"

"Yes, but—"

"My mind is made up. I won't spend another night here."

"But there's no one at Melcombe, my lady. Mrs. Melcombe is in Bath with Lady Beaminster, and the young masters are either still there with her or have returned to Eton."

"I'm aware of that, but it makes no difference. You're to send a footman to secure a post-chaise for me. I want it here in about an hour's time, and when it arrives, I require you to load it with all my things, *my* things, not anything I've been given since my marriage."

Ann was too overwhelmed to speak.

"I also need the town carriage brought to the door in a few minutes' time."

"The town carriage, my lady?"

"Yes, for I intend to visit York Street."

Ann was aghast. "You can't do that, my lady!"

"No? I think I can do it very well. If I see him with her, then it will be easier to leave him."

"Please don't go."

"I have to." Rowena went to the wardrobe and selected the only gown that remained from Melcombe. It was the one she'd worn the day Justin proposed to her.

Ann came to assist her out of Emily's riding habit, but Rowena shook her head. "I'll do it myself; you attend to my instructions."

"Very well, my lady." The maid went to the door, then turned to look at her. "I . . . I'm so sorry this has happened, my lady," she said quietly and then went out.

"So am I, Ann, so am I," Rowena murmured, inhaling the faint trace of lavender that clung to the gown from the muslin bags in her wardrobe at Melcombe. She was going home. And it was a home saved from debt by her bitter experience of marriage. Justin had told her Melcombe was secure now, no matter what happened, and no doubt from now on he'd regard such an expense as worthwhile if it relieved him of a wife whose notorious conduct in St. James's Park had led to his exclusion from Almack's!

Justin stood by the fireplace at York Street, one booted foot on the fender, one hand leaning on the mantelshelf. Another generous glass of cognac in his other hand, the firelight flickered over him as he gazed silently into the flames. His shirt was undone and his crumpled neckcloth hung loose. His coat lay untidily over a chair.

Chloe didn't know quite how to gauge his mood. The edge had gone from the joy she'd felt when he'd arrived, for he was remote, as if an invisible wall had been raised between them. It wasn't like him to drink such large measures of cognac, or so many. It would be wrong to say he was in his cups, but neither was he entirely sober.

Henry watched as well, having positioned himself in the corner near the door. His lips pursed thoughtfully, and his ghostly fingers drummed upon the arm of the chair. For all his talk, bedding Lady Westcote didn't appear to be Alderney's immediate concern. As for the mistress, she was clearly perplexed as to how to seduce her lover back into her arms. Long may she continue to be perplexed, for the last thing the ghost wanted was her success. Whatever lay at the core of this cataclysmic falling out between husband and wife, Henry felt the Alderney marriage wasn't yet lost beyond redemption. But it would be lost if Justin turned to his mistress.

The wraith knew his spectral powers could be used to prevent Chloe's achieving her purpose now, but he wanted Justin to realize it was wrong to stay here. Henry was surprised at himself, for restraint wasn't usually part of his inventory. Had all this concerned anyone other than a member of the Melcombe family, retribution would have been forthcoming before now. But Justin was Rowena's husband, and she clearly still loved him. For that reason, and that reason alone, Henry stayed his hand.

The concerned spirit gazed intently at Justin, willing him to finish the cognac and go, but it was replenished.

Chloe put a slender hand upon the glass. "You don't need any more," she said softly.

"I know, but it's helping."

"Is it? Can you honestly tell me you feel any less pain now than you did when you poured the first one?"

He put the glass down. "You're right, of course," he murmured.

"Come to bed," she whispered, slipping her arms around him.

But he shook his head, suddenly knowing he could never make love to her again. He no longer felt the same fierce desire for her that had seared him at the beginning of their liaison, and now her husband was looking for divorce, he knew it was wrong to put her in such a position. It had been different when she and Westcote had been content to disregard each other's liaisons.

She ignored the shake of his head and reached up to kiss him, but he stopped her. "No, Chloe. Believe me, I'm thinking of you as much as myself. If I loved you, it would be different, but we both know I don't. I've desired you, but that's hardly the same thing, and it's certainly not worth the risk you would be taking now."

"Risk?"

"You must know of Westcote's devotion to Lady Jane Pankhurst."

"She's a passing fancy, that's all."

"I think not. He's looking for evidence in order to divorce you."

"Westcote will never divorce me," she replied scornfully.

"I'm telling you only what I've been told."

"I'd risk everything for you," she whispered. Her arms still around him, she pressed closer, her body molding voluptuously to his.

"You play the siren so well, Chloe," he murmured, holding her for a moment.

Henry sat forward urgently. Resist, damn it! Don't give in to your base male urges!

The ghost need not have worried, for Justin was determined not to succumb. He tried to move away from her, but she clung to him.

"Justin, you came here to be tempted, did you not?" she breathed, putting her lips to the pulse at his throat. She tasted his warmth, her body alive to him, but she couldn't help knowing he wasn't responding. She moved tactfully away then, affecting not to have noticed anything amiss. "I . . . I was thinking of staying at Clanwood for a while," she said lightly.

Henry sat back with relief as the immediate danger was temporarily averted.

"Clanwood?" Justin looked at her.

She gave him a reproachful look. "Surely, you haven't forgotten my ancestral home? Mine, not Westcote's; he never comes there," she stressed.

"Ah, yes. I wasn't thinking," he replied absently.

"Well, I was, to the extent of asking you to come with me." She was at her most fascinating, caressing him with the warmth in her eyes and the softness in her tone.

He smiled, but shook his head. "No, Chloe."

"Why not?"

"I've already explained why not, and apart from that I've no intention of leaving London now because it will be seen as running away. My marriage is probably already spoken of as a laughable misalliance, but I won't have it said I can't face the gossip."

"Perhaps you'd appear not to be giving a damn," she suggested slyly.

"Leave it, Chloe, for I won't change my mind."

His firmness stung her a little. "Dear Rowena certainly has you in her palm, doesn't she?"

"She's my wife," he replied shortly.

Jealousy flitted keenly over her. "She isn't worth it, Justin. She married you to save her precious home, and she's been dallying with Andrew Kemp even though you've only been married for a month or so. As to having had him in her bed on the very day you—"

"That's enough, Chloe!"

"You have to face it, Justin—she's made a fool of you!"

"And I made a fool of her by saying nothing about you," he replied, turning away and running his fingers through his hair.

"Is that so blameworthy?" she asked, anxious to allay his conscience. "You haven't been with me since your marriage, but she's been encouraging Kemp." She put her arms around him from behind, resting her cheek against his shoulder. "I love you, Justin; you mean everything to me."

He gave a short laugh. "Dear God, those words again!"

"Again?"

"It doesn't matter." He disengaged her arms and flung himself on the sofa.

"Must I beg for your favors, my lord?" she breathed, injecting the huskiness into her voice that always aroused him in the past.

"Perhaps my favors aren't worth begging for tonight, Chloe," he murmured, leaning his head back and closing his eyes. He wished he hadn't taken so much cognac, for it was making him a little drowsy. He felt incapable of responding to Chloe, even though, as she'd pointed out, that was why he'd come here. He'd wanted to pay his wife back in kind, to bed his mistress just as Rowena had been bedded by Kemp. Wretchedness welled up inside him. Rowena and Kemp. He couldn't bear to think of anyone else's hands touching her, defiling her. No act of love had ever meant as much to him as his wedding night. The pleasure, the tenderness, the exquisite consummation, and the joy all had combined to affect him as never before. To lie with Rowena was to know ecstasy. To be inside her, enveloped by her warmth, was to be in heaven itself.

Chloe undid the front of her low-cut bodice. "Your favors will always be worth begging for, my lord," she murmured, sinking to her knees as her rose-tipped breasts were revealed. Then she put her hands upon his thighs, her fingers spread to caress him.

His thoughts were still of Rowena, and he made no move to stop her.

Henry felt uncomfortable as he watched. Alderney was weakening, and the woman was accomplished at her art, more accomplished than any woman should be! The ghost was so intent upon the scene on the sofa that he didn't hear the carriage draw up in the street outside, nor was he aware of Rowena entering quietly through the unlocked outer door without announcing her arrival. No one realized she was looking into the drawing room, not even Henry, for the open door stood between her and his corner.

Chloe was encouraged by Justin's quiescence and knelt up to slip her knowing fingertips toward the buttons of his breeches. It was then she saw Rowena's reflection in a wall mirror. She was startled, but gave no sign of it. So Lady Alderney had followed her husband, had she? Well, let her see something to make her journey worthwhile! Reaching over so that her exposed breasts pressed against him, she kissed him lingeringly on the mouth.

His eyes were still closed, and it was Rowena's lips he felt. Her name wept silently through him, and when Chloe's tongue pushed exploringly into his mouth, he held her close, his fingers winding in her hair as he returned the kiss. *Rowena, oh, Rowena, my love . . .*

Rowena was untouched by emotion as she watched. Inevitability's cold cloak settled over her. What she was seeing now would continue to take place whether or not she stayed. But she wouldn't stay, not with a husband who cruelly put his vanity and mistress before his wife and the truth.

Turning, she left as silently as she'd come. She felt the icy touch of snowflakes against her face as she hurried back to the carriage waiting in the street.

Chapter 38

But as Rowena drove away from York Street, sanity swept over Justin as he realized it wasn't his wife he caressed. The spell snapped, and he was suddenly sober. He pushed Chloe gently but firmly away and then got up to put on his coat.

She was seized with dismay. "You're leaving?"

"Yes."

"No!" she cried, trying to cling to him.

"I shouldn't have come in the first place." He put his hand to her cheek. "Forgive me, Chloe, but I can't stay with you."

Henry, who still knew nothing of Rowena's brief presence, smiled with relief. That was more like it! Alderney was redeeming himself at last.

Chloe was choked with disappointment. "Can't? Or won't?" she said bitterly, getting up to retie her bodice with shaking hands.

"As I said, I shouldn't have come here. It wasn't fair to use you."

"But I want to be used!" she cried. "Don't you understand? I'm prepared to take you on *any* terms!"

"Please, Chloe, don't say anything more," he said quietly as he donned the coat.

"You're going back to her?" The question was raw.

Henry held his breath. Say yes, damn it!

"Not tonight. Too much was said, and I need a clear head. I'll go to White's."

"But you *are* going back to her?"

Justin didn't reply, but his reticence was only too indicative of his intentions. For a moment she considered telling him his wife had been there a moment before, but almost immediately she decided against it. If he knew Rowena had just been here, he'd probably go straight after her, and there'd be a joyful reunion. No, better to say nothing, and to let him go to his club. That way he'd still have spent the night away from St. James's Square, and his precious wife would draw her own conclusion!

He bent his head to kiss her cheek. "Good-bye, Chloe," he murmured and then left her.

Her eyes glittering bitterly, she picked up a little bronze figurine and hurled it at the mirror. The glass shattered and cascaded over the floor. Resentment and frustration tightened her heart, but then a thin smile appeared on her lips. She wouldn't spend the night alone! There was still Andrew!

She hurried from the room, calling for the maid who always remained discreetly out of sight. "Jones?"

"Milady?" The maid came quickly.

"I want someone to go to Mr. Kemp's lodgings in Conduit Street to tell him to come here tonight, not Westcote House."

The maid curtsied and hurried away.

Chloe went back into the drawing room and picked up Justin's empty glass. Another thin smile touched her lips as she turned it upside down. Tonight she'd lie with the man who'd tried to take

Rowena Melcombe by force, and she'd do it in the bed she'd shared so often with Justin. She'd satisfy Andrew's every desire, and she'd revel in the knowledge that he was the one man Justin should hate above all others, the man whose life he'd saved, but who'd have been left to perish if the truth had been known.

Henry hovered nearby. He was conscious of the waves of hatred and spite emanating from her, and his wraith's eyes were cold as he studied her. She wasn't merely a woman scorned; she was an unprincipled, dangerously calculating bitch who'd stoop to anything to get what she wanted. He could tell she knew far more than she'd admitted to Justin, and that a great deal of what she had said was untrue. It all centered upon Kemp, whose accomplice she had to be. She most probably knew what had happened in Melcombe!

For a moment the shade was on the point of making his awesome presence felt, but again he stayed his hand. All in good time. Lady Westcote would be punished, but the scale of her punishment must reflect the extent of her crime. As soon as he found out all there was to know, the time would be right to wreak vengeance upon this beautiful but deadly woman.

Contenting himself with breathing coldly over her and making her shiver, he glided away into the night, intending to return to his frame in St. James's Square. He didn't know it, but he was about to be summoned away by the Powers-That-Be, and it would be dawn before his task was finished. By then his precious frame would be on its way to Melcombe with Rowena.

As Justin drove to White's and Henry glided up into the snowy darkness above York Street, Rowena had almost reached St. James's Square. She felt hollow inside, leaving only the shell of the happy bride who'd come to London only a day or so ago. A day or so? It might as well have been a lifetime.

She leaned her head back against the upholstery. Her heart beat slowly, its strength drained by unhappiness. She couldn't even cry anymore; she'd gone beyond tears. Justin's name sounded distantly in her head, reminding her of the joy she'd lost and longed for still. But she wouldn't fight, not when he'd made it so clear he held her in contempt.

The London streets swept past in a blur of noise and lights, but at last she saw the frozen lake and the square. The post-chaise she'd ordered waited outside the house, and the yellow-coated postboy tended the blanketed horses as her carriage drew up. She alighted, gathering her cloak around her as Ann hurried out to her.

The hopeful maid searched her mistress's eyes, but the hope died as she saw nothing had changed. "We're still leaving, my lady?"

"Yes, Ann, we're still leaving."

"Everything's ready, as you instructed."

"Thank you, Ann. Did you remember Henry Melcombe's portrait?"

"I . . . I wasn't sure whether to bring it or not, my lady," the maid confessed. "You said not to pack anything you didn't have before."

"I know, but I doubt if Lord Alderney will wish to keep a Melcombe portrait," Rowena murmured. "Have it brought out."

"My lady." The maid hurried away again, and Rowena followed her into the house.

She moved from room to room, remembering how she'd been so briefly happy in them all. The bedroom was last, and she couldn't bring herself to look at the bed as she went to the dressing table and took off her wedding ring. The inscription seemed to mock her. *If in love thou constant be, My heart shall never part from thee.* How ironic Justin should choose such words. She'd been constant, but he hadn't. Placing the ring on the dressing table, she walked swiftly from the room.

She emerged from the house to find two footmen carefully loading Henry's portrait into the chaise boot. Ann was waiting and followed her into the vehicle. Rowena didn't look back as they drew away. It left the square and passed along King Street, where the hallowed portals of Almack's stood on the southern side. She stared steadfastly at the seat opposite.

Soon the chaise was bowling out of London, coming up to a spanking pace along the highway to the west. Its lamps cut through the darkness, shining on the snowflakes that still fluttered aimlessly in the air, and the postboy urged his team to greater effort. He and his kind were not known for their caution and always drove wildly. The chaise swayed alarmingly, and Ann had to cling nervously to the handgrip, but Rowena was oblivious.

London slipped farther and farther behind, and the January night closed coldly over the open highway as Lady Alderney left her husband to his mistress.

And left Henry Melcombe's as yet unaware ghost without his frame. The phantom was now in great danger, for the frame was vital to his existence. He was free to move about as he pleased, provided he and his frame were never more than fifty miles apart. If that happened, disaster would befall him. Ghosts who haunted their portraits could not haunt anything else for long. They faded slowly and wretchedly away and were lost forever in the endless realms of eternity.

Rowena's chaise had still been waiting to leave when Henry first started to glide back to St. James's Square, but then he felt the familiar tingling sensations preceding a message from the Powers. Their communications simply came over him, and he knew exactly what was required. This was what happened now. He realized his presence was required at Westminster Abbey, where a pitched battle was in progress between local gargoyles and a raiding party from Canterbury. With a sigh he turned back. Plague take gargoyles! Thames mud evidently hadn't proved a sufficient deterrent, so he'd have to be even more firm! He flew swiftly away from St. James's Square.

It was a bloody conflict, with shrieking, squealing, and vicious clawing, but humans were unaware of the noise and turmoil in the night sky over London. Dogs howled and barked, however, and carriage horses refused if they were urged anywhere near the scene. The stench of brimstone was all around as Henry gave a terrible bellow and swooped toward them. Instant silence fell as reptilian heads turned, then with frightened squeaks the gargoyles scattered, some back to the abbey, the rest toward the river and their distant lair in Kent.

Henry wasn't fool enough to think they'd go all the way back to Canterbury unless pursued. No, they'd be up to all sorts of mischief, and so he was obliged to give chase. Canterbury was on his fifty-mile limit, but he didn't know that it was now beyond that because Rowena had taken his frame with her.

He set off after the fleeing gargoyles and was still well short of Canterbury when he felt the sharp tug of his frame. Realization swept alarmingly through him, and he turned to fly back to London as quickly as he could.

Chapter 39

Dawn had long since broken when the ghost arrived wearily back in the capital. The snow had stopped falling, but now lay more thickly on the ground, although the roads were still clear. He was very tired, but more relaxed now, for there was no longer any pull from his frame, and he thought he must have imagined there ever had been.

At last he flew to St. James's Square, but as he entered the house, he soon found his frame had gone. So he hadn't been mistaken! He swept from room to room, just in case it had been re-hung elsewhere, but there wasn't any sign of it. Nor was there any sign of Rowena! He inspected the bedroom, and when he saw the wedding ring on the dressing table, he knew she'd gone back to Melcombe, taking his frame with her. He'd have to follow, not only to stay with his frame, but also to try to persuade her she was wrong to leave. The time had come to speak to her again.

His feelings were mixed as he hovered there, for although he knew he could at last return to Margaret, he was also dismayed that Rowena had decided to abandon her marriage. He was uncertain what to do, but then the door opened and two maids came in to tend the fire.

"Wot d'you reckon 'is lordship will do, eh?" one of them asked as they knelt by the fireplace.

"Gawd knows. I didn't think 'e'd go back to that Lady Westcote, but 'e did. Talk about not wasting time! 'Ow long was 'e been back in town? Two days? Seems 'is new wife couldn't have pleased 'im much." The second maid grinned and winked.

The first one sat back on her heels. "Well, no one expected the match in the first place, so I s'pose no one'll be surprised she's already gone back where she came from."

"Maybe 'e'll go after 'er," her companion suggested.

"You reckon?"

"Well, 'e might. She ain't gone far yet, only to the Golden Cross in 'Ounslow."

Henry relaxed a little on learning this. Hounslow wasn't very far away, so his frame was well within reach.

The first maid spoke again. "I know she ain't gone far yet, but them yellow bounders don't hang around," she reminded her friend.

"If 'is lordship wants to catch 'er, 'e will, but that's not to say she'll want 'im to catch her, not after she went to York Street and saw 'im with Lady Westcote," the other girl observed practically.

Henry's spectral heart sank. Rowena had gone to York Street? He couldn't believe it.

Wheels rumbled outside. "Maybe that's 'is lordship now," the first maid said, hurrying to the window.

Henry followed and looked down at the town carriage drawn up at the curb. It wasn't Justin, who'd been driving his curricle. The ghost's brows drew together as the coachman climbed down to open the vehicle's gleaming door. A dandified gentleman alighted. Henry stared blankly at him. Who was this?

The maid supplied the answer when she glanced back at her friend. "It's that Mr. Jermyn, the one wot called last night wanting to speak so urgently to 'is lordship. 'E said 'e'd call back this morning, but I didn't reckon it'd be this early. Wonder wot 'e wants?"

Henry watched the gentleman below pause to flex his fingers in his gloves. There was something unpleasantly anticipatory about the fellow's smile, the ghost thought, deciding to see what the call was about. He had time yet before he needed to reach his frame. He glided from the room down to the entrance hall just as Jack Jermyn's cane sounded at the door.

The footman who answered was so unprepared for such an early caller he was still straightening his wig and smoothing his hastily donned coat. He was taken aback to see Jack standing there.

"Mr. Jermyn? I . . . I fear his lordship still isn't here."

"I'll wait." Jack stepped into the hall, holding out his cane for the man to take.

"But we've no idea how long he'll be," the footman explained.

"I'll wait," Jack repeated, removing his hat and gloves and pushing them into the man's hands as well.

"As you wish, sir." The footman didn't know what else to do, for he could hardly eject a gentleman by force.

Jack toyed with his cuff. "Is Lady Alderney at home?" he asked suddenly.

"No, sir."

"I thought not. She left yesterday, did she not?"

"I, er, I believe so," the footman confirmed awkwardly, not knowing what else to say.

Jack smiled a little. When he'd come to see Alderney the
evening before, he'd seen the post-chaise being loaded. He'd lingered out of sight nearby and seen Rowena return in the town carriage before leaving in the chaise. She hadn't gone to a dinner
appointment, not with all that luggage!

He nodded toward a nearby door. "That's the library, is it not?"

"Yes, sir."

"I'll wait there."

"Sir."

Henry followed as Jack strolled to the door and went inside. A
maid was just finishing the fire, and she hastily completed the
task and left with the bucket of ashes. New flames crackled and
spat behind the wire guard, and light flickered over the shelves of
gilt-embossed volumes. The window overlooked the garden behind the house, and the morning sun sparkled on the covering of
snow.

Jack went straight to the decanter to pour himself some cognac.
It was never too early in the morning for him; indeed liquor frequently replaced breakfast at the start of his day. Taking a large
mouthful, he savored the smooth but fiery taste and then swallowed it with audible relish. He was looking forward to informing
Alderney about Chloe's conspiracy with Kemp. He would have
relayed the tale yesterday had he been able to run his quarry to
ground. But it was morning now, and soon his quarry would come
to him.

Henry took his place on the pelmet, watching as Jack made
himself comfortable in a leather armchair by the fire and stretched
his legs out as if he was in his own house. What was this fellow
up to, the ghost wondered? He had the look of a cat at the cream.
Henry's spectral intuition quivered, telling him this was to do
with Rowena.

Rowena herself was at that moment still asleep at the busy
Golden Cross Inn. Hounslow was a very prosperous town on the
route west and was a place of inns, stables, and smithies right on
the very edge of Hounslow Heath, an expanse of open land that
stretched for five bleak miles beyond the town. The heath was notorious for highwaymen and footpads, and only well-armed vehicles dared traverse it after dark, which was why Hounslow itself
boasted so many important inns and posting houses.

The Golden Cross was busy throughout the night. Hooves clat-
tered in the yard, wheels rattled, ostlers and waiters shouted, and
ticket office bells rang out at regular intervals. Rowena's room

was on the third floor, and in her dreams the sounds of the inn became the merriment around the Halloween bonfire at Melcombe.
She was back in her bedroom at the manor house, and turnip
lanterns glowed on the window sill. The flames in the fireplace
swayed slowly, as if time itself was held in check.

She was naked, with comb and apple in her hand as she stood
before the cheval glass. The gentle firelight moved beguilingly
over her, now shining on her breasts, now casting them in
shadow. A frisson of anticipation passed excitedly through her,
for she was about to make Justin come to her. Her pulse quickened as she raised the apple to her lips and began to draw the
comb slowly through her hair. Suddenly, she was no longer looking into her own eyes in the mirror, but into his. The apple and
comb fell from her fingers, and she turned toward him.

He caught her outstretched hand, drawing her close and pressing her to his warmth. Fresh excitement began to course through
her as his mouth moved over hers. She could feel every firm line
of his body and the delicious sensation of his masculinity rising
needfully toward her. Her lips parted as she drew his tongue into
her mouth, and her body curved richly against him, her breasts
thrusting close so he felt her arousal.

She was lost in the heady mists of desire, her lips aching with
love as she kissed him. His hands moved seductively over her,
and then he held her hips to his, his pulsing virility pressing between her legs. Their passion increased, and she clung to him as
he laid her gently on the bed, standing over her for a moment as
she reached up toward him. Their fingers touched and entwined,
and her breath slipped out on a sigh of love as he came down to
her.

Their lips seared together, seeming almost to fuse with the
flame of their shared desire. She wanted him, wanted him inside
her . . . But just as her trembling body received him, the dream
began to fade. He was vanishing in her arms, becoming ethereal
as she tried desperately to hold him.

"Justin!" she cried out with a sob and was suddenly awake, sitting up in a strange bed, tears wet on her cheeks. She stared
around her. Where was she? For a moment confusion gripped her,
but then she remembered. Oh, how much she remembered.

"My lady?" Her cry awoke Ann on her pallet at the foot of the
bed.

More tears welled from Rowena's eyes, and she hid her face in
her hands, her tangled hair spilling over her shoulders.

The maid scrambled up to hurry to her. "My lady?" she inquired again, putting a tentative hand on her mistress's shaking shoulder.

Rowena struggled to quell the sobs and after a moment managed to collect herself somewhat. "What . . . what time is it?" she asked.

"It's early yet, my lady."

"But it's daylight. I . . . I think we'll continue the journey as quickly as possible. Unless—" A thought occurred to Rowena. "Has there been more snow?"

The maid went to the window and drew the curtains back. "Only a little, my lady. The road is clear."

Rowena threw the bedclothes back. "We'll leave now."

"Very well, my lady."

Rowena went to the window and stared out at the snowy scene behind the inn. The rooftops of Hounslow were coated with white, and beyond the town was the heath, an undulating vista of thickets, gorse, hollows, and streams. She gazed toward it, but with eyes that didn't see. Justin was all around her, and her body yearned for him. But all she saw was the way his arms had embraced Chloe as he kissed her the evening before . . .

Memories of Halloween weren't Rowena's sole preserve at that moment, for the power of love and desire can sometimes match the power of those in the hereafter. It needed no ghost this time to cause Justin to share the dream.

He'd fallen asleep in an armchair in the subscription room at White's. Low male voices murmured at the far end of the candlelit room, where a group of gentlemen were still seated around a gaming table. Outside it was daylight, but to them it was still night, and a fortune rested on the turn of the next card.

His sleep had been dreamless, but suddenly he was with Rowena again. The enchantment of Halloween filled him, and his desire for her was so strong, it ruled him completely. Nothing mattered but being one with her again, of surrendering his very essence to her. He could taste her mouth, feel her warmth, and his whole body seemed to throb as he carried her to the bed. She was so eager, so wanton, and so precious to him. He went down to her, and her thighs parted for him. The sweetness of her body awaited, but as he began to enter her, she began to fade, slipping inexorably away into nothingness.

His eyes flew open, and he sat forward with a gasp. Desire still pounded through him, and he remained where he was for a long moment until the intensity of the feeling began to fade. He ran his fingers through his hair. Dear God above, it had happened again. He'd dreamed the same dream and been denied consummation at the same point . . . He'd also been reminded of just how fierce and compelling a passion he felt for her. No other woman affected him as she did, or aroused him as she did.

"Rowena," he whispered, exhaling slowly and then getting up from the chair. He had to go back to St. James's Square now. He couldn't wait any longer to see her. She was his wife, and he wouldn't surrender her to another. A faint self-mocking smile appeared on his lips. How the mighty had fallen. Here he was, the future Marquess of Exford, one of London's leading gentlemen and a favorite among the ladies, brought to his very knees by a sweet country creature who'd conquered him with a glance. He loved her completely, and if he hadn't fully realized it yesterday, by God he realized it now!

He strode from the room, and his departure wasn't even noted by the group around the gaming table. Indeed, had someone called "Fire!" it was doubtful they'd have glanced up from their cards.

Chapter 40

Henry was still seated upon the pelmet in the library at St. James's Square, and Jack was stretched out comfortably in the armchair. Both felt as if they'd been waiting an unconscionable length of time when Justin's curricle was heard outside and the footman welcomed his master home.

Jack sat forward immediately, and the ghost assembled himself for the imminent meeting.

Justin had noticed he had a caller. "Whose carriage is that outside?" he asked the footman, his tone a little impatient because he was so anxious to see Rowena.

"Mr. Jermyn has called, my lord. He insisted upon waiting in the library."

Justin's irritation was almost tangible. "Very well. Is Lady Alderney—?"

"My lord, I'm afraid her ladyship isn't here," the footman interrupted in some embarrassment. He explained what had happened, then added. "The maids found this in the bedroom," he added.

There was a moment's stunned silence. "Her wedding ring?" Justin breathed, his voice only just carrying to the listeners in the library. Then he recovered slightly. "I, er take it she's gone back to Melcombe?"

"Yes, my lord. She took a chaise and told her maid she'd spend the night at the Golden Cross at Hounslow."

"Have my traveling carriage made ready immediately."

"My lord."

Justin's boots rang on the tiled floor, and then he flung the library doors open. "I haven't much time, so what do you want, Jermyn?" he asked without preamble, not only because he wished to rush after Rowena, but also because there was very little love lost between him and his visitor.

Jack rose swiftly to his feet, noting as he did so that Justin's appearance could only be described as ragged. "Er, good morning, Alderney."

"Well?"

"I understand your wife has left town," Jack remarked.

Justin became still. "And of what concern is that to you?"

"None, except that I believe I know why she's gone."

"I'm not in any mood to play games, Jermyn, so please get to the point." Justin's tone was dangerously quiet.

"I have information you're bound to find interesting. It concerns a conversation between Chloe Westcote and Andrew Kemp."

Henry sat up alertly, and Justin closed the library door and went toward his visitor. "What conversation?"

"I overheard it early in last November and have been out of town since, but I think you should be informed."

"How noble, to be sure," Justin murmured, knowing self-interest was Jack's creed.

"Alderney, those two have been conspiring to discredit your wife."

Justin held his gaze. "Go on," he said softly.

"It seems Kemp is, er, infatuated with Lady Alderney and returned to Melcombe last autumn in order to seduce her. He failed because she'd fallen in love with you, and so he came back here to London to enlist Chloe's help. He still intends to succeed with your wife if he can, and to that end he thinks to drive a wedge between you and her. Forgive me if I'm blunt, but I'm one of the few who happen to know Chloe is your mistress and that she'd do anything to keep you. Lady Alderney is a rival she wishes to dispose of, and so it benefits her to help him."

Justin went to the window, leaning his hands on the sill to stare out. He was ice-cold with fury, but as yet had an iron grip upon himself. He paused for a long moment before speaking, and when he did, his voice was almost too calm. "How can I be sure you're telling the truth?"

"I'd hardly come here with a cock-and-bull story," Jack replied.

"You would, if it was to your advantage, so don't treat me like a fool, Jermyn. I think you'd better tell me exactly why you've chosen to tell me this." Justin turned to face him.

"I haven't got any ulterior motive," Jack replied steadily.

"You swear you overheard Chloe and Kemp discussing a plot against my wife?"

"Yes. They said they'd wait until you and Lady Alderney came to London, then Kemp would compromise her, and Chloe would see to it you heard a suitably damning version of events."

Henry's rage began to gather hotly, but one glaring question remained unanswered. Why hadn't Rowena denied Kemp came to her bed in Melcombe when on Kemp's own apparent admission, he'd failed to seduce her.

Justin's lips were set in a thin line, and his eyes as frozen as the arctic. "Jermyn, if you've uttered so much as a single lie—!" he began.

Jack's nerve faltered, but he held his ground. "I swear it's the truth, I wasn't mistaken in my understanding of their intentions. I don't profess to know if they've done anything yet, but your wife's sudden departure without telling you would suggest they have." He hesitated uncomfortably. "Forgive me, but I couldn't help overhearing when you returned. It's clear you had no idea she was leaving."

Justin turned away again and closed his eyes. Oh, Rowena, how could I have failed you like this?

They both heard another knock at the front door, and then George's voice as he was admitted.

Jack swiftly prepared to play his trump card before George was announced. He knew that once Justin heard what Kemp had done at Melcombe, and that Chloe knew about it, the Countess of Westcote would never again receive so much as a nod from the man she craved so much. "There's more, Alderney, but I shrink from telling you," he said urgently.

Justin turned sharply, detecting the odd note in the other's voice. "Tell me."

"Something happened at Melcombe before your marriage. Kemp forced his physical attentions on your wife. He went to her room to have her whether she would or not, but she struggled, and he failed in his purpose. He admitted it all to Chloe."

Justin stared at him. "Do you swear this is the truth?" he breathed.

"Yes."

Henry was very still. So that was why Rowena had shrunk from explaining what happened! The spirit's rage smoldered, and his eyes became firebright. Sparks of energy scintillated over him as all his powers began to gather. But his surge of bitter energy was invisible to the occupants of the room.

George entered and immediately halted as he saw the thunderous expression on Justin's face. "Good God, what is it?" he asked.

Justin continued to hold Jack's gaze. "Where can I find Kemp?" he demanded.

"He has rooms in Green's Lodging House, Conduit Street."

Justin turned to George. "Will you be my second?"

"Your second?" George stared at him. "What's changed things since we last spoke?"

"Kemp attempted to rape Rowena, and for that I'll kill him! I want you to accompany me to Conduit Street now. He'll either meet me this coming dawn, or I'll put an end to him sooner."

George was alarmed by his white-hot and yet icy fury. "Justin, are you absolutely sure of your facts?"

Jack bowed. "I'm afraid there's no mistake."

Justin looked at George again. "Will you oblige me in this, George?"

"You know I will."

"Thank you."

His jealous mischief done, Jack prepared to leave. "I don't believe there is any further need for my presence," he murmured, turning toward the door, but Justin spoke to him.

"We have unfinished business, Jermyn."

"Unfinished business?" Jack felt a cold finger run down his spine.

"On your own admission, you overheard all this early last November, which means you've kept it to yourself for at least two months."

Jack's unease intensified. "I . . . I told you, I was out of town."

"A man of honor would have conveyed such facts immediately, but you chose to delay. I'm no fool and can put two and two together. You've failed to bed Chloe, and this is your revenge."

Taken by surprise by the accuracy of the deduction, Jack didn't reply.

The thinnest of smiles touched Justin's lips. "Honor has very little place in your philosophy, does it, Jermyn?"

"Look, Alderney, you've misjudged me, I swear—" Jack began, backing slowly toward the door.

"No, sir, I haven't misjudged you, and the only reason I don't intend to call you out as well is that I'd probably never have found out about all this if you hadn't told me. But that doesn't mean I intend to let you off scot free."

Jack's face went pale as Justin advanced toward him. "Alderney, I—"

George was disturbed as well. "Leave him, Justin, he isn't worth it!"

But Justin crossed the final few feet and without warning brought such a pistonlike fist up to Jack's jaw that the force of the blow jerked his head back. With a grunt he staggered, then his knees sagged and he slumped to the floor.

Justin looked down witheringly at him. "I wish to God I felt better for doing that," he breathed, then strode to the door and called the footman. "Get some assistance and have this maggot taken out to his carriage!"

The footman stared past him at Jack's crumpled body. "Er, yes, my lord!" he gasped, and then hurried away.

George looked urgently at Justin. "The outcome of any duel isn't a foregone conclusion, so have a care. I've made it my business to find out about Kemp, and he isn't a dunce with pistols."

"I'd still call him out even if he were the finest shot in England," Justin replied in a tone so controlled it was almost matter-of-fact.

"I know you would." George put an understanding hand on his shoulder.

"George, I came back here this morning to mend the rift with Rowena. I spent a very sobering night at White's and knew even before Jermyn said his piece that Rowena was all I wanted."

"What exactly did Jermyn tell you?" George asked, stepping aside as two footmen came to carry Jack out.

Justin explained briefly, then gave a pale smile. "I've been a fool, and now she's gone."

George stared at him. "Where?"

"Back to Melcombe, where else?" Justin drew a long breath. "I'll go after her, but not until I've dealt with Kemp. As for Chloe—"

"Chloe? You surely don't *still* mean to see her?" George cried incredulously.

"See her? George, I wish to God I'd never set eyes on her in the first place. Only the fact she's a woman protects her from my vengeance now, of that you may be sure." Justin paused and looked anxiously at him. "What if Rowena won't forgive me, George?"

"I'm sure she loves you, Justin."

"I've given her good reason to despise me." Justin lowered his eyes for a moment and then collected himself. "Come on, I mean to descend upon Conduit Street without further delay."

George nodded. "We'll take my barouche."

As they drove away, the footmen were still trying to bundle Jack into his carriage.

Chapter 41

Henry had followed every word and action with great intensity. He'd been savagely pleased when Justin knocked Jack down, and at first bloodthirstily approving when he'd announced his intention to call Kemp out, but then he'd been dismayed to learn of the latter's apparent prowess with pistols. Duels were notoriously risky, and it wouldn't do for the odds to favor Kemp! What purpose would that serve? Rowena was in love with her husband, and he with her, so they must be brought together in life, not at Justin's graveside.

The duel must therefore be prevented, but Kemp still had to be punished; indeed he must pay the ultimate penalty for his cowardly crime. Chloe had to be punished as well, but in accordance with the level of her offense, and Henry knew exactly what to do. Erupting from the house in a blaze of ghostly malevolence, he sped to York Street, where he found Andrew and Chloe still asleep in the bed where she and Justin had so often made passionate love.

With a grim smile the phantom left again, this time for Westcote House. Gliding in through an upper window he found Chloe's husband alone and snoring in his huge four-poster. The silky tassel of his night cap had fallen across his face, his mouth open in a most undignified manner. Henry flapped impatiently around him. Now to find out if the fellow could hear ghosts as well as see them.

"Lord Westcote?" he said into the sleeping man's ear.

The snoring caught on a grunt "Eh? Wassermarrer?"

"Wake up, sir," Henry commanded.

Lord Westcote's eyes flew open, and his face drained of color. "Is my time up? Have you come for me?" he asked timorously.

"Come for you? No, damn it, I'm not the Grim Reaper! I'm hear to help you."

Lord Westcote sat up and stared at him. "I recognize you, you were at the opera house!"

"Yes."

"Wh-why do you want to help me?"

"You want to be free to marry Lady Jane, don't you?"

Lord Westcote gaped at him. "I, er, well, yes."

"And you know your wife is unfaithful, but cannot prove it?"

"Yes."

"Well, if you accompany me now, I can provide you with all the proof you need."

"Accompany you where?"

"York Street. She's with her lover, Andrew Kemp."

Lord Westcote searched the wraith's face. "Are you certain?"

Henry nodded.

"Very well." Lord Westcote flung the bedclothes back, then padded to ring the bell. It was cold in the room because the fire had burned low, so he went to stand with his back to it, raising his nightgown to warm his bare buttocks.

It was a few minutes before his sleepy valet answered the summons. The man couldn't hide his surprise on learning that his master intended to go out so early, for it was unheard of that Lord Westcote should leave the house before noon.

Henry hovered impatiently as the business of dressing proceeded at what seemed like a snail's pace. "Oh, do get on with it!" he cried at last.

"I don't intend to go out looking like a sack of rags," Lord Westcote replied.

The valet looked at him in puzzlement. "No, my lord," he murmured.

Henry fluttered restlessly up and down. "You do want to be there before Kemp leaves, don't you?" he grumbled.

"I'm being as quick as I can," Lord Westcote said, frowning at him.

The valet was bewildered. "My lord?"

"Oh, I'm not talking to you!"

"You aren't, my lord?" The valet's jaw dropped.

"No, I'm talking to him." Lord Westcote jerked his thumb toward Henry.

The valet looked uncertainly toward the empty corner.

Lord Westcote sighed. "Oh, it doesn't matter. You can't see him. There, is it finished now?"

"Yes, my lord."

"Very well. Have my phaeton brought around immediately."

"My lord." The valet escaped thankfully.

Ten minutes later, when the phaeton drove smartly out of the gates, Henry was seated next to Lord Westcote, urging him to drive as quickly as possible.

York Street was quiet, and the curtains were still drawn at the house behind the brick wall. Lord Westcote reined in and made the phaeton fast, then, following Henry's instructions, he made his way around to the back of the house. Chloe's maid was in the kitchen having her breakfast of tea and buttered toast. She leapt to her feet in alarm when she saw her mistress's husband, but Henry had primed Lord Westcote with what to say. In order to prove Chloe's guilt, another witness would be required, and who better than her ladyship's trusted maid? Loyalty to her mistress didn't figure high on the girl's list of priorities, and without hesitation she accepted a bribe and then showed Lord Westcote upstairs. She knew nothing of his invisible mentor.

The two in the bed awoke with a start as the bedroom door was flung open. Chloe gave a horrified gasp and clutched the bedclothes to her breasts. Her face was a study in mortification, and Andrew was so dumbfounded he stared openmouthed.

Lord Westcote had conveniently forgotten all his own infidelities as he smiled at his dismayed wife. "Thank you, Chloe, my dear, for I now have proof and a witness to your adultery. I fear it's going to be very unpleasant, and your name is going to be chewed over with great relish. Indeed, you won't have a name when it's over."

Chloe couldn't speak. All the horrors of a scandalous divorce passed before her eyes, and it wouldn't even be Justin's name that was cited, but Andrew Kemp's!

Lord Westcote beamed at Henry, and then he and the maid withdrew from the room, closing the door behind them. The phantom didn't go, too, for his attention was on Andrew. Chloe's punishment was mapped, for she was ruined, but Andrew was about to be snuffed from this world! Henry despised the man who'd assaulted Rowena, despised him for his cruelty, his lust, and his cowardice. How poor a creature he was to try to force a helpless woman. Well, help had come now, and Andrew Kemp would never again lay violent hand upon the fair sex.

Chloe had tearfully thrown the bedclothes aside to scramble into her clothes. She was panic-stricken and wished with all her heart she'd heeded Justin's warning. But it was too late now. She paused to toss a vitriolic look at Andrew. All was lost, and for *him*!

Andrew also got up and didn't sense the malignant presence in the room as he dressed. His mind was racing. Westcote was bound to cite him, but would such a scandal necessarily harm his reputation? Maybe it would be enhanced! Who knew? Buttoning his shirt, he struggled into his waistcoat and then picked up a brush from the dressing table to drag it through his tousled hair.

Henry heard Lord Westcote leaving, taking Chloe's treacherous maid with him. It was then the phantom howled into ghastly action. Concentrating all his immense power, the specter manifested himself, looming tall and menacing to shimmer transparently in the middle of the room. He towered there, his aspect hideous and his eyes grisly as he gave a thunderous cry that seemed to shake the very house.

Chloe screamed and fainted, but Andrew knew no such escape. His face ashen with dread, he stared at the unspeakable being directing its malevolence toward him. His mouth ran dry, for he knew he faced death itself.

Suddenly he found the strength to move. Dashing to the door, he fled down the staircase. Henry followed, bringing with him the breath of the tomb. He reached out to touch the fleeing man, and Andrew screamed as he felt the spectral hand upon his shoulder. Stumbling and staggering, he ran to the front door, screaming again as Henry tugged at his clothes and hair and gave another monstrous cry that resounded through the building.

Sobbing with terror, Andrew ran out to the street. He paused to glance back, but Henry was there. Dread robbed Andrew of the vestiges of caution, and without looking he ran into the road. A carriage was approaching, and the coachman had no chance to rein in. He tried to shout a warning, but to no avail. The lead horses struck Andrew, knocking him to the cobbles. Their hooves trampled him, and then the carriage wheel bumped over his limp body before the vehicle halted. Andrew lay like a bundle of rags, his dead eyes staring up with indescribable terror.

A woman screamed, and then several men came running to see what had happened. No one saw Henry, who had now resumed his usual invisible form and was gazing down with satisfaction at the result of his revenge. He straightened his tricorn and brushed his coat, congratulating himself upon one of the most rewarding minute's work he'd ever done. The Powers had sent him on many a similar mission, but this had been personal.

Now to pursue Rowena to the Golden Cross at Hounslow, for not only was he concerned about his frame, he also knew she could hear him when he spoke. She had to be told what had really happened, and that Lord Alderney loved his wife and wanted her back.

George's barouche was still waiting outside Green's Lodging House in Conduit Street for Andrew to return. The minutes ticked by, and Justin's anger and impatience increased.

"Where in God's name is he?" he exploded at last, flinging the door open and climbing down to the pavement.

George followed him. "Justin, Green himself said Kemp left word he'd return this morning, and there doesn't seem to be any reason why he should lie about such a thing."

"I'm going in to question the fellow again," Justin declared, turning toward the door of the building.

George caught his arm. "No! In your present mood you'll hang the man on the wall if he doesn't give you the answers you want to hear."

As he spoke, a pale-faced footman ran past them and into the lodging house. A moment after that they heard Mr. Green's dismayed cry.

"Dead! Kemp? And still owing me rent!"

Justin and George exchanged glances, then walked swiftly to the doorway.

The lodging house owner was livid. "God damn him to hell and back! Three months he owed!" Then he saw George. "Well, sir, you'll have a long wait now, and no mistake. It seems our Mr. Kemp has gone and been killed. Ran in front of a carriage in York Street, he did."

Justin's lips parted. York Street?

George looked at the footman who'd brought the news. "What exactly happened?"

"Well, it's a bit of a mystery, sir. I was just taking a message to an address in that street, when a carriage drove past me. At the same time Mr. Kemp came running out across the pavement as if he'd seen a ghost. He didn't look where he was going and dashed out into the road. The coachman couldn't stop, and it was over in a moment. There was a constable in the street at the time, and when I told him I recognized Mr. Kemp, he told me to come here and let someone know what'd happened." The footman was shaking so much he had to sit down. "Then there was this scream from the house Mr. Kemp had run out from. A lady stood at an upstairs window, and she had the vapors good and proper when she saw. Someone said it was Lady Westcote and that Lord Westcote had just called briefly, but I wouldn't know. All I know is that Mr. Kemp ran from the house she was in, and there were tongues wagging before I left."

Justin looked away. Westcote had gone to the house? Foolish Chloe. How like her to vent her spite and jealousy by having Kemp to warm her bed last night. Kemp, of all men. How she must be regretting it now. If she'd taken the warning about Westcote's desire for divorce, she wouldn't be in this position today. Now her name was going to be bandied all over London.

George took his elbow and steered him back toward the barouche. "I don't know what's been going on in York Street, but I *do* know you're well out of it, my friend. You're also saved from a duel with Kemp."

"Your faith in my shooting accuracy is really quite touching," Justin replied.

"I'm just relieved fate has intervened. I didn't care for the thought of pistols at dawn, not once I'd learned he was reckoned a very good shot." George held his gaze. "What now?"

"I have to go to the Golden Cross at Hounslow. Rowena is there."

"Then don't let's waste any more time." George opened the barouche door and waited for him to climb in. Then he nodded at the coachman. "Did you hear that?"

"The Golden Cross at Hounslow? Yes, sir."

"Then make all haste."

"Sir."

The door slammed, and the vehicle drew smartly away.

Chapter 42

Henry reached the Golden Cross in time to see Rowena and her maid emerge into the crowded yard, where their post-chaise waited among the clutter of vehicles.

The postboy was suffering the aftereffects of too much ale the night before and was too disgruntled to assist his passengers, choosing instead to stand by the lead horse and leave the women to fend for themselves. Henry frowned at him, then glided next to Rowena. She wore a cloak, and her hood was raised against the early morning cold. Her pale face and her eyes still bore the marks of her tears.

The ghost floated around her as she prepared to climb into the chaise. How could he speak without frightening her? He knew she'd hear him, but that he'd remain invisible. It was one thing to imagine one had heard a portrait say something, quite another to hear a disembodied voice. He glanced at the maid and to his relief saw she'd gone to give the surly postboy a piece of her mind. The specter knew it was now or never. Rowena was going to have a shock however he approached her, so better to get it over and done with.

"Rowena, can you hear me?" he asked gently.

She gasped and whirled about. "Who's there?" she asked, glancing around the busy yard.

"You can't see me, I fear, but I'm here all the same," he said.

Her eyes widened still more. "Who are you?" she whispered, her voice almost lost in the noise of a departing stagecoach.

"Don't be afraid, Rowena, for I mean you no harm. Don't you remember hearing me speak to you at the Hanover Square rooms when you purchased my portrait?"

"Henry Melcombe?" she breathed incredulously.

"Your servant, my dear." He swept her an invisible bow, but then he saw the maid returning. "Rowena, we must talk privately, for although you can hear me, your maid cannot, and she's bound to think it very strange if you appear to be conversing with someone who isn't here."

"Sir, it *is* very strange to be conversing with someone who isn't here," she replied. This wasn't happening. Henry Melcombe couldn't possibly be speaking to her like this! Was she taking leave of her senses?

"Make an excuse to return to the inn. Go back to your room and have the maid stay away," he instructed urgently.

"But—"

"Do it, my dear, for it's imperative I explain certain things to you. For the sake of your marriage you must listen to me."

She hesitated, but then made up her mind and gave the maid an apologetic smile. "Ann, I fear I cannot travel just yet after all."

"My lady?"

"I . . . I feel a little unwell and couldn't face the road. I'll take the room again for a while."

"But, my lady—"

"Inform the postboy he must wait, and then you can do as you wish for a while as I will not require you."

The maid stared at her. "Very well, my lady."

Rowena turned and walked back into the inn, where the astonished innkeeper gave her the same room again.

When she closed the door behind her, she leaned back against it and glanced uncertainly around. "Are . . . are you still here?" she asked.

"Of course, and let me say I believe you can hear me because we are of the same blood. Your father once heard me, too, although he didn't like what I had to say."

She remembered. Poor Father, no one had believed him . . . She looked hesitantly toward the place Henry's voice seemed to come from. "Why are you speaking to me?"

"Because you're making a dreadful mistake by leaving your husband."

"How do you know about that?"

"My dear Rowena, at this moment I know far more than you do about your marital tangle, enough to be able to state quite categorically that you have nothing to fear from Lady Westcote, and that your husband loves you so much he was prepared to fight a fuel for your honor."

She gasped. "A duel? Is he—"

"Don't alarm yourself unnecessarily, my dear, for no challenge was issued, nor will it be now. But that doesn't alter the fact that Lord Alderney would have faced Andrew Kemp for what he did to you in Melcombe."

Her lips parted. "Justin knows about that?"

"Oh, yes, but it's a long and complicated tale, and we may as well be comfortable. There are two chairs by the fireplace; you take the one nearest the door, and I will take the other one."

When they were seated, he told her everything he'd learned.

Rowena listened incredulously as the story unfolded. Chloe and Andrew had conspired so callously to ruin her? Andrew was dead? Lord Westcote was going to divorce Chloe? And Justin loved his wife after all . . . ? But then tears stung her eyes.

Henry broke off, looking at her in puzzlement. "I see no reason to cry, my dear, for surely you should be happy?"

"You say Justin loves me, but he still went to her at York Street."

"Nothing of consequence took place, my dear."

"I cannot agree, sir, for I saw them together."

"I know you did, but if you'd stayed longer, you'd have seen him spurn her. He suddenly came to his senses and left, not to go back to St. James's Square admittedly, but he felt he should be more sober than he was before seeking a reconciliation with you. He spent last night at White's Club."

Hope began to kindle within her. "That is the truth?"

"Indeed so, for I'm not in the habit of telling lies," he replied huffily, but then his tone became more kind. "My dear, your place is with the husband you love and who loves you. He told George that after he'd faced Kemp, he'd come after you, and since there can no longer be a duel, then I'm certain he's already on his way here to find you. He knows in which inn you intended to spend last night."

She couldn't speak. A great weight had suddenly been lifted.

Henry waited for a moment, then looked intently at her. "Now there is something I must ask of you, my dear. Will you promise to send me back to Melcombe as soon as you can? You see, I can't go more than fifty miles from my frame, and I want to go home more than anything else. I miss Margaret so very much, and then there are all the others whose acquaintance I wish to make."

"The others?" She stared at him.

"Oh, yes. Actually Melcombe possesses a number of family specters. Any Melcombe whose portrait hangs in the house is still to be found there, although he or she cannot go abroad more than once or twice a year and cannot do a great deal in the way of haunting, *et cetera*. Halloween is a favorite time, of course," he added, thinking fondly of the Halloweens he'd known at Melcombe during his lifetime.

Halloween. Rowena turned her gaze toward the fire, remembering that was when it had all started. There had always been a mystery about the sequence of events that day, for how could she possibly have dreamed about Justin before actually meeting him? Now she began to wonder if there was much more to it than mere chance . . .

Henry observed her thoughtful expression. "Is there something on your mind, my dear?"

"May I ask you about the specters at Melcombe?"

"I don't know them, my dear," he reminded her. "Don't forget, my frame has always been in London, never in Melcombe."

"But you know what things they might be able to do?"

He was curious. "Why do you ask?"

"Because I now think there wasn't anything accidental about the way I met Justin. Oh, I think it was chance that he actually came to Melcombe when he did, but after that, everything was manipulated by unseen hands."

"Manipulated? In what way exactly?"

"Just as Halloween commenced, I had a very strange dream. At least, I think it was a dream, I'm not really sure anymore. I'd decided to test the old Halloween charm of standing in front of a mirror with an apple and comb—"

"Ah, yes," he interrupted. "Many a maiden has seen her future husband that way."

"And countless more have waited in vain, but I saw Justin. More than that, I . . ." She broke off quickly, hot color rushing into her cheeks.

"Go on, my dear."

"I . . . I don't think I should."

He smiled. "So it was *that* sort of dream, was it?"

She was hugely embarrassed. "Yes."

"And you didn't actually meet him in the flesh, as it were, until after that?"

"The next day. I was in the church vestry, thinking about the wretched financial fix the family was in, and suddenly he came in. He said he'd been chasing his hat after the wind had blown it away . . ." She paused again. "But it wasn't windy outside," she added.

Henry was intensely interested now. "Let me summarize. Your family was in financial difficulties, it was Halloween, you er, 'dreamed' of Justin, and he then came to you by chasing a wind-blown hat on a still day?"

"Yes."

"My dear, I fancy you're right to suspect unseen hands, and if I were to guess whose hands, I'd hazard they were Lady Margaret's, for the whole business smacks of her. As I've already said, every specter is allowed a day or so a year in which to leave its frame, and Halloween is a favorite time. She'd very probably go abroad then, especially if the Melcombe family was in dire straits. Was the house itself in danger?" he asked.

"Yes."

"Then the specters would indeed have been alarmed, for themselves as well as for the family, and Margaret would be capable of conjuring dreams, raising winds, moving objects, and so on." He chuckled a little. "It would be just like her to think of marriage as a solution. I'll warrant she couldn't believe her good fortune when a gentleman like Justin turned up."

Rowena was more than a little anxious. "Sir, does this mean that the love Justin and I have for each other isn't real after all? Is it an illusion?"

He smiled indulgently. "You fear you're both enchanted?"

"Yes."

"Then cast that fear aside, Rowena, for your love is genuine. A wraith may be able to create favorable illusions and circumstances, but true human emotion must come from humans themselves. Whatever you felt when you first saw Justin's reflection in the looking glass came from the heart itself, my dear, not from any supernatural force." Henry leaned his head back, recalling his own earthly life. "It's a strange coincidence, but it so happens that I was once damnably jealous of one of Justin's ancestors, a previous Marquess of Exford by the name of Kit. He was plaguey handsome and possessed of devastating charm. I loathed him because he was Margaret's love before she met me."

"But she married you, sir."

"Yes, she married me, and now I long to be with her again. Until you found me, I'd become reconciled to my existence, but you've brought back sweet memories, and now all I want is to go home again, even though it will mean forfeiting many of my privileges."

"Privileges?"

"If I go back to Melcombe, I'll become like the other ghosts there. I'll only be able to leave my frame from time to time, not at will as I do now, and I'll be able to speak to my fellow specters, but not to you. It's one of the rules."

"There are rules?"

"Oh, yes, my dear. The supernatural code of conduct is just as tedious as its counterpart in this world, and those who transgress are punished as effectively." He drew a long breath. "So, my dear,

I have your word you'll send me home to Melcombe without delay?"

"Yes, of course."

"Then I believe I'll have a little nap in my frame."

She got up anxiously. "You're leaving me now?"

"Yes, for my work is done. All you have to do is await your husband's arrival, and then mend your differences."

"He *will* come?"

"Oh, yes, my dear, he'll come. And I suggest that when he does, you make proper use of that bed!"

Chapter 43

George's barouche arrived in the yard, and Justin looked at his friend as the vehicle came to a halt.

"I pray she hasn't left already."

"If she has, we'll follow," George replied, opening the door and alighting. Then he glanced across the yard and smiled. "I think we can say she's still here, for I believe that's her maid."

Justin climbed swiftly down and looked where he pointed. "Yes, it is," he said and without further ado pushed his way through the press of people and vehicles to where Ann was flirting with one of the ostlers.

"Ann?" Justin said as he reached her.

She turned with a gasp. "My lord!"

"Is Lady Alderney still here?"

"Yes, my lord, but—"

"Where will I find her?"

The maid was reluctant to reply.

"Please tell me, Ann, for I mean her no harm. On the contrary, in fact, and if you won't tell me, then I have only to ask the landlord."

"She's in a room on the third floor, my lord. The last door on the left."

He hurried away and she called after him. "My lord, she isn't feeling well . . ."

But her words fell on deaf ears as Justin entered the inn. George remained by the barouche, tipping his top hat back on his head and folding his arms as he prepared to wait. He prayed Justin and Rowena would resolve their differences, for in his and Em's opinion Lord and Lady Alderney were a perfect match.

Justin reached Rowena's door, and there his courage almost failed him. He'd accused her of unfaithfulness with Kemp, and even gone so far as to hint that Kemp was merely one among many. Maybe that was something she couldn't forgive. But at last he raised his hand to knock.

"Justin?"

"Yes."

"Please come in."

Relieved, he opened the door and saw her. She was standing by the window in her lavender and lace gown, and her long hair was brushed loose about her shoulders. She gazed uncertainly at him and gave a hesitant smile.

Gladness surged through him, and he closed the door and went to gather her in his arms. He held her tight, exulting in her warmth and in the sweetness of her perfume. When he spoke, his voice was choked with emotion. "Forgive me, my darling. Forgive me for doubting you, for accusing you so basely . . ."

"I should have told you what happened at Melcombe, but the longer I left it, the harder it became to say anything."

"I know," he said softly.

"I wasn't encouraging him; I didn't even want to speak to him, but he made it seem as if I—"

"I know, my darling." He explained briefly about Jack Jermyn. "So you see, it was all a despicable plot to drive us apart, and it so very nearly succeeded."

"I believed you when you said Lady Westcote was still your mistress."

He drew back a little. "My pride was wounded because I thought you and Kemp were lovers. It's no excuse for lying to you, but I couldn't help myself. I should have told you earlier about my relationship with Chloe, but I left it and left it, then found it impossible to say at all.

"Just as I did over my secret. We're both guilty of not mentioning things we should have," she said quietly.

"She doesn't mean anything to me now, you must believe me. I know I went to her last night, but I didn't stay."

"No, you went to White's Club," she said, drawing slowly

back. She had to tell him everything, about Henry, about the Melcombe ghosts, and about the dream. "Justin . . ."

He looked keenly at her. "Am I still unforgiven over Chloe?" he asked, misunderstanding the change in her.

"It's not that." She held his gaze. "There are things I have to tell you, strange and unbelievable things, but unless I tell you everything now, then—"

"Tell me. Whatever it is, I'll understand."

She smiled a little. "Will you? Justin, I didn't lightly use the words *strange* and *unbelievable*."

"Tell me," he pressed gently.

"First I must ask you something. Did you dream about me before we met?"

He stared, then nodded, "Yes, I did, but how—" He broke off, remembering how he'd once suspected she'd shared the dream. "You dreamed it, too?"

She nodded. "Except it wasn't really a dream, not in the strictest sense of the word."

He searched her face. "What are you saying?"

"Justin, I want you to know what's been happening around us since Halloween." She paused. "Do you believe in ghosts?" she asked then.

"Let's say I'm skeptical."

"Then what if I told you I knew exactly how Andrew Kemp died? And I know why Lord Westcote went to the house in York Street and saw Lady Westcote and Andrew Kemp in bed together? And that I even know how you took your leave of Lady Westcote last night?"

"I don't know what I'd say, except I'd wonder greatly how you came to know all that when you weren't present."

She held his gaze. "Justin, I heard it all from a ghost. Please don't look at me like that, for it's the truth. Supernatural powers have been at work on our behalf, and it started on Halloween. Maybe you don't want to believe me, for I can hardly believe it myself, but there are ghosts at Melcombe, and when I found Henry Melcombe's portrait, I found his ghost, too. The Melcombe ghosts brought us together, and he has been helping us as well. How else can you explain how I've learned so much about things that happened when I wasn't there? And how else can you explain the dream we shared. We recognized each other that day in the vestry, and it was because we'd been together in our dreams. Justin, Lord Westcote went to York Street because Henry Melcombe took him there in order to ruin Chloe, and Andrew

Kemp died because Henry frightened him out of his wits. It was Henry's punishment for what they did to me." She turned away. "You think I've taken leave of my senses, don't you?"

"No. Rowena, I believe every word you've said," he replied quietly, remembering how the footman at Green's Lodging House had described Andrew's death.

She whirled gladly about. "You do?"

"Yes." He smiled a little wryly. "I've always prided myself on being able to find a logical explanation for everything, but there isn't anything logical about the way we met, about the dream we shared, or, indeed, about Kemp's demise, which I have heard described in detail, and which couldn't really be accounted for until you told me about Henry Melcombe. Maybe the explanation is incredible, but I believe it."

"That's how I feel about it all. I didn't know there were ghosts at Melcombe, and I didn't even know about Henry until he came here to the inn to tell me I was wrong to leave you."

"I have Henry to thank?"

"We have both Henry and his wife, Lady Margaret, to thank. *She* conjured up our dream and raised the wind to make your top hat blow into the church. At least, Henry and I believe she was responsible."

"I knew there was something other-worldly about Melcombe. Even George felt it when he and Em came for the wedding, and there's no one more down-to-earth and levelheaded than George Rathbone. I remember we were walking in the garden before the ceremony, and he mentioned feeling a strange atmosphere about the village. Melcombe is no ordinary place, Rowena, and if you say there are ghosts, then I know there are."

"Henry wants to go home there now." Rowena held his gaze. "And so do I, Justin."

"To Melcombe?"

"There's no one there at the moment, so we'd have it to ourselves."

He smiled. "No one there? You've just told me it's populated by a small army of phantoms!"

"Friendly phantoms. Please, Justin, can we go there?"

"Of course. But first, I want you to wear this again." He took her wedding ring from his pocket.

She gazed at it, then raised her eyes to his face. "Are you quite sure?"

"More sure than I've ever been. I love you, Rowena, and I want you to stay my wife." He went to her, taking her left hand and slipping the ring on her finger. Then he raised her palm to his lips, kissing it tenderly.

Suddenly she was in his embrace. Their mouths met, and his arms were tight around her as they kissed. They'd both feared never to hold each other again, and so there was an added sweetness to the embrace. From fearing they'd parted forever, they suddenly knew the future was theirs. Joy mingled with desire, and their need was imperative as they removed their clothes. He lifted her onto the bed, and she drew him down toward her, her breath escaping on a quivering sigh as his lips moved over her breast. Delicious waves of desire shivered through her as he drew gently upon the nipple, sucking it up into his mouth. Her eyes were dark with passion, and her body trembled with eager anticipation, just as it had in her sleep the night before.

But fulfillment wasn't denied her this time; he was very real in her arms, his body fusing with hers in an ecstasy of emotion. His hand was upon her thigh as he parted her legs to sink his urgent manhood deep into her. He slid in slowly and to the hilt, but their shared need was too imperative to linger. She begged him to take her, and he began to thrust forcefully, driven by the overpowering demands of his flesh. Each thrust raised her to new heights of pleasure, and when the final moment came, she clung almost weightlessly to him as ravishing waves of joy washed endlessly over her.

They continued to hold each other afterward, their heartbeats gradually lessening to a gentle rhythm, their bodies warm and lazy. Neither of them spoke, for there was no need. They understood each other as never before, for all secrets had been unlocked and allowed to fly away.

There was no snow at Melcombe as the carriage drove through the January twilight at the end of its long journey from London. Melkery Beacon stood out against the sky, and stars had begun to glitter overhead. Rowena's head lay on Justin's shoulder, for she'd fallen asleep not long after the carriage had begun the long climb out of Dunster.

His arm was around her as he gazed out at the remembered countryside, so shadowy and enigmatic in the fading light. He wondered what Henry's reception had been at the manor house, for the impatient ghost had flown ahead from his frame the moment the carriage was within fifty miles of journey's end. Justin rested his cheek against Rowena's hair, smiling a little as he thought about the unlikely conversations he and the phantom had conducted through Rowena during the drive. It had been most in-

teresting, for Henry had been more than willing to talk about the
supernatural world that marched alongside the present.

It was a world of specters, demons, devils, and gargoyles, where
the Prince of Darkness was opposed by the veiled and hidden
Powers-That-Be, masters of the arcane and upholders of the un-
written laws. It was a fearsome place that had always existed, and
always would. Here in Melcombe, where the heights of Exmoor
seemed to keep the present at bay, that other world was closer than
anywhere else. He was conscious of its presence now, just as he'd
sensed something different when he'd been here before.

He glanced out as the carriage passed the Red Lion, and suddenly he saw a mirage of bonfire flames reflected in the inn's
windows. Turning toward the green, he saw Halloween. It was
chimerical, a transparent image through which he could see the
cottages beyond. Turnip lanterns glowed, and rowan branches
were fixed to doors. He could see the guisers and the Devil's
Mare and hear the laughter and music as the villagers celebrated
the ancient festival.

Then his lips parted with surprise as he looked beyond the arc
of firelight and saw his own likeness. He was with Rowena, and
they were locked in their first embrace. It was a moment he remembered so well, for he'd just told her how much he longed to
take her in his arms.

Magic was all around him again now, and he aroused Rowena
from her sleep. "Wake up, my love. Do you see what I do?"

She stirred sleepily and then her eyes opened. She looked out at
the green and sat up swiftly. "Yes, I see it, too," she breathed,
reaching out instinctively to catch his hand.

The carriage drew up outside the manor house, where more turnip
lanterns glowed on the gateposts. Justin alighted and turned to hand
Rowena down. They walked toward the door, and it opened before
them. The house was lit by countless ghostly candles, their flames as
ethereal and lacking in substance as the scene on the green.

The Powers-That-Be had bestowed their favor upon the Melcombe ghosts, who had all been permitted to leave their portrait
frames for this one magical night. A spectral ball was in progress,
with sweet music that was inaudible to the human ear. The invisible dancing came to a halt as Justin and Rowena entered, and
silent voices greeted them.

"Welcome home, welcome home . . ."

Unaware of the spirits all around them, Justin relieved Rowena
of her cloak, and she smoothed the rich folds of her cerise angora
gown. Justin took off his overcoat and laid it on the table next to

her cloak. The purple of his tailcoat seemed almost black in the candlelight.

Rowena remembered that Henry had been sure Lady Margaret had instigated everything, and so she looked up at the portrait. "Thank you," she murmured with a smile. She didn't sense the lady's phantom standing almost at her shoulder. Nor did she know that Henry was there, but most of all she didn't know her own father was close enough to have touched her.

William Melcombe's eyes were misted with loving tears as he gazed proudly at his daughter. She was now assured of a happy future, and his own past failings would never again be referred to by his fellow specters. He wasn't Silly Billy now; he was the father of the future Marchioness of Exford!

Justin drew his wife's palm to his lips. "If it's Halloween again, my love, let us complete the dream."

She smiled, and he led her toward the staircase. They didn't hear the ghostly ball commence again behind them or see the generations of Melcombes dancing the night away.

More candles glowed in Rowena's old bedroom, as dreamlike and fanciful as everything else. An apple and comb lay on the floor by the cheval glass, just as they had on Halloween when Lady Margaret set everything in motion. There was no need to speak. Rowena slipped out of her gown before picking up the apple and comb and standing naked in front of the mirror. Justin undressed as well and stood beside her.

She loosened her hair so it fell about her shoulders. "Take me now, my Halloween husband," she whispered, turning toward him.

The comb and apple slipped from her hands as he kissed her.

Ghostly elation stirred through the house, and Lady Margaret glanced coquettishly at her husband. "We did well, did we not, sir?" she declared, tapping him playfully with her fan.

"Very well indeed, my dear."

"We *all* did well," William reminded them.

Henry nodded. "Yes, and now we have the whole night ahead to enjoy ourselves. We must make full use of this unprecedented occasion, for it may be centuries before the Powers are again disposed to indulge us like this." He turned and clapped his hands to the phantom orchestra. "Play on!"

The shades continued their ball, and Lady Margaret looked coyly at her beloved husband. "Well, sir? Shall we adjourn to my frame?"

"What are you suggesting, madam?" he inquired, feigning surprise.

"I'm suggesting we do what Rowena and Justin are doing, sir, or have you perhaps forgotten how to?"

"Forgotten? Madam, I'm about to show you that I'm as ardent a lover as ever," he declared.

She smiled as he took her hand and led her up from the crowded floor to her frame.